The Proximate Voices

Book V of

The Voices Saga

William L Stolley

iUniverse, Inc.
Bloomington

The Proximate Voices
Book V of The Voices Saga

This is a work of fiction. All of the characters, names, incidents, organizations, and dialogue in this novel are either the products of the author's imagination or are used fictitiously.

iUniverse books may be ordered through booksellers or by contacting:

iUniverse
1663 Liberty Drive
Bloomington, IN 47403
www.iuniverse.com
1-800-Authors (1-800-288-4677)

ISBN: 978-1-4620-0813-1 (pbk)
ISBN: 978-1-4620-0815-5 (ebk)

Printed in the United States of America

iUniverse rev. date: 04/05/2011

"The microcosm is a universe of infinitely tiny proportion. It exists in spaces measured smaller than the dot of an "i" on this page and yet is as complex in structure as an entire galaxy. These relatively uncharted frontiers beckon the 21st Century explorer into this gigantic world of the miniscule." WLS

Contents

Chapter One

The Armor Cracks

An icy cold wind pressed down on the complex of buildings at the end of an inlet bay in northern Labrador – a private undisclosed military base located north of the Cirque Mountains. The snowstorm that raged this evening was not the kind where pretty snowflakes twirled around a picturesque countryside. A strong forceful wind blew down from the Arctic and brought with it a major blizzard that dumped tons of the white precipitation in heavy clumps – typical wintery stuff for this time of year in early February of 2019. A storm like this could last for days. The last outside flight to land – which arrived three days ago before the storm hit – brought fresh food, supplies, and plenty of sanity in the form of reading material.

Since this was probably the most top-secret and least known base of operations in the world, security was extremely strict. General Andrews banned the use of all personal electronic devices: cell phones, personal pads, electronic readers, anything of that nature. The laptops the staff possessed displayed only classified material. No one on this base could surf the internet. What entertained the personnel amounted to reading material in the form of books, magazines, or newspapers – those still available in print form.

Only the small building near the entrance was visible. The rest of the base lay hidden on the other side of an embankment. Inside this smaller building, another world existed that went far below the surface. The warm, sleek, multi-level, modern ambience belied the plain unadorned one-level exterior behind a wall of tall barbed-wire fences and surrounded by invisible lasers that prevented unwanted encroachment. One lonely country road wound through the wilderness and eventually led to this desolate place, strategically located between the four major powers that oversaw its expenditures – the United States, England, Germany, and France. Yet, only a handful of men loosely associated with those governmental purse strings knew of this building's existence or its dark purpose – the closely guarded secret of a unique and special organization meant to carry out the clandestine, away from the public, away from legislators, away from government officials who might interfere with its twisted plans to subvert and eliminate.

A young man, wearing a black non-descript uniform with a pressed white shirt and long thin black tie, leaned back in his chair, his feet propped up on an electronic console, while he read the magazine in front of him. He appeared to be in his middle twenties, had closely cropped blonde hair and broad shoulders. He had a bland typical American face, a healthy complexion, and a keen mind for observation, his primary task. He was bored with having to stare at screens all day. He knew that the "intelligent" computer before him monitored the activity and performed any alerts they might receive. He was considered the necessary "human" element, to be on guard in case the computer did not correctly respond. Besides, he reasoned, the one satellite in orbit for the new "obs" division, of which he played an important part, had yet to come online. They were still running diagnostic programs and working out the kinks in the relatively new system.

The career NCO was both rugged and handsome in an Oklahoma homespun kind-of-way. Born and raised just outside Tulsa, he wrestled in high school, won some awards, and after graduation, headed into military service, just as his uncle and cousin did. After taking some aptitude tests, a special officer showed up to interview the fresh recruit at his training barracks. This special officer privately met with the eager 19-year-old and explained his reason for being there. The older man told young Gary Peterson that he had the right kind of mental toughness they needed for a new mission under development. Six years later, Cpl. Gary Peterson had a secure job with the promise that one day, he could enter officer's training candidacy and earn some real money, the funds for which were completely paid for by this organization. Until that time arrived, he performed mundane jobs such as this one.

He did not look up at the large screen display that showed the entire globe and the movement of every satellite, jet airliner, and stray piece of junk that moved in the space above the planet. Instead, his clear blue eyes stared at the new spring catalogue from an electronic supply company that arrived by the usual delivery. He slowly turned the precious pages of this treasured object, as they seldom received mail of any kind in this god forsaken secret place. He dreamed of one day filling his living space with the latest gadgetry, when all hell broke loose.

"Eh! Eh! Eh! Eh!" his console sang to him.

He moved his head around the catalogue to look at the control panel. A flashing yellow alert light told him that some phenomenon in the atmosphere was unusual enough to trigger a programmed "track" function.

"Probably some deer hunter in his private plane flying through a restricted airspace zone," he muttered as he sat up.

All at once, the large screen on the wall in front of him zoomed from a broad view of the planet and focused on an area over the Pacific Ocean. If he wanted to, he could call up displays that showed visible light, radar, infrared, UV, water vapor, and other frequency ranges of images onto the screen in front of him.

"Alert! Alert!" the big screen cried out to him.

He looked up at the huge image on the wall and his jaw hung slack. He could not believe what he saw. The computer automatically adjusted the image and zoomed in across the world as it tracked an unknown object moving at an extremely high rate of speed. Whatever this unknown was, the NAT-IX satellite told him it was not a rocket and not an aircraft – at least not of the type that matched any identity profile on record.

"Analysis in progress…" the board said as it began to follow the object.

"What the hell?" he wondered as he put down the catalogue.

"Non-belligerence determined." These words flashed next to the moving object. "Origin unknown. No weapons systems detected. Unknown propulsion system. Intersect course based on current trajectory: North America. Probable landing site: western sector of the United States. No city specified as target, repeat, no city is targeted!"

Only a second or two passed when the computer flashed the words next to the object that no one in the military wanted to see. In large letters, "UFO" flashed on the screen. The computer just did its worst to the young corporal. It labeled the object as an Unidentified Flying Object, a label that usually ended up in military review boards and close-door congressional hearings. The last thing he wanted to do today was file a thirty-page report that followed the current reporting protocol for UFO's.

"Damn! Now what? Can't you come up with a better label than that one!" he declared, disgusted with the computer program and the NAT-IX satellite. "Is the whole system out to ruin my day?"

He quickly typed in "re-analyze" and tried to force the system to change the label. Yet, he no more than hit enter, when the same readout occurred and the label immediately popped back into "UFO" mode. He tried again but the computer refused to change.

"Speed: exceeds Mach 10" the board flashed next to the object.

"That's fast!" he thought. "What the hell is that?"

He sat down at the keyboard and quickly typed…

"Is that a meteor or a satellite on re-entry?"

"Negative," the computer immediately spit back. "No heat or chemical signature. No wake detected."

"No heat and no wake? But, how could that be… at that speed, the atmospheric friction alone would be enough to generate…" he considered.

He glanced over at the special direct line he had to his superior officer. He flipped up the cover, took in a deep breath, and closed his eyes. His thumb punched the red button, which activated a direct line to the captain's office. He had never used it since he started this specific job over a year ago when they first constructed the big screen and activated it.

"Hello?" a voice said to him. "Who is this?"

"This is Spec Obs, sir."

"It's late… you're lucky I was in my office…"

"Yes, sir… Captain, I think you should look at this," Corporal Peterson said through the emergency com line.

"What is it? Is it an attack?" Captain Brighton wondered, his voice anxious.

"No, sir… nothing like that," Cpl. Peterson replied.

"Good! I'm a little busy," Brighton breathed a sigh of relief.

He had mail that he wanted to read, too. He savored and slowly turned each page of his furniture magazine. He had dreams of retiring to Scotland one day and making his home one he could put in a magazine. He called England his country, but he had a soft place in his heart for Scotland, home of his ancestors.

"I can't explain it," the corporal said, "…some kind of atmospheric phenomenon. You'd better see for yourself! Please hurry, sir!" Peterson implored.

"This better not be a UFO," Brighton said as he cut the line and put his furniture magazine away.

Corporal Peterson shut his mouth and did not reply. The initials "UFO" kept flashing next to the object as it moved across the screen.

The captain started up the hall toward the special observation room, known on the base as "Spec Obs." Most soldiers called it the dead end room, as those assigned to that job never received promotion. The "Spec Obs" crew – along with other crews on staff there – was selected to serve a special function in this kind of remote location. They were intelligent men who placed high on their aptitude tests and had one other asset the military had in mind when they considered this remote location. These men didn't mind not having any women on the base.

The captain was not one of these men. He resented the idea that no man around him desired female companionship. He and a few officers were the exception.

"They didn't tell me about that part when I hired on," he mumbled when he made the discovery.

While he tolerated the men around him, he kept to his room mostly when he was not on duty and did not fratronize. Still, he could not argue with the large raise in salary; and he did go out with women when he went on leave, which was fourteen months ago.

Brighton stood on the footpads in front of the entrance door. Sensors read the security badge on his chest and scanned his face. He did not need to enter a keypad code. A security computer measured his height, weight, his uniform, his face, and matched them in a database.

"Speak," it requested.

"Captain Brighton, Spec Obs Division Commander," he said and held up both hands.

Laser light shot out from the wall on either side of the door and scanned the palms of his hands. In seconds, the door to "Spec Obs" opened and he walked into the most sophisticated spy center on the planet Earth.

"Let's see," he said as he paused by the unmanned entry desk. He touched a screen, which pulled up the current assignment list. "The person in charge at this time of day would be..." he thought as he looked over the duty rooster, "Corporal Gary Peterson, American chap, well groomed, nice fellow... probably one of those gay ones," the captain privately considered.

Peterson looked over at the man in the entry and notice that his "Brit," commanding officer, Captain Brighton, stood there looking over the rooster display.

"Over here, sir," Peterson beckoned.

Captain Brighton, medium height, fit, with a thin mustache and thinning hair on his middle-aged head, walked over to stand beside Cpl. Peterson. He looked at the corporal rather than up at the large flat screen and wondered what all the fuss was. He was reluctant to ask the corporal about his private life. He could get into big trouble prying about his subordinate's private lives, as the military now considered that harassment. The corporal looked back at the captain and gestured toward the screen.

"Sir," Peterson said and pointed.

Brighton glanced up to examine the detailed image. He seldom came into this room and could not tell what the screen displayed. The image and numbers meant nothing to him.

"What's all the fuss?" he asked as his eyes wandered all over the gargantuan screen. "I don't see anything unusual."

"There, sir," the corporal said and indicated a small "zoom box" that highlighted an object in motion.

A very large screen that spread across one whole end of a very large room dwarfed the two men standing before it. The huge image that currently filled the display showed the Pacific Ocean. Row upon row of detailed readouts overlaid the entire left side of the screen. Its gargantuan image overwhelmed the captain's ability to make sense of it. He looked at the left side. Brighton watched as streams of data poured out in a continuously moving list of data that ran down the screen.

"What is all of that? That's your specialty, corporal. Is that non-sensical junk spewing out from our NAT-IX satellite?" Brighton asked. He did not understand the data stream.

"Yes, sir," Peterson replied.

"Can you clear that off the display?" Brighton requested.

Peterson touched something on his console that removed most of the onscreen clutter. He expanded the view of the "zoom box." The two men stared at the clarified image, puzzled and confused, as they tried to make sense of the oval-shaped object that flew across the screen at a very high rate of speed, faster than any known aircraft in existence. Next to it, the letters "UFO" flashed in yellow. When he saw the letters, Brighton ran his hand down his face to keep from loosing his temper out of frustration.

"What the devil is that?" Brighton wondered, "and please don't tell me it's a UFO!"

"That's why I called you, sir," the corporal said. "Even if you don't like the label, I'd call that highly unusual."

"Start a recording…" Captain Brighton ordered.

"The system is way ahead of you, sir," Cpl. Peterson informed him. "It started the recording the moment its sensors came on line."

"Do you have a point of origin?" Brighton asked.

"Unfortunately, the satellite didn't pick it up right away," Peterson replied. "Based on its trajectory, the computer places its point of origin back toward either New Zealand or Australia."

"Australia?" Brighton replied, surprised. "Shouldn't be hostile then… should it?"

"I would not think so, sir," Peterson said rather absently.

"Could it have been launched from a sub?" Brighton speculated.

"I doubt that, sir," Peterson quickly spoke up.

"Why not?" Brighton asked.

"You can only launch a rocket from a sub," Peterson pointed out. "A rocket would leave a vapor trail, have a heat signature. The read out display, which you ordered off the screen, showed that information."

"Oh… well… put it back up," the captain said.

The corporal touched his control panel and the read out resumed.

"You see, sir? No heat signature. Can you see that?" Peterson pointed.

Brighton scratched his chin and furrowed his brow.

"Yes… I see your point. Can't be a new experimental jet, can it?" He asked his resident expert.

"Pentagon's got some space spy planes that can go nearly as fast… but not in the atmosphere. Look at its altitude of 40,000 feet…"

"Metric, soldier," Brighton corrected.

"That's about 12,000 meters… sir," Peterson corrected. "It's not in space. It's in the upper atmosphere… and whatever it is," the corporal continued as he checked the computer evaluation, "it isn't a rocket or a jet aircraft."

"How do you know that?" Brighton shot back.

"Because NAT-IX says it's not leaving any chemical trail either, sir," Peterson told him. "It isn't even leaving a wake, which should be impossible."

Brighton gave the corporal a confused expression.

"Anything that moves through the atmosphere creates a wake… Doesn't it? How is that possible?" the captain asked, his eyes narrowed on the object. "Are you certain that isn't a glitch?"

Yes, sir," the corporal quickly answered. "I ran diagnostics."

"You say it's not leaving a chemical trail? No heat signature at all?" the captain asked, incredulous.

"No, sir," Peterson said and gestured toward the read out on the screen. "We aren't just scanning this object in the visual or infrared range. This image is only available in the new multispectral imagers that have yet to go online with the defensive grid. Its signature is either far into the red or into the blue end of the EMS. Do you want me to sound the general alarm, sir?"

Corporal Peterson flipped up the cover of a special card insert slot and started to take off the ID badge on his chest, capable of activating the alarm system, which would notify NORAD and the Defense Department.

"Not yet…" Brighton added as he waved his hand at the corporal. In his mind, this object represented more of a curiosity than a threat to national security. "You did say the computer analyzed the data and stated its place of origin as Australia and not China or India," the captain asked as he turned toward Cpl. Peterson, "…and definitely not a submarine?"

"That's right, sir," the corporal replied. "Had it launched from the sea, NORAD would have broadcast an alert."

"For some reason," the captain said as he stared up at the moving sphere, "I agree with the computer. I believe the object to be non-belligerent. I mean if this read out is true… then this object is invisible… to a fighter jet or missile defense system, I mean."

"I believe you are right, sir," the corporal replied as he pulled his hand away. "I didn't think about that."

"…and normal interceptor tracking couldn't hit it," Brighton offered as he referred to missile command that tracked and fired its rockets at hostile targets.

"Again, captain, I believe you are correct," the corporal responded. "I could pipe this in to the general's office, or over to NORAD, sir, if you require another opinion," the corporal urged.

"Let's not be too hasty," Brighton said as he turned to face Corporal Peterson. "Wait a second, what did you say?" he asked as if he just woke up. "Do you mean to tell me that neither the NSA nor NORAD is receiving these images, soldier?"

"No, sir," Peterson confirmed. "This is our private satellite, NAT-IX, secretly launched three weeks ago by ARANE. General Andrews intends to use it exclusively for Spec Ops. We're still working out the alignment problems, sir."

Brighton walked closer to the screen. The luminescent bubble moved very fast as it streaked passed Hawaii. The computer projected its entry destination into North America at a point just north of San Francisco.

"I've never seen anything move that fast. What is its speed?" he asked.

The Corporal glanced up at the readout. "At its peak, the spherically shaped object exceeded Mach 10," he told his superior.

"Exceeded Mach 10?" Brighton said, whirling around. "Did you say at its peak?"

"Yes, sir, the object is slowing down..." the corporal pointed out, "using a controlled braking maneuver."

"A rocket can't do that!" the captain exclaimed.

"I know that, sir," the corporal replied.

"Are you certain we can track this with our new satellite?" the captain interrupted.

"For a while, at least," the corporal stated, "I'm not sure if the satellite is in proper position to track it beyond the middle of North America... uh, oh," Corporal Peterson added.

Brighton closed his eyes and refrained from biting his tongue.

"Don't ever say 'uh, oh' in my presence again. I hate that expression," he said with his quaint British accent. "What the devil is happening now?"

"The object is losing altitude. I would say that it is going to land," the corporal pointed out.

"Or explode!" Brighton added as his hand rushed to pull his own key from around his neck and plunge it into the console's slot.

Oddly, the corporal changed his demeanor. He reached out and stayed the captain's hand by placing his own hand on the man's arm. The two exchanged glances. The touch of Peterson's hand on his arm made the captain shudder.

"What do you mean by this gesture, soldier?" the captain demanded, yet nervously swallowed hard from discomfort. "He's got a firm grip for being... gay," he privately thought.

"I doubt the object is going to explode, sir," Peterson said as he nodded back toward the screen. "The computer was correct to label the object as nonbelligerent."

"Why?" Brighton questioned.

"No explosive device would come in at such a sharp vector or at that speed. It's slowed to less than Mach one," the Corporal explained. "That's a controlled landing speed, not a collision speed," the corporal said and pointed, "Look!"

The two men watched as the elongated sphere headed inland toward the Rocky Mountains, yet it moved significantly slower as it lost altitude.

"If that were an attack, other systems would have detected it, wouldn't they?" Brighton asked.

"I'm not certain, sir, on how to respond to your comment. As you said, it appears somehow to be invisible. No technology on this planet can do that. It seems we have a bona-fide UFO on our hands, possibly an alien spacecraft that is about land..." Peterson started.

"No," Brighton said dismissively and cut him off, "don't even suggest it. Aliens, my foot! I don't believe in such a thing. This is a glitch in the computer system. I'm telling you that what we've seen is simply some new aviation device from DARPA or the Air Force. They test things all the time. I refuse to believe that is an alien spacecraft."

"Whatever they are, they've dropped out of range. Their gone," the corporal indicated. "About 500 meters above the surface, they vanished."

"Gone?" Brighton asked, this time genuinely confused. "I thought you said you could track it!"

"The NAT-IX can track anything, even to Kansas, but something happened..." Peterson said as his voice dropped.

"What?" the captain demanded.

"I believe they've landed, sir," Peterson reported, "looks like, southwestern Kansas from the last position."

"Aliens... UFO's... no vapor trail, no wake... this is highly suspicious..." the captain thought as he scratched his eyebrow. Brighton turned to the corporal, his face full of determination. "I have an idea..." Brighton said and looked the corporal in the eye, "and I want you to be a part of this. Are you with me? No, hanky-panky."

The corporal inwardly blushed. He knew exactly what the captain meant. Nevertheless, he thought his personnel file was a secret. He tried not to let his face show any change so that the captain would still wonder. Somehow, he managed to fool the older man with his stony expression.

"I don't know what you mean, sir," the young man replied.

Brighton stared at the corporal's perfect straight face and figuratively blinked. For the time being, any doubts he may have had about Peterson's private life he set aside. He took in a deep breath and continued.

"I want a copy of that recording on my desk in five minutes. I intend to take this information straight to General Andrews," the captain ordered.

"What do you think it is, sir?" the corporal asked as he inserted a chip to make a transferable copy.

"I believe we've just witnessed something that could change the course of humanity," Brighton told him.

"If you don't mind me asking, how?" Peterson questioned.

"We may have an individual, possibly a scientist from Australia, who has created an aircraft capable of circumnavigating the globe in less time than it takes to have lunch," the captain stated. "That is what I believe, not an alien… a very clever person."

"…and can elude detection, ordinary detection, that is," the corporal added.

"True," the captain echoed.

"Why land in America?" Peterson asked.

"I intend to find out," Brighton said with a low voice. "Where is the general?"

"Probably asleep, sir," the corporal said.

"I won't wake him tonight," the captain said. "Mention what you have seen to no one. This is strictly top secret from this moment on; and I want no report filed through normal channels for now. Download all of the read out into a memory chip… you know, one of those portable ones. Remove the log information. Then call for a replacement and log out. Bring that information chip to my office. You and I are about to become a very important part of this organization… if I have anything to say about it."

Chapter Two

An Alien in Our Midst

Villi swooped around in a slow arc as the strangely shaped aircraft headed down out of the sky. He programmed the computer to open automatically the fuselage's wings when the aircraft dropped below Mach 1. Its wheeled, spindly, insect-like legs slowly lowered while the large oval-shaped craft with its fully extended boxy wings moved on the flight vector to their destination. The team left after breakfast in Australia. Here, the hour was late in the evening and dark outside. In the distance, they could see wide patches of winter's white blanket scattered about the countryside. At around 500 meters, the aircraft entered the protective shield that not only hid the village of Rollo; it provided perfect weather year round.

Michael, Su Lin, Cecilia, Zinian, Zhiwei, and Chou rose up out of their seats and entered the back of the pilot's cockpit. They stood behind Villi as he gently steered the big aircraft toward the hanger, whose large mouth-like gates parted as the ship descended. They could see lights on in several homes scattered about Rollo. Master Li alerted Running Elk as to their arrival. She, in turn, woke several others and so on. Despite the late hour, a group of determined people crossed the stretch of land between the northern parkland and the entrance to the vast underground hanger complex. Michael and Cecilia held hands. The whole group leaned on one another and welcomed the sight. The ordeal in Australia had been a trying one.

Villi could just make out the artificial moonlight that reflected off the mirrored surface of the "duck pond" in the north park. The peaceful scene welcomed the young Russian in a familial way, as if the village itself reached up with its collective arms and embraced him. The underground hanger's huge gray metallic doors magically slid apart as the aircraft approached. The strangely shaped craft entered the opening and softly landed on the platform. The elevated round platform moved the aircraft further into the interior and headed downward until it locked into place, while Villi sat back and relaxed.

"Destination reached," the ship's computer reported.

"Start shut down procedures for the super conductors," he instructed. "Begin power down protocols of all systems."

"Acknowledged," the computer replied.

"Rollo," Villi sighed as he glanced back over his shoulder at Su Lin. "Good to be home."

Villi was not the only one in their group who held that sentiment. The entire group felt good to be back in their oasis of safety and beauty.

"Home…" the other psychics echoed.

They had just finished a long and arduous journey. Australia was in the middle of its summer. The desert region had been especially hot and dry this season. They flew down to confront a terrible rogue psychic and to welcome a new member into their ranks. Fortunately, they stopped the rogue psychic before he could wreck too much havoc on the region, although he did inflict terrible damage on the city of Brisbane.

"Strange request of Master Li," Villi thought when he recalled the flight home. "He linked to me 'Let's see how fast you can go!' Odd, he never made a silly request like that," he thought. "We made it home in record time," he considered as he closed off the flight controls. "I didn't think this baby could go faster than when we traveled to Australia. Coming back, we clocked our fastest time yet! I can't wait to tell Edward and Victor!"

Yes, they had arrived home in Rollo, Kansas, headquarters to the WPO – this village created by the Native American Comanche and the nine original psychics – their secret community tucked away in an obscure and largely ignored part of the American west. This was February 2019, and the outside world had changed very little from the previous decade of the 21st Century, certainly not in a fantastic way, unless you lived in Rollo.

New York was not a city with flying cars or magically moving sidewalk belts that whisked people around the city. Many cars still used gasoline, although the number of electric cars now numbered nearly forty percent of all those driven. Some countries, such as those of the European Union, used syn-fuels, and a few countries had even begun to use fuel cells. Governments hadn't changed much either. While political parties in power seemed to swing back and forth, the world continued as it had been for decades with only cosmetic changes.

In Rollo, you could say the opposite was true. Contact with other worlds via Galactic Central transformed the village in one filled with technological and biological marvels. The psychics completely controlled their environment.

From the way their plants grew at fantastic rates of speed, to how they lived in their self-cleaning homes filled with a myriad of electronic gadgets, Rollo would be a place unrecognizable to outsiders. A person could travel around town on an antigravity hovercraft, watch true three-dimensional curved television screens without glasses, and enjoy a daily generous slice of climate-controlled abundance. Tucked away in the corner of America's breadbasket, Rollo represented an idyllic paradise: no disease, no poverty, perfect weather, perfect health, an endless supply of food, and plentiful employment that involved only maintenance. The citizens of Rollo could do what they wanted, when they wanted… except leave… but then, who would want to.

Two young Native American men, Villi's assistants, ran out to greet the newly arrived psychics as the clear bubble-nosed craft moved inside the hanger. When the village transitioned two and a half years ago, they were teens, hell bent on going to Kansas City and a life of delinquency. That changed when Villi took them under his wing and taught them aircraft mechanics along with martial arts. Like many of the other Native Americans, the young men or women stayed and enjoyed their new life here instead of leaving to the outside world. Some worked construction projects. Some worked to maintain the parks. Some cooked or baked meals that families shared. Some worked in the manor house. Some maintained the greenhouses. Zhwei had two assistants in security. Zinian had his work crew headed by John. While, Villi's two assistants helped to maintain this huge hanger complex.

"Villi!" Victor and Edward shouted and waved from the control room above the platform.

When the team left for some crisis, no one in the village knew if they would return. Imagine the relief they felt when the people who saved their village from self-destruction returned home in triumph from another mission. It was no wonder or surprise to anyone onboard the aircraft when such a large crowd of people turned out to welcome them home at such a late hour in the evening.

Villi glanced out of the cockpit and acknowledged his helpers as the platform swung the clear nose of the large steely gray oval aircraft around to face the control room.

Victor and Edward ran to the elevator and soon joined the gathering party of friends that waited for the side to open. The two crewmen stabilized the aircraft's special engines so that the ambient heat on the outside of aircraft's hull did not disturb the temperature of the superconducting cores. Despite the fact that a psychic bubble minimized friction around the craft, the crew had to maintain the difference in the two temperatures. They started the liquid nitrogen preservation process that kept the special engines in stasis.

They donned their safety gear as the computer protocol requested it. A yellow caution light came on.

"Whoa!" Victor said as he looked at the read out. "Look at this!"

Edward walked over and glanced down at the panel.

"I wonder why he did that?" the young man questioned his boss.

The computer attached special hoses to the rear of the aircraft. A great hissing noise followed as the extremely cold liquid poured into chambers that flanked the engine cores.

"Is it my imagination or did we take less time coming back?" Michael asked his pilot friend.

Villi, in the process of directing his ground crew, stopped to link back.

"Master Li requested additional speed," he informed him. "He offered no explanation other than to hurry," he told his friend. "If you'll excuse me, Michael..." Villi said as he turned his attention back to his ground crew. "As soon as you attach the thermal conductors and stabilize the readouts, we can safely depart the aircraft," Villi requested.

"Sorry, Villi," Victor replied when he realized the core's temperature had skyrocketed to 96 degrees Kelvin (-177 C or -286 F) during the flight. "You must have pushed the engines to their limit," he pointed out. "It should only take a few minutes," he relayed, "the readings surpassed safety ratings."

"As I thought," Villi mumbled but hoped that Master Li had not heard his comment.

Finally, Edward spoke into his com-link mouthpiece.

"The cores have reached 69 Kelvin, which is their optimum. Those are safe levels... and Running Elk tells me that if I don't allow you to open the doors this instant, she will," he added.

"Acknowledged," Villi chuckled.

He signaled back through the fuselage to the passengers that it was safe to proceed. He touched a control and dropped the clear firewall that surrounded flight deck during take offs and landings.

Sensing Running Elk's urgency, Master Li used his mind to open the aircraft's side door. A staircase extended down from the oval shaped fuselage. Master Li stepped out first. A cheer went up from the crowd when they saw his kindly face. He slowly descended the steps and spied Running Elk as she emerged from the group of Native American friends. Her keen eye thoroughly examined Li's exterior to make certain nothing bad happened to him in Australia.

"Welcome home," she said, relieved.

"Good to be here," he told her.

Though intimately linked via a private connection, Master Li and Running Elk never showed any physical affection toward one another in public. They did not hug, hold hands or even embrace. Running Elk brushed the Comanche children forward. They ran to and surrounded the elderly man who made them all see a shower of flowers cascade like rain out of the air. The whole group of friends saw it, too. The adults laughed as the children chased the imaginary flowers only to grab at air when they tried to catch one.

"Hooray! Master Li has returned!" the children cried.

Villi left the pilot's cockpit and descended the steps with Su Lin. She seemed tired and listless after their ordeal in the outback.

"You ok?" he linked to her.

"Sure," she linked back, yet blocked most of her thoughts.

Rollo's two most famous couples thrived on open communication – Cecilia, Su Lin, Villi and Michael were very close friends and frequently mind shared. The isolation that the women created during the trip baffled the group's leader and the Russian ex-cop.

"Strange," Villi thought regarding her block. "She's usually quite open."

Michael and Cecilia departed the aircraft after Villi and Su Lin.

"You're oddly silent," Michael linked to her.

Cecilia, normally a psychic chatterbox, did not link or say anything. She seemed drawn toward Master Li. She let go of Michael's hand and moved near Li.

Master Li, who only seconds before accepted a kiss on either cheek French-style from Star Wind, turned around and looked back toward the aircraft at his assembled team. Running Elk sensed trouble in his mind and saw concern on his face.

"What's wrong?" she asked.

Master Li shook his head and frowned. He could not explain it to her without saying too much in front of the others. The trip left him feeling tired and weak. He glanced over her shoulder and saw many familiar faces of the manor house staff, the work crews sensed weariness on Cecilia's face. Li smiled and waved at their Native American friends when a sudden queer expression ran over his face. He spun around and pointed at a stunned Cecilia.

"Aliens in our midst!" he cried out.

Everyone in the hanger froze. Since Master Li was an expert when it came to blocking, the psychics could not understand his meaning. He walked over to Cecilia. Su Lin defensively moved up to her side. Li shot her the same look of shock on his face.

"Did you think you could hide them forever?" he put to the women. "I wondered what troubled me on that flight home," he said aloud so that everyone on the hanger deck could hear, "that pounding urgency to return home," he continued as he paced back and forth. "I felt a change in the air for two days. I've been so preoccupied with my other gifted colleagues… I did not put two and two together," he added. He turned to the women and broad smile crossed his face. "May I make the official announcement?" he requested.

The two women exchanged glances as if they shared an intimate secret and then nodded their approval.

"Thank you," he said as made a gesture with his arms. "It gives me great pleasure to report that a transformation has taken place," he announced to the gathering. "We have two new visitors." He bent over and whispered toward Cecilia's stomach. "Welcome little one," he said. He reached out and placed his hand on her abdomen.

Cecilia's eyes started to water. Again, she only nodded. Emotion caught the words in her throat.

"Master Li… I…" she linked as she glanced over at Michael.

"You have a child, growing inside your body," he told her.

"Yes, it's true," she finally declared. Her eyes searched Michael's face for a reaction.

Michael dropped the luggage in his hands. He had not expected this. He rushed to her arms. He embraced and held her as tears streamed from her eyes.

"This is only half the story," Master Li said aloud.

He moved over to Su Lin and repeated the gesture he made on Cecilia.

"You've been hiding a secret, too, haven't you?" he confronted her.

Su Lin glanced over at her friend, Cecilia.

"Yes," she stammered, "I wanted to tell you…" she started when she glanced over at Villi.

"What?" the pilot cried out. "Is it true? You're pregnant?" he said as he embraced Su Lin. "Whoopee!" he cried, his shouted word echoed around the great open space.

The rest of the group and bystanders rushed in with congratulations. They all wanted to express their happiness for the two couples. The joy seemed contagious as they embraced one another. The Rollo group united around the happy event. Even Han dropped his usual formality and gave Su Lin and Cecilia a friendly hug.

The world's first truly psychic women would bear the world's first psychic children. The joyous moment was brief. The group notice Li's face changed to one of concern as he kept his focus on the children within their mother's wombs.

"This is a troubling development," he said as he linked with the psychics. "These children are not dividing cells. They have rapidly advanced in less than a week, faster than ordinary human children would have grown. Already, they are aware of their environment, even with only minimal development. At this rate, they will be fully formed infants in only three or four months," he told them. "They will need special care, as do the mothers. I sense great psychic strength. Both father and mother must keep these growing infants aware of the caring world around them, so that the raw input they perceive will not frighten them. No other child ever experienced what will be their level of awareness, for these individuals will remember everything of their existence, even their time in the womb..." he linked. Once more he began to pace and his thoughts drifted.

No one moved. They watched and studied Master Li. Finally, he stopped and glanced up. He noticed that the two couples stared back at him. Without a word of expression, they understood the full ramifications of his intended speech, for psychics express not only thoughts but also meaning when they communicate.

"This is no ordinary pregnancy... and these will be extraordinary children... Michael, Cecilia, Villi, Su Lin... do you understand?" he put to them.

They nodded in reply. At the same moment, they turned their focus inward to the developing fetuses.

Han glanced over at Master Li. With an almost accusatory tone in his thoughts, he practically glared at his mentor.

"What did you do to them, old man?" he privately wondered.

A memory came back to Han, one he was not meant to retain. He blocked his thoughts and momentarily turned away. He remembered something that happened several days ago, when the entire WPO membership came to visit due to Master Li's request. Han went to bed after dinner. The rest of the guests went to library. Li joined them after he spoke to the Rollo group about preparations for Australia. Something happened in the library that night. He sensed it from his room. However, he was not present. He knew that Li used the other member's energy to perform some alteration. What Li did he could not say. Perhaps he erased the memory of what he did from their guests' minds, Han speculated. His focus went from the two perpetually youthful couples over to Master Li. The elderly sage did not look in Han's direction.

"This situation bears study," Han thought.

Master Li suddenly shifted his attention skyward. He lifted his eyes toward the heavens. Zhiwei sensed trouble. He looked up as well.

"What is it?" Zhiwei whispered.

"I fear other changes have taken place," Li said with his head tilted back, "changes that will impact our lives." He glanced over at Zhiwei. "I am not certain what I sense..."

As head of security, Zhiwei knew he would need to start an investigation immediately.

"I will begin new scans at once," he thought to Li.

The elderly man paused a moment, glanced around him at the eager welcoming faces, and then shook his head.

"We have only just returned home," he said as his expression changed to calm. "Here I am, sounding like the harbinger of doom and gloom. Relax; enjoy some solitude with your loved ones. This investigation can wait for a few days," he told his head of security.

Trusting Master Li's words, Zhiwei turned to his Native American girlfriend and kissed her. Chou went to meet up with Star Wind. She patiently waited next to her mother. They embraced and kissed. This was the first time they had separated since the wedding. Zinian held his Native American girlfriend close. The two hugged and kissed just as the others did, having missed each other. Only Han remained a bachelor, unable to release the memory of his deceased wife, which kept him from making any formal commitment to another woman.

Running Elk walked beside Master Li as they strolled from the hanger to the manor house. She spread a coat over Li's shoulders, although the weather inside the dome was a comfortable 20 degrees Celsius (68 Fahrenheit).

"Lovely night for a walk," he linked to her and motioned to the north park. As soon as they rounded a corner on the path through the woods and away from the sight of others, her hand found his.

Normally generous with his exchanges, Li did not share any thoughts with Running Elk about Australia; or what happened just now in the hanger. She did not mind. She was content to hold his hand and have him home. Yet as Li walked beside her, he could not shake the feeling that someone watched over them.

Chapter Three

A Subtle Difference

Five years passed since that fateful night in February 2019, when the Rollo team returned from its adventure in Australia. Many changes took place during that period: around the planet, in the WPO, and even in Rollo with the peculiar births of not just two, but eventually five psychic individuals. Their very presence changed the dynamics within the organization.

Halfway around the world on the planet's second largest continent, some other startling changes took place in April of 2024, changes that would mark this year as the most fateful since Michael Tyler first heard his Galactic Central voice at age ten.

Late one evening, two citizens in the land-locked country of Mali huddled over a machine whose display screen glowed in a darkened laboratory. They worked in a small clinic just west of central Gao, a moderately sized city located on the eastern side of Mali and situated on the great Niger River. A large black man wearing a long white yet soiled lab jacket sat on a stool. He peered intently at the image on a display screen. He had a kind face, with graying temples and very dark skin. His eyes, bloodshot from strain and lack of sleep, focused on the complex image that shone before him.

A young, black female, small, demur, and simply dressed, also wearing a lab jacket, stood by his side as she had for the past seven years – his trusted assistant, Kim. While they often worked together after hours in the intimacy of the lab, they had a very cordial yet platonic relationship, casual and informal.

"You should have reason it out by now," she said as her hand reached out and lightly touched the controls.

"If every puzzle revealed an easy solution," he sighed as he glanced away for a moment and rubbed his eyes, "we would not strive to find unknowns like this one."

He returned to the image for a moment longer before frustration forced him to push away. He sat up and leaned his large frame back. He stretched his big arms out and sighed.

"I'm wading through a pool of mud," Salla Motambou commented.

"Struggle builds fortitude," Kim said as she leaned against him.

Salla smiled slightly before he returned his gaze toward the screen.

"Where did you hear that rot, Kim?" he spoke over his shoulder.

"It's on the wall in your office," she answered as she patted his broad shoulders before she moved on. "Besides, I believe you mentioned this virus is different from any you've seen, isn't that so?"

Kim flipped a switch that turned on the room lights.

"I'm not sure," he said, squinting. "It's funny, but from what I've seen so far, this virus vaguely resembles another…" his voice trailed off as he concentrated on the screen.

Dr. Salla Motambou knew the nuances of almost every African virus that existed. After all, he spent the last seven years of his adult life in Africa studying both simian and human viruses alike, especially those specimens taken from the surrounding countryside of his homeland, Mali.

This evening he and his lab assistant, Kim, prepared the stage to display a recent acquisition for detailed examination – a new specimen brought to him by special messenger from up river. He anxiously anticipated its view with his digital electron microscope, thanks to Kim's help.

Salla often worked late in his lab. Still early by his standards, a few minutes before eight o'clock, Salla remained fixed on comparing this new specimen to others in his vast collection. He dedicated his life to the study of virology. The numerous commendations, awards, and citations on the wall proved that his passion paid off handsomely, including a prize rarely accorded in a person's lifetime – the great Nobel in medicine for his work on an inclusive serum that would give immunity from all viruses. Whenever he received a new viral specimen for study, such as this one that arrived from upstream, he treated that day as a birthday or holiday, as he considered them gifts.

After he prepared the stage, he turned on the electron microscope and zoomed down, closer and closer, until at last he spotted the culprit as he suspected he would, tiny in comparison to the gargantuan blood cells around it. He frowned when his closer examination revealed details he did not expect to see, not just one isolated virus, but hundreds, thousands, perhaps millions in this one small drop, a troubling development.

"This is not good," he thought as he puzzled over the sheer numbers present.

He presumed he would search for hours before he spotted the culprit. Instead, he instantly found so many. The mystery now lay in why. Why were there so many viruses… and why did they rapidly attack just the red blood cells? Salla needed to know the answers and soon, for privately he feared the worst could happen… epidemic.

"Their structure seems oddly familiar," he said as he took out a pad to take notes.

At first, he believed the microorganism might be the same virus he studied for years, Ebola. This virus had similar structure and seemed to carry out a similar purpose. He peered intently at the screen in front of him; its bluish-white hue cast a large shadow on the wall behind him, which outlined his large form. Yes, he knew that virus well.

"You certainly resemble my old friend…" his thoughts trailed off. He adjusted his stool and moved in closer. "I've a strange feeling you're something new and not one of my usual specimens."

Over the past decade, Dr. Salla Motambou studied many viruses but concentrated his efforts on Ebola. He published his findings in scientific journals around the world. Although he did not publish his personal feelings, he feared the Ebola virus might mutate into a wild strain and quickly spread through the world. He spent those last seven years trying to prepare for such an eventuality.

Yet, for all his vast knowledge, Salla really did not recognize this object on the screen. He feared he might have discovered a variant. If that was the case, the results could be catastrophic and newsworthy. However, before he could make any announcement, he would need to study this virus for many days before he came to any conclusions.

Once more he rubbed his poor strained tired eyes as his day that began fourteen hours ago finally seemed about to end. His large black face aged a great deal from its former handsome and youthful state. The corners of his mouth that once easily curved up now slackened from frequent disappointment and sorrow. The chin so firm and proud began to sag. Dark circles filled in the skin under his eyes from lack of sleep.

"Can I help you with anything else, Dr. Motambou?" his assistant asked, her voice intruded on his concentration.

"Would you mind shutting off the lights, Kim," Salla requested. "The glare on the screen hurts my eyes."

"Yes, doctor. Did you find anything unusual in the specimen?" she hesitated at the light switch.

"You prepared a good sample," he informed her. He did not wish to reveal more to avoid the spread of fearful gossip. "Just turn off the lights before you go. I want to study this preparation a bit longer."

"You've put in a long day," she replied softly. "We can always examine it tomorrow."

She waited for a reply, but Dr. Motambou remained focused on the screen and had already tuned her out.

"Oh, by the way, take extra precautions as you leave," he mumbled absently. "I'm not certain what we have."

"Of course," she said and remembered something important. "Don't forget the time, Doctor Motambou. Your wife will be upset if you are late for this evening's dinner."

"Yes, yes, good night, Kim," he absently spoke. "Don't forget the lights. You may go."

He acted as though he had not heard her. She stared at his back for a moment before she switched off the lights and slipped out the door.

The screen clarity improved in the total darkness. His eyes barely focused on the image. Salla considered himself fortunate the virus survived in a dormant state and not an active one.

Somehow, fortune favored Dr. Motambou in many ways. Few private researchers in Africa possessed a digital electron microscope of this caliber. Even fewer had their own privately funded laboratory to perform independent studies at their leisure. So, how did such an esteemed physician and viral researcher come to live in the eastern part of a lowly country like Mali and be equipped with a top of line electron microscope and sophisticated laboratory?

Dr. Salla Motambou began his climb into the elite prestigious world of respected viral researchers many years earlier, when as a little boy, curiosity drove him to seek answers that each leaf, each insect, and each microbe seemed to hold in store in for him. His story began on the opposite side of Mali, in the west, on a small farm far away from any large village or town. He was much smaller then, a scrawny skinny boy with an insatiable inquisitive nature...

Chapter Four

From an Acorn

In October of 1985, Salla Motambou was born on a small family-owned farm located thirty-two kilometers (20 miles) outside the village of Kita, about 208 km. (130 mi) west of Bamako, the capital city of Mali. The people who lived in this area were quite impoverished. In 1985, they had no schools, hospitals, running water, or even electricity for that matter. Most people lived in "mud" huts or houses. At night when the sun went down, the area grew very dark unless one sat near the fire that burned in the cooking pit located outside the hut that Salla called home from the time of his birth.

His father should have been a farmer, like many of his neighbors and his father's father had been. Their farm was special, for it had a well, the only source of water within a ten-kilometer radius. After Salla's grandfather died, his father inherited the well. He started to sell the previously free water to the same neighbors he once called friends. Therefore, if anyone wanted fresh water, they paid Salla's father or had to locate another source. Soon, the money he obtained from the well gave him the opportunity to have more than one wife. He eventually brought home three wives.

By having the only freshwater well in the area, Salla's father possessed a profitable means of support. Instead of helping his large expanding family, the pitiless monster took his gains and gambled on the weekends in the nearby village of Kita. Over the next 10 years, those three wives bore him 15 children, Salla being the youngest. Salla's father ruled over his household as a tyrant. He beat his wives and children anytime he pleased. As a child, Salla entered a life full of hazards. Not a day passed when Salla did not go to bed hungry or he was beaten because his siblings accused him of wrongdoing to avoid their own beating. The night brought different horrors.

A woven mat covered the floor of his father's bedroom. He and the wife in current favor slept on padded pillows filled with finely chopped dried straw. The children and the other two wives not in current favor huddled together in the other room on a dirt floor. They shared their living quarters with insects that crawled around them throughout the night. Sometimes Salla woke to find bites on him that itched for days.

When his father went to gamble in Kita, Salla's mother and the other two wives remained home. They worked the land around the hut and raised the food needed to feed Salla and his siblings. Unlike other providers, Salla's father seldom bought home meat for his family from Kita's markets, except when he stayed on the farm for any length of time. He preferred gambling and prostitutes instead of caring for his family. He only returned home to collect the well fees and reassert his authority over the family.

By the time Salla reached his tenth birthday, he did not behave as his brothers and sisters did, with cynicism and contempt. At this age, Salla began to notice and appreciate the living world that grew in his environment. He loved to explore, possessed an insatiable curiosity about plants, insects, and studied animals, too, to see how they functioned. Teased by his parents and siblings as a daydreamer, they often made him work hard tasks, such as pulling water out of the well, digging latrines, fetching firewood, and weeding the garden.

As he worked tirelessly on his monotonous tasks without complaint, he constantly focused his attention on nature. From the tiniest leaf to anything that crawled or flew, Salla carefully scrutinized specimens as if cataloguing the biological spectrum of their farm. His ability to recall facts outshined his uncanny faculty to study them. Yet, the little boy remained silent around his family lest they beat him for being outspoken.

Unfortunately, the first time he caught and studied a frog, his father happened to be home. He spied Salla's activity and severely beat the boy for being lazy by "wasting his time." He forced the 10-year-old boy to sleep outside the hut that night, alone. The moist grass felt cool to his bruises and bleeding welts as he lay on the ground. He looked up at the night sky and watched the stars.

"If only someone would come to take me from this place," the boy prayed. He stared up at the sparkling heavens that spread across the blackness of space. He closed his eyes and tears slid down his face.

By some strange turn of fate, a missionary wandered into their region the following morning. Slightly naïve yet genuinely warm-hearted, this white-skinned Englishman named Jonathan Ramsey with his receeding hairline and graying hair, already into his late-forties, took his passionate religious fervor to Africa. He volunteered to spread the word of the gospel for his church.

Jonathan started out his adult life as Dr. Ramsey, an English country doctor, whose private practice eventually failed after ten years due to increasing debt and mismanagement, common to many physicians actually. Jonathan did not fare well in the love department either. Married only a short time before his medical business collapsed; his wife of two years left him and took nearly all of his assets. He spent the next few years, working hard in a local clinic to pay off his debts. However, the idea of being a country doctor disheartened Jonathan. He eventually gave up his dream of practicing medicine and became a minister in the Church of England.

In the summer of 1995, Jonathan volunteered to go to Mali as a missionary, working on behalf of the church. He tried to use what medical knowledge he retained from his practice to help the disadvantaged in many of the small villages he visited. He often cleaned and dressed infected wounds, or treated children with dysentery when some charity donated the medical supplies. Mostly, he taught cleanliness while he preached his religion. Most of the large communities spoke French. In the provinces and out in the countryside, the natives spoke Bambara and dialects varied from village to village.

When he came upon Salla's farm, he no longer had the guide that brought him to this part of Mali's countryside. He couldn't afford to pay the man with the little cash he had left. He saved it for his trip home. Acting alone, without an interpreter, he convinced the three wives that he was there to help them. He spent an entire day examining all fifteen children and even the wives once they realized he was a doctor. The father was away in Kita gambling. Although the women feared the father's reaction should he find out about the missionary, they nonetheless allowed Jonathan to stay while they sent one of the children to watch the trail should the father return.

Jonathan examined Salla last. The shy child hung back and observed the Englishman all day until he finally found the courage to step forward.

"You're a brave one," Jonathan stated when Salla probed his bag. The missionary used his stethoscope to "auscultate" or hear the heart and lungs of the women and children. While the little boy watched, he observed the missionary and carefully listened as he spoke.

When Jonathan finished Salla's exam, the boy retrieved and picked up the stethoscope, just as he had seen the missionary do. He placed the buds in his ears and put the diaphragm on his chest. His eyes grew large and round when he realized that the instrument amplified the sound of his heart. The missionary looked down at the boy and wondered how much he grasped.

"You're listening to your heart," Jonathan said in English and pointed to his own chest.

He formed a heart with his cupped hands and moved his hands in rhythm, squeezing them together.

"It pumps your blood. Lub-dub, lub-dub… Hear it beat?"

He saw the boy's head tilt as if puzzled by what he'd said.

"I don't know why I bother to explain things. You can't possibly understand me," Jonathan said aloud.

He took back the stethoscope from Salla and placed it back into his carrying bag.

"H...h...heart," the young boy stammered as he pointed to his chest.

Jonathan's head jerked around, completely taken aback. Did that little black child speak to him in the Queen's English?

"Yes, heart," he pointed again to his own chest. The boy said nothing, so the minister patted him on the head and said slowly, "Very good."

"G...g...good," the boy tried to repeat.

This response shocked the missionary.

"Yes!" Jonathan exclaimed, astonished at the boy's level of understanding. "That's amazing. You're an amazing little fellow."

"A... a... amazing." Salla struggled to annunciate.

Now the missionary frowned in reaction. He had not expected to find any child as exceptional as this in the wilderness. Had he actually comprehended the meaning of the words, or did he simply mimic the sound?

Salla reached inside the missionary's bag and picked up a glass thermometer in a clear plastic case.

"Let's see if you can get this one," Jonathan thought as he decided to try an experiment. "Thermometer," the man of the cloth instructed. He took it out and pointed to the long glass tube that he placed in Salla's hand.

This time Salla examined the device in his little hands. His eyes carefully explored every detail. He noticed tiny writing along the white side on the back. On the front of the long tube, he noted numbers and a red-colored liquid partway up from a bulb at the base. He flipped the tube back over. His eyes examined the back once more. Then he cocked his head to one side. He glanced up at the older man, and instead of repeating what the minister said; Salla stammered out a different word, a word he heard the missionary say when using the device.

"T...tem... temp... tempa-chure," he spoke in slow hesitant English. He pointed to the numbers along the side, "D... de-grease."

"I'll be da..." Jonathan caught his speech before he swore. He squatted next to the small child. "I'll be a monkey's uncle! How the devil did you know to say that?" He stared at Salla with complete disbelief as if he could not believe his eyes and ears.

"You teach?" Salla quickly interjected.

"Do you mean to tell me that you have a grasp for the English language just from sitting here and listening to me examine your brothers and sisters?" the missionary asked with incredulity. "Why that's... that's..."

"N… not… p-possible," Salla answered as his little brown eyes slowly filled with water. The boy nervously glanced around as tears fell down his face, afraid he might be beaten.

Jonathan recognized Salla's apprehension as he witnessed the women beat other children when he first arrived. He also saw the scars on Salla's bare back and knew what they were.

"This brilliant little boy is trapped on a dirt farm in the poorest country of Africa," he thought. "God brought me here for a purpose…"

Jonathan decided to act on Salla's behalf. He felt compelled to change the boy's situation. Eager to lift the young boy out of his predicament and encouraged by his potential, he approached the family with the idea of sending the boy to school in Bamako, the capital city.

"Excuse me," he said

He interrupted the women as they prepared the family's main meal of the day. He tried to speak in French, but the women only laughed at him. Jonathan knew only a few phrases of Bambara, the local language. Finally, they stopped to listen to the missionary.

"We must discuss this little boy," he tried to say and knew from their puzzled expressions they did not understand him. "Boy…" he pointed, "… is very smart… smart…" he added by pointing to his head. Once more, they laughed at him.

Salla stood behind him. Jonathan reached behind and pulled the little boy to his side. "He has a brilliant mind," he began. 'Head!' he spoke in Bambara.

They believed Salla had a disease of the head. The women nodded their heads in agreement and the children tittered with laughter.

When Jonathan noticed how wide he hit that mark, he tried to clarify.

"I want him to attend school… school… in the city…" he struggled.

Seeing his attempts at speaking got him nowhere, he tried to explain by drawing in the dirt, when Salla pulled on his coat.

"I can help," the boy said with such conviction in his eyes, Jonathan turned to him for assistance.

"You can translate?" the missionary asked Salla.

The little boy nodded.

"Very well, explain to them. I want to take you to the city and place you in school. Can you tell them that?" the missionary requested.

He wondered if the boy grasped what he said. Salla nodded, and then began to speak. He went on and on in his native tongue. The women interrupted and started to argue. Salla turned back to the missionary.

"They say – my father – will not – allow," the boy told him, his speech hesitant.

"Where is he?" Jonathan asked.

"He will return this evening," the boy replied, disheartened.

"I will wait and speak to him," the missionary told the boy.

When Salla told his mother what the missionary intended, she stared down at the boy and then at Jonathan. She realized at that moment, it was a chance for her son to escape the poverty that trapped her and the entire family.

"Tell him to wait over there," she asked Salla to translate.

Jonathan sat under a nearby tree and read the Bible while the family ate. He refused to take any food they wanted to share with him. He managed to make a cup of tea with a tea bag and some boiled bottled water from the things he took from his backpack.

The father arrived later that evening, drunk and angry with the missionary for interfering with his family. An argument broke out between the obstinate the man and his wives.

"You work too hard around the farm," he turned on the boy. "I cannot replace you. The others are lazy. You stay here!"

The boy stood still. He shook his head in defiance of his father's wishes. The drunkard picked up a stick to beat him. He felt certain the boy responsible for the Englishman's decision to remove him from the farm.

"Defy me!" he yelled at the boy. "I will beat some sense into you!"

Although a peaceful man, Jonathan, clearly a head taller than Salla's father, stepped between him and the boy. He vigorously protested this rough style of treatment.

"You'll not strike the boy!" Jonathan spoke with conviction.

"He disobeys!" the father cursed in his native tongue and tried to reach around the minister and grab at Salla.

Jonathan grabbed the stick with his right hand and yanked it away from the father.

"If you must strike anyone, strike me. I encouraged him!" the missionary stated and waved the stick over his head.

Salla's father stopped and stared up at the minister for a moment, uncertain of his next move. He did not know what Jonathan said or intended. He only knew that a man much larger than him held the big stick he used to beat his wives and children. Jonathan decided to act. He had an idea.

"How much is the boy worth to you?" the minister asked. He dropped the stick and pulled out his wallet. "I have cash," he said and took out some English pound notes.

The entire family stopped still and silent. They all stared at the fistful of foreign money and then looked over at Salla. No one knew the amount. They only knew that foreigners were often wealthy. His mother practically pushed the boy into the missionary's arms.

"How much money will you take for the child?" he asked. "Five pounds? Ten?" he said as he pulled out note after note.

The family greedily stared at the wad of cash. Salla looked first at the money, then at his family.

"Twenty English pounds," a small voice spoke.

"Twenty pounds!" Jonathan protested. He glanced down and noticed that Salla spoke. "That's all I have!"

"You must provide for my family," the boy answered the question growing in Jonathan's mind.

"I…very well," the Englishman gave in. He pulled all the money out of his wallet. "They must sign a paper for your…"

"They will sign," Salla spoke up as he glared at his family, "if they want the money." He quickly rattled something off in the native tongue.

The father's face broke into a smile. He drooled over the prospect of having so much money. This amount constituted what a person with a job might earn in several months. The boy sensed this represented a fortune to his brothers and sisters as well. Salla wondered what would happen once he and the missionary left. A fight over the money would most certainly break out. He wondered who would win.

Ramsey hastily drew up a paper whose language would formalize the deal with Salla's adoption. Families often sold children into servitude at that time. The wives each witnessed the document.

"I hope I'm making the right decision," Jonathan whispered.

The moment he completed the negotiations, Jonathan decided to leave before the father changed his mind. Salla said goodbye to his mother. She pushed him away. Neither she nor the others showed any emotion.

As soon as the missionary left, the father jumped up and down for joy.

"I will go to Kita and have the best time of my life with this money… this enough to last me for a week!" he bragged.

Anger built up in the oldest wife as she watched him. For years, she toiled in the fields and suffered his physical abuse. Suddenly all the emotion she felt inside overflowed into action. She picked up a large log from the fire pit and swung with all her might, striking the man's head. The log struck with such force that it broke into two pieces. His neck snapped to one side. The gathered family heard a loud crack. With a grimace, the father fell over, killed instantly from one blow. The pound notes drifted to the ground from his open hand.

"I didn't mean it," the horrified woman said as she backed away.

She turned toward the jungle and intended to commit suicide. She feared the authorities would discover her murder and punish the entire family. The other two wives restrained her.

"What are you doing?" one said.

"I must atone for my sin," she cried and tried to break free.

"For committing justice?" the other wife spoke. "No one here will ever speak against you. You saved us, sister. Believe me," she assured her.

The older woman glanced around the room. The other children nodded agreement. No one would mourn the evil man's passing. They all felt relief.

"In fact," the middle wife spoke up. "We must quickly make a large fire." The others caught on to her plan.

Soon they created a large pyre that raged. They swung the man's body back and forth until they flung it on top.

"You suffered the most," the youngest wife said as she picked up the money from the ground and pushed it into the older woman's hand.

The eldest wife looked down at all the money in her hand and started to weep.

"From this day forward, we will make this home a loving place, no more cruelty and beating," she told them. "Let us never discuss what took place. We are free from tyranny. Justice is done. That is all that matters." She held up the cash. "Water is free for all who wish it. We will use this money to start another business she said, and all of you will help make it a success."

She sat them down and explained how they could make wares to sell in the marketplace at Kita using the cash to buy their basic materials.

"I did not know you knew of such things," the youngest wife said.

"What you do not know can fill many jars," the older woman replied.

The younger wife laughed in reply. The other two wives took the husband's meat he brought home from Kita to make a general stew for all to share. The eldest wife stared up the road toward Kita.

"May God protect you, Salla," she said.

Walking through the jungle with the older man, Salla felt uncertain about his new life. He had never been this far from the farm. He wondered how this stranger would treat him.

"What is your name, little one?" Jonathan asked as they walked up the road.

"Salla," the boy softly spoke.

"Well, Salla, I foresee a great future ahead for you," the minister stated.

Jonathan Ramsey cut short his missionary journey through the countryside. Instead, he brought Salla to the city of Kita on foot, and then arranged for a driver to take them to the capital city. When he returned to Bamako, he went straight to the Anglican branch of the church.

Soon after they arrived, Jonathan began to search the records for the bright young boy's sponsor. The church often connected childless couples with younger orphaned children when they could not conceive. Working with the local minister, Jonathan quickly found a fine loving family able to look after the small boy and raise him as their own.

After they spoke to Salla for only a few minutes, the middle-aged couple valued the young boy's obvious intelligence despite his older age. They promised the church that they would take good care of him.

Jonathan would not be able to keep track of Salla's progress. Once in Bamako, he received word from the church that they recalled him to England and wired him the money for the ticket. He promised Salla he would return one day and hoped his costly investment in Salla had been worth the trouble.

"I will make you proud," the tearful boy whispered when they parted.

Chapter Five

A Life Spent Searching

THE FIRST DAY IN HIS new home and Salla already feared how his stepparents might treat him. He moved hesitantly about the house, uncertain how to behave, lest they severely punish him. No adult ever treated him with any kindness.

The middle-aged couple, Mr. and Mrs. Robert Motambou, put through the official paper work to formally adopted Salla. An upper middle-class family, modestly successful, they had a comfortable but not overly expensive house in a nice neighborhood on the outer edge of Bamako.

When they brought Salla home, they took him through the house to show him the different rooms.

"This is the living room," Mrs. Motambou told him, "the kitchen is in there," she pointed. "We sleep upstairs. Your bedroom is up there. Would you like to see it?"

He simply stared at her. They did not know how much French he knew and tried to speak to him in Bambara, but he remained unmoved.

"Just show him," Mr. Motambou spoke quietly as he raised his eyebrows in expectation.

"Salla, come with me," Mrs. Motambou said and led the way.

They took him upstairs to a modest room at the top of the stairs. Inside, Salla noticed a nicely furnished but rather austere setting. Good furnishings were expensive and difficult to obtain. However, to Salla, these accommodations seemed quite luxurious compared to life in the hut.

As the young boy stood in the doorway, his eyes focused upon a steel framed bed with white sheets, a pillow inside a plain white cotton pillowcase, and a tan woolen blanket spread out on the bed. The walls held a fresh coat of light yellow paint. Flowered curtains trimmed with lace around their outside edge hung on either side of the window. The floor was not dirt, but clean planks of stained and polished wood.

In addition to the bed, a small dresser stood off to one side with a vase filled with dried blue flowers on the top. Next to the bed sat a wooden nightstand, open in the front with a washbasin and a water pitcher resting inside. A towel and wash cloth lay next to them with a bar of white soap. Mosquito netting, gathered at the middle, framed the simple bed on either side like a canopy.

Salla was afraid to speak or comment. He looked around and thought this must be where his stepparents slept.

"This is your room, Salla," she showed him and gestured.

She put her arm around Salla's shoulders and practically pushed the young boy further into the room.

"I know it isn't much, but it is all we have to offer. I hope you like it," Mrs. Motambou stated.

"Is this where you sleep?" he asked, still uncertain about the room.

"No, Salla," the woman informed him. "This is where you will sleep. This is your bedroom."

"Me? Alone in here… with my own bed?" Salla asked.

His eyes filled with tears. All of his life, Salla slept on the floor with his brothers and sisters and two stepmothers in the same room. The idea of sleeping on his own bed in his own room overwhelmed the little boy. He turned and hugged his new mother so hard around her waist, his little boney arms dug into her flesh.

The woman did not mind. She stroked the grateful boy's head while he sobbed into her dress. She glanced over at her husband in the doorway as the two exchanged glances.

"There, there, Salla," she said reassuringly. "You are home now and everything will be fine from here on."

That turned out to be an understatement. This place seemed like heaven to Salla. In return for their generosity, Salla showed his gratitude in many ways. He picked up his clothes and took them to the laundry without being asked or reminded. He even tried to wash them out of the basin in his room before his mother stopped him. Whenever he could, Salla helped his mother in the kitchen and in the yard. He carried home any shopping she did. She never once had to ask him.

"Salla helped me at the Townville market today," Mrs. Motambou informed her husband that evening after they put Salla to bed.

"Oh?" he looked up from packing his pipe with tobacco.

"Yes, but I must tell you. He was the only barefoot child at our market," she pointed out. "A little girl with her mother made fun of him."

"Oh…" the father quickly caught on. He realized they had not purchased the young boy any new clothes.

By the end of that first week after he received his government paycheck, Salla's father brought home some new clothes and shoes for the boy. Salla never had a pair of shoes, having something cover his feet felt strange but good.

"They'll protect your feet from stones," his new father explained to the puzzled expression on the boy's face.

Again, the boy wept out of gratitude. This time he held Robert Motambou so tight, the man cried, too. Having a parent show love and affection were difficult concepts for Salla to accept. The proud young man paraded around the house all evening, marching in his new shoes, showing off to his parents how he appreciated their gift, which made the couple laugh at how the child welcomed the simple a gift.

That evening, after he dutifully performed his "chores" around the house, Salla's father called the boy into the living room.

"Salla," he began, "We have another surprise for you." Robert and his wife exchanged knowing smiles. "I've enrolled you in school. I don't know where they're going to place you. But I feel we should try to start you as soon as possible with that curious brain of yours. You will begin your studies in a few weeks. I stopped by the university library and brought this home."

Salla furrowed his brow as his father produced something Salla had never seen, a book.

"Come here, Salla," the man motioned to the sofa.

Salla curled up into the nook of his side as the man wrapped his big arm around the child.

"We learn to read by understanding that letters are symbols, which stand for something. We put these symbols together to form words. Then we take those words and make sentences whose meaning conveys the thoughts of the author. That is how the rest of the world communicates or speaks to each other. They learn to read and write," the man told him.

"Yes, father," Salla replied.

"Rather than learn French, I brought a book on English. This is the language of learned people," he told the boy. "This is their alphabet. Let us begin… A, B, C…"

Salla listen to his father, watched the page, and absorbed everything he heard or saw that evening. They went through the English alphabet and discussed how to pronounce certain letters in different ways. Although most people in Mali spoke French, Robert tried to find books on their native language, Bambara, which were rare at the library. The father challenged Salla on what he knew. The boy surprised Robert when he replied nearly everything verbatim. Then they tackled a few simple words and their meanings. The Motambou's were very pleased with his immediate progress.

During the following week, Robert Motambou tutored the boy every evening after supper. Salla progressed so rapidly, that by the end of a week, he could read on his own.

"Where is Salla?" Robert asked his wife as the two cleaned up the kitchen after dinner one evening.

"He is in the living room, reading… one of your books. I hope you are not offended. I gave him permission," Mrs. Motambou said.

"Of course not," Robert said. He leaned over and looked through the dining room toward the chair where Salla intently stared at a book in his lap. "By the way… which book did he choose?" curious which book Salla chose.

"I don't know," his wife replied. "Why don't you go and see?"

The fact that his child could read he found amazing. When he finally stood before Salla and noticed the book in his child's hands, the moment overwhelmed the civil servant.

"Can you understand that book?" his father asked.

"Oh, yes, father. I find the story fascinating," the boy lucidly replied. From memory, he recited the opening line: "It was the best of times, it was the worst of times, it was the age of wisdom, it was the age of foolishness…" he quoted.

"It was indeed," Robert Motambou said as he shook his head, overwhelmed by Salla's quick comprehension. "Can you understand the setting?"

"The French Revolution," Salla quickly answered. "The peasant class rose up against the tyrant king due to inhumane treatment… Am I correct, father?"

Robert Motambou stood there with his jaw slack, flabbergasted.

"I believe it's time we took Salla to the university library," Mrs. Motambou stated, to which her husband readily agreed.

The following afternoon, she took Salla into the city. She drove onto the university grounds, having obtained permission, where she located the university's library, the largest in Bamako. Her husband, Robert, was one of the first graduates from the relatively new school. She took the boy by the hand and led him through the campus to the building whose location she sought.

As they walked inside the library building, Salla saw the rows of books on shelves behind the main desk. He stopped and stared at them, transfixed, as if someone had glued his feet to the floor. He shook all over with his eyes fixed dead ahead.

"Your child," the man at the front desk said.

Mrs. Motambou glanced down and noticed Salla frozen to the spot, shaking and staring.

"Salla? Is anything wrong?" she asked.

She lifted his chin and noticed the young boy started to weep.

"Salla, what is troubling you? Are you ill?" she asked.

"No, mother," he said quietly. "I didn't know such a place existed," he told her and indicated the books he saw on shelves up ahead.

"Go inside," she encouraged and watched him enter the stacks.

Salla slowly moved from one shelf to the next. He would methodically pull books out, flip through them, carefully place them back, and then move on to the next.

"Are you finding a book you like?" she asked, wondering when he would make a choice.

He looked over at her, his face a mixture of excitement and emotion.

"I like all of them!" he told her.

After seeing how enthralled and overjoyed Salla felt being in the library, his new mother brought Salla as often as she could. She let the boy check out as many books as the library permitted, as they did not loan books out the way American libraries do. A person had to leave a promisary note to pay for books lost, stolen, or damaged. Still, they decided to take the chance as Salla treated each book with such reverence.

Mr. and Mrs. Motambou were not only stunned at Salla's rapid progress in reading, but also by his retention. The child remembered practically everything he read, and could recite whole portions of literature, point out scientific principles, and perform mathematical calculations as if by magic. In a very short period, the boy genius rapidly advanced in a variety of subjects to the point where if he asked his father a question, Robert could only shrug. Impressed with this sudden vault in understanding, Salla's father stopped by the local school to ask the counselor for an evaluation of his son before the start of term.

"I'm sorry to take up your valuable time," Robert humbly approached the important man. "I would like you to evaluate my son," he requested. Robert took his lunchtime make this meeting possible.

"For what purpose?" the man asked. "I thought you told the administrator the boy never attended school. He'll have to start out like the rest of the children in the lowest grade."

"I know what I said before," Robert began, "however something about the boy has changed."

"What is it?" the administrator asked.

"That is why I want you to evaluate him," Robert stated. "I believe you'll find him… different… and enlightening."

"Does he know how to read?" the man asked.

"Let me put it this way," Robert said when he started to leave. "He learned how to read in about three hours."

"You mean months," the man said with disbelief.

"Salla is a refreshing change from other children," Robert replied and left the administrative counselor to wonder what he meant.

Eager to evaluate the boy, the counselor agreed to meet with Salla before the start of term. After he spoke briefly with him, he administered several tests to Salla. When the boy quickly finished and passed all the ones for elementary school in a matter of minutes, the counselor gave him the upper grade exams. Salla took slightly longer with these, but passed all of them without one mistake. This accomplishment astounded the counselor.

"One hundred percent… no one has ever taken these exams and made no mistakes. We purposely throw in a few problems to see if some of the children can reason them out. But this… This is amazing!" the man declared when he reviewed the papers three times.

He examined the boy's body and clothes to see if he cheated somehow. When the truth stared the counselor in the face, Salla's natural gift forced the man to conclude that Salla needed special attention.

"Wait here," he ordered.

The counselor retained Salla in his office while he entered the teacher's private lounge, their midday meeting place. During their lunchtime, the counselor bragged about Salla's feat to the other instructors gathered. Upon hearing the story, one of the secretaries called her friend at a nearby private school. Another called the local paper, and a reporter showed up, requesting to interview the boy.

As rumor spread throughout the school, the instructors filled the break room to overflowing while they poured over Salla's test results. After seeing the results, each teacher demanded to have Salla for his or her class. However, the counselor decided to take Salla over to the local private academy meant for upper class children. Only children who met their criteria could attend when the secretary of admissions called the family back for an interview, which seldom happened – even in Mali they were that exclusive.

With the child in hand, the public school counselor met with the head of the private academy. He pleaded Salla's case.

"He cannot pay," the counselor told the head academician. "I would simply beg your indulgence to interview the boy."

"I'm a very busy person," the man told him. "However, since you have roused so much interest, I will speak with him for a few minutes… but only with the boy. How old is he?"

"Ten, sir," the counselor said.

"Ten, you say," the head of the school replied. "Send him in."

A few minutes came and went. An hour later, the head of the school emerged from his office, stunned.

"I've known many people in my day. I've met Bishop Tutu and even heard Nelson Mandela speak," he said, "but I never met a human being with more insight. This boy is remarkable. For being ten, he sounds like a wise old sage. You were right. We must have this boy. I will arrange for a private sponsor."

To his parent's amazement and delight, Salla started at the local private academy for privileged children, sponsored by a local patron. Despite his age and lack of social skills, the young boy progressed through his courses faster than any student in the history of the school ever did.

Within a year, he mastered both the French and English languages and began the study of Latin and Greek origins on his own time. By the time he turned twelve, Salla started to take college level courses. He memorized pages of books as if preparing for state board exams.

No professor at the school ever saw anything quite like Salla. He made quite a stir in the capital city as news of his prowess spread. Mr. and Mrs. Motambou quickly took pride in being parents of the smartest child in Mali. As a result, Mr. Motambou received advancement in his job position and a raise of his salary where he worked. Salla brought goodwill and good fortune to the Motambou's.

After a few years of formal study, Salla further distinguished his record outpacing every student in the region. The academy encouraged the young boy to move onto a higher seat of learning.

By the time his fourteenth birthday arrived, Salla enrolled in a special honors program at the University of Bamako (Mali) created just for him. Salla achieved celebrity status. Scholarships completely paid for all of his schooling.

By the time the twentieth year of Salla's life rolled around in 2005, he graduated as the youngest student in the history of the medical school with a Sigma Cum Laude, having also served his internship at the same time! He started on staff at the local hospital while also performing research at the university.

Shortly after his graduation, a visitor arrived from England. Bishop Ramsey, promoted two years earlier, intended to locate the little boy he rescued from the jungle a decade earlier, and inquire as to his progress. When he arrived in Mali, he had heard nothing about Salla or his life with the Motambou family.

"We are so pleased you chose to attend our parish, your grace," the young black minister said as he welcomed the older Englishman to his church. "We were a little surprised by your unannounced visit."

"I hope I didn't inconvenience you," Bishop Ramsey stated.

"Oh, no, your grace, your presence is always welcome here," the local minister told him. "We made some arrangements. We have a place for you, should you chose to stay. However, my staff and I are puzzled as to why you made your visit now?"

"I worked here nearly ten years ago as a missionary," the bishop told him.

"I was not aware of that, your grace," the minister smiled.

"Yes, perhaps the previous minister failed to mention that fact," the bishop explained. "At any rate, I wandered onto a remote farm and found a little boy there. Bright chap, little Salla was his name. I believe he went to the Motambou family. They used to be members of the church. What has become of him?"

The minister stood before the bishop dumbfounded. He swallowed hard and could not believe his ears.

"Your grace discovered Dr. Motambou?" he said, aghast. "I had no idea!"

"Doctor?" the bishop questioned.

"Doctor Motambou is the brightest resident in the hospital," the minister spoke with pride. "Everyone wants to be his patient. They say he can cure anything."

"Hmm," the bishop considered this new information. "A doctor, you say? Well, I'm not surprised. He showed great promise when I met him."

The minister giggled like a little girl.

"Surly your grace is joking," he said, nonchalantly. "He is one of the greatest minds in the history of our country. They want him to run for public office but he refuses. He says he wants to go into research."

The bishop found this new information startling to say the least. He thought about this news for a moment.

"I just remembered something," Bishop Ramsey said and briskly walked back to the car. The driver still had his bag and waited for him outside in the heat.

The bishop stepped into the back seat and opened his portable telephone. He pressed a long series of numbers. For several minutes, he spoke with a party very far from Mali, going on and on about a young man he promised would astound the party that he spoke to on the other end of the line. When he closed the phone nearly ten minutes later, he smiled and immediately wondered what Salla's reaction would be.

Bishop Ramsey called the Motambou residence. He spoke with Mrs. Motambou on the telephone. They arranged for tea later that afternoon. She promised the bishop that Salla would be there. The aging couple waited on the front porch for him when he arrived. The house seemed the same at first when his car pulled up. Then he noticed several significant changes, such as the paved driveway, new siding, along with a new roof. The windows had new curtains, even a new, screened, front door. The bishop felt certain Robert Motambou had benefited from his son's success, too.

The Motambou's welcomed the Bishop inside their small home. They brought him into their dining room where they set the table for tea. He noticed a tall handsome young man, with broad shoulders, large hands and feet, standing next to one of the chairs, staring at him with a toothy smile.

"Salla?" the bishop guessed.

The big man's smile broadened, as he stepped forward. Impressed with the young man's clean and orderly appearance, the bishop extended his hand and shook Salla's large black hand, giving him a warm greeting.

"You've grown!" Jonathan exclaimed.

"Yes, I have, your grace," Salla replied with a deep baritone voice as he nodded his head.

"I've been hearing so many good things about you, young man," the bishop began.

"It is an honor you have come to see me," Salla interrupted. He started a speech he prepared. "I can never express the gratitude I feel toward your grace," Salla began. "I would still be struggling for survival on a dirt farm if you hadn't spent your last dime to free me."

"Best investment I ever made," the bishop smiled back.

Salla nearly cried as he spoke. The bishop remained standing and smiling, not knowing if he should sit or continue to stand.

"I have something for you," Salla said as he reached inside his suit coat pocket and pulled out several large bills of currency in his hand. "Consider this a down payment, your grace, on a debt long overdue," Salla said as he held out twenty British pounds he must have obtained at a local bank.

The bishop felt so moved by Salla's gesture that he fought back his own tears. He pushed the money back into Salla's large hand.

"Take money from my best student? You're going to need that money, my friend," the bishop said.

The Motambou's gestured for the Bishop to sit down. The bishop and Salla sat as Mrs. Motambou began to pour tea.

"But your grace," Salla began to protest. "I must return the favor that you did for me."

Bishop Ramsey held up his hand and silenced Salla. He gazed upon this large man and tried to remember the little boy he once knew when he first arrived in the city of Bamako over ten years ago. He glanced over at the numerous plaques and honors on the wall that attested to Salla's many accomplishments over the past ten years.

Bishop Ramsey nearly burst with delight inside, as he wanted to tell Salla his news. However, he kept his exterior calm.

"Salla," the bishop began, "do you trust my judgment?"

"Of course, your grace," Salla replied.

"Then you must trust me now," the Bishop spoke with earnest. "I'm sending you on another journey, consider it a new challenge," he told him. "This is only the beginning of great things for Salla Motambou. A mind like yours needs the best instruction in the world, and you're going to get it, if I have anything to say about it."

"What are you saying?" Salla asked.

"I called an old friend in America. She and I discussed the matter. They are willing to sponsor your advanced training at a very prestigious medical school," the bishop explained. "Is this something of interest to you?"

"Would you want me to leave?" Salla asked and turned to his parents.

"You must follow your dream, Salla," his father said, "wherever it leads. You would learn a great deal more in America than you could here, son."

His mother nodded her agreement, crying tears of joy for her son. Salla turned back to the bishop.

"Your grace," Salla said bowing his head. "I cannot find the words…"

He took the older man's hand and held onto it, kissing it, weeping.

"Salla…" the bishop said and felt uncomfortable at the humility of the prostrating young man. "Please, Salla," he pulled his hand away. "This is something you have earned. Besides, America will give you the tools to accomplish many great deeds." Here the bishop spoke with rousing feeling. "Now go and achieve success in your field, never forget your people."

Salla rose up. He towered over the bishop; tears trickled down his face. "I won't disappoint your grace. I will try to do my best in America."

"I have no doubt in my mind that America will be surprised by its new African visitor. I think you will take America by storm. Good luck, Salla," the bishop smiled. He rose and embraced the young man.

The move surprised Salla. Local bishops never showed this type of informality. He embraced the bishop back, wincing back more tears, knowing with a trip to America, he could realize his dream of becoming a research scientist.

Based on his mentor's advice, Salla reluctantly left his loving adopted parents behind and went to the United States. Shortly after he arrived, Salla demonstrated to all concerned his prowess in medical knowledge. He easily passed his boards and obtained his medical license to practice in America. He remained in the states to take a residency at Johns Hopkins. Within three years, he managed to impress the medical community with his extensive skill and craft, for Salla excelled in his profession – as a diagnostician, as a surgeon, as a medical practitioner – no physician at the hospital complex surpassed his skill.

As his reputation of excellence spread, patients clamored for his services and other doctors waited in queues for his advice. Many offered him positions in their practices. He could have started in any medical specialty. Yet, neither money nor social position enticed the young Malian. Despite the generous offers that poured in, Salla chose to continue his goal of viral research. He had one particular place in mind next, England. He wanted to study with some of the world's leading virologists.

Before Salla decided to enroll in yet another institution, he sought out the advice of his old friend, the bishop. He wrote the bishop and explained in a series of letters (as the bishop did not own a computer) how he longed to study virology in England. The bishop replied and carried on a lengthy correspondence with Salla that lasted for nearly eight months. Finally, an invitation along with a first class airline ticket arrived. The bishop requested Salla's presence at his home in England. Without even a place to stay, Salla abruptly cut his ties, said goodbye to his American friends, and thanked them for their hospitality.

Upon reaching his destination at Heathrow, Salla made a beeline to his mentor's house. Bishop Ramsey, currently retired, lived in a modest dwelling in an area southwest of London. Salla took a train from London. As he looked out on the English countryside that passed by, he wondered what the bishop had in store for him. Despite the pouring rain, he managed to flag a taxi from the station and made his way to the bishop's cottage. Naturally, Salla's arrival at the bishop's house coincided just in time for afternoon tea.

"Salla my friend," the older man exclaimed when he answered the door. "I am so glad you wrote me at length about your aspirations. I tried to have things ready for you," Bishop Ramsey stated and gestured for Salla to enter. "Just in time for tea," the bishop added.

"Thank you, your grace," Salla replied. He placed his suitcase on the floor near the front door.

"No formalities," the bishop requested. "We're old friends."

The bishop's physical appearance startled Salla. The man had aged a great deal since Salla last saw him. Snowy white hair framed a thin pale face that still beamed at the sight of the big black man.

"I'm so grateful you wrote me about your desire to enter research," the bishop began. "I think that is a laudable goal." He stood back as Salla shook the cold rain from his overcoat before he entered the bishop's cottage.

In the past three years, the bishop managed to raise a significant amount of money from his friends in the medical field, which filled the church's coffers, enough to keep the ailing man out of a nursing home. In return, the church rented a small old cottage so the bishop could spend the remaining days of his retirement in comfort.

"What's this?" a loud voice with a heavy brogue cried out. "I t'ought I felt a draft! You sit while I help the gentleman with his coat..."

The bishop had an old Irish woman for a housekeeper and cook, Mrs. Thomas. Her husband of forty years passed away only a year ago. The bishop took pity on her when the bank took possession of their heavily mortgaged home. She was a feisty thing with a temper to match. The heavy woman, wider than she was tall, spread out her apron with her stubby fingers and smiled at Salla when the tall man ducked to come through the doorway. She immediately closed the door behind him and hung up his coat.

"Dat's better. I'll have a nice hot cup a tea for ya. Have a seat," she said and practically pushed Salla into the living room.

The inside of the cottage had that cozy feeling throughout, with a stone face around the fireplace, a woven rug at the foot of a large overstuffed chair and ottoman nearby. A small table with a shaded lamp sat near the puffy chair where the bishop sat. A stack of books with markers in them indicated the bishop's current reading list. The mantel over the fireplace had a pendulum clock that chimed on the quarter hour.

The moment the bishop resumed his spot in the large comfy chair positioned near the fireplace, Mrs. Thomas rushed over to him, seeing to his needs.

"Keep dat cover over yer lap, or you'll be catchin' a draft!" Mrs. Thomas practically scolded. She rushed into the kitchen and returned with the tea service that she had ready for Salla's visit. She plopped down the tea tray full of goodies and large pot of hot water covered with a tea cozy. She took the tea, added two heaping spoonfuls to the pot and replaced the cover. Then she adjusted the blanket in the bishop's lap as if he had not done it properly enough for her.

"The way you coddle over me, you'd think I was two!" he protested.

"The way you fuss, you act like it!" she shot back with a stern look.

The bishop opened his mouth to reply and closed his mouth when he decided it was foolish to debate her. Mrs. Thomas, having won the argument, turned to Salla and poured out his tea through the strainer. She gave him a slice of her pound cake.

"Sugar?" she asked.

"One, please," Salla replied.

Mrs. Thomas added a teaspoon, but didn't offer Salla any cream. Yet, when she turned back to the bishop, she poured his tea and added plenty of cream and sugar before she placed a larger slice of cake on his plate without saying a word, her generosity a bit one sided. The bishop shook his head. He looked over at Salla and shrugged. The big man could only smile as he watched how Mrs. Thomas attended the bishop.

"Will you be wantin' anythin' else, your grace?" Mrs. Thomas asked in her heavy brogue. "Otherwise, I'll be goin' to afternoon mass."

"Thank you, no, Mrs. Thomas. Say hello to Father Mulligan for me," Ramsey added.

"Dat I will, your grace," she said as she waddled to the door. She put on her coat, threw a scarf around her neck, and put on a large rain bonnet before she exited out the front door, pulling up an umbrella at the last second.

The moment she left, the bishop fixed Salla's tea by adding some cream to it. The two old acquaintances enjoyed Mrs. Thomas splendid tea and cake while they reminisced about their lives. Salla filled the Bishop in on his job offer from Johns Hopkins and his life in Baltimore for the past three years. He tried to speak of things he did not include in his letters, although Salla saw very little of the American historic city. He spent most of his time in research studies toward his doctoral thesis on diseases with a virus origin.

"Oh, by the way, did you receive your retirement gift?" Salla asked him.

"You mean this box?" Bishop Ramsey replied and pulled out the beautiful stained and polished wooden box marked, "Rémy Martin – Louis XIII – 750ml." The bishop struggled with its weight. "Heavy!" he said.

Salla reached over and helped the other man with the beautiful cut glass object.

Salla smiled broadly, "I thought you'd like it."

"Like it…" the bishop said as he set it aside, "flabbergasted would be the proper reaction. The moment I opened that package, I discovered I have new friends from the local postman to the constable to the parish minister, all wanting me to uncork the bottle when it arrived!" he said with a chuckle. "Now, let's return to your aspirations…"

The bishop knew the young man dreamed of becoming a research virologist from the numerous times he mentioned that fact. While he had strong credentials, Salla had not applied to any of England's great schools, such as historic Cambridge or the equally prestigious Oxford.

"Do you know where you'll go now?" the bishop asked. He poured out more tea and took another piece of cake on the side plate. He handed the steaming cup over to Salla, this time he added a generous portion of cream with the sugar. Salla thanked the bishop. He stirred his tea and looked off at the grate full of glowing orange coals, his mind distracted.

"That's what I wanted to ask you," Salla responded. "You've helped me so much in the past. Frankly, I need your advice. What would you recommend, your grace?"

"You've mention virology research so often in your letters. I've kept them all by the way," Bishop Ramsey said as he leaned over and picked up a different decorative box. He opened the lid and held up a stack of letters bound in a wide pale blue ribbon.

Salla smiled, "You kept all of them?"

"Of course, I treasure everything from my favorite pupil," he spoke quietly and placed the letters back into the box. "Besides, in this electronic age, who writes letters any longer? These are precious documents," the bishop stated with a sly grin.

He leaned back in his chair and sighed. He punctuated the moment with silence. The fire crackled in the iron grate, the special logs he ordered for the occasion nearly burned up. The bishop's eyes seemed caught by the fire's magnetism.

"If I were going to study virology," he said. "I would only consider one place in England… Oxford."

"Why chose Oxford, your grace?" Salla asked before he took a bite of cake.

"If I were a man with as much curiosity as you posses, I would want to study with the top virologists in England. Oxford is, in my humble opinion, the greatest seat of learning in the civilized world. A man can satisfy his curiosity, and perhaps discover greatness. Who knows where an education from Oxford will lead?" the bishop speculated.

"I will follow your advice, your grace. I will apply to Oxford," Salla said as he raised his cup. "Hopefully, I can convince the acceptance committee to…"

"Indeed," the bishop interrupted with his raspy voice.

He reached down next to his chair and slid his hand under a folded blanket. He pulled out a large leather valise. A dark burgundy leather portfolio had a golden seal embossed the middle. The official seal would be unmistakable to those Englishmen who recognized its familiar shape.

"I felt in my bones you would like the idea of Oxford. I hope you won't be cross with me. I took the liberty of speaking to members of the acceptance committee. A London solicitor helped. We've had all of your transcripts sent from America and Africa. These are your papers and your visa. Welcome to Oxford, my very dear friend, Salla. It's about time you came to England!" the bishop said as he handed over the package.

The big young man accepted the heavy object and opened the binding to find an acceptance letter on the inside with his name on it. As Salla read down the page, the bishop continued to address him.

"They gave you a full scholarship, my lad, with funds provided by several physicians on both sides of the Atlantic," the bishop explained. "It seems your reputation precedes you. You see, I went to Oxford about six months ago and attended a medical luncheon. I'm still on a few lists from the old days when I was a physician. I spoke to the dean in question. I called you one of the greatest research minds of our age and named the list of honors you had received. Afterward, the professors inundated me with their plans for you to attend their college. Seems they all want you as their research partner..."

The bishop noticed Salla staring at the paper in front of him. The young man said nothing. He kept reading the same line over and over that showed how much money they had allocated to his study. The amount astounded the young African.

"I understand that with all the hours you worked for John Hopkins, you never asked for a dime – only a bed to sleep on and a meal now and then in the cafeteria. Depite the billing they did on your behalf, you refused any payment for your services. For three years, you worked and studied without a break. The Board of Regents feel they owe you a great deal. They've offered you a handsome package," the bishop put in. "Congratulations, Salla."

He reached over and shook Salla's limp hand. Salla could not speak. Surprised by all this generosity, he finally grasped onto the bishop's hand, when a strange feeling came over him, like a dark foreboding cloud of doom. He sensed spreading illness in the man he knew as Jonathan Ramsey. He realized now why he had retired so relatively young and why he aged so prematurely. Cancer rapidly progressed through his body. It would only be a matter of weeks, months or perhaps a year before it took him. Salla knew this would be the last time he would ever lay eyes on his friend. A moment of joy suddenly became a moment of sadness. He wondered how he gained so much information simply from holding the man's hand. He began to wonder if that was how he knew so much about his patients back in America and Mali.

"Your grace, I don't know what to say..." Salla replied. His eyes began to water.

"Now, now," Bishop Ramsey said as he patted his hand, "they'll be none of those. This is a joyous occasion, one that calls for a celebration... and it needs something stronger than tea."

The bishop reached over and opened the beautiful stained wooden box. Inside he pulled out a red velvet box and opened the lid. Set within a white satin interior, the bishop carefully lifted out the large beautifully decorated crystal decanter. He took a sharp knife from the drawer and gently broke the seal at the top.

"Salla," he requested. "Fetch two glasses," he asked and nodded toward a nearby curio cabinet. "My housekeeper brought her Irish crystal with her when her husband died."

Salla rose, crossed the room, and took out two cut crystal goblets. He brought them back to the place where he and the bishop sat. He placed them on the table next to the bishop and resumed his seat.

"Did you know," the bishop began as he poured out the rich dark amber liquid, "Winston Churchill drank this on the day he won the election in 1951 – I believe it was the only time he ever capitulated to the French. This is certainly as momentous an occasion," Jonathan said. He smiled as he poured two generous portions into the bottoms of the glasses.

Sall watched as the bishop sniffed the glass once, twice, and a third time before he took a small sip. For the moment, Salla followed the bishop's lead. Salla never drank anything alcoholic in his life, although in this instance he dare not refuse. Besides, he wondered how often a person sampled 100-plus-year-old French cognac. A simple toast followed the first sip and then the bishop offered yet another.

"I see a very bright future for you," he said and raised his glass. "To virology."

"To virology," Salla echoed.

The two men savored their rare drink while the Bishop related some history regarding Oxford. They talked for another hour until the bishop finally fell asleep in his great over-stuffed chair. Salla covered him up just when Mrs. Thomas returned from church.

"Don't fuss," she said as she shook out her shawl and hung it up. "I've given you the room at the top of stairs," she whispered. "I'll take care of the bishop. By the way, congratulations, doctor. We're very proud of you. I lit a candle at church for you and his grace."

"Thanks, Mrs. Thomas," Salla whispered back. He picked up his bags and retired to the guest's bedroom.

After spending the night, Mrs. Thomas roused Salla early. She served a light breakfast of muffins and kippers. She called a taxi and sent Salla off to the train station with good wishes and a ticket to Oxford. Within the hour, Salla sat in his rail car, gazing out at the English countryside that sped by as he made his way to Oxford, England. The trip took a series of trains but he finally arrived. On the last leg of the journey, the bishop purchased a compartment ticket for Salla, which allowed him privacy. He felt his anxiety level rise as the train whisked him away toward one of the most famous cities in the entire civilized world.

When Salla's train pulled into Oxford station, a portly balding middle-aged man dressed in a black waistcoat greeted Salla. The man pulled out a gold pocketwatch, popped open the cover, and glanced at the time before he returned the object to his vest. From all appearances, the man looked from another time, formally dressed, impeccably groomed with a serious straight affect on his face. He seemed to recognize the African the moment Salla stepped from his rail car.

"Pardon me, sir," the man said as he stepped forward.

"Yes?" Salla replied. He wondered why a well-dressed gentleman should address him with such formality. He had grown accustomed to the informal casual American lifestyle.

"You must be Doctor Motambou," the smartly dressed man properly pronounced.

"Yes?" Salla asked.

"I am Radcliff," the man told him with a thick upper class British accent. "I'm assigned to help you with all of your needs, sir."

"You mean help me find my way around?" Salla asked, misled by his comment.

"I mean everything, sir," Radcliff told him. "I'll be doing your cooking, laundry, cleaning, and anything else you wish, sir."

"A domestic? Oh, I don't need one," Salla said and started to dismiss him, while he grabbed his bags. However, Radcliff also reached out and took the handles. For a moment, Salla wondered if there would be a tug-o-war.

"Begging your pardon, sir, we do things differently in England," Radcliff said quietly. "When a person as important as you comes to Oxford, England rolls out the red carpet. My job is to help you concentrate on your studies. You may call me your butler, your valet, or even your personal assistant, but I can assure you; I take my job very seriously. I will see to your every comfort."

"Very well," Salla gave in. "But I must give you a bonus for your trouble," Salla added.

Radcliff smiled, "If you insist, sir."

The two men smiled at the same time as Salla finally let go of the bags and stepped back when he saw the fight a futile gesture. Radcliff took his bags toward the private car he had waiting for them. On the way to the school, Radcliff informed Salla of the living arrangements made on his behalf.

"I understand you've been enrolled in the Sir William Dunn School of Pathology, Doctor Motambou," Radcliff explained. "Doctor Shackleforth, Dean of the School, is looking forward to making your acquaintance on Monday. You have an eight o'clock appointment with his staff."

"Thank you, Radcliff," Salla replied.

"That gives you the weekend to become acquainted with the university and your living quarters," Radcliff suggested.

"My living quarters?" Salla inquired.

"You weren't expecting a dormitory apartment, were you, sir?" Radcliff wondered.

"Well, I..." Salla started.

"You have a two bedroom flat with adjoining living quarters, where I'll be staying," the gentleman stated. "I'll explain the layout better when we arrive. I hope you find the quarters satisfactory, doctor. I can assure you, they are more than adequate. The Duke of Windsor once used those quarters, along with many other royal personages," Radcliff informed him.

"May I ask who is responsible for this?" he wondered.

"You might say that several persons anticipated your arrival, sir," Radcliff ambiguously stated.

Salla leaned back and smiled.

"Does this mean I've finally arrived?" Salla muttered. He gazed out the window of the private car and watched the city of Oxford pass.

"Beg your pardon, sir?" Radcliff asked, seated beside Salla.

"Oh, nothing," Salla replied, "call it wish fulfillment."

He tried to remain as reserved as Radcliff did, however inside Salla wanted to burst out with an enormous roar of approval.

From his very first day, Salla Motambou fell hopeless in love with Oxford University, with its rich historic traditions and great variety of talented intellect. He settled right into his new apartment that had once been the residence of future kings. In addition to the finely crafted antique furniture, Salla marveled at the details from the decorative pewter plates around the light switches to the sterling silver candelabra. Shiny copper pans hung down from racks inside the most organized kitchen he had ever laid eyes on. Radcliff beamed with pride when he saw the look of satisfaction on Salla's face.

"I happened to be gourmand," Radcliff boasted. "Lunch, sir?"

"I can hardly wait," Salla replied, eager to sample Radcliff's artistry.

On Monday, he thoroughly enjoyed his first meeting with the department heads. They exchanged humorous historical anecdotes as they tried to help him feel at home among them. Salla expressed his appreciation of his reception and his willingness to start his work at once. They were impressed with Salla's level of intelligence, his command of the English language, and his incredible sense of medical knowledge.

"Do you have a goal... a personal project you wish to persue?" one of the men asked him.

"If you are asking me do I have a purpose in mind for my research... I do. I believe we can find a substance that will bind the receptor sites of all viruses and render them ineffectual..." Salla began.

Just as he started to speak, the dean noticed how every member of his staff leaned forward, as if Salla were about to reveal some great secret. He quickly stood up and cut the young man off.

"Yes, yes, yes..." the dean interrupted. "Research can begin tomorrow, Salla. Join us for dinner tonight," he said, "and no shop talk. Bring your best stories."

The staff and faculty quickly took to Salla's simple disarming charms. The young African freely indulged his curiosity and wasted no time as he plunged headlong into viral research. He worked and studied very hard for two years without taking a single day off, except when the labs closed for holidays. He surpassed everyone's expectations, while he simultaneously contributed valuable research to several projects outside his own. He gained such a likable reputation that faculty members clamored to claim Salla as their discovery. At the end of those two years, Oxford awarded him an advanced degree in Virology. His papers on virus theory caused a stir worldwide and brought fresh interest in Oxford's science departments as well as new cash flows from industry contributors. Salla turned out to be worth every penny invested in him.

He fulfilled his dream when he discussed his theories in the presence of Nobel Prize winners such as doctors' Watson, Crooks, and Shackleforth, the renowned world leaders in viral studies. Salla gained an immeasurable wealth of knowledge and experience at Oxford. By offering to work on the research of others, he also gained important friendships as well; for these men had not only worldwide reputations, but also contacts with viral researchers from universities around the globe. During this period, Salla quickly gained a reputation on his own. He lingered on at Oxford after he received his degree. He still had a large amount left in his endowment and decided that since they continued to provide his apartment and Radcliff, he had no reason to look elsewhere. He no longer pursued any further academic pursuits. This afforded him additional time to help others finish their projects. Meanwhile, he waited for a private research opportunity to open outside the scholastic world of Oxford.

During his entire tenure at the university, Salla wrote Bishop Ramsey nearly every week. Despite Salla's gloomy outlook for the man, the bishop continued his correspondence with the virologist throughout this two-year period. While he did not attend Salla's degree ceremony, the bishop sent word of his admiration for his friend. In turn, Salla kept in touch with the elderly man by writing letters and informed him of his progress while he expressed his gratitude for this opportunity. The bishop always wrote back to Salla. The young doctor often looked forward to the day when the letters usually arrived, though lately the bishop had not written. The absence of letters bothered

Salla. He thought he would make his way south and drop by to check on his old friend.

One afternoon, Salla returned to his flat early. He wanted to take the afternoon off to see a cricket match. The moment he arrived at the house, however, Salla sensed change. He could feel tension in the air. He wondered why Radcliff had not met him at the door and took his things as he always did. As he stood in the foyer and removed his coat, he noticed Radcliff speaking with another man on the sofa in his living room. Radcliff stood up when Salla entered. His face held a dour expression. Salla did not recognize the other man.

"Radcliff?" Salla questioned when he entered.

"A gentleman to see you, sir," Radcliff offered. "Mr. Atherton Harcourt is a senior member of the university, sir. He wishes to discuss a matter of some delicacy with you. I'll be in my quarters if you need me."

Radcliff inclined his head respectfully and quickly exited.

Salla felt confused by Radcliff's abruptness, as over the past two and a half years they built up a casual rapport and became good friends. Salla could see by the somber mood in the room that something seriously troubled the other man who stood before him. Salla glanced down and noticed the beautiful box he had seen at Bishop Ramsey's house, which held the letters he'd sent to the bishop. The lid was open and with two stacks of letters inside, one bound with sky blue ribbon, his American letters, and another stack bound with yellow ribbon that had English postmarks. Salla realized why he had not received a letter from the bishop lately. He looked into the face of the somber man and guessed the dark purpose he had yet to perform.

Mr. Harcourt motioned for Salla to sit.

"If you would, sir," the man calmly spoke.

Mr. Atherton Harcourt immediately turned to Salla.

"I regret to inform you that your friend, Bishop Jonathan Ramsey, passed away yesterday morning," he said quietly.

Mr. Harcourt produced a thick brown leather portfolio sealed with a family crest impressed into red wax.

"The bishop's solicitors left this for you. His instructions were explicit." He handed the package over to the stunned young man. "You were to receive this on the event of his death, my condolences to you, sir."

The man stood up and left poor Salla all alone. Salla remained on the sofa with the folded portfolio in his hands and wept. The man who helped the little boy from a life of misery had died. For the first time in many years, Salla felt like the frightened little boy on the farm again, wanting to flee another punishment, to run away from the pain and hurt to somewhere, anywhere, until he felt safe once more.

A soft knock at the door broke the silence.

"May I come in?" he heard Radcliff quietly speak.

"Of course," Salla said as his voice choked with emotion.

The door slowly opened. Radcliff's face gave away his empathy.

"If I can help…" he offered. "Why don't I make a pot of tea…" Radcliff said but saw these words had little effect on Salla. "I guess what I'm trying to say is, please feel free to…" his words trailed off.

"You've been a friend and companion these past two years, Radcliff," Salla admitted as he turned his face away. "I know you wish to help. However, right now, I believe I want to be alone, if you don't mind."

"Very good, sir," Radcliff replied. "I understand your grief. If you need me… well, you know," he told him.

Salla went to the window seat and gazed out at the gathering clouds that cast gloom over the once bright and sunny day. He remembered the first time he saw the bishop… a tall slender middle-aged man who appeared as out of place as a white blossom in Salla's very dark world. He recalled the excitement in the bishop's eyes when he brought the news of Salla's scholarship in America; and he recalled the last time he saw the bishop, when the elderly man, whose spreading illness made him appear older than his age, shared the rare cognac with him in celebration of his acceptance at Oxford.

Salla bowed his head and wept. Lightning flashed outside the window. The rain that dripped down the pane of glass mimicked the young African's sadness. Only the loud rumble of thunder finally shook Salla back to his senses. His eyes fell upon the thick envelope in his hands. He broke the heavy red seal and removed several pieces of heavy parchment paper. Salla recognized at once the Bishop's beautiful calligraphy. He practiced the art the last few years of his life.

On the cover page, in beautiful cursive letters, read the following:

"Jonathan Ramsey, M.D., Bishop Esquire, Retired, Church of England. The documents herein are the property of one Salla Motambou, currently of Oxford, England. Only he may receive these documents in the event of my death."

The next document had the official government seal of Mali at the top of the page. Salla frowned. What had the Bishop done? Salla examined the document more closely. This official paper spelled out the specifics of a deed, allocating a large parcel of land in eastern Mali near the city of Gao to the bearer of the deed, Salla Motambou.

A hand written note attached had just one sentence.

"Go back to Mali one day, my son, and bring some hope to your people." His Grace, the honorable Bishop Jonathan Ramsey.

"One day I will return, your grace," a melancholy Salla spoke softly as he bundled the paper together and slid it back inside.

Chapter Six

The search ends

After the many years of assisting others at Oxford and Baltimore, Salla finally struck out on his own with a different goal in mind – he wanted to make a career out of viral research. He wrote the Motambou's in Mali that he intended to find a job. He thanked his stepparents for their support. As soon as he received an income, he told them he wanted to repay their kindness. Ultimately, he wished he could return to Mali and build a world-class medical facility. Broke yet hungry for adventure, Salla sought to obtain employment of the kind he knew would advance his theories in virology.

"I'm not entirely without funds," he wrote in his letter. "A firm in Paris made me an offer. They send me 'traveling money' in the form of five-thousand pounds Sterling. I used it to pay Radcliff the bonus I promised. Now I am broke. However, I'm certain I can find a ride to Paris."

Despite being in his young mid-twenties, Salla Motambou's reputation preceded him. Without even knowing a thing about the company in question, he made up his mind to take any job they offered, based soley on comments made to him by his collegues. After he said goodbye to his English friends, he set out for Paris, France with one purpose – to work professionally with the top viral researchers at the famed Laboratory Institute d'Paris, a division of Ossures Pharmaceuticals. He would put his research to work creating tools for the pharmaceutical industry. His friend took him as far as the "Chunnel," where Salla caught a train to Paris. He emerged from the station in the heart of the city.

It was a sunny, beautiful day when Salla stepped outside. He took in a deep breath and set out to explore the famed city he had never seen. He wasn't interested in the usual tourist places. He wanted to walk along the Champs Élysées and wander into shops. He hadn't spoken French since he left Mali, although he retained it. Now he could freely converse in a language he found quite comfortable. He stopped by a café. The smell of coffee, baking bread, and confection lured the young man to sample the culinary delights on display.

"Je voudrais café au lait et un croissant! (I would like coffee and a croissant)" he said with a broad smile as the French rolled off his tongue with ease.

"Merci, monsieur," the shopperson said.

"Je vous en prie," Salla rattled back as he accepted the change.

Salla sat outside and watched the bustle of the city, delighted with the sophistication of its citizens and the cosmopolitan feel of Paris. Something about the place called to a kindred spirit inside him. He slowly savored each morsle as he nibbled off the pastry and sipped his coffee. He felt the first moment of joy since the bishop died.

After his brief reverie, he decided to walk to the famed Laboratory Institute d'Paris. Salla did not mind the walk. All along the way, he submerged his mind in the French language, its culture, and took in all the conversations around him.

"Bon jour," he wished those he passed and ignored the comments of "tourist" behind his back.

He casually walked along for several blocks until he finally stood before the ornate entrance to the established Laboratory Institute d'Paris.

"What a quaint old building," he noted.

Classic Romanesque architecture, clinging ivy covered the walls and colonnaded buildings, which gave the appearance of a palace. Salla walked up the long granite steps and noted the polished plaque before entering the tall brass doors, "established 1758" it said.

"Before the United States was a nation," he thought.

He crossed the marble-floored entry and slowly approached the receptionist while he enjoyed the splendor of the exquisitely decorated lobby with the busts of Nobel Prize winners. At the same time, a security guard approached.

"May I help you?" the guard quickly spoke up. His eyes searched all over Salla, which made the researcher feel like a suspect.

"My name is Salla Motambou," he answered. "I have an appointment." He started to walk forward when the officer stepped into his path and started to ask for identification.

"Just a moment," the receptionist spoke up when she overheard Salla speak. She pulled up some information on her computer screen. The picture of Salla stared back at her. She could see his complete profile.

"Oh, yes, they're expecting you," she said to him as the security guard backed away. "Straight ahead, doctor, to the elevators. I'll tell them you are on the way."

"Which floor?" he asked. He eased past the security guard, who still scrutinized the black young man.

"They know," the receptionist told him.

Salla marveled over the centrally located display that showed the institute's great accomplishments as he walked through the lobby. A large glass case held the golden trophy of France, heralding the discovery of the infamous HIV virus, the root cause of Acquired Immune Deficiency Syndrome. The gleaming figure of gold stood alone, spotlighted on a pedestal and surrounded by replicas of five Nobel Prizes received by individuals who once worked here, the most ever awarded to any single private institution in Europe.

He sighed as he gazed at the display. A life's dream would come true for Salla if the institute offered him a position. For the past two years, he secretly desired to work with the world-renowned researcher Camille Ossures, the famous French virologist. He heard several of his English colleagues mention her name on different occasions, each time with a certain gleam in their eyes. Yet, research positions with Ossures Pharmaceuticals, the parent company that owned the institute and its recently acquired nearby university, were seldom open and difficult to obtain, even for someone with Salla's reputation. He had only accepted an offer to interview. The institute did not promise any position.

Camille Ossures, the daughter of a wealthy French pharmaceutical giant, inherited a vast fortune when her father passed away. As a "genius" teenager, she studied abroad with special tutors in Germany, Switzerland, Sweden, and Russia before she returned to Paris when her father died. Rather than relinquish her inheritance, she took over his company in what later became a famous trial played out in the press. The young woman convinced the judge she could best serve her father's intentions for the firm. Once the corporation began to expand under her leadership, she later purchased the Laboratory Institute de' Paris and made it a permanent part of a new expansion that combined the institute with her corporation.

Her rising business success in just a few years took the entire French financial world by storm. Youthful in appearance, a striking beauty from birth with a vivacious personality, every eligible bachelor in Paris wanted Camille Ossures on his elbow. Not only did she epitomize contemporary French intelligence; Camille also had a reputation for being charming and witty. She always drew a crowd when her charismatic figure strolled into any social gathering.

Salla did not expect to meet the famous French industrialist when he stepped into the elevator. He reached to press a button when the top floor light came on. He nervously glanced at his reflection in the mirrored surface.

"I wonder if they're watching me now," he thought as the elevator rose.

When the elevator doors opened, Salla stepped into the reception area of a large executive office suite. A young woman approached him. She had an electronic organizer in her hand and a warm smile on her friendly face.

"Dr. Motambou?" she asked and extended her hand.

"Yes," he answered, taking it. "Is this Camille?" he wondered.

"I am one of Ms. Ossures assistants. My name is Marla," she said. "We've been expecting you. Please come with me."

Although the young girl spoke to him in broken English, he knew this was not the famed Camille he'd heard so much about.

"Have you been to Paris before?" she asked him.

"I arrived earlier today," he replied in French. "I'm sorry if I took too much time sightseeing before I came to the institute," he said. "I had lunch at the Café Etude. Veuillez m'excuser si mon français est un peu rouillé."

"Oh, a very nice bakery," she said, pleasantly surprised he spoke fluent French. She spun around to face him. "You're French is very good."

"It is the national language of Mali," he told her. "I learned French and English at the same time."

"Are you planning to stay in Paris?" she asked.

"I assume I will go back to England after the interview," he said, slightly deflated.

"I hope you can take in more of the city before you return to London," she said.

"Me, too," he replied. He thought it would be a shame to return to England without the position. However, knowing the institute's history, he already accepted this fate as a possibility. "I suppose I'll have to rent a flat in London," he thought, "and look for a research associate position."

"If you'll follow me," she said, "I would like to show you around the institute."

The receptionist pressed on and Salla fell into step behind her. As they walked along the corridor together, the young woman stopped from time to time and relayed the history of the institute to Salla. He learned the story behind each prize he saw in the lobby. She kept her remarks and the tour brief. She never mentioned anything about a research position or with whom he would interview. He thought it best not to ask questions. She took him to a private elevator where they descended to a lower level than the lobby.

When the doors open, he immediately sensed a difference. The hall was wide, extremely clean, and well organized. Every surface shined. He saw no desks or employees. He did see screens along the hall that spouted out schedules and deadlines. She paused before two large frosted glass doors. She turned and faced a black panel on the wall while she held up her security badge. A green light came on over the doors.

"That's all I have for you, sir," the young woman stated as she gesturing toward a door. "If you'll step through, they are waiting for you."

"Thank you," Salla stated as he walked toward the parting doors.

Salla stepped into a large open area that contained the most sophisticated, clean, and orderly laboratory he had ever seen, a modern facility with the latest equipment. A large group of people had assembled and faced him. The moment he entered, they burst into applause. A beautiful, tall, slender woman dressed in very stylish clothes stepped forward. She gently took Salla's elbow and turned toward the group.

"Ladies and Gentlemen," the woman began, "I give you the finest virologist on the planet and the newest researcher for Ossures Industries, Salla Motambou!"

Several people stepped forward as the room again applauded enthusiastically. They patted Salla on the back and offered congratulations. For a moment, the woman allowed the group to offer their support before she thanked them and whisked Salla off to a side corridor where they walked in silence to a different private elevator. Salla waited for the woman to address him but she said nothing. When they approached the polished brass doors, the woman inserted a key, and turned to Salla.

"How did you like your new laboratory?" she asked.

"That is a lab?" he replied. "It's very... clean," he said and hesitated to add more.

"I hope you like it," she said softly to him, "I built it just for you! I've been looking forward to this day for over a year."

Salla did not know what to say. He simply stared at her with disbelief on his face.

The woman smiled slightly before she resumed her regal bearing. When the elevator doors opened, Salla noticed the inside of this elevator seemed more like a small den that a conveyance. The two sat on a velour settee as the elevator ascended slowly for a long time. He noted plants in the corners and even a coffee machine!

"How cozy," he thought.

When the elevator doors opened, the two walked into a spacious office. A wide window faced the familiar skyline of Paris and in the distance, the Eiffel Tower protruded onto the horizon. The woman walked toward the huge flat desk that Salla assumed must be hers. She spun around with her hands in the air.

"Welcome to Paris," she smiled broadly.

"Thank you... Ms. Ossures?" he wondered.

"That's fine... you may call me Camille, since you will be my best researcher," she told him. "We will be working on the most top secret program in the world… a general cure for viral sicknesses," she said, with a sly grin, "one that would apply not to just one virus, but a vaccine good for *any* virus… Interested?"

Salla opened his mouth. That was his goal, the same one he tried to convince the men in England to pursue, base on his theory. But before he could answer, she quickly moved around her large desk and crossed toward him. Camille vigorously shook his hand never giving Salla a chance to speak.

"I cannot begin to tell you how excited we are that you have chosen our laboratory to continue your research in virology. Dr. Shackleforth gave a glowing report of your work with him. I've been following your progress for some time and if you'll pardon my intrusion, I used part of your theoretical applications to start my… our new project." She noticed that Salla still stared at her and did not speak. "You do wish to work for me, no?"

"If you will have me," Salla began humbly, a bit overwhelmed by Camille's beauty and assertive charms.

"If I will have you?" Camille laughed. "Salla, I would fight for you. What is it you want, money? A larger private lab? Direct corporate funding? A government contract? Publication? Right!" she rubbed her hands together. "If it is within my power, I will find a way to give them all to you!" she exclaimed as she smiled. Her outward jovial manner seemed refreshing to Salla after being around reserved Englishmen for so long.

"Your project sounds intriguing," Salla mentioned softly. "If I could just study some African viruses, I'd feel honored to help you."

"Oh, Salla," Camille came closer and draped her arm around his shoulder. She guided him to her window that overlooked the city of Paris. "I offer you the world and you take only that which will help me? I think you underestimate your value. I can assure you, the honor is all mine. However, if you want to study African viruses, as I read in your future goal paper, perhaps we can set up a separate lab for that, too."

"Then…"

"…it's a deal," she said and shook his hand. She smiled and informally hugged him from the side before she released him. "First, we must go out and celebrate. I just nabbed the best researcher in the world for my new research associate, and you, my friend, are going to make a lot of money for the first time in your life! By the time we finish, our medicine will revolutionize the drug industry and be used in every country on the planet!"

Salla seemed surprised by this news. He had not realized he was going to draw a salary. This would be his first paying job outside the piecemeal work he performed at clinics to help defray his costs. All this time he had survived on grants, scholarships, and gifts. Now he would be working for a large private corporation and taking home a paycheck.

"So… I have a job?" he mumbled.

"Oh, oui, mon bon ami (Oh, yes, my good friend)," Camille continued in French, having heard he was fluent. "You have one of the best jobs at one of the best companies in all of France. We produce many lines of pharmaceuticals. Drug companies from all over Europe and America come to us for our research. We have patents on hundreds of processes and new formulations. No one will know how to make our serum… but us! Five Nobel Prize winners worked for this lab! Perhaps now we have a sixth, no?"

Her smile appeared both broad and genuine. Her slender but shapely frame floated about the room while her original-design outfit flew around her like a movie star dancing on a Hollywood set. In every sense, she overwhelmed Salla.

"Last year, I turned down 200 applications from top researchers from over a hundred universities who submitted their names for a position," Camille exclaimed to Salla. "We've had only one research position open. My employees are so happy, they tend to stay until they… well, until they pass away, usually from old age! Yet, when I heard from Dr. Watson last year that you expressed a desire to work here, I decided to create a completely new position, just for you. Voila! Just like that!"

She snapped her fingers and added laughter that sounded like music to Salla.

"Thank you, Madam Director," Salla spoke shyly.

Camille sighed in reaction to his quiet nature. Most men would have reacted with more bravado.

"Oh my," Camille said quietly. "I most wholeheartedly welcome you to Paris, Salla Motambou. I am so glad you have come to work for me," she told him.

Before he could answer, Camille touched a button on her desk. Her special electronic office communicator came to life. She rapidly fired off a few orders in French to the person on the other end. The person spoke back and they seemed to argue for a moment in a rapid pattern of speech that amused Salla. Finally, Camille reached for a pile of papers on her desk and tossed them into the air. She did not care where they landed. She cut off the phone and extended her hand to Salla.

"Come," she said at last. "No more work for a while. Let us flee this stuffy office and celebrate."

Salla gazed out at the cityscape of Paris.

"Where to?" he asked.

"You must be joking. I will show you all of Paris. I have just taken the day off to be with you, Cherie. We will paint the town red and perhaps cause a scandal or two, no? Tonight you stay in my guest suite at The Ritz, which I reserve for out of town guests. Tomorrow, we will discuss your new residence. N'est pas? Come!"

Camille took Salla by the crook of his arm. The couple spun around and swept from the room to the private elevator. In one of the lowest levels, the door opened into a garage where a limousine waited for them.

"Charles," Camille stated as they approached the car, "this is Salla. Salla, Charles, introductions over. Let us start with lunch. My favorite spot, Charles, please call ahead for us."

"Oui, mademoiselle," the chauffeur bowed and quickly moved to open the door for her.

In minutes, they arrived at the Solé restaurant. The maître'd escorted the couple to a private table. During lunch, Camille informed Salla that as part of his duties, she suggested he see patients at her research hospital while he took part in the private research studies at the Institute's testing facility.

"I have an idea on how you can get started, if you are open to suggestion," Camille offered.

"Certainly," Salla responded.

"We're backlogged on human trials. I know its paper intensive, but perhaps with that highly organized brain of yours, you could tackle it," she offered.

"What about my license?" he inquired.

"My dear, they will quickly grant you that. Your credentials Salla are more impressive than the head of our board," she said and smiled. "As I understand it back in America, you could have taken over as head of Johns Hopkins, No?"

"Well, I..."

Camille broke into light delicate laughter that belied her height and stature. It sounded like music to Salla's ears. He enjoyed her laughter. It had a disarming quality. Salla told her he did have a license to practice medicine in the State of Maryland and in England. A medical license from America was usually good enough to go anywhere else in the world and practice.

Camille Ossures, it turned out, had many contacts in the French government. For a process that normally took weeks, if not months, Camille put through Salla's French medical licensure practically overnight. True to her word, Camille set up Salla in a townhouse apartment in the city, one of several such investments she owned. Within two weeks of his arrival in Paris, Salla began work with a busy schedule as both a physician and researcher. He saw patients in the morning for research studies while he performed viral research in the afternoon. Once she saw his progress and organization skills, Camille completely relinquished her research to Salla, which freed her to concentrate on the business side of her corporation.

One afternoon, Salla looked up and noticed that work in the lab suddenly stopped. He glanced over to the main doors in time to see Camille walking toward him. She waved a piece of paper in her hand.

"What is this?" he asked when she drew near.

"Your first check," she told him. "I thought you might like to frame it, since it is the very first time in your life you ever made money."

"I sold goods in the market place when I went to school in Bamako," he said with a slight grin.

"I'll bet you didn't make this much," she said as she held out the check.

"Fifty-thousand Euros? What is this?" he wondered.

"Consider it long overdue payment for services rendered," she said as she turned on her heels and left Salla with a surprised expression on his face. "Don't ever cash it," she told him as she headed for the door. "I've opened an account in your name. Just frame it, Salla. Trust me. You're money is already in the bank."

Therefore, he hung it up in his office along with a staged photograph of Camille handing him the check. She added a note: "To my dear friend and colleague, Camille Ossures."

In addition to the lavish office suite at the institute, Camille completely furnished Salla's Parisian apartment. At times, she even provided a chauffeur driven car when she invited Salla out for the evening. They attended concerts, shows, and events where Camille introduced the young physician to the Paris elite. Salla managed to impress the smart set with his command of language and his vast level of medical knowledge, while he kept his personal opinions poignant and brief.

Camille soon discovered that she and Salla were kindred spirits when it came to discussing many subjects outside of research.

"When did you develop a taste in opera or ballet?" she asked, surprised.

"I used to take the train to New York on the weekends…" he began.

"You've been to the Met?" she wondered.

"Oui…" he told her.

"We must go to the opera here," she declared. "I am a patron. My father's contributions helped to remodel the opera house in '97," she told him. "I own a permanent box!"

Soon, Camille stopped by to pick up Salla nearly every night after work so the two could dine at some different restaurant around the city. However, on this particular night, Salla sensed Camille had something she wanted to say. She took him straight to the Solé with hardly a word. She ordered a private table. He could tell she had much on her mind. Camille had their dinner ready by the time they arrived, so the waiter served them at once. Once he left them, Camille breached the silence.

"Salla..." she began.

"Yes," he responded as he dabbed his chin.

"We are friends, are we not?" Camille put to him as she glanced up from her dinner plate.

Salla stared back at her for a moment, uncertain where this conversation might lead. Her personal tone made him feel a little uncomfortable.

"Yes..." he replied as he reached for his wine glass, "friends."

"I... I want to make this clear from the start, Salla," she said in a low voice so that no one else could hear, "I want us to be friends and only friends... not lovers."

Salla choked on his wine. He set the glass down and wiped his chin.

"You are the most beautiful woman I've ever known, Camille," Salla began. "I've never thought of you as anything but my sister."

A moment passed when Camille simply stared at the young black man. All at once, she broke out laughing, which attracted attention from the wait staff. She did not care that others watched them. She heard the rumors from her office staff. Since she had an open relationship with them, they were the first to tell her things, such as the rumor going around Paris about Salla being her lover.

"Oh Salla, that is the kindest and most cruel thing I have ever heard a man say to me," she blushed, "thank you, anyway... brother."

She called for the waiter usually assigned to her table.

"Chilled champagne," she requested. "We have a celebration," Camille said smiling at Salla. "I have a new brother."

"Oui, mademoiselle," the man nodded. He rushed from the room to fulfill the order and to repeat what he just heard... that they were not lovers but in fact just good friends.

This talk of lovers made Salla reflect. For all of his success, he never sought a companion. In fact, he never had an intimate relationship in his life. He was always too busy with scholastics for any personal interaction. While a few women flirted with him, he tended to ignore them. For the first time in Salla's life, he had some leisure time to enjoy his life, only to discover a void. Later that evening, as he stood in front of the window and gazed out on the night landscape of Paris, he wondered about his future and what fate held in store for him.

"If I could meet someone like me, with similar interests, that would be nice," he thought.

For a man in his mid-twenties, Salla felt the same longings most men feel. These feelings simply arrived later in Salla's life. He sighed as he pondered his future.

"What woman would want me?" he thought.

Feeling dejected, he turned away from the bright lights of the city. He retired to his bed early, resigned to get a good night's rest.

"Am I that repulsive no woman has ever been attracted to me?" he wondered as he lay in his bed. "I should be content with my life and forget all about women."

Chapter Seven

The First Solid Evidence

On a bright wintry morning in February 2019, Captain Brighton, brimming with confidence, headed up the hall to the security briefing, where he knew General Andrews, the top commanding officer of this secret NATO operation, had just ended his daily briefing. The night before, Corporal Gary Peterson, the handsome young blonde corporal from Oklahoma, discovered an unidentified flying object in the sky over the Pacific. He handed Captain Brighton not just new and vital information, but perhaps the roadmap to promotion.

This information was just the kind of thing that either bolstered a man's career in the world, or moved him to the side while others led in his place. Brighton recognized an opportunity when he saw it. He knew how to take advantage of a unique moment like this.

As a brace of officers made their way from the room, Captain Brighton approached the General with a slim silvery laptop tucked under his arm. The general tarried a moment longer while he gave last minute instructions to his assistant. Brighton waited until he had the general's attention.

"General, sir," Captain Brighton stood at attention. "I have something that needs your immediate attention."

The general glanced up at the British officer. He would have preferred an all-American team. He did not like the idea of having French, German, and British officers in his midst, especially when it came to sharing classified material. Unfortunately, he had no choice. The huge funding it took to run an operation of this magnitude required different sources. The general looked down his nose at the pipsqueak.

"What is it, Brighton?" the General barked. "I'm a busy man!"

"As you know, sir, I am in charge of the new satellite surveillance systems known as spec obs. We just put the NAT-IX satellite into orbit," the captain began.

"Yes?" he said gruffly as he turned his focus to the captain, "What is it you want?"

"Well, sir," the captain explained, "NAT-IX started to take scans of the Pacific the moment it went active. As you know, it's not interfaced with the rest of the defense grid. Last night, it caught something very… unusual."

"Get to the point," the general impatiently requested as his aid stood next to him. The rather plain young man with short black hair and glasses closely guarded the general's valuable time as his first priority.

"I have some images of an event, sir," Brighton stated while he glanced around him. "For your eyes only."

The general waved his hand and dismissed his aid, who peevishly left the room. The lad added an expression of disgust on the way out.

"Sorry about that," the general said, "He's a pain in the ass, but he's a damn good organizer. He helped turn this place into a well-oiled machine. I don't care what their orientation is, I could never argue with efficiency. Go ahead," he indicated the laptop.

The captain opened the slim silvery device and started playback of the recorded image. As the image played, the captain explained the visual.

"We caught an object moving through the atmosphere," he said and pointed to the ghostly image that moved across the screen. "General, the object achieved speeds that exceeded Mach 10… at 12,000 meters!"

"Exceeded?" the general questioned, "must have been a satellite re-entering the atmosphere…"

"No, sir," Brighton interrupted. "It was a controlled aircraft…"

"That's not possible at that altitude and speed," the general stated.

"In this instance, we believe it is the case, sir," the captain continued, "We could not identify the type of craft. NAT-IX detected no chemical or heat signature, so we ruled out both jet aircraft and rocket. We also eliminated a ramjet as none of our current systems has such stealth technology. We still do not know its origins, although the computer stated somewhere in the southwest Pacific, which rules out China and India, sir. Cpl. Peterson made this recording when he reported off shift. Evidently, the system felt the object non-belligerent. It set off no alert! I thought you should see this information right away."

"What do you think it is?" the general questioned.

"Peterson is an expert trained in recognizing such craft. We've both analyzed the image. We're not exactly sure what it is, general," the captain continued. "Since it left no contrail or heat signature, it is difficult to say. With no vapor trail, we also ruled out a comet-type asteroid. Cpl. Peterson states an ordinary object would have left a wide heat plume. Our satellite could only see this using the new multispectral range finder. One interesting note, it entered American airspace without triggering any alert or alarm."

That caught the General's attention. He took a closer look at the flowing images on the screen.

"Are you certain NORAD didn't spot this?" the general inquired.

"They did not see it," the captain told him, "nor did the Pentagon, the NSA, homeland security, or anyone else. We are the only ones with this information, sir."

"Come again?" the general carefully examined Brighton's face.

"That object passed through the entire defense grid, general, completely undetected," the captain confirmed.

"Why didn't you notify command immediately about this?" the general demanded.

"That is why I am here," the captain explained. "Sir, this object made a soft landing in southwestern Kansas," the captain pointed out, "the automated satellite warning system regarded it as controlled and benign."

"Are you telling me that you have proof of a genuine alien UFO?" the general said, his eyes going back to the screen.

"I'm not ready to draw conclusions yet, sir. We've had no reports of any unusual activity in Kansas. I ordered a ground satellite surveillance scan of the area in question," Brighton told him. He reached over and touched the screen. He switched the image on the screen to stills of the ground that showed fields of cultivated plants and grain silos with an occasional farmhouse. "We scanned every square inch of land with our best high-density camera and found no ship on the ground or any trace of a vehicle landing," the captain reported. "We found no airstrips, no hangers that could hold a plane, and no bases within 200 kilometers of a probable landing site."

"Let me see that traveling image once more," the general requested.

The captain changed the image on the small screen back to the satellite-tracking image. The general nodded and muttered as he stared at the continuous loop flow of images. The screen showed a silvery sphere fly across the Pacific Ocean, only to disappear into southwestern Kansas. He began to hum and rub his finger on his chin.

"Who's seen this?" the general asked.

"Cpl. Peterson, myself, and you, general," Brighton pointed out.

"...and that's all?" Andrews questioned.

"Yes, sir," Brighton responded.

"Good," the general said, "let's keep it that way, for a while."

The captain watched as the general reached over and closed the lid to the laptop. He glanced up at the captain.

"Very well, Brighton, you've got my attention," the general said as he waited to see what the captain's next move might be. "Now what?"

"Don't you think we should investigate this phenomenon, sir," the captain suggested.

General Andrews paused a minute and sized up the man in front of him. He recognized ambition when he saw it. He could use a man like Brighton to shore up the strength of his command.

"Right you are, Brighton," General Andrews took over. "You seem like a very intelligent man. I want you to look into this with everything we've got at our disposal, including ground investigative teams and specialized agents. Tell no one our objectives." General Andrews stared Captain Brighton in the eye. "Are you familiar with our agents?"

"Yes, sir. But, I can think of only one suited for this job," the smart captain replied.

"Then get busy… find him," the general said as he rose. "Keep this project between you and me….and that Peterson fellow," the general added. "Arrange any funding you need through me as well. I have codes that will alter where and how you spend your money so that the bean counters cannot trace it. Get to work, Brighton. Let me know what you find out there. Dismissed."

Chapter Eight

When Trios Collide

When informed of the limited offer for a two-year scholarship, Filla Zambi proudly claimed, "That is all the time I need." After extensive screening, Camille Ossures chose only one candidate for the Ossures International Scholarship Fund during the summer of 2014 – a young woman from Africa. Her high marks in school, the highest in aptitude testing, and an impressive personal interview singled her out when five finalists came to Paris. Four returned home without funding. Only one stayed, Filla.

At first, Camille received monthly reports on her progress in passing. However, after just six months, the entire university campus buzzed with her name. She had perfect scores on every exam and perfect attendance in all of her classes. Professors found that she not only retained everything she read, she also remembered their lectures as if she had a recorder for a mind.

Her career counselor wanted to inquire as to Filla's goals. When he questioned her ambitions, she answered: "I want to start a hospital in my country. I want it to be the best hospital in the region, in the nation, in all of Africa." Ambitious, indeed. Upon hearing those remarks from Filla's counselor, Camille appreciated the young woman's gusto for life and her keen perceptive intelligence.

On a whim one evening, she invited Filla to dine with her at the Solé, Camille's restaurant in downtown Paris. Ten minutes into the meal, both women knew they had found their best friend. On practically every subject that came up, they agreed except one – men. Camille spoke of this one and that one. She had a current boyfriend but she never wanted a serious relationship. Filla had never been with a man. She blushed when she emphasized the word, never. Camille on the opposite side of the coin was definitely more gregarious.

"I love men for companionship, but never marriage. I'm not that kind of woman – one who settles for domestic life with children – not me," she told her new friend.

"Oh, I don't know..." Filla sighed. "If I found the right man, I think I could be a good wife," she stated. Camille's eyebrows went up. "If he let me run a hospital, didn't expect me to cook or clean, and had no interest in children, just good clean sex!"

"My kind of man!" Camille quickly shot back.

The two women laughed. They were professionals and intended to remain that way. If the men in their lives could accept that, all the better.

Filla and Camille saw each other frequently after that evening. They often dined out on Tuesday or Thursday evenings, when Camille did not have a date or Filla had an exam. They discussed what it took to run a hospital. Since Camille owned one of the largest teaching hospitals in the city, she was eager to hear what Filla had to say about it. Filla would only offer suggestions on how she would run a large hospital in a hypothetical way so she didn't offend her friend.

Filla's two years of scholarship time passed all too quickly for Camille. Filla not only worked on her graduate degree in Hospital Administration, she had her sights on completing her dissertation at nearly the same time. Her plan was to return as quickly as she could to Africa. Camille feared that when the spring of 2016 rolled around, she would lose her best friend.

Then Salla came to town and Camille's life changed again. All at once, Camille found she had two new friends... two friends who had similar problems forming relationships and similar backgrounds. It didn't take her long before she realized the strange but wonderful coincidence of their origins, too.

One evening in April, when the two women dined together...

"I graduate in May. Are you ready to..." Filla began.

"I want you to stay..." Camille cut her off.

"You know I can't," Filla responded. "I promised my family and the government I would return to oversee construction of a new hospital..."

"Listen to me first," Camille interrupted. "You've impressed just about everyone connected with the university and the hospital, Filla. However, if you return to Africa too soon, you will take only scholastic expertise with you. I spoke to my hospital administrator. He would like you to work with him for the next year as his assistant. It's a salaried position... probably long hours, but you'll have hands on experience..."

Filla rose from her seat. She leaned over and gave Camille a hug.

"You just don't want me going back to Africa," she whispered in Camille's ear.

"Perhaps," Camille replied when Filla pulled away. "Still… I'd like you to at least go to Africa prepared."

"I accept," Filla finally relented.

Grateful her friend would remain in Paris a while longer, Camille concentrated on Salla, integrating him into his new lab. Daily she traveled from the lab to the hospital, looking in on her friends' progress. Nevertheless, Camille kept her opinions about her two friends separate from them. Filla and Salla lived in two different worlds. They never saw one another. Salla's world was all laboratory. Filla helped the administration in the daily operations of the hospital.

Summer passed into early fall. Before the start of mid-September classes, the university announced the retirement of a professor. On that day, both Salla and Filla received invitations in the mail to attend a "going away" party for the doctor. Since he worked in research *and* taught at the university, both Salla and Filla knew the man. During the week that followed, Camille subtly yet strongly hinted to both of her friends that she would like them to attend. When she saw their names show up on the RSVP list, she changed the location and offered to throw the party at her Paris townhouse.

In the past five years since she took over Ossures Pharmaceuticals Incorporated, Camille gained a reputation for having some of the best "A-list" soirees in Paris. She usually invited a wide variety of intellectuals, politicians, financiers, and a few artists to mix things up a bit. If you were anyone in France, you went to one of her parties where even the President of France might show up coming through the back door entryway, as Camille owned the entire block around her townhouse and could provide some of the best security in Paris.

Camille sent her car for Salla to make certain her best researcher would show up. By the time Salla arrived at the party, the evening's festivities had already started. Camille sometimes used this townhouse as a gallery for new artists. She displayed their artwork on the walls or positioned them in display cases near the corners of the large yet homey open front room, where her partygoers gathered. While she seldom stayed at this particular address, she brought her full staff from her country estate to prepare and serve hors d'oeuvres along with dinner for this evening's guests. The moment she saw her favorite researcher enter, she crossed over to the foyer and warmly greeted Salla with open arms.

"Salla!" she cried out.

"Camille," he quietly replied.

If Camille placed that much attention on someone, it turned heads. However, no one at the social gathering actually knew the tall broad-shouldered black man who entered to such a warm reception. She fluttered up to him, wearing another of her very expensive original designs. Camille loved new designer clothes. Every time Salla saw her, she wore something different and exciting. Once when he asked her about them, she replied, "I auction them off every month to my rich friends and give the proceeds to the disadvantaged. Is that so terrible?" He could not dispute her logic.

After their brief exchange at the door, Camille continued to greet new arrivals and entertain her guests. Salla quickly retreated to a corner of the main room as he felt somewhat a social butterfly. Despite his recognizing several people, he shied away from interacting with this room of hobnobbing notables.

The three people of interest seemed in different worlds. Salla was most comfortable in his lab or in private one-on-one interactions. Since he rarely attended parties, Salla did not have the same social skills people that Filla possessed so naturally. Filla Zambi, on the other hand, often attended Camille's parties. Most of the people in the room knew her as Camille's best friend. Camille, on the other hand, worked the crowd as a consummate politician would. She expertly socialized while at the same time effortlessly floated from group to group, joking, laughing, and being her usual charming self.

A waiter offered Salla a tray whose glasses held many different kinds of wine, which the waiter readily pointed out. As he settled on a glass of port from the tray, Salla glanced up through the crowd and spotted her for the first time. When Salla initially beheld Filla, her very beauty astounded him. He had never seen such a beautiful African woman. In that moment, he could see nothing else in the room except her.

In Salla's eyes, Filla resembled an ancient Egyptian Queen with her light-bronzed skin, small nose, and high cheekbones. Her brilliant perfect smile matched her radiant beauty. Filla stood out from the crowd like some sparkling jewel washed ashore on a deserted beach, impossible to miss. In this room mostly filled with bankers, politicians, artists, and intellectuals, the young African man could see only one person. Filla struck Salla as the epitome of pulchritude.

"The gods breathed life into a statue of perfection," he sighed.

He wanted to introduce himself, speak to her, say anything. Yet his shy nature took hold of his throat and held him glued to the spot where he stood. He took a big gulp of wine and gathered his courage. When his host glanced his way, Salla sought her help. He motioned to Camille and caught her attention. She came to his side and noticed an immediate change in her friend's expression.

"Well, Salla, you've come alive, my friend! Has something caught your eye?" Camille asked with a wry smile on her lips. She could see how he gazed in Filla's direction.

"I feel as if I started out this evening on my way to a boring party, took a wrong turn, and showed up here by mistake," Salla remarked, as he never took his eyes off Filla.

Camille covered her mouth and laughed so gently that only the person next to her would have heard it.

"I don't believe your heart will survive the evening unless you find out the lady's name, is that it?" she asked her friend.

Salla turned his attention to Camille. She knew him all too well. He cleared his throat.

"Ever since I arrived at the party, I've felt you've been up to something." His eyes met hers. "You didn't arrange this, did you, Camille?"

"I'll let you in on a little secret," she whispered in his left ear. "Her name is Filla, she is single..." She moved around behind him. As she spun away, she whispered in his other ear. "... and I did."

Salla heard her laugh as she moved away from him. He grinned a little broader.

"So she *did* arrange this... and her name is Filla..." he thought, as he slowly stumbled and clumsily made his way through the crowd toward Filla. He accidentally bumped into people as he worked his way through the tightly packed space. "Excusez-moi... je vous demande pardon..."

For the first time in his life, he felt a strange sense of attraction about a woman, more than just a passing interest. He could not wait to meet her. All at once, Salla suddenly stopped dead in his tracks. He could not describe his feelings. Was this love he felt, or just physical attraction? What did he feel? His strange feelings tortured him. He felt something else inside his mind when he saw Filla – something he could not, or would not recognize. The experience reminded him of when he was a boy on the farm, how he knew the answers to things, and did not understand why he knew them; or how he knew a person's illness with only a cursory touch, or his rapid diagnosis of the bishop. Perhaps this intuition he possessed might explain why school came so easy and why his research won both fame and recognition.

Salla realized his mind had drifted and he snapped back. He glanced around the room until he found her. Normally, he never spoke to strangers, let alone a beautiful woman of Filla's caliber. Yet, his feelings for Filla began to fill him with new sense of boldness and courage. He had crossed to within speaking distance and thought he would introduce himself before she continued to move on through the room, the same way Camille did. She started to turn away from him. He felt the opportunity slipping away unless he spoke up. He garnered his last ounce of courage and swiftly moved around the last person between them to block her. He tried to make it appear as if he bumped into her accidentally.

"Excuse me," he said as if he behaved a bit clumsily.

Filla quickly moved her drink hand away so as not to spill it. Salla knew this was his chance.

"I've never seen you before," he blurted. "Are you a student here at the institute?"

His dry voice cracked, so he took a quick gulp of his wine.

"Pardon me?" she said as she turned her head to see what ungainly oaf nearly knocked her over.

"I'm sorry," he said as he pulled back. "My name is Salla," he held out his hand.

"Filla Zambi…" she answered and did not take his. "Do I know you?"

"I saw you at one of the institute's symposiums," Salla blurted as he tried to recover. He searched for some thread to start the conversation. He felt this was a safest way he knew to open with her. Most of the students attended one of the symposiums held every month at the Institute.

Filla, politically savvy, knew when a man made a pass at her. She also knew every guest speaker for the last two years. Camille made her the chair for the committee that booked them. She realized he was on uncertain ground.

"That's right," she said as she politely looked up at him. "I usually go every month."

She tried to determine his motive for striking up the conversation. People were always trying to gain favors because of her close relationship with Camille Ossures. She decided to pin him down.

"Which symposium was that? The one on world hunger?" She asked.

Salla nodded, "Yes, that's the one, world hunger. Good speaker."

Filla knew there was no symposium on world hunger, not this past season.

"I don't recall seeing you there?" she went on. She almost turned away at that moment, when a strange thing happened. The room seemed to slow down until the action around them came to halt.

Across the room, Camille, and a financier she invited, discussed the funding of a new design project related to one of her guests. She stopped in mid-sentence when a sharp feeling cut through the room. It felt like a knife that stabbed inside her mind. She twisted her head toward Salla and Filla. Time stood still. The three seemed independent of the events around them. Suddenly, a great pulse of energy passed between the three that carried with it understanding and a connection that went beyond familiarity. For a brief yet prolonged second, their minds connected in a new foreign way – nothing else in the room mattered.

"Salla!"

"Filla!"

"Camille!"

Then just as swiftly as it occurred, the feeling vanished. Camille turned back to her guest. She realized the event passed so quickly, nothing changed around her except her heightened senses. Sweat broke out on her face. Her stomach lurched. She could feel her composure collapse.

"Camille?" the banker asked when he saw the color drain from her face. "Are you alright?"

"I just remembered something…" she muttered. "Please excuse me…"

Flustered, Camille made a polite excuse and ducked into a nearby restroom off the foyer. She locked the door behind her, reached into the linen closet, and took a washcloth. She turned on the faucet, put cool water on it, and rang it out before she lightly placed it against her flushed cheeks and the back of her neck.

"What happened out there?" she wondered as she stared in the mirror. "How strange," she thought, "how very strange."

This event struck the beautiful young industrialist too personally. For a moment, Camille closed her eyes and recalled the trauma of hearing a voice that spoke to her when she was a teenager. It frightened the young woman during a difficult time in her life. Her mother and father whisked her out of France to avoid any social embarrassment. They took her to a psychiatrist's clinic in Switzerland. She could still hear her own voice when she called after her mother.

"Mamma! Mamma! Don't leave me!" she screamed. Yet she heard nothing in reply except the fading sound of her mother's highheels as they clicked on the polished tile floor.

The sounds from that day echoed in her thoughts when Camille opened her eyes and tried to remain calm, despite her shaking hands.

"That happened a long time ago. You are the CEO of a major corporation and you have a room full of guests," she thought as she grasped for the concreteness of the room and stared at her image in the mirror. "I must regain my composure."

She took the washcloth and placed it in the hamper. She stood up tall before the mirror, took in a deep breath, smiled and exited. She hoped the feeling was only a temporary one.

Meanwhile, Salla stood still as he faced Filla with a blank stare. Salla blinked his eyes.

"What was that?" he thought.

He shook his head as if the action would rid him of the sensation.

Filla did not move. She hoped the feeling would go away if she held still. She realized that Salla had not answered her question from a moment ago.

"I must say something," he thought. "Symposium! What made me say that? That was a stupid thing to say."

Salla started to squirm, not certain how to pose his reply.

"Well, you know how these symposiums are. They all seem the same..." he casually tossed out.

At that precise moment, Camille returned to the room. She signaled the staff and they called the guests to dinner.

Salla breathed a sigh of relief.

"Saved by the dinner bell," he thought. "Shall we?" he said to Filla, and motioned toward the dining room.

Filla realized that she had been staring at Salla for some time, yet somehow she did not mind that fact. As if a vale of mystery lifted, she found the brutish big man strange but somehow also attractive, although she could not explain her feelings.

She did not take his arm, nor did she look away, intrigued instead by Salla's face. Filla suddenly had a very strong emotional attraction toward this brash young man that she could not explain. Rather than move, the couple stood still and gazed into each other's eyes.

The dinner guests moved toward the main dining room while Salla and Filla remained as the last two people in the room. Camille stood in the archway to the dining room. She noticed how the pair could not take their eyes off one another.

She loudly cleared her throat. That sound brought Filla back to her senses, breaking her eye contact with Salla. She glanced around and noticed only the two of them standing there. She blushed and took Salla's arm. He escorted Filla into the main dining room as they searched for their seats.

Camille directed her forty-two guests to their prearranged seat, twenty guests on either side of a long table with Camille at one end of the table, and the guest of honor at the other end. As much as she tried to fulfill the demands of her eclectic gathering, Camille could not keep her thoughts or her eyes away from Salla and Filla.

"I've done my part," she thought. "The rest will be up to you two."

Salla and Filla approached the two remaining open seats, delighted when they discovered them next to one another.

"Funny," Filla remarked. "Your placard is next to mine."

"Yes, that is a coincidence," Salla replied.

He held out Filla's chair for her.

"May I?" Salla slipped and spoke in Bambara, one of Mali's local languages. He could not explain why he chose to speak in his native tongue. He had not done so in a while.

Filla turned abruptly and glared at Salla. She answered him in Bambara.

"Did you just speak my language?"

"Your language?" he continued in Bambara. "That's all I spoke as a child."

"Mali?" Filla questioned as she stared at Salla, shocked.

"Yes?" Salla answered with trepidation. "You?"

She nodded. The pair burst out laughing. Salla and Filla realized this was no coincidence. Someone steered them together on purpose.

Simultaneously, they glared in Camille's direction. The hostess seemed too busy as she discussed something with the current winner of the Paris Prize in Literature who sat on her right. Camille briefly shot a glance in their direction when she noticed the two faces from Mali seated together. She gave them a knowing nod.

"I guess since we've been thrown in together like this, we'd better make the best of it," Filla said sweetly to Salla as she raised her glass.

Salla raised his glass. "Agreed," he responded and took a sip of wine.

Camille gazed at the impressive display of guests she invited. Many layers to the social strata gathered around her table. Despite the varied level of intellect and different backgrounds, her guests' behaved quite amiable. The conversation proved both lively and spirited as the food and wine flowed. Soon the room's air filled with laughter and gaiety.

During dinner, something definitely clicked between the two Africans. An ease of communication flowed between them that went beyond normal attraction. Perhaps the fact they could speak in their native tongue and dialect made the difference.

"I feel relaxed speaking Bambara tonight," Filla said in her native dialect.

"It sounds beautiful," Salla replied in Bambara. "I'd forgotten how much I missed it till you replied."

"I don't believe anyone can understand us. I think we're the only ones here speaking Bambara," she observed.

Salla became so enthralled with her that all he could do was nod.

"Please tell me about your home, your family, and how you came to be here from Mali," Filla asked.

To Salla, her face appeared so innocent and pure in the soft light of the dining room. How could he refuse such a request?

"Did you say your name was Zambi? That does not sound like someone from Mali," Salla addressed first.

"My family moved from Ethiopia in 1970, before the uprising. Salla sounds east African as well," she pointed out, although Filla still did not know Salla's last name.

"I do not know my father's history," he started. "We did not practice any religion. I began life on a dirt farm west of Kita. My family had no money. We were very poor. We lived in a mud house."

Salla described the hard life on the farm without going into too much detail. He spoke eloquently of the day that changed his life, when Bishop Ramsey visited and then later when he met his new parents.

"I was the youngest graduate at the University of Bamako Medical School..." he proudly stated when Filla cut him off.

"Oh, my goodness," she nearly choked. "Did you say your name was Salla?"

"Yes..." he softly replied.

"Salla... er, Dr. Salla Motambou?" she spoke up.

"Yes..."

"*The* Dr. Motambou?" she asked, as something akin to fear spread across her face.

"Yes, did I say something wrong?" he responded.

"Why didn't you tell me you were the famous Dr. Motambou?" she wondered, becoming a bit upset.

"...because I..." he swallowed, nervous from her reaction. "I didn't realize I was so famous," he said as his face fell. "I suppose I should have mentioned it. I apologize."

For a second, she judged his humble expression and then her features softened.

"No, doctor, I am the one that should apologize," she said as she realized he spoke sincerely without guile. "I simply did not realize who you were. Forgive me for interrupting. I should have known. You were saying... please continue."

He glanced at her a moment, dabbed his chin, and resumed his personal history. This time, Filla sat enthralled with the fact that this man whom she liked and felt this attraction toward, should also be one of the most famed researchers in the world, featured in the New England Journal of Medicine, New Age, JAMA, and other leading periodicals as one of the most brilliant physicians of the 21st Century.

"After I obtained my medical degree in Mali," he continued, "I went to America and specialized in viral research at John Hopkins while I obtained my advanced medical degree. For a while, I worked in a variety of settings, mostly for the experience. After that, I left America intent on extending my research in virology..." he continued when she interrupted.

"Wait," she broke in, "Camille said something to me about this brilliant virologist. I actually read an article about your work at Oxford – your paper on the theory of viruses and a possible overall serum that would inhibit all viral replication. I've heard people say you were destined to win the Nobel in medicine. I had no idea you were him… that is…" she stumbled, very unlike her usual poised manner.

"I'm not that special," he said as he cast his eyes down.

"Oh, but you are," she objected. "It's no wonder Camille snatched you up so quickly. You are a catch," she said as she measured him up. She glanced briefly over at Camille, who returned a quick wink. Filla continued; "Well, Salla, you weren't the only one to quickly advance. I graduated from high school at fifteen, completed four years of college in two years, and started my master's degree program here before my nineteenth birthday."

"Indeed," he commented.

"Yes, but I chose a different path from you," she told him. "My focus is hospital administration. I will turn twenty-one next summer and already have my doctorate in hospital administration."

"Very nice," he politely observed. "Your family must be proud."

All at once, the conversation between them fell into silence. The couple politely turned to the people on their opposite side, only to find those people around them engaged in other conversations. Filla turned back to Salla as he did to her. The two smiled and shrugged.

"How do like Paris?" she spoke up. "Quite a change from England, I would imagine."

"Paris is definitely less reserved than England and more open than America," he told her. "I was very nervous about what to expect when I arrived. Camille helped to change all that."

"She does like to get involved," Filla threw out.

While their conversation continued along the same vein, the conversation began to take a personal note. Each one probed the other's opinion of this thing or that, preferences, likes, dislikes and so on. No matter what they said, they listened intently to what the other person said.

When the evening ended, neither Salla nor Filla wished to part company. They remained at the table while everyone else drifted away after dinner. Each one felt as if they found a long lost relative with so much to say – catching up on missed experiences, reminiscing about home – personal things neither wanted to end.

"I think everyone else has left," Filla spoke up as she glanced around the dining room. "It's late. I suppose it's time we leave, too."

"I'll get your coat," Salla offered.

He headed over to the yawning servant in the corner and quickly returned with both their coats. Salla helped Filla into hers. They lingered near the front door, the last of the party to depart. Filla offered her hand and thanked Salla for the wonderful evening.

"It was a pleasure to meet you, Salla," she said as she extended her right hand in courtesy.

Like a perfect gentleman, Salla bent and placed his lips lightly over her hand. He straightened, hesitated, and wondered what to do next. Should he offer to escort her home? Should he attempt a kiss? Would that be too intrusive since they just met? An awkward silence followed.

Camille moved toward Salla's side.

"I'm so glad you could come, Filla," she said as she stood next to them. "Did you want to give Salla your card in case he might want to contact you about someone in Mali?" she asked innocently.

"Oh, of course," Filla said as she fumbled with her purse.

Salla sighed deeply, grateful for his friend's intervention. He watched anxiously, unable to muster the courage to ask for her telephone number. Filla found one of her printed business cards. She took out a pen, and quickly added her personal phone number on the back.

"Thank you Salla for a wonderful evening," she said and handed him the card. She turned to Camille. "A very interesting guest list, I underestimated your ability to invite all the right people." She glanced toward Salla and then walked out the front door.

Camille raised both her eyebrows to Salla.

"Well?" she asked.

He simply sighed in return, content with everything in his life at that moment. From the front door of her building, he looked out at the city lights of Paris. He turned back to her and shrugged.

"Good night my lovesick friend," Camille laughed.

She spun Salla around and pushed him out the front door. He floated down the stairs on a cloud without saying a word of goodnight to Camille. Tired but amused Camille watched her friend walk away from townhouse and gasped as he nearly kept going into traffic.

"Salla!" she cried out.

He snapped out his dream, pulled back just in time to miss a passing motorist. He sheepishly smiled up at Camille and waved goodbye. He quickly hailed a cab and left. Camille stayed in her doorway a moment longer. She brushed her cheek lightly with her hand. The light of the room behind her outlined her slender silhouette.

A strange sensation came over the Parisian CEO, more like a chill that forbade some ominous event. As she watched Salla's cab fade into the night, she had the strangest feeling she would never see Salla and Filla again. Camille rubbed her flesh up and down, trying to warm up before she stepped back inside. Her maid waited at the top of the curving stairs to assist her nighttime retirement. She decided to spend the night in one of the townhouse's spacious upstairs bedrooms.

She slowly made her way up the stairs to the private bedroom, grateful for the maid's help after she dragged her tired body to the top.

"What a night," she thought. "I couldn't possibly top this evening," she thought as she pulled on her satin nightgown and prepared for bed.

"Pleasant dreams," her maid said and quietly closed Camille's door.

"Dreams…" Camille's thoughts drifted as she closed her eyes. "Dreams…"

Chapter Nine

Manufactured death

March 23, 2024, about five minutes before seven in the evening, somewhere near the center of Novgorod, Russia, two men sat in a compact vehicle and watched the front of a clothing store. They sat at this location for nearly three hours and very nearly ran down their charger to maintain heat inside the vehicle. The dark tinted windows prevented anyone from seeing inside. They watched and waited for the right moment to act.

"Cold… isn't it?" the tall black man commented as he rubbed his gloved hands together.

He felt uncomfortable in such a small car, with his legs bent up. He tried to shift, only to resume the same spot. His flesh ached from being cramped.

"You are not Russian?" the driver asked sarcastically as he knew the answer. Russia had very few black men in positions of power. "This is nothing. Every day in Russia is cold. We are used to such cold."

"Это не мой первый визит в Россию (This is not my first visit to Russia)," the black man stated and continued to speak in Russian. "I have been here many times. I visited Moscow in 2016… a special assignment."

"You were part of the Blankton assassination?" the driver wondered.

The large black man coldly stared at the smaller driver.

"You know better than to discuss such things in the open," the black man admonished. "True, I'm originally from a warmer climate. But no matter how times I visit, I simply cannot get used to the cold…"

"Seldom will you hear a Russian complain…" the driver said and stopped speaking when he noticed movement across the street. "You play chess?"

"I was chess champion of England… for a while," Reg confessed.

"Oh! Then you have made your gambit here. No?" the man squeaked with delight. "I know a man who was cousin to Flatenov…"

"The Russian tournament player?" Reg inquired.

"The same… he knows all the man's moves… Uh, oh. There she is," he gestured with his head.

A woman paused outside her shop and glanced around. For some reason, the night seemed darker on the street for Elaina. She looked up. Two of the streetlights did not work, a task handled earlier by the black man. She turned the key and bolted the door to her shop. She dropped the ring of keys in her heavy coat pocket.

Her breath filled the air in front of her like heavy smoke, the outside temperature dropped quite low for this time of year. She pulled her collar up around her neck as she walked down the sidewalk to the alley where she parked her car. She quietly cursed the city for not fixing the streetlights.

"I must call in the morning," she thought. "It's so dark, I can hardly see where I parked."

She walked up the length of the old brick building and headed to the back. The alley had only one way in and out. Two tenants lived on the ground floor in the back of the building, behind her store. She noticed their lights out and thought they must be away.

As she reached for her door, a hand slipped around her face and held a cloth against it. The woman kept her wits and did not panic. First, she knew to hold her breath. She also knew some martial arts moves and stomped down on the stranger's feet while she placed a jab into his side.

However, this stranger knew a few moves, too. A professional assassin, he performed this maneuver many times. His feet deftly moved aside. He easily deflected her elbow while his hand pressed hard against her face. Struggling to break free and forced to breathe, she gasped for air, the last thing she did before the fast-acting drug filled her lungs. Soon, she fell limp in the large black man's arms.

He picked her up like a limp doll and thrust her inside her own vehicle. He found the key ring inside her pocket. He started the car and headed off across town to her private residence. At the base of the stairs that led up to the second floor landing, the large black man paused. Alone, without the driver nearby, he did something he knew no one else could do – he reached out with his mind to sense his surroundings.

"The target is watching television," he thought, "and distracted."

Carefully, with very deliberate steps, he silently crept to the door, gently inserted the woman's apartment key, and quietly pushed open the door. Inside, he saw a man leaning back, repose on a sofa, watching television, the woman's husband. The black man produced a gun from his right coat pocket. He reached up, took the woman's hand that hung down from his shoulder, and placed it around the gun. With a few pulls of the trigger, the silenced pistol shot its bullets into the man's head and chest.

Like throwing a weighted sack, the man tossed the woman off his left shoulder down on the sofa next to the dead husband. He removed the silencer and placed the gun in her hand. He left the note that would explain how the woman killed the man. Despondent, she took her life with a vial of poison he placed in her hand. He let it drop to the floor and roll away as it normally would.

Searching, the assassin found the electronic key card in the man's belongings. He placed this into his coat pocket and quietly slipped back out of the apartment before he returned to his partner who waited below.

"Let's go," the big black man said to the driver. "This address," he told the man and shoved a piece of paper into his hand.

"This is way out in the country…" he started to speak, when the large black man placed his big hand over the man's mouth. When the driver glanced over at him, the big man put a finger to his lips and shook his head. The driver caught on.

He put the car in gear and drove across town and out to the country to an obscure unmarked road with a fading sign that stated, "Authorized personnel only." The driver turned up the road, shut off the car's lights and stopped when the black man signaled him to stop. The big man stepped out. He crept through the woods, parallel to the road. The black man flanked a booth that held a guard on duty. A compact car cautiously approached a guard post. As the vehicle pulled before the lowered gate, the driver saw the assassin quickly enter the booth and remove the guard as a threat. The gate went up and the black man returned to the car.

An evening's snow began to fall. Beautiful light flakes drifted down from the thick gray gathering clouds with hardly a breeze to scatter them. The driver continued up the road, which wound further into a dense forest as snowfall began to pile up and cover the ground. They drove the remaining distance and eventually entered a large compound surrounded by tall fence. What had once been a teaming hub, filled with research scientists, was quiet now, with a minimum number of security guards around the long-abandon secret cold war facility. This location was one of the last laboratories on the "set for destruction" list. Stripped of most personnel many years earlier, it sat alone with few people employed here any longer. The only one scheduled to be on duty this evening was the custodian whose ID badge rested inside the black man's coat pocket.

The agent instructed the driver to pull into one of the parking spaces outside the large building. He killed another security officer on duty and one other custodian on duty after he slipped inside and disabled the security recording system. Using the special key he took off the man in the town of Novgorod, Reginald Atwater entered the inside of the laboratory. He went to one of the cold storages, removed the cover and pulled out a container that rested inside the boiling "liquid air." He opened the container and removed several coded vials before he placed the container back inside the extremely cold liquid. He reached into his inside jacket pocket and produced a carrier made to transport the vials. He placed all of them in the carrier except one.

He took a single vial and placed it on a lab warmer. He watched as the tiny vial changed color from blue to clear. He held the small amount of clear liquid up to the light.

"Factory made instant death," he said and laid it down.

He walked over to a nearby cabinet and removed a small mechanical device. Rolling up his sleeve, he took another vial from this cabinet marked "Forbidden" in Russian. He used the device to inject his arm with a single dose from the cabinet's vial. He took all the remaining vials in the cabinet except one and smashed them on the floor.

"Oops," he muttered, "no more antidote."

He waited as the warmth in his arm spread throughout his body. Once a few minutes passed, he took the thawed vial from the counter. He walked over the storage container and reached down to the base. Rather than disconnect the power, which would trigger an alert in Moscow, he placed a small device with a transmitter. He pressed the side and it began to count down from 9999…

"I am ready," he thought.

Before he returned to the car, he slipped two white filter plugs into his nose. He opened the car door and slid into his cramped seat while at the same time he reached into his right pocket and fingered the thawed vial.

"Did you find them?" the man asked.

"Oh, yes," Reggie replied. He carefully pulled the vial from his pocket and popped off the top without the man next to him seeing what he was doing. "Drive over there for a second," he said as he pointed to a corner of the small parking lot adjacent to the building.

"What for?" the driver asked as he put the car in gear.

"Just do it," Reg gestured.

Not wishing to pick a fight with an expert hired killer, the Russian man pulled the car over to the far corner of the lot. He turned to question his accomplice, when he clutched his throat and made a gurgling sound. Reggie leaned back and watched as the man's eyes widened with the realization the other agent infected him.

"I…I… thought you were my friend...d…d," the driver struggled to speak as blood surged into his throat and turn his speech into a death gasp.

Coolly, Reggie reached across the man, opened the driver's door and pushed his convulsing body out onto the fresh white blanket of snow.

"I had to make certain it worked," he said.

Reggie stepped out and walked around the car. He stood over the man and dispassionately watched the driver's body writhe in the snow. Bright red blood spurted from his choking mouth and nose. It leaked around his eyes and dripped from his ears, then every orifice gushed blood. Reggie took the open vial and dropped it next to the corpse.

"They'll believe you broke into the lab and tried to steal the item," he thought. "I believe that is checkmate. Goodbye, Dmitri," he said.

He sprayed a special mist from the lab on his clothes and carefully walked away in reverse on his toes, not pressing his feet all the way down. Once he made his way back to the building, he walked out the way they drove in. As he walked out, he placed a finger along his nose and forcefully ejected the plugs from each nostril with his own lung pressure. He squirted a special gel onto his hands and rubbed them together before he rubbed his nostrils. He did not wish to carry contaminates on any part of him. He passed the guardhouse and the entrance. Not far up the road, he came to another side road off into the woods, where he parked a car the day before.

He returned to his apartment on the edge of town, where he carefully went over the place to make certain he left no trace behind. He half smiled when he heard the sirens go off and the fire brigade head out of town. He knew the device he left in the lab did its part by igniting the gas line inside the lab. Investigators would say the line ruptured and caught fire.

He drove north to the little town of Lipovo on the Koporskaya Guba (Baltic Sea). Reggie took out a small self-inflatable raft with an electric motor before he pushed the car off the end of a private dock into the sea. For two hours, he slowly made his way out to sea before he activated a small device in his pocket.

An hour later, a small six-man submarine surfaced. Reggie scuttled the raft. The sub brought the agent safely across the Baltic to the neutral sovereignty of Finland, about 130 kilometers on the other side of the sea. No one aboard the sub questioned Reginald Atwater or discussed his mission. Reggie blankly stared off into space as Finland grew near. He knew the next part of his mission would be the most difficult. Inside his coat, he held one of the most closely guarded secrets in the world and one of its most terrible creations.

Chapter Ten

Three New Voices

When Salla woke the morning after Camille's farewell party, he heard a sound so abrupt, so close, and so intimate that its immediacy startled him.

"Good morning," a female voice said.

With his eyes closed, his hand thrust out into the space next to him for fear he slept with Filla last night. Nothing. He suddenly sat up and looked around his bedroom. He saw no one. Yet, he distinctly heard the female's voice in such close approximation that it felt as if she spoke directly into his ear from close range. He looked under his bed and did not see anyone. Was she in his closet he wondered?

"How are you, dear? Sleep well? I made you some coffee," the female voice continued.

Salla flipped the covers back as he thought the woman might be hiding there.

"Don't bother to get up. I've got the paper for you," she said.

"What is this?" he shouted. "Where are you?"

No reply. He went mad with fear and kept shifting in his bed, his eyes darting around the room, although he did not see anyone. Salla rose and slowly moved toward his bedroom window, where he could see across the breezeway into his neighbor's bedroom. With their curtains open, Salla noticed the wife stood next to the bed and spoke to her husband. She had a cup of coffee in one hand and the newspaper in the other.

"Here," she said as she tossed him the paper and set his coffee down. "You handsome hunk of man," she thought.

Her thoughts rushed to his brain.

"What the hell?" he thought with disbelief. He backed up so abruptly that he plopped down on the side of his bed. "How is this possible?"

As he stared out the window and tried to deny the proof of his eyes that he could read her thoughts, they continued to flow unabated into his mind until they gradually began to fade away. He laughed at his own reaction and calmed down.

"Easy Salla," he said for self-reassurance. "That was scary. For a moment, I thought I could hear her thoughts!"

He lay down on his bed and started to close his eyes when he heard a voice laugh in his head.

"Now what?" he declared as he sat back up and carefully peered out the window.

"This isn't your next door neighbor," a different female voice spoke.

This was not the neighbor. This was a new voice; a voice that sounded familiar to Salla. The voice giggled.

"Hey!" he spoke up. "If I didn't know better, I would say… say… say!" he thought as he recalled his dream from last night. "Maybe that wasn't a dream! Perhaps I *was* with Camille and that Chinese man… and… and…" He heard the giggle once more. "Filla?" he thought hesitantly.

"Good morning, Salla," she replied.

"Good Morning you two!" a voice far stronger than Filla's intruded.

Camille Ossures spoke to them in their native Bambara.

"Did you sleep as strangely as I did last night?" she asked them. "Or was I the only one who imagined that we traveled to a distant world and spoke with some overgrown sponges living in big liquid tanks?"

Filla laughed, "I would hardly call the voices of Galactic Central sponges."

"True, but that's what those things resemble, do they not?" Camille shot back.

"I believe they have a brain similar to ours in construction but much larger and far more complex," Salla pointed out, as bits and pieces of his 'dream' last night began to surface.

"You would know about anatomy, my learned friend," Camille added. "Actually, I wondered if you two could join me on my terrace for breakfast. I have a feeling that there is much for us to discuss, such as how someone connected our minds and why this should happen at this time in our lives."

"I wondered the same thing," Filla put in.

"I'll get dressed and be right over," Salla added.

"Me, too," Filla spoke up.

The pretty, young African jumped into some casual clothes and threw her hair back. As she exited her building, she started to call for a cab on her cell phone. Surprisingly, a taxi waited for her outside her building.

"Did I call you?" Filla asked when she opened the door.

"Yes, ma'am," the driver answered in French.

When she arrived at Camille's, she started to pay when she paused to regard his meter. The driver never turned on the meter. It read all zeros.

"I don't owe you anything, do I?" she suggested.

"No, ma'am," the driver said. He pulled away without question after she stepped out.

The front door to Camille's townhouse stood open, the butler already held it open for her. Filla practically flew up the four flights to the roof, surprised to find Salla and Camille already engaged in thought as they sat around a table. Filla plopped down into one of the chairs.

"You'll never guess what just happened?" she linked to them.

"You didn't pay for the cab," Salla linked to her mind, "because you suggested the idea to him."

"How did you know?" Filla questioned.

"I did the same thing. We have the ability to influence the behavior of others, as if they thought of it instead of us," he answered and cast Camille a side-glance. "We have other abilities, too."

"That will save us some money on cab fare," Filla thought.

"It seems we have much to discuss," Camille offered.

The glamorous Parisian wore a pair of dark sunglasses and a lovely checkered sundress. She also wore a wide brimmed hat to shade her eyes. She picked up and rang a crystal bell next to her. For being September, a lovely warm sunny day with hardly a cloud in the sky greeted the three as they gathered that morning on the terrace. Camille sipped her coffee while she gazed out on the city skyline. Confidence filled her mind. She felt all of Paris at her feet as new power pulsed inside her mind like a great throbbing generator, waiting for some purpose.

Her butler came out on the terrace and took breakfast orders from Salla and Filla while the three quickly got down to business.

"This is amazing," Camille linked as she sat in an unladylike fashion with one foot propped up on an adjacent chair. She looked from Salla to Filla like an excited schoolchild. "Have you tried to do anything else? I've read the minds of my servants," she linked to them.

"Well, I accidentally read the mind of my neighbor this morning," Salla said. "The experience embarrassed me. I didn't realize what was going on. I thought I'd slept with the woman!"

Camille laughed and almost choked on her coffee. Filla giggled.

"I must apologize," Filla linked to him. "I listened in without intending to, Salla. It just happened that our minds were linked together when I woke," she said rather shyly. "What brought all this on?" she wondered turning to Camille.

"I don't know about the two of you, but I've felt all my life as if I had something that made me special," Camille confessed. "Now I realize what I had wasn't just a feeling. This ability, once lying dormant in my mind, is very real and tangible. We are psychic beings, very different from the rest of humanity, and we are not alone."

The other two nodded back to Camille, which confirmed they knew.

"You mean the oriental man?" Salla questioned.

"He spoke to me in Chinese?" Filla asked. "I understood him."

"You heard correctly," Camille linked. "Moments after our... conversion... we heard from the leader of a group on the other side of the world," she informed them. "They've just begun to set up a new community of similarly gifted individuals in America."

As Camille said this, she shared the experience of her interaction with Master Li, linking last night's events to Salla and Filla. They had also felt the strength of his contact.

"The man's name is Li Po Chin, once a college professor in Harbin, China," she began. "He now lives in America with this new group. He contacted me this morning before you awoke. We've exchanged a great deal of information. The fact that many psychics are emerging at this time may not be a coincidence. He has some very interesting theories. I'll fill you in later," she told them. "I found Li... very enlightening," Camille privately confessed to the other two as the maid and butler brought in breakfast. "Did you ever hear voices in your youth?" she put to the other two.

"Yes," Salla said and glanced over at Filla. She also nodded.

"When I was a young woman," Camille linked to them, "I shared the news of this new voice with my mother. My parents argued over how to treat this 'sickness' as my father called it. My parents left me in Switzerland, where psychiatrists performed experiments on me. It was a horrible experience, one I will never forget."

Filla and Salla exchanged knowing glances as they had similar traumatic circumstances that surrounded their youthful experience with hearing voices.

"When you first arrived in Paris," Camille linked to them, "that same troublesome voice returned and scared me out of my wits. I was afraid I would go insane. I carefully watched your progress and did not realize that fate intertwined our lives for a reason. After last night, I knew it was destiny that brought us together."

"You heard your voice recently?" Filla asked.

"Why didn't you mention it?" Salla wondered.

"I couldn't begin to guess its bearing on our relationship," Camille said as she sipped on some coffee. "Li told me he accidentally triggered a psychic event at the party last night because the three of us were so close. Now we have to figure out where we go from here," she thought to them.

The other two began to ponder that problem.

"Do you mean how this new ability will affect us?" Filla asked.

"Of course, everything is changed!" Cecilia declared. "I run a large multinational company. I've already been on the phone with a client this morning and discovered the man lied to me about several important details. Do I call him out on it, or do I pretend that I am unaware of his thoughts, his true feelings? Frankly, I'm at a loss. From this moment on, I will know if a person is sincere or deceptive. Worse, I'll know that person's darkest fears and most perverse fantasies if I choose to probe their mind. I'm stuck with an ethical dilemma. Should I fire my maid if she lies and tells me she is sick while rushing out to meet a lover? How will I react when it happens, as surly it will? Everything about my life is going to be completely different from this moment on."

Camille sighed and stared into her coffee cup.

"Yes, I see," Salla said slowly. "My place within the institute will change," he said regretfully. "It's not a question of money or even friends, but what I'm going to do with this new power." He pushed his breakfast plate away, stood up and began to pace. "I want to do some good," he linked to them. "I want to go back to Mali and help my country. Mali is one of the poorest nations on Earth. They could use a little advantage."

Filla gazed at Salla with a profound respect as he spoke. It had been her lifelong dream to return to Mali and start a hospital.

"How would you like to be my Chief of Staff and start a hospital with me?" she asked reaching out to him.

"You'd want me?" Salla gazed longingly into her eyes.

Her love blazed into his mind. The feeling washed over him like a big wave. Salla opened up his mind. Filla felt the energy flow between them. She realized Salla was no longer a stranger to her mind or her heart. He was the man she loved now and would always love. Yet, Salla realized he could not abandon Camille. In the midst of this mutual admiration, he knew he could not simply back out of commitments he made.

"I can't drop everything and go to Mali," he said as he glanced over at Camille. "I'd have to finish my research first."

"I could stay until next June, finish my apprenticeship with the hospital administration," Filla offered.

Camille only smiled, nodded, and sipped her coffee. She did not link her intentions. The other two, content she approved of their suggestions, turned their attention to the fresh breakfast. However, neither Salla nor Filla could keep their thoughts apart for long. Camille could hear them… it was if they played a subtle mind game of foreplay. She turned inward.

"I believe that 2016 will be a great vintage year," Camille privately observed.

She nibbled on her croissant and tactfully gazed away at the city while she closed her mind to the other two. She sent out a call, millions of light years away.

"Tell me more about this technique that Li called blocking," she requested of her voice.

CHAPTER ELEVEN

HE'S A NATURAL

AS THE TWENTIETH CENTURY ENDED, years before Michael Tyler experienced his conversion or Master Li turned on his bright psychic mind, other psychic men and women with darker purposes walked the planet. They did not recognize the weird metallic voice in their head, although they possessed the necessary conduit to do so. They held their own agenda in the presence of such newly awakened power. These "rogues" ignored any off world intrusion with its moral codes. Instead, they set about using their power for personal gain and self-gratification, either to obtain wealth and possessions, or to seek out the perverse.

Li's maniacal cousin in China had been one case. His psychic girlfriends, whom he managed to manipulate, sought out pleasure over reason. They lived in a constant world of mental fantasy in pursuit of physical satisfaction. Had they been free to roam China, no telling how they would have influenced the formation of the Chinese state government? Only captivity held them in check.

Najib sought his own materialistic path in Oman. As a prince of the realm, he sought power over others. He frequently bent his mind to torture as a release for his abilities, and took great pleasure inflicting pain.

Cyrus, the rogue in Australia, began his onslaught two years before the WPO formed. His twisted world consisted of money, sex, and power. He sought to eventually rule over all humankind with a planned disaster that very nearly took place.

When Michael first went in search of Li, Villi's presence and discovery made Galactic Central realize that humans had the capacity to block their probes. No other psychic species before the humans of Earth could do such a thing. Villi surprised Michael's voice. He was one of those rare individuals who did not hear a metallic voice in his youth. After they converted Li, they advised the sage to "probe your planet and find these silent psychics." When the Rollo group completed the Australian mission, Master Li thought he rid the world of its last rogue psychic. He was wrong, completely and utterly wrong.

Reginald Atwater's family migrated from Nigeria to England years before the state of Connecticut released Michael Tyler from his asylum. Starting in his childhood, this young black boy quickly demonstrated strange abilities. Yet, unlike Li's Chinese cousin, this rogue psychic had no emotional attachment to the world around him. He had a cold and cruel side to his nature, which his psychic ability only reinforced. He first became aware of his power at the age of ten, when he could make birds fly into buildings or dogs attack one another.

At the ripe age of twelve, he made certain the family car crossed the train tracks at precisely the right time to eliminate their interference in his life. He managed to step out of the car and coldly watched as his parents perished when the train struck their vehicle. Now orphaned, English Child Services placed Reggie into the protective custody of a ward home. He attended a public school created to serve as a helping ground for parentless children. As a ward of the state, he scholastically surpassed every student in the special school. When he beat every child and adult supervisor in a local chess tournament, it brought him to the eye of a counselor who brought in a sociologist friend of his to evaluate Reg. Impressed with his incredible intellect and rapid advancement; the state sociologist enrolled Reggie in the English public school system.

However, Reginald Atwater came to the attention of British government officials and the intelligence community when the 12-year-old took the chess world by storm and handily won the English tournament in a matter of minutes. Chess officials looked on stunned and repeatedly watched the video replay to understand how and why the two players moved so fast.

"Either the other chessmaster acted stupidly, or the boy is extremely talented," one official put it.

Despite the award recognition, Reg did not receive the monetary part, which instead went into a trust to pay for his education. In public school, Reg excelled even faster since he had access to more information that included computers. When tested by the school officials, his psychological profiles went off the charts. Rumors began to spread among the students that Reginald could easily intimidate his opponents by making them feel afraid. Even staff members were afraid of Reg. He had no friends. No ordinary psychologist or psychiatrist could handle the aggressive lad.

One of the school administrators called an official he knew in the

British military. Once the man appraised Reggie, he knew what to do. The following day, a government official quietly showed up with two men. They were behavioral scientists assigned to his case. After extensively testing him, they concluded that "Reggie" displayed genuine psychic ability, the first fully documented case on record. In test after test, he made extremely accurate statements that convinced the government scientists he needed special attention.

They pulled him from public school and raised the boy in an isolated building where they could carry out further psychological testing. His file, code-named "PSTILL" (psychic stasis within temporal illogical lobe locations) grew so large that they had to alter a storage room on the site to hold the volumes of observation and test files. He physically and mentally progressed at a faster pace than other boys his age did. By age sixteen, he resembled a fully-grown man in his mid-twenties. He had a huge frame, stood over 215 cm in height (approx. 82 inches or 6 ft 8 in) and weighed 110 kilograms (approx. 240 lbs). Far from flabby, the teen was all muscle and keenly aware of his prowess. The project scientists decided to enroll the big teenager at Cambridge, where he surpassed everyone's expectations by acing all of his courses. Within two years, he mastered fluency in over twenty common languages, including French, Chinese, Japanese, Sanskrit, Greek, Latin, Russian, Arabic, and Hebrew.

Unfortunately, he also expressed sociopathic attitudes in his relationships with others. The emotionally charged teen picked up a female during one of his evening jogs around the campus. He brought her back to his private rooms, where he brutally and sexually assaulted her. Afterward, he walked her back to where he found her. Somehow, she could not recall the rough experience, only that she could not explain the discomfort she felt. Nor did she ever seek medical help. She had no idea that a man had raped every one of her orifices.

No one would have known about the incident, if the scientists in charge of his case had not placed a video recording system in his apartment and discovered the act after the fact. They watched and witnessed his brutal rape of the woman over the period of two hours. Curious as to why she did not report him, they interviewed the woman on another pretext and discovered she had no memory of the event.

The two scientists in charge of Reggie's case intended to "sweep the matter under the rug." However, the military division in charge of Atwater's care discovered the video and ordered the scientists, who were supposed to keep track of the teenager, to find out how Reggie managed to sneek a woman into his quarters without their knowledge.

"I understand Reginald Atwater violated some girl on campus and you were sent to investigate. What did you find out?" a military major in charge of the secret operation asked the scientists.

"He's quite clever," one the scientists said.

"I've never seen a man with such prowess," the other scientist seemed to brag.

"Enough of that talk!" the major snapped. "What about the woman?"

"Oh, she'll say nothing about Reggie…" the other scientist spoke up. "We found her… in her dorm room on campus… asked if she knew Reggie… showed her a photograph… she has no recollection…"

"None?"

"None!"

"Hmmm…" the major contemplated.

The government considered Reggie too valuable to discipline him or charge him with a crime. They had other purposes in mind for his peculiar talent. They intended to groom him for work in the spy agencies as a specialist.

"What else can you tell me about the development of Reginald Atwater?" the major requested. "We can cover up the molestation of the student. Easy enough…"

"You mean since he did most of the work for us," the first scientist commented.

"…when he somehow erased her memory," the second scientist chimed in.

"Will he be a problem to handle in the future?" the manager asked.

"I don't think so," the second scientists replied. "I suppose that his attack was to be expected… eventually… considering he is a teenager and he had never been with another woman sexually. It was bound to happen sooner or later."

"I don't believe this young man has any emotion in regards to his consequences," his colleague responded. "He's never expressed regret for his actions. As an assassin, I believe he would kill without hesitation. What a cold hearted bugger."

"I believe our modification work is done," the second scientist stated. "Perhaps it's time to contact MI-6 and put him in the field," he suggested.

"He's only 18! Do you think he's ready?" the manager wondered.

"Yes!" the two scientists replied.

They were eager to be rid of Reggie. Like others who had interacted with Reg before them, they were suspicious that Reg had manipulated their minds, too. They transferred the big psychic at the age of 18 to MI-6, where he spent the next two years training to be a spy. He injured one instructor after another until the entire squad refused to train with him. Once more, those in charge asked the question of Reggie that all of his superiors needed to answer…

"Do you believe he's ready?" the division chief asked his commander.

"I pity the target," the commander in charge of training told him. "I've never seen such an intelligent yet cold blooded killer in my life."

"Then by all means... let's send him on a mission!" the chief ordered.

After two years of training, MI-6 gave Reg a single assignment along with a license to kill. Out in the field on his own, he demonstrated tendencies that even division chiefs at MI-6 found repugnant, such as his bloodlust for killing without remorse of any kind. He carried out his first assassination so well and with such stealth, no one suspected anything except that natural causes took the person's life. He seemed perfectly suited for spy work – secretive and psychologically paranoid, Reginald Atwater turned out to be the best assassin the secret government department ever deployed.

All of this took place before Master Li, before the WPO, and before Galactic Central decided to make a pact with a homeless man about to commit suicide outside Hattiesburg, Mississippi. Once they converted Michael Tyler, Galactic Central cut off any communication with these rogue psychics. The potential of Earth's psychics frightened them, but especially the psychic Reginald Atwater. They felt that if they tried to open contact with him, he would quickly infiltrate their ranks. Their hope for Earth lay with psychics whose profile lent itself to self-sacrifice and high moral standards. Reginald Atwater seemed to be the epitome of its antithesis.

Prior to Captain Brighton's transfer to NATO, he worked briefly with the British military arm of the secret service. When General Andrews asked Captain Brighton, which agent he had in mind to start the investigation of the new project, Brighton only considered one agent for the special highly secretive mission. He drew up his plans for the operation and returned to the general for approval.

In the early spring of 2019, Captain Brighton stood inside General Andrew's office, and explained his idea of how to tackle this special problem – the location of the speedy "ghost ship."

"Sir," Brighton saluted.

"Go ahead," the general mumbled, "although I consider this entire episode a waste of time. It was probably a glitch in the system... that's all."

"This is such an unusual case with so many unanswered questions. I believe it calls for an unusual agent, someone with the ability to go beyond the ordinary abilities of most men. I'd like Reginald Atwater for the job," the captain requested.

He had never seen the general with this expression of both fear and concern on his face. Few people ever mentioned Reggie's name aloud, as MI-6 considered the demented psychic the most classified secret in their arsenal. They called him by his code name, if they mentioned a name at all.

"How do you know of this… agent?" the general retorted, unwilling to repeat the name for fear a listening device might pick it up.

"Did I say something wrong?" the captain wondered.

"This agent you mentioned," the general continued, "is only known by a few people. I repeat, how did you come to have knowledge about this agent?"

"I have contacts… back in England," the captain said. "The people I knew did not mention his name. I discovered the unspecified file on Atwater when I worked at the NATO branch which set up this organization of yours, general," he went on. "I had and still have a level five access, sir. I'm supposed to be a strategy specialist. I believe that is why they placed me here, isn't it?"

The general stared at Brighton for a moment and realized he had underestimated the man's cleverness. He took in a deep breath and decided to reveal what he knew.

"We never mention this agent by name, Brighton," the general said and made a note. "His file is considered one of the most secret of secrets. Besides, this isn't exactly his line of work. We've no need for an assassin of his caliber. But, you never know… I'll see what I can do to obtain his services… temporarily, of course. Meanwhile, you are not to discuss this with anyone, especially Cpl. Peterson."

"Yes, sir," Brighton replied. "I understand he can perceive things other men cannot," the captain expressed. "Perhaps we should bring him into our organization," he suggested. "He may help us with future projects."

"You have a point," the general considered. "I'll place a call this morning. I suppose I could use this agent for some of our planned missions. I'll need the appropriation first. This may take a while. Let me get back to you."

"Yes, sir," Brighton said, saluted and exited.

"Atwater," the general thought. "I never thought about him… the freaky psycho which the spy agency had trouble directing in the field. He disappeared on them twice and then showed up as if nothing happened. If we do go in for surgical strikes, I could use his talent for more than one mission. I wonder if MI-6 will give him up."

At the captain's request, General Andrews sent a meeting request directly to Britain's MI-6 and received an immediate reply.

"PSTILL at your disposal," the message came through to the general and then vanished from his inbox.

Despite Reggie's top clearance, he was not aware of this new NATO organization. A secret organization with even more anonymity than MI-6 immediately perked Reggie's interest. With the agency's permission, they arranged a meeting with General Andrews, Captain Brighton, and Reggie. The three met in secret at a pre-arranged rendezvous in Iceland. During this meeting, the two men promised Reg more money than he earned at MI-6, including fringe benefits, such as permanent luxury apartments in London, Hong Kong, and Rio. From those locations, they could send him directly to the required assignment. They promised him great latitude in carrying out his missions. The general needed someone very good at assassination, which he hoped to develop as one of his organization's secret primary objectives. MI-6 seemed all too eager to dump Atwater off on someone else. In the last two years, he not only made seventeen kills in the field, he also caused 54 collateral deaths not included in his contracts. Despite these "murders," the government considered Atwater too valuable for discipline.

At the March 2019 meeting, Atwater agreed to all the general's terms. He officially transferred his service from MI-6 to NATO's nameless secret service. MI-6 expressed no regret to his leaving.

"What's my first assignment?" Reg asked them.

"I'll let Captain Brighton explain it to you at a later date," the general stated during the secret meeting.

"Whatever you wish," Atwater told them.

Reginald came and went from the Labrador facility with relative anonymity. He had a private jet aircraft at his disposal and clearance for practically any airspace he desired. He never presented an ID and the security officers never asked him for one, as General Andrews instructed them not to bother the agent. Finally, after a few weeks while Reggie set up his new living arrangements, Brighton called Reggie in for another private conference with General Andrews.

At this meeting, Brighton pulled out a flat hand-held display. He played the image that started this process two months earlier. The two officers watched Reggie's reaction as he took the display from Brighton and went over the video several times.

"This is very interesting," Reggie told them.

"You are one of four witnesses," the general informed him. "This is highly classified."

"I'd like to begin my investigation in Kansas," Reg told them.

"Take your jet," the captain broke in. "You have clearance. I'll have a team on the ground to meet you."

"You were confident I would accept the assignment," Reggie stated.

"No," the captain replied, "I was prepared in case you did. I am a strategist, not a mind reader or a psychologist, Mr. Atwater. These are your general orders," he said as he handed the agent a seal envelope. "Discuss your mission with only the general or me and no one else. As of today, this is mission is like its manager, the most secret of all secrets held in the world. Understood?"

"Understood," the big man replied. He rose and left for the airstrip.

As the captain and the general watched Reggie retreat from their room, the general wondered aloud, "Can we trust him?"

"I believe no one else is more suited for this job," the captain stated.

"That is exactly how I wish you to think," Reggie thought as he boarded the jet.

Hours later, the jet landed at a private airstrip outside Dodge City. A man with a State Police car and an officer's uniform waited for Reg. The man handed them over without speaking and left. It was Brighton's idea to have Reg pose as a Kansas State Trooper and drive around. Atwater drove southwest to the area in question. At first, he drove past Rollo. When he checked his location on a GPS receiver, he saw nothing of interest from the road. According to the location on the satellite photographs, he should have spotted something that held a large aircraft. Yet, he saw only an outcropping of rock surrounded by grassy fields.

He turned around about five kilometers past the so-called landing spot and started to head back to Dodge City. As he slowly tooled up the highway, he sensed a strong psychic presence along the right side of the road. He slowed down and stopped on the berm. He turned on his radar equipment and pretended to watch the road for speeders. Movement caught his attention in the field off to his right. He tried not to be obvious, but he definitely saw something move.

As he sat and focused his senses, he began to see the faint presence of other psychics and the details of buildings, very large buildings. He could only make out the presence of those individuals who used psychic energy. However as he began to concentrate, he did not simply see a ghostly image of this village, gradually he saw through the holographic ruse and observed the complete village that finally came into view. When a Native American man walked up the highway and crossed over into the field, the same pedestrian disappeared inside the projection. The power behind the illusion alarmed Reggie.

"What the hell is going on over there?" he thought for a moment, before he proceeded any further with his line of thought, his natural sense of paranoia kicked in. He stopped his current thought process and emptied his mind. "If I can see them, they can probably see me," he thought. "That means they can hear my thoughts, too." He changed his tact. "Well, I believe I've sat here long enough… this is not much of a speed trap…" the state trooper thought. After a few minutes, he gave up on the location and drove on.

Once back in Dodge City, he boarded the private jet and flew directly to the secret organization's headquarters in Labrador. He requested an immediate private meeting with Captain Brighton upon arrival. When he walked in, he noticed General Andrews also seated in the room, eager for Reggie's report.

"Tell me what you found," the general requested.

"You were right to send me, sir," the tall black man answered with a swagger.

He reached over and took one of the general's cigars off his desk. He struck a match and began to puff on a cigar. While that irritated the captain, the general secretly admired Reggie's guts.

"What's going on down there?" the general demanded. He did not have time to play games. "Just what was that flying sphere?"

"First off, what you refer to as the sphere is only an energy shield used to hide a new type of flying aircraft designed for fast travel. They also use a similar energy device to hide their village from our radar and most satellites. How they create this dynamic field is unknown to me. I could not linger or properly scan their village. I did not want to alert them to my presence."

"Them?" the captain said. "Who are they?"

"Village?" the general interrupted. "What village? I thought it was a grassy plain with a strange rock formation?"

Reggie looked from one to the other and half smiled before he answered. He had all the cards and could reveal his hand how he chose.

"Yes, gentlemen, they have a very quaint village… made up of Victorian mansions, tree-lined streets, along with a unique and quite extraordinary group of individuals, gifted with abilities that surpass mine," Reggie told them. "I'm not certain how many live there."

"Aliens?" the general asked. Reg noted his level of anxiety rising.

"Quite human, general," Reggie answered. "However, they possess advance levels of technology scattered everywhere about the village. The place is cloaked behind some kind of holographic generator…"

The general started to laugh when Reggie cut him off.

"I never joke about such things," he said with such seriousness that it wiped the smile off the general's face. "You brought me here for a reason. I know what I saw… and you should listen very carefully if you value your lives. They have advanced technology, decades, perhaps centuries ahead of us."

"That's impossible!" Brighton declared.

"Would you like me to personally demonstrate what I can do to a man?" he put to the captain.

A bead of sweat broke out on the man's forehead as he backed down from Atwater's forceful nature. Even the general squirmed slightly before he thought of what Reggie said grasped its significance.

"Do you know what this could mean…" the general began as he gazed off into space while his imagination ran wild. "Why, if we had access to that technology…"

Reggie cleared his throat and hoped to bring the general back to earth.

"Wait, general," Reggie said as he tried to pop the general's bubble, "I'm just getting started. I want you to hear everything that I discovered about this village before you go off on a safari for stalking new technology," Reggie explained. "You need to understand a few things about this group."

"What's wrong with them?" the general asked, confused.

"You may not believe this, but in addition to the very quaint little picturesque village, complete with brick-lined streets and Victorian mansions they've created," Reggie explained, "they also have an unlimited supply of power, water, and food… whose sources are also unknown to me."

"You're kidding," the captain spoke up.

"If you could see their world, you'd find it's actually quite beautiful. From the road or from above, no one can see the place. I located their projectors," he said as he pulled out one of the satellite photographs from the file on Brighton's desk. Reg took a colored marker and began to draw on the photograph.

"This is how the town is laid out… streets, houses, one really big building at this end, and these power sources. The projectors are here, here, here, and here." Reg drew in small boxes on the photograph. "Those are the only ones I saw. The power sources themselves are unprotected. If the right shell exploded next to one, the projection that surrounds the village might collapse."

"Are you serious?" the general demanded. "How do you see these things and our most advanced satellite surveillance system can't?"

"Isn't that why you hired me, general? I can see and hear things that no ordinary person can. I believe I've proved that to the government many times," he leaned back in his chair, blew out smoke, and glanced from captain to general. "Would you like to me to prove that here… right now?"

Neither man disputed Reggie's claim of seeing a village or anything he boasted, so they allowed him to continue.

"Go on, Reg, no one here wishes to question your peculiar talents," Brighton said as he glanced sideways at the general.

"The reason your satellites can no longer see the town is due to these projectors," Reg told them. "They shoot out a field that forms a barrier around the village. It could repel a bullet, but I don't believe it can repel a powerful shell fired at it. However, I didn't test it. Most of the projectors are directed outward, but some of these point up," he said as he indicated two additional locations. "I believe they create the overhead image specifically aimed at fooling satellites."

The captain leaned forward.

"Are you certain they were unaware of your presence, Reg?" the captain begged. "What I mean is, were you able to observe and get out without them knowing who you really are?"

"I believe I did," Reggie told them, confident. "I felt a probe or two, but

I managed to keep my thoughts focused on being a state trooper. Besides, I don't believe they personally probed me. I think I activated their security system. I felt nothing personal in the contact... it's difficult to explain to a normal person."

The general and captain again exchanged brief looks.

"From what I could discover, their technology is highly advanced, general," Reg said. "As far as I'm concerned, I believe they pose a threat to our national security."

"They're really not aliens?" the captain asked.

"No, Captain Brighton," Reggie replied. "I used to believe I was alone in the world," he said unfocused. Then he quickly resumed his cool character. "I was wrong. The people of this village are special people like me with incredible mental ability. I would even venture to say that I believe their abilities far surpass mine."

"Do you realize what this means?" the captain began before the general waved his hands to shut him up.

The general got up and paced about the room. He picked up the photograph that Reggie drew on. A terrible feeling began to rise inside him and filled him with dread.

"Tell me more about their security," the general requested. "This shielding technology could be an incredible advantage if we could capture it," he commented.

"General, they possess abilities that go beyond shield technology," Reggie stated. "You could send the whole army against them and with just their minds, they would turn them away, or even worse, make them attack each other," Reg impressed upon him.

The general pulled a cigar from the box on the desk and chewed nervously on the end. He did not have Reggie's boldness to light up in front of his subordinates.

"This is a strategic nightmare," he mumbled. "Right in the heart of our nation... a group of individuals poised to take over, building up their forces..."

"General," the captain spoke, "they must be stopped. This could be the spearhead of some kind of alien invasion."

Atwater laughed at the two men for a moment before his expression turned to stone.

"Do I look like an alien to you?" he asked them.

The captain shook his head. Although Atwater worked for them, the captain feared the large black man and his capacity to do terrible things.

"Believe what I say, captain," Reggie said. "These people are not aliens.

They're human beings with extraordinary power… consider them a new breed. Others may exist in various stages of development. I'm not certain."

"Can we reason with them, Reg?" the General asked.

"I don't think they want anything to do with us, general. That's why they settled away from humanity. They prefer isolation," Reggie told them. "They want to be left alone."

"Do you think they are a threat?" the general asked.

"Anyone with advanced technology and unwilling to share it with a friendly country like America is a threat, general," the captain spoke up. "Who could stop them?"

"I want you to concentrate on this issue, Brighton," General Andrews declared, "while keeping it secret, of course."

"Yes, sir," Brighton replied and glanced over at Atwater.

As the meeting broke up, other important matters pulled General Andrews away, especially since his division scheduled another secret classified NAT-IX satellite launch next week. In a world full of governments that constantly and secretly tried to undermine each other, Andrews had plenty of missions for which he could use Reggie, other than chase strange rumors in Kansas.

Outside the office, after the meeting, Brighton requested Reg remain at the headquarters compound for a few days.

"I'd like you to review some of our protocols, go over the rules…"

"Is this a delaying tactic?" Reggie put to him.

Brighton couldn't lie. He wasn't very good at it. So, he nodded.

"…until we can work out your new assignment, Reg," Brighton promised.

"What about Kansas?" Reggie asked him.

"Since you don't believe they are an immediate threat, you've convinced the general. He runs things," Brighton comment. "He'll let us know when he wants another recon visit."

However, Reggie could tell that Brighton was not convinced of their benign status. In his mind, he believed that these "psychics" were actually aliens who had mated with humans to produce "warped" individuals. He wondered about Reginald's origins as well. Still, he believed in the military chain of command. He decided to let the matter rest as long as the general was content to do so.

While Captain Brighton did not completely confide in Corporal Peterson, he promoted Peterson to his personal assistant and transferred the other male secretary he had in his office. He explained to his new special assistant that a secret organization existed in southwestern Kansas, one capable of threatening the nation. He swore Peterson to secrecy and gave him a Level 3 security access. After a series of meetings between Atwater, Peterson, and Brighton, the three men concluded that at some future point in time, the military must destroy the entire community. The only question that remained in their minds was how they would do it.

"Let's nuke 'em," the corporal suggested.

Atwater raised his hands and shook his head.

"Sending a nuclear weapon into the heart of America won't work," Reginald informed them, as he was familiar with those protocols. "First of all, you need the President's authority. Second, igniting a nuclear warhead on American soil is not a good thing; think of the fallout going over the rest of Kansas. It could kill millions and the political fallout alone would end our little program. Third, they might be able to turn a rocket around and send it back at us," the knowledgeable spy stated. "We have to be subtle about this," he explained. "Brute force will only explode in our faces. This may take us time to find out their weaknesses before we can devise a plan that will take them all out, if necessary."

"They could strike us at any moment," Captain Brighton fearfully insisted.

"I don't' think so captain," Reg calmly informed him. "They've built a school, a medical clinic, and beautiful houses. There's certainly nothing threatening about them. Besides, I didn't detect a single weapon or any malice of thought."

The captain shifted uneasily in his chair. These strangers made him feel uncomfortable. More than anything, he wanted his hands on their advanced technology… before they sold it to a foreign power. Reg could sense his envy that bordered on jealousy. He tried to calm Brighton.

"I agree, sooner or later we'll have to do something," Reggie commented. "But if we go charging in there without a special plan in place, we might alert them to our presence and force some kind of radical reaction," he told the two men. "Do you want to provoke a war between these people with their advanced technology and us? They may be able to take us out remotely and in a matter of minutes… the shortest war in history. Do you really want that?"

Brighton realized that Reggie thought along similar lines as he did when it came to strategy. He shook his head.

"No, you're right, Reg," he said. "How much time until you can devise a plan?" the captain asked.

"Months… perhaps two… three years," Reggie said as he looked away. "This plan must be perfect down to the last detail. It will take time and special circumstances to execute. We'll only get one shot. After that, they'll know about us knowing about them and possibly come after us if they feel threatened."

"Months…" Corporal Peterson sighed.

"Years..." Captain Brighton echoed.

"Years," Reginald affirmed. "This is a long term commitment, gentlemen. From time to time, I must go to Kansas and monitor their progress. You'll have to monitor any flights they make, too. Have NAT-IX bypass the main display and pipe that information directly to this office."

The other two nodded agreement.

"Oh, I've been informed that we have a new code name for this operation," the captain told them, "NIMBLE (Non-Invasive Mobile Bifurcating Lab Extension)."

"What is that supposed to mean?" Reggie asked.

"Who knows? I don't make this stuff up. Others perform that function. However, I want you to take over a new sub-division of my section we are creating just for you. Those were General Andrews' orders. I am going to give you a budget, too," Brighton informed Reginald. "After all... you are the only person who can see these people and know they are there... we must trust your word," Brighton said as he glanced over at Peterson.

Reggie caught the skepticism in his voice.

"What are you getting out of this?" Reggie asked him pointblank, "a promotion?"

"Possibly..." Brighton said as he tried to evade the big man's probe.

Reggie glanced over at Peterson. He had been very quiet during the meeting. The corporal heard about Reg's ability to read minds. He tried not to think of anything. Unfortunately, that was not enough to keep Reg from discoving Peterson's secret.

"So you butter your bread on both sides," he thought. "Big deal. You'd be surprised. Lots of guys think about doing it with another guy, Peterson. You're not alone."

He stood up as if to indicate he felt the meeting over. Peterson and Brighton returned to the captain's office. In addition to his quarters, they gave Reggie an office as well. He went there to consider his future with the organization.

"Plans," he thought as he closed the door and began to pace, "I need a plan... and more information... I'll have to budget trips to Kansas," he thought.

His printer began to spit out paper. He went over and looked down.

"For your eyes only," the paper stated, "New assignments for Reginald Atwater," it stated and gave a list of new meeting times with the general. At the bottom, it further stated, "Atwater to head Project NIMBLE."

"So... he doesn't trust the captain," Reggie thought. "I'll need that plan sooner than I thought."

Now with the official code name of "Nimble" in place and a budget to draw on, Reginald Atwater took over the project. He met with Corporal Peterson occasionally to give him updates. Peterson informed Reggie on any flight movement to and from the Kansas location. The corporal passed on the contents of those meetings to Captain Brighton. In turn, Brighton's role in the organization changed. Andrews assigned him to more complex and security conscious tasks. General Andrews allowed Atwater to monitor the ongoing situation in Kansas. Brighton realized that the general wanted Reggie to take over the matter. He no longer considered "Nimble" a priority project.

As Reggie predicted, weeks turned into months, months turned into years – five years to be exact. The project fell into limbo. Peterson and Brighton put in many hours on other assignments for General Andrews and had very little time for the "strange folks" in Kansas. If Reginald Atwater knew anything or made surveillance, he did not mention the fact in any of his reports.

Four people within the clandestine NATO organization remained the only people in the world aware of the strange town's existence. Reggie and the others believed the Kansas location the only one in the world. When an occasional detectable sphere came or went from Rollo, they flew to places outside the United States so quickly that their satellite surveillance could not follow them until they returned. Even NAT-IX had trouble locating the "mysterious spheres." When they did appear, the recently promoted Sgt. Peterson, who commanded the special UFO position from the captain's office, told the other men in spec obs that these were computer glitches.

"We're having trouble with the programming. We can't seem to eliminate ghost images… thanks for reporting them," he lied.

Therefore, the destinations as to where these ghost spheres went remained a mystery. However, the flights infrequently occurred during this five-year period. Ultimately, NATO added four NAT-IX satellites to cover the globe.

The village in Kansas may have died a bureaucratic death, when all at once…

The spec obs red light on Sergent Peterson's desk lit up. He flew down the hall, dismissed the man on duty and notified Colonel Brighton at once.

"Colonel, this is Sergeant Peterson. You need to come to Spec Obs at once, sir!" Peterson's voice boomed into Brighton's office. "They're flying all over the place!"

"Who is flying where?" the colonel responded, somewhat frustrated.

"Sorry, sir, but the screen is going wild with flying spheres," Peterson told him. "It's Nimble, sir."

"What?" he declared. "I'll be right there!"

General Andrews promoted Brighton to colonel about the same time he promoted Peterson to Master Sergeant. However, with Peterson now in charge of spec obs "UFO reports," neither man heard much about the "flying spheres" any longer. This news almost came as a shock to the colonel. When Colonel Brighton entered the surveillance room, he saw ghostly spheres flying in and out of southwestern Kansas almost continuously as they rapidly headed to points east and west beyond America's borders.

"Damn!" he said and stamped his foot. "I was hoping they left the planet."

"They?" Peterson questioned.

"Nevermind… just give me a copy of that video!"

Brighton brought the latest visuals to the general. He re-focused the general's attention on this invisible village as the source of the flights.

"This isn't a glitch general when we witnessed so many spheres leave and return to the same location simultaneously. They're definitely up to something. All this activity points to some kind of preparation, perhaps an invasion if you ask me," the colonel pointed out.

"Get Reginald Atwater in here!" the general requested.

"He's out on assignment," Sgt. Peterson pointed out.

"Recall him!" the general demanded. "Send the signal."

"Yes, sir," Peterson replied. He put two numbers into a hand held device. Agent Atwater responded and acknowledged his impending return.

When Reggie showed up at his office the following day, General Andrews sequestered him in his office for nearly two hours before he released him to Colonel Brighton. Reggie left the general's office shaken. Not only did the general inform him about the new UFO sightings, he had a new assignment that involved something he had never done. Things had rapidly changed in his absence. He realized he had to accelerate his plans for Kansas. He tracked down Brighton and Peterson and arranged a private meeting in the surveillance room. General Andrews ordered Sgt. Peterson to take over 24-hour duty of spec ob with the computer on night watch.

"General Andrews informed me that multiple spheres are active," Reggie commented when he entered the surveillance room. He watched as a new sphere came into view over southwest Kansas. It streaked off to the west and headed out over the Pacific Ocean. "Where is it going?" he asked.

"We don't know, sir," Sgt. Peterson informed Reggie. "We've tried to follow them, but they go so fast the NAT-IX satellites lose their ability to track them."

"I thought you said activity stopped," Reggie inquired.

"This is the first time in nearly five years spec obs reported this much activity," the colonel told him. "We thought we should bring it to your attention."

"We've noticed rare occasional flights, but never this many in such a short period," Sgt. Peterson told him.

"Where does the computer think they're headed?" Reggie wondered.

"That one headed toward China. The previous trajectory headed to Europe… the computer guessed France," the sergeant pointed out. "Notice I said guessed."

"France? Did you say France?" Reginald questioned. "During the meeting, the general didn't say the spheres were traveling to France," the agent said, almost as if he were thinking aloud.

"We aren't certain they are going to France," Brighton pointed out. "The computer only states the most likely point of touchdown."

"Why is France so important?" Sergeant Peterson wondered.

"I suppose I can tell you. I just received new orders for an assignment in Paris," Reggie told them. "General Andrews ordered me there for target observation," he explained. "Some geek scientist from Africa is receiving the Nobel prize in medicine. He's staying in Paris for a few days. They want me to observe him."

"I know I shouldn't ask…" Peterson started.

"This isn't top secret," Reggie told him, "more like babysitting. I'm to observe from a distance and not appear in any press coverage. The scientist probably received the usual death threats… just routine safety precautions," he said. "That's all."

"Do you think they're related," Colonel Brighton asked.

"No," Reggie replied and did not elaborate.

Reggie lied to his team. The general's assignment had nothing to do with death threats. Some NATO officials within their organization expressed concern about this Nobel Prize winner and his political leanings. The general's words still echoed in his mind…

"A French NATO officer, uh, how should I say this, expressed concerns about the liberal attitude of Dr. Salla Motambou," General Andrew told him. "His research into viral vaccines led Ossures pharmaceuticals to clinical trials on a serum that might mean the end to all forms of influenza and colds. Both scientific circles and the world of finance buzzed with the possibilities for the vaccine. However, in our strata, we fear the scientist could render some biological weapons useless while giving Carte Blanche to some of our enemies. What if they had samples of this new vaccine and then tailored viruses to kill others while they administer this new vaccine on their own people. They could infect our populations and remain immune with disease resistance. Look into it, Reg. I believe this Dr. Motambou bears watching," the general ordered.

By the meeting's end, General Andrews assigned Reginald Atwater to "watch over Salla Motambou" in Paris before the scientist went on to Stockholm to accept his prize.

"Find out which side he's on," the general requested and winked at Reg. That usually meant he wanted the spy to use his ability to read minds.

Reggie left the meeting with Peterson and Brighton armed with new suspicions. He already knew about the scientist from his file. He knew Salla came from the neighboring country of Mali, as Reg was born in Nigeria. Yet his grandparents came from Somalia. He wondered about Salla's origins. While he did not suspected anything different about Dr. Motambou, the man's remarkable and easy rise through the scholastic world mirrored the ease Reg had in school.

"Could it be?" he wondered on his way to his jet. "Are there others like me… like them… out there… scattered around the globe?"

He flew to Europe and began his surveillance. On his first day in Paris, he discovered the true underlying cause of Salla's genius… and to his surprise, also discovered that his wife, Filla, and their important friend, Camille Ossures, was also psychic.

"No wonder she's a billionaire," he thought. The moment that realization occurred, Reggie knew the Kansas psychics were only the tip of the iceberg, metaphorically speaking. "Therefore, the flights from Kansas were to visit their friends. But why now?"

He reasoned that the Kansas psychics and the three in Europe were somehow connected and more than just friends. They must have a financial connection, too. He thought that Camille must be a front… that they used her to make money and finance the operation.

"If I were to eliminate her… or better, use her as bait, I could lure the other group out of Kansas and into a trap…" he thought and reconsidered. A better idea occurred to him; one so diabolical, it would take additional planning. However, Reggie felt that given enough time, he could pull it off. If he did, he would become the most powerful psychic in the world and the richest. The day after the ceremony in Stockholm, Reggie flew back to NATO's secret quarters in Labrador brimming with news.

"I must meet with General Andrews," he told an aid when he disembarked from the plane. "Tell him it is urgent… tell the general I've grown nimble… he'll know what I mean," the secret agent told a subordinate. Moments later, the general put his calendar on hold and took the private meeting with Reggie. He invited Brighton in for consultation.

"Go ahead, Reginald," the general ordered, "you have the floor."

"This Salla Motambou and his wife, Filla… they're similar to the Kansas group… they're psychic," he began.

"Are you certain?" Brighton responded.

"Not only that, but their friend is psychic, too," he informed them. "Camille Ossures is one of the most powerful women in France. That is not the best part. The reason you saw so many spheres is that the Kansas psychics arrived for the Nobel ceremony. They're all friends. They used portable fields to remain invisible…"

"Invisibility," General Andrews said as he gazed off, "can you imagine? If we could get our hands on their technology…"

"I can't imagine what that would mean for our side," Brighton wondered with the same dreamy expression as the general had.

"Dr. Motambou has an open mind, and I don't mean broadminded. I managed to hear many of his thoughts," Atwater informed them, which made the other men exchange glances. "I know why the Kansas psychics remained grounded for so long. It seems they have been busy. They've had some births… five children in total, and not ordinary children. These new little psychics possess very strong power… possibly more than their parents do. They left them behind. They didn't know how dangerous they would be in public."

"He told you all of that?" Brighton asked, incredulous.

Reggie winked and touched his temple.

"Well, that's it," General Andrews stated. "Our course is set. We must have access to what they know," he said to Reggie.

"…and I know just how to get it, general," Brighton broke in.

"Brighton?" the general questioned.

"It suddenly dawned on me how we could obtain the very things we want," the colonel said.

"Keep believing those are your thoughts, Brighton," Reggie thought when he planted the idea. "What's your plan, colonel?" he asked aloud.

"Isn't it obvious? We lure the psychics away from Kansas on some pretext," the colonel began. "Europe is too crowded. They seem to like this doctor. Mali is the more likely place where we would have advantage… if we lay a good trap. We could place their African friends in danger. They'd feel obligated to rescue them. With the pair isolated in Africa, they'll be separated from their brethren, which makes them easier targets for our… Reggie," he suggested to his best agent.

"Those people won't leave their children unguarded," the general said. "We must find a way to separate the parents from the children."

"These psychics are very intelligent," Reggie spoke up. "They'll suspect a trap, if the Motambou's suddenly disappear without a trace. Therefore, we'll have to make one trap an obvious one and the real trap more devious," the man said as he ran his finger along his temple. Reggie recalled a file he once read. It had to do with a Cold War research facility in Russia. He thought about this ever since he followed Salla to Sweden. "Since Dr. Motambou likes viruses, we'll give him one… one that will wreck havoc in Africa… one that will spread fear and panic. What parent would bring their child to an area infected with a deadly virus? And what psychic parent wouldn't defend his world against such a threat?"

"What do you mean, Reg?" Brighton asked.

"I know of a lab… from the cold war… stuff created by scientists long ago… tailor made for situations like this," he recalled. "I can get in and out with our Baltic connection. I can bring back vials of the stuff," he told them. "We could infect the region near the Motambou's."

"Mass murder?" Brighton questioned. "We can't justify…"

"You want someone else to obtain this information? We don't know what we'll find in Kansas… a treasure trove of advanced technology, Brighton. What price would you put on it? What do these people mean to the rest of the world anyway?"

Reggie entered his mind once more and changed his sympathies.

"I see your point…" Brighton mumbled.

Reg turned to the general.

"You can authorize an international quarantine of the area, general, and cut off communication," Reg pointed out. "I'll handle the rest. I'll take the Motambou's prisoner. I can interrogate them anywhere… probe their minds, find out everything we've wanted to know about their organization. After I nab our prey, you only have to lift me out." He saw the skepticism on their faces. He had to add another point to seal the deal. "It beats trying to bomb southwestern Kansas with a deadly weapon. This way, if there are any collateral casualties – and I'm not saying there will be – but they'll be Africans, not Americans, British, or Europeans… who cares about them?" he put to them.

"Yes…. I see…." General Andrews stated.

"I don't get it," Brighton questioned. "What about the Kansas psychics?"

"Don't you see? Once we lure them to Africa, we bring them to our trap and then…" Reggie smiled. He leaned back in his chair and put his feet up.

"And then what?" Brighton asked.

"Then we kill 'em!" Reggie said and grinned. He broke into laughter. The general and Brighton exchanged nervous expressions as they did not wish to offend Atwater. Yet, from where they sat, his laughter bordered on the maniacal.

Chapter Twelve

The Proximate Voices

By the time November of 2016 rolled around, the Rollo psychics had established a new community in southwest Kansas. They befriended the local Native American tribe of Comanche, started to use the new invention of the fusor, stopped a hurricane from destroying New York City, and followed up with a second visit to Paris where they established the first charter for the World Psychic Organization. While in Paris, the Rollo psychics met the three psychics who lived there: Camille Ossures, Filla Sambi, and Salla Motambou – remotely converted by Master Li. During that visit, the assembled group of psychics dedicated their lives to the provisions of the first charter. This became the start of the fledgling WPO, which consisted of the original Rollo nine psychics plus the three in Paris. At that time, they were not aware of any other psychics in the world, at least any ready for conversion.

From November of 2016 until the following spring, Salla promised Camille he would try to finish his research for Ossures Pharmaceuticals and Filla pledged to remain on staff at the hospital as well. The three psychics had many mental interactions, although it became clear very quickly that Salla and Filla interacted on a completely different level than they did with their friend Camille. Being psychic helped the two Malians bond even closer. If Filla decided to leave for Mali and fulfill the contract she made with the government, it would mean separation by a great distance. All three psychics avoided the subject for as long as they could put it off. Camille had a corporation to run. Salla started simian trials on the new serum he devised that spring and Filla worked to complete her apprenticeship, although the point of experience seemed mute in light of downloads from Galactic Central. Weeks turned to months as they focused on completion of their tasks before the elusive time when Salla and Filla had to depart.

When spring rolled around, the activity in the lab increased ten fold. Salla did not emerge from the lab for an entire month. He had a bed brought into his office and worked feverishly, non-stop for days, taking only naps for rest. Worried for his health, Camille infiltrated his staff with her assistants who peppered Salla's co-workers with constant questions about his progress. One afternoon, Filla burst into the lab when she heard that Salla had not slept in three days. She bodily dragged him from the building, forced him to eat some soup, and put him to bed. He slept for 18 hours straight and then slipped away from her, heading right back to the lab. After that, he barred anyone on his staff from mentioning his health status to anyone outside "or you will be immediately fired!" he told them.

When she saw how overburdened Salla became, Camille brought Salla a bright new gifted student. Like Filla, she won that year's scholarship, this time the student's specialty involved research. Salla welcomed the highly trained help. Linda Schlosberg from the Netherlands proved herself worthy of the praise that preceded her. Salla felt so confident in her ability to run the lab that he hoped she would take over the trials sometime in June, so that he could return to Mali with Filla.

Late in May 2017, one of Salla's assistants let slip the news of the serum's success in the trials when lunching with Camille's private secretary. Once he realized his error, he pleaded with the woman to keep the news to herself. However, the dutiful assistant ran back to her boss and told her of the breakthrough. When Camille heard the news of Salla's preliminary results, she decided to pay a surprise visit to the research lab. Salla did not wish to share any results with anyone. While he felt confident his new serum would work, he informed his staff that he wished to purify the formula further to eliminate side effects.

On this particular day, Salla worked under a "draft hood" trying to purify his formula to minimize the side effects. He did not see the whirlwind as it approached behind his back. Everyone around him stopped working. One of them tried to gain his attention.

"Salla," a colleague whispered.

"Not now," he answered with his face in the vented chamber. "I'm in the middle of something crucial."

"But Salla, the CEO is here!" the woman told him.

Salla pulled his head out and yanked off his gloves. He could sense her strong presence as it drew near. By this time, Camille had become a powerful psychic.

"Camille?" he asked as he looked around. At that moment, a yellow light started to flash on the console next to the chamber. He glanced over just as his experiment reached its crucial phase. "Damn!" he exclaimed and started to don his gloves.

"I'll take over," his colleague Linda offered. She placed the bulky gloves on her hands and immersed her head into the chamber.

"Thank you, Linda," he said as he turned toward the entourage.

"I sense tension and exasperation," Camille's voice linked to his mind. "It must be Salla Motambou!"

No one else heard this. Only Salla heard Camille's remark in his mind. He grinned when he heard her thoughts.

"I hope I didn't disrupt anything," she openly apologized as she walked up to him.

Salla pulled off his goggles and shook his head.

"I can always duplicate the experiment. Besides, my colleague, Linda Schlosberg will carry on," He sighed. "Have you met…"

"I know every person in my employé," she retorted. "I'm on the scholarship selection committee."

"I forgot. I'm sorry. We haven't spoken in three weeks. How are you Camille?" he wondered as her group gathered around them.

"Is it true what I heard… about the serum?" she asked.

"The results are extremely encouraging," he told her. "This could be the breakthrough we've sought since the beginning… if the trials bear fruit," he stated cautiously. He did not wish to exclaim that no simian who received the vaccine had died or was sick, not one, a rare occurance in research trials. If he openly spoke of this, he knew that someone present might leak the information to the press. He glanced around at the staff. They knew he thought any talk of a breakthrough was premature.

"I always knew my investment in you would pay off," she said as she placed her arm around Salla's shoulder.

Salla laughed that someone with such ethereal beauty and so usually reserved could behave down to earth at times. He guessed that was part of her charm.

"Our friendship is productive, too," Salla privately replied.

"Oh, Salla, I'm so proud of you," she said as she gestured toward his workstation. "Look at what you've accomplished. Your genius paid off, not just for us, but for humanity. I'm sending this work to Sweden for consideration."

Salla blushed. He could not speak. His voice completely choked with emotion when she mentioned the prize every scientist seeks. He humbly remained silent.

All at once, the entire lab burst into applause around him. Other co-workers walked up to congratulate Salla. Whether he ever won a prize did not matter. Acceptance by his peers paid him the highest compliment of all. He felt completely overwhelmed by their spontaneous reaction.

"I declare this lab a Salla free zone!" she said aloud. "Your boss is on hiatus… for a few hours at least. Come on!"

Camille whisked Salla from the lab. She took him to a tailor's shop where she had them make a beautiful jacket and matching pants while they waited. Afterward, she took him to her restaurant, the Solé, where Filla waited for them to arrive. Despite Master Li's advisory not to drink alcohol, Camille ordered up some of the best wine she had from her cellar. She asked that the waiter "pour small portions" into their glasses.

"By the way," Filla spoke up as the three started hors d'oeuvres, "congratulations, Salla," she offered as she help up her glass. The three took small sips of the exquisite and rare beverage.

"Thanks," Salla stated. He glanced over at Filla. Her mind seemed isolated and her thoughts, distant. All three seemed to block the other out.

"Need I remind you that I finished my apprenticeship," Filla added.

"What?" Salla spoke up. "I thought I had another month…"

"Sorry," Filla said as she set her wine down.

"No, it isn't that I object. It's just…" Salla could not find the words.

"You still plan on going to Mali," Filla asked him. "Aren't you?"

Camille and Filla both stared at Salla. He swallowed hard, torn between the opposite desires that both women seemed to press upon him.

"Of course," he said aloud. He wished at that moment he could link with Filla.

"My work in Paris is finished. I must return to Mali," Filla spoke hesitantly. "Salla?"

Salla had been working so hard on the viral research project that he hoped to obtain an additional grant to continue his work. He did not wish to leave and start a hospital in Mali. He knew that if he left Camille, it would prolong the release of the serum to the market. He would disappoint one or the other.

Camille stayed silent and blocked. She did not tell Salla that only yesterday she easily obtained funding to green light the project's test phase well into the next year. She felt certain that if Filla left, Salla would go with her and that would complicate their lives. They meant so much her.

Salla could not bear to look at either woman.

"Salla?" Filla called after him.

"I'm sorry. What?" he replied and tried to appear unmoved.

"You didn't answer me," Filla said.

"The trials on the new serum must continue," he muttered. "I feel very positive about the results we've seen. It should only take about a year or so before we publish the results."

"A year?" Filla expressed her frustration. "I've stayed nearly a year longer than I intended… I promised my mother… the government…"

She wondered how Salla be so thoughtless about her feelings. Did he change his mind? Perhaps she underestimated his dedication to her versus his research.

"I have a surprise," Camille suddenly spoke up. "I have tickets to the opera!"

Filla dabbed off her chin and stood up. She would no longer look in Salla's direction.

"I thank you for your hospitality," Filla said to her friend. "Please excuse me, Camille. I'm sorry about the opera tickets, but I must go and start preparations to leave France," she added. "I intend to return home."

Camille and Salla stood out of courtesy. Without another word, Filla walked out of the restaurant.

"Did I say something wrong?" Salla responded.

"My darling Salla," Camille began as the two resumed their seats. "You're a brilliant man, but in all those books you read, didn't they ever mention tact when it came to women?" she shook her head.

"I've been thinking about my project," Salla confessed. "She blocked me out. I couldn't link with Filla."

"Sometimes it doesn't take a psychic to read disappointment on a face," Camille quietly linked to him.

"Why should she…"

"She wants to go away and start a new life with you. Filla is in love with you," Camille quietly linked. "It's easy to see why…"

She and Salla stared at one another for an uncomfortable second. He suddenly realized that given the right circumstances, he and Camille might have become lovers as well as friends. Camille purposely broke eye contact.

"Go to her," Camille said and glanced toward the door.

"Camille… I…"

"Go…"

The large black man rose, bowed to his friend and left.

Camille gazed at the two empty place settings and realized in that moment how much she would miss her friends. She snapped her fingers to the waiter.

"Bring me a dessert menu," she requested.

"But mademoiselle… you never eat dessert…" the waiter pointed out.

"I'm breaking many precedents tonight, Michel… besides, I only want to taste it," she said so seductively to the young handsome waiter that he blushed and scampered away for the menu. "I wonder if he likes the opera."

Back in her apartment, a frustrated Filla went to her desk and began to fill out the necessary forms for her transfer back to Mali: bank information, her passport, visa, medical clearance… she had been out of the country over three years. A hundred things went through her mind until she thought of Salla.

"What will I do if he stays?" she thought. "…leave behind what could be my only chance at happiness? I never thought I would say it… but I need Salla. What if he choses to stay? What will I do? What can I do?"

She felt desperate. She wanted to link with the man she loved. She wanted to strip off her clothes and throw herself at him. They had only kissed. She wanted passion. Her body was on fire and she felt Salla hardly noticed her at dinner. Perhaps she should not have blocked him during dinner with Camille.

Filla sat at her desk, upset, depressed, and on the verge of crying.

"I do love you…" she quietly spoke as she ran her fingers along the frame of his picture, "you big, gentle man."

She took in a deep breath and turned away, determined not to cry. She started to review her list of things to pack, when the doorbell rang. She jerked her head around as if someone shot her full of electricity. She knew who stood outside. For a second, she did not move. The bell rang again. She crossed the room and opened the door. Salla stood there with the most pitiful expression she had ever seen, like some dewy-eyed dog that wanted a bone. She didn't know whether to laugh or cry. She only knew he was here.

"May I come in?" he quietly asked.

"Yes," she answered and turned away.

She could not sense Salla's mind. He blocked his feelings from her. Before Salla could say a word, Filla spilled her pent-up feelings.

"I know you want me to stay, Salla, but I promised everyone in Mali I would return. They've waited very patiently for me. But, I have no more excuses to stay. My mind is made up," she passionately spoke as she paced. "Mali is my home. My people need me. They need a hospital… a place where they can find decent and basic health care." She turned to face the man she knew as a friend, her mind full of conflict. "They need us now more than ever," her wide misty eyes, pleaded with him.

"Have you any staff for this new hospital of yours?" he asked.

"Of course not," she stamped her foot. "We haven't even built…"

"I'd like to apply," he spoke in a soft voice. "I have a deed…"

"What?" she asked as she gazed into his eyes. "What did you say?"

"The bishop willed me the deed to some property near Gao. We could start there," Salla offered. "It's remote, not Bamako, but I believe…"

"You would do that for me?" Filla responded as she moved closer.

"I don't want to lose you. I would do anything for you, Filla," he whispered, his head down.

"Oh, Salla," she cried and practically pushed him over.

She threw her arms around Salla's big shoulders. With the side of her face pressed against his chest, she could hear his heart beating. She glanced up and he gazed down at her, their lips nearly touched. They wanted to kiss with passion. They had never truly kissed that way. Instead, they pushed away. Yet in that moment, they simultaneously opened their minds. Their thoughts, desires, hopes and dreams began to intermingle. The feelings that passed between them were so personal, they bordered on the physical. The crescendo was all too brief. The two psychics mentally broke apart. Filla straightened her hair while Salla adjusted his new tie and cleared his throat.

"That was close!" he thought, trying to catch his breath.

"Are we too old fashioned?" Filla wondered via a link.

"Not in my mind," he agreed with her.

"It's not enough to want sex. You have to be committed to the rest," Filla wisely linked. "Is that what you are saying?"

Salla nodded his agreement.

"I can't stay in Paris if you leave. I can't live without you, Filla. I'd like you to come with me... in the morning... when I give Camille the bad news," he requested. Filla silently linked her agreement. "I see we both have some preparations to do," he added.

Across town, Camille looked over at the young man passed out on her bed sheets. She discovered on their way from the restaurant that he did not like the opera. However, he liked other things that were good for her at that moment. She would be kind to Michel and let him down in the morning.

Meanwhile, she needed to cool off. She silently left her bed behind and stood on the edge of her balcony. With a wine glass in her hand, she gazed out at the skyline and secretly eavesdropped on Filla and Salla. She tipped her head back. She didn't care that she took in a large drink of wine. The bottle on the table floated over to her hand. She refilled her glass and sent the bottle floating back. Her manipulation of psychic energy came easily to her. She sighed when she thought about her friends leaving Paris.

"Oh, my friends... I had to introduce you... and you had to fall in love..." she thought as she took another drink. "What must be, had to be, I suppose," she considered. "How I will miss both of you..."

The lights of Paris glittered in the cool evening. The sounds of the bustling city drifted up from below. Camille could only think of how lonely she would feel without her special friends to share in psychic links. As she stood there in her flimsy chemise, she started to take another large draught when a cold breeze blew through her terrace. A chill ran through her, so she sought warmth under the covers with Michel.

The next morning, when Salla and Filla appeared in the lobby, the security guard, now very familiar with Dr. Motambou, directed them to Camille's private elevator. When the doors opened, the CEO stood before them and warmly greeted the couple.

"Filla... Salla... please come into my office... sit down, I want to speak with you," she warmly spoke.

She could tell by their faces that neither slept due to anxiety. Salla rehearsed his speech most of the night, afraid he would offended one the best friends he ever had. Filla could not make eye contact and tried to block her thoughts, though she was not very good at it when it came to Camille's level of power. Camille noticed Filla and Salla barely let go of each other's hand.

"Who am I to interfere with love?" she thought as she sat.

"I have some bad news..." Salla began.

"That you wish to leave," Camille broke in to help ease her friend's fear. "Salla, we are psychics," she linked. "It is impossible to hide our intentions."

"It's not that I don't want to stay..." he started to apologize.

"Yes, Salla really wants to stay Camille..." Filla joined in.

"I understand... perfectly..." Camille replied to both, "and I understand how you arrived at this decision."

"You do?" Salla and Filla linked together.

"Yes, I do," Camille reassured them. "How could our understanding of each other be clearer? I understand your feelings for one another, your motivation to leave, and your strong emotional ties, which Salla has never been able to express very clearly until he became psychic. You didn't have to explain it. I sensed it. Now, how could things be any clearer than that?" Camille blocked the next thought from them. "No matter what happens or how far away we are from each other, we will always be this close," she thought. "I love you, both."

She rose and had to turn away so they could not read the sadness on her face. She went to her executive refrigerator and found the expensive bottle of champagne she asked her secretary to stock before she arrived. She brought it back to her desk along with three glasses.

"I can't give you a proper French send off without some wine," she thought to them. "I would be shirking my patriotic duty if I did so."

Using her mind, she popped the cork, and poured out the golden bubbly liquid, handing each a taste. Filla marveled over her control.

"We may soon find ourselves far apart," Camille told the lovesick couple as she raised her glass. "But our minds will always be connected as if we were in the next room. In medicine, they say that something is proximate if it is close. The voices in Galactic Central are distant. Yet, we will always be close if we have each other as friends… to the proximate voices."

"To the proximate voices," Salla chimed in.

"The proximate voices," Filla echoed.

They drank their toast, set their glasses down, and all three hugged for several moments. They wondered if this might be the last time that they were ever this close again. Filla started to cry when Camille consoled her through her thoughts.

"We have these," she said as she took out the black card that Chou gave all three when the Rollo group visited Paris.

"True," Salla said as he took his card out. Filla fingered hers in her hand. She always kept the precious device on her person, afraid that if anyone else touched it, the card would turn to dust as Chou warned her.

"Filla, I promise you, I will contact you every day this way," Camille told her friend, her expression sincere. "I know how these things slip men's minds. I want to keep in touch with you, too. Eh, Salla?"

Salla smiled back at Camille's way of charming him.

"I'll try," he meekly replied.

Filla and Camille turned to one another. For nearly three years, Filla helped Camille in so many ways. Ever since their conversion, the two women were closer than they had ever been. Salla closed his thoughts to them and allowed the two friends a few minutes of privacy. Filla practically flew into Camille's arms and they held each other tight.

"I will miss you," Filla whispered into Camille's mind.

"We shall never be far apart," Camille said as she pulled away and fought back her tears.

Filla moved next to Salla and held his hand. The meeting ended. Salla and Filla had to find the Mali embassy in Paris and arrange for their return. Two days passed and the friends hardly linked to Camille during that period. Salla transferred control of his lab over to his assistant, Linda. She closely followed his work over the past few months. He had very little to do in the way of an explanation. She understood his goals and the time trials. The Ossures Pharmaceuticals board promised Salla they would not rush his product to market. However, when word leaked out about the serum to the press, Ossures' stock soared… and once they began to manufacture the serum, the sales had the potential to make everyone involved very wealthy.

On the third morning after their meeting with Camille, Salla and Filla stood ready in their apartments for the arrival of their taxis to the airport. A knock sounded on Filla's door about an hour before her arranged time. She opened the door to find Charles, Camille's chauffeur, and the limousine parked in the street.

"What's going on?" she asked.

"Mademoiselle Ossures would like to fly you and Salla aboard her private jet," the driver informed her. "May I load your luggage?"

"Thank you, Charles," she replied. "My bags are over there."

Filla looked out the front window of her apartment and saw Salla already in the back seat. He had the limo's dark window down and waved to her. An hour later, the private jet plane taxied down the runway and took off for Africa. In mid-flight, Camille contacted Filla via her black card. The young African woman took out her card in the secluded cabin. The card expanded with a three-dimensional image of a smiling Camille.

"I just wanted to make certain this thing would work from a distance," she mind-linked to Filla.

"We'll save lots of money on long distance bills," Filla kidded as she reached out for the image only to have her hand pass through it.

"Have a safe trip… I'll miss you…" Camille linked as she choked back her emotion.

"We will… miss you, too…" Filla linked back.

Camille could not prolong her contact without weeping. She and Filla cut off their communication.

Once they arrived back in Mali, Salla and Filla were greeted at the airport like celebrities, as Camille tipped them off. The couple officially announced their engagement to the local press a few days later. They would have the ceremony take place at the local Anglican Church. Since Camille could not attend the wedding, Filla arranged for a special pocket in her wedding dress. She kept her card active so that Camille could witness the ceremony from afar via psychic link.

Filla and Salla married in Bamako a month after they arrived in Mali. Instead of taking a honeymoon, the newlyweds drove the highway along the Niger River until they came to Gao and searched to find the plot of land left to Salla by Bishop Ramsey. When they pulled into town, a huge banner across the main street read "Welcome Mr. and Mrs. Motambou." The Regional governor of Gao, a dignified man dressed in a suit approached Salla and Filla, surrounded by well-wishers. He handed them an envelope with Salla and Filla's name on it.

"We've been anticipating the arrival of Mali's most famous couple," he said with a smile as he held out the envelope. "Welcome to Gao, honored guests."

Salla and Filla thanked him. When Salla opened the envelope, the note inside read:

"You didn't think I would send you back to Africa without a wedding gift, did you? All my love and best wishes for your union, Camille Ossures."

The envelope contained a certificate of deposit with a large amount made out to "Drs. Salla and Filla Motambou" as Filla had her Ph.D. The couple realized that with this amount of money, they could start construction of the hospital. Camille also included a list of donors willing to contribute to their cause on an annual basis. Filla began to cry.

"Oh, Salla," Filla said as she wrapped her arms around her new husband. "Isn't it everything you've always wanted?"

This time they took their time with a long passionate kiss. The Regional governor coughed uncomfortable with the newlywed couple expressing their love so openly.

"Did you know we were married a few days ago?" Salla said to the man as the couple broke apart.

"I would never have guessed," the regional governor quipped.

On that plot of land, they decided to open the first regional free hospital on the eastern side of Gao. The couple stayed extremely busy for the next two years. They organized construction of the new hospital with Filla in charge of administration while Salla headed up hiring staff that included importing physicians and nurses while they arranged for the transfer of medical equipment and supplies. On the west side of town not far from the river, Salla found a parcel of land to build a private laboratory where he could continue his study of viruses while it also doubled as a lab for the hospital. One evening before local work crews completed the the lab's foundation, Villi flew Zinian and two of his crew into Gao. They created some special items for Salla that he could use and added a safety device that would prevent the spread of any foreign microbes he kept on site in case of an insurrection.

True to her word, Camille used her card device to contact Filla every evening just before bedtime. Salla chimed in on the calls to Paris from time to time. He and Filla also sent weekly reports to the WPO headquarters in Rollo on their progress. The trio remained close friends and shared many of their challenges and experiences as time passed. They tried to make the distance between Mali and France seem as if they were next door neighbors.

Months turned to years as the Motambou's operated the region's only hospital and enjoyed success in their various ventures, thanks in part to their friend in the corporate world, Camille Ossures. Despite their distance apart, they remained in mind-link with one another, keeping their friendship alive. Salla continued to offer Camille suggestions on the serum, while Camille and Filla discussed their private life once Salla departed their party line.

When April of 2024 arrived – over eight years after he turned psychic and seven after he left Paris – the committee in Stockholm awarded Salla the Nobel Prize in Medicine for his work on the new anti-viral serum. Tahir flew from Egypt to Mali and delivered the couple to Paris, where they met up with many WPO psychics who flew in especially for the presentation. After an all too brief reunion, the entourage flew via a privately owned but very public jet airline to Sweden where Salla left the plane into the arms of the local press. The following day, he graciously accepted the prize. Shortly thereafter, he and Filla flew back to Africa, where the famous scientist received a huge celebration in the streets of Bamako that lasted for two days.

By the time Salla and Filla returned to Gao, the scientist thought he had reached the pinnacle of his career and they could settle down into a life filled with purpose yet obscurity. However, Salla was wrong. Only a few days after they returned from Bamako, a special delivery package arrived at his lab from up river… a package that brought with it, a curse on their lives and their country.

Chapter Thirteen

Expansion

THE STRANGEST BIRTH IN THE history of the human race took place in the summer of 2019, when an infant son reached through the birthing canal for the hand of his father who helped the newborn as he wiggled his way out. Less than four months passed since conception. Yet the child inside Cecilia developed into a full term baby aware of its surroundings.

A mother normally pushes out a human child from the womb via a series of contractions that take place over a period of hours. However, in this instance, a child born of genetically altered psychic parents had been in mental contact with since a week after conception. He learned about the outside world with his parents as his guide. He bonded with his mother in a way that no ordinary woman on earth would ever experience. When it came time for his birth, both parents and the child agreed to the method and the process they would employ.

Although uncomfortable at first, Cecilia did not experience any pain when her son traveled out of her uterus via her vagina. The two worked slowly together and blocked the nerves in her canal to make the event a blessed one that concentrated on the birth instead of the pain. The infant reached out with both of his tiny hands for his father's fingers. Gently, with the help of the mother, the child wiggled and squirmed his way out. Michael used no pressure on his newborn son's hand as he helped to guide the infant.

The child, Mark Tyler, knew his name long before his birth. The process of being born did not frighten him. He knew what to expect. With calm deliberation, his head emerged. With eyes still closed, he ejected the fluid from his lungs and took in his first breath of air. Anxious, his parents, and their psychic friends, watched and waited for Mark to complete the birthing process.

"I can breathe air," he calmly linked to them.

The entire room let out its collective breath, which they held sympathetically. Smiles broke out as Michael continued to wipe his child's face with a soft warm cloth.

"Welcome to the world, son," Michael linked to his mind.

"Welcome, son," Cecilia echoed.

This calm procedure resulted in the birth of Mark Tyler, the world's first fully formed Level IV psychic child at birth without a conversion. For the past few months prior to this event, Cecilia and Michael taught their son the use of language as well as how to use his psychic ability, while still in his mother's womb. Mark spoke to his parents day and night, until he understood the concept of rest and sleep cycles. When he detected them asleep, he learned not to disturb them. In addition to language, he also learned patience. He gained an understanding of the world around him through the mind and eyes of his parents. Surprisingly, Mark also had a voice at Galactic Central from the moment of his conception. Master Li requested the child's GC voice remain mute until after his birth, so that Mark would rely on Michael and Cecilia for all communication and support.

When the day of his birth finally arrived, all of the Rollo psychics, including his yet unborn cousin still in Su Lin's womb, attended the anticipated event. Friendly faces greeted Mark Tyler when he wiggled his way out of his mother's body. Instead of the usual crying and fussing child, he smiled and waved at them, unable to form words with his new mouth and lungs. Until he could open his eyes and properly use his vocal chords, he instead linked his feelings in regards to being outside his mother's womb. Without a fanfare of words, the child conveyed to their psychic friends his feelings of ease and peace.

All during the birth Master Li remained in a corner of the room. He did not comment or offer any remarks. He silently watched as Mark emerged into the world and beheld his father with his eyes for the first time. Still wet with fluid, the father took his son into his arms and cuddled the child. He detached the chord with a special medical device provided by Cecilia. Michael gently proceeded to clean Mark's body while he provided the child warmth against his bare skin. With the sight of his face and touch of his father's hands, Michael and Mark completed the father-son bond that first started as a mental link between them months ago.

Sharing the moment, Michael passed his son to the mother. Mark glanced briefly at his mother's face before he understood his next obligation – undertake nutrition. At once, he suckled at his mother's breast as she had instructed him to do prior to birth. Their eyes again briefly met as the child snuggled into her chest, his new home, while he drew nourishment from her bosom.

From the back of the room, Master Li stepped forward. Sensing his presence, the others moved aside.

"Congratulations," he linked to both parents and child.

The elderly advisor moved in for a closer examination. While the others could not perceive his intent, Li could see further into Mark's mind than anyone present. Li saw only intelligence, curiosity, and a sense of well being. It warmed him to discover such a balanced individual. He took heart in knowing that Mark had a great future before him.

"Welcome to the world, Mark Tyler," he linked to the child's mind.

In this quiet moment, Villi offered his congratulations.

"Chip off the old block of stone!" he said and took Michael's hand.

He looked at his friend's face as Michael beamed with pride. Words could not convey the deep feeling of satisfaction that passed between the two friends.

"Won't be long now," Michael replied.

Before Villi could respond, Zinian, Zhiwei, Han, and Chou added their congratulations to the couple via links, including a curious female child yet to make her exit from Su Lin's body. That would take place later in the week, for another anticipated gathering. The female child patiently waited inside Su Lin as her parents instructed. She actually felt grateful that Mark went first. Mey Li (may-lee) saw how easily Mark handled the birthing process. She would follow his example.

"It is Mey Li's turn next," Han observed.

"She is ready," Su Lin remarked.

"We set Thursday morning as the delivery time," Villi reminded them.

"I look forward to meeting her," Master Li added.

"So will we," Mark, Cecilia, and Michael chimed in.

Since these events concerned the psychics of Rollo, they decided to make the event private until after the birth to accept the community's appreciation and offers of joy. Master Li made that sentiment clear when he called for a village meeting in the Main Street Park prior to the births. The meeting brought every person to the concert shell so that Li could explain the arrival of the new children, Mark and Mey Li.

"These children are very special," he told the large gathering. "You will find them very different from the rest of us," he explained. "Please be mindful of your thoughts. They will not understand the courtesies we take for granted. They will probe you. Do not be offended if this happens. It will take time to establish discipline. Once they understand the importance of their power, we can safely integrate them into society. Until then, their parents shall be responsible for their actions. If any of you encounters any disturbing thoughts, dreams, or hallucination, I want you to report them at once to any of us. Do you understand?"

The village returned a unanimous agreement. They gave the two couples at the end of Main Street their privacy and kept their distance. When Master Li announced the births, many questioned the premature status.

"They grew at a faster rate," Li explained to them. "They are human beings with a slight difference. Because of their power, no one knows what to expect. That is why we must exercise on the side of caution," Li said to allay any fears.

After their births, the children integrated rather quickly into the Rollo community. At six months, they could walk and fluently spoke English as well as French and Chinese. By the time their first birthday rolled around, Su Lin enrolled Mark and Mey Li in a special pre-school class that alternated with her, Cecilia, Villi, and Michael as at-home instructors.

Oddly, about three months later, both mothers experienced a second fertilization. Cecilia and Su Lin became pregnant a second time. After only four months, they gave birth to two more children: Sandra, a daughter for Michael and Cecilia; and Xiong Po (chong-poe), a son for Villi and Su Lin. While the two couples seem busier than ever raising their children, Star Wind discovered only weeks after Sandra and Xiong's birth that she was pregnant. She carried her child slightly longer, taking an additional month. She delivered Robert in a more traditional fashion with some struggle that took place between child and mother.

As the other two couples did, Chou linked with his son Robert as soon as the child began to form thoughts. At first, Robert had trouble with the birthing process as he did not have the same level of connection with Star Wind. However, Chou guided his son during the birth and the child received encouragement from his psychic cousins as well. Robert eased his mother's pain and managed to make the transition a smooth one. Master Li noted that Robert had the same level of psychic power as the other children did.

The five children grew quickly both physically and mentally. The parents did very little travel during this period. If a crisis arose, others in the international psychic community handled any involvement. They kept in contact with Zhiwei, Master Li, or Han who offered their guidance in return. At the end of three years, Su Lin discovered that the five children presented a special challenge for her current level of teaching ability. She went to Artane and requested individual tutors for these "special" children. Their intellectual capacity and their ability to reason outstripped those of their parents at its current pace. Master Li gave his permission for the children to spend part of their day off world in a "classroom" of sorts on the most knowledgeable world in the universe.

The rest of the time, the children did what other children do – they played outside with their friends, while they also promised their parents restraint on the use of their power. When the children questioned this restriction, Master Li intervened on the parent's behalf.

"I have ten times the power you will ever have. Do you see me bringing down the heavens?" Master Li put to them during a private session. "We must use the utmost restraint and patience when we exercise our power in a world occupied by those who do not understand us," he told them.

"Yes, Master Li," they chimed in response.

When the spring of 2024 rolled around, the children unanimously agreed to comply with Master Li's wishes… for a while at least.

Chapter Fourteen

Conduit of Death

Late April 2024 marked an early return to the rainy season in Mali, which usually did not start until June or July. The Niger River swelled and expanded, which allowed travel by river in large boats, similar to ferries. During this period, merchants preferred to send their goods by river versus by the unreliable road from Bamako, which often flooded out at times. As it had for decades, the Niger River still acted as the main highway for commerce during rainy season between the capital city of Bamako and Gao.

The city of Gao prospered since Salla and Filla arrived, thanks to the help of their friends from Europe and America. The couple brought doctors and nurses from other countries on a rotating basis to staff their eighty-eight bed facility. Their medical staff treated literally thousands of patients since they erected the largest building complex in Gao. In turn, the hospital attracted other businesses that flourished and helped the community of Gao to grow into a relatively modern city compared to its previous more elemental existence. This was the home of a Nobel Prize winner. Many people in the medical profession wanted to work with Salla, even in a place like Gao.

People around the globe used the serum that Salla's work produced. However, due to some side effects, not everyone could take this new form of immunity – a simple test revealed who could take the serum, limited to about half the world's population. Yet, in all of these many cases, people who took the serum no longer had to take a series of shots for immunity to viral diseases that included influenza and the common cold. Ossures Pharmaceuticals reaped billions in profits and became the largest such corporation in the world in terms of gain.

In Gao, Filla headed the hospital's administration and handled the business aspects of the institution. Working with her contacts in Bamako, she encouraged the government to establish a military garrison a few miles east of the town, which brought security and stability to the region. That led to an increase in the overall prosperity for the city. One could say that since the Motambou's arrived, they became two of Gao's leading citizens. People in the region openly recognized the couple wherever they went.

Unfortunately, their workload took a heavy toll on their marriage. Salla performed numerous surgeries and made medical rounds during the day. Most evenings he spent in his lab to continue his research in virology. When she wasn't recruiting physicians, nurses, and running the hospital, Filla frequently traveled to Bamako to seek political and financial support. Their jobs kept them so busy that they hardly had time for a private life. Only social functions, like the formal dinner scheduled this April 2024 event at the regional governor's house, brought Salla and Filla together. Dignitaries from the central government, important people that Filla contacted to help pass certain legislation or receive funding, were also present at tonight's festivities. Naturally, they all wanted to meet the reclusive Nobel Prize winner, since he was now the brightest star in all of Mali. Salla had become a source of national pride, which made Filla's job easier when it came to raising funds.

On this warm night in late April, Filla mingled through the crowd, working her charm before dinner, as she knew Salla would join them soon. Wandering through the guests, she checked this one's vote on a certain bill and that one's opinion on legislation. The entire time she kept an eye on the wall clock. The regional governor nervously glanced at Filla and then at his watch. She knew he wondered about Salla's whereabouts. Filla smiled in return and shook her head. Salla still had not showed and it was eight o'clock.

Across town, Salla could not tear away from the electron microscope display screen. A special messenger arrived with a desperate sounding note hours earlier. With the help of his assistant, the intrigued researcher accidentally discovered the unexpected – a similarity between a virus he knew and one he suspected might be a new variant. He stared at the electron microscope image and took some micrographs. He compared the images of this specimen to other logged images for cross-reference.

In his focus on the moment, Salla forgot to utilize two vital components that he possessed: he could have accessed his black card and used its database for comparison analysis, and he forgot to look at his watch. He promised Filla he would arrive at the party on time. Perhaps his own pride stood in his way.

"What are you?" he thought as he pondered the image. "This doesn't make sense. They're all dead. It's as if they quickly replicated, served their intended purpose – which destroyed most of the red blood cells – and then somehow they shut down. But why?"

The cumulative burden of a long stressful day combined with a lack of rest filled his mind with uncertainty. Salla could no longer concentrate. He drew psychic energy from the city, which only revived him a little.

"That's it!" he finally said as he pushed away. "I can't think. Into the disposal..."

He nearly discarded the specimen and shut down the microscope when he noticed another detail that he overlooked. Certain markers appear on ordinary viruses as being natural. However, some parts of viruses can show signs of manufacture to an expert eye. A flash of brilliance filled Salla's mind. His eyes widened as his face drew closer to the screen. He finally saw them, the markers, created by lab technicians to identify this virus as created for a specific purpose.

"You are not Ebola at all. Man-made?" he conjectured.

The idea of a manufactured mutation suddenly occurred to him.

"A biological weapon," he whispered. He looked away and tried to reason it out. "How did it come to Mali? Who released it? Why?" He glanced over at the screen. "If this is true," he thought, "that would make this strain extremely contagious and deadly... a manufactured virus for the deadliest of games – war! And we, the innocent, are trapped in the middle of it. Why? Why here? Why now? And why Mali? Who would do such a thing?"

Salla realized that this was not just some ordinary lab creation. It took years of research to create such a tailor-made biological agent, the kind used for warfare, the kind of research that only devious scientists who worked for militaries with large budgets could manufacture such a specific deviant.

"I thought agreements shut down most of those facilities," he considered. "This could be the first salvo, a testing ground to see if these viruses work... We are a prelude to *war...*" he whispered the last word aloud with the breathlessness of a dying man. "Oh, my god... If that is the case," he thought, "then we're all in danger..."

Dr. Motambou's forehead broke into a sweat as he pushed away from the screen. His head jerked toward the door.

"Kim!" he thought of his assistant. "I've got to warn her." He turned and looked over at the note, "and what of Beluna," he considered.

His mouth grew dry as he recalled the note that accompanied the specimen. Beluna Boodona worked as a nurse specialist in the field. She went from small village to small village as the only connection between the Gao Regional Hospital and the remote areas more than two hundred kilometers away. She had once been on staff and now worked as a field nurse. She remembered that Dr. Motambou specialized in treating patients with hemorrhagic fever. She had the presence of mind to take some blood samples from a recent case and sent them via a special messenger along with a note.

He glanced down at the nurse's note lying on the counter.

> *Dear Dr. Motambou- April 24th 2024*
> *As you may recall, I am a nurse working in a village at the junction of the Moballa tributary. I remembered you treated patients with Hemorrhagic Fever. Yesterday, some villagers found a ferryboat floating down the Niger, all aboard dead. They called for me to examine them. I could not estimate the length of their illness before they expired. I noticed each person had dried blood coming from the ears, mouth, nose, and around the eyes. I managed to draw a sample before the villagers pulled me away. They burned the boat and the people onboard. Please use caution when handling. Also, all traffic along the road has ceased. No truck or car has come from the west for days. The cell phones and landlines no longer work. Please respond via messenger. If you could tell me what to expect, I would greatly appreciate it.*
> *Sincerely, Beluna Boodona, R. N.*

"That was yesterday," he said thinking aloud.

The chiming of an old clock in the corner of his cubical shattered the silence of the lab. Eight loud tones rang out which shook the studious doctor from his concentration. Salla knew the old clock ran slow. He glanced down at his watch. The wristwatch read a few minutes after eight o'clock.

"Oh, no," he let out a groan. "She's going to kill me!"

He had instinctively put up a powerful block around him to cut off any distractions. The moment he let down his block, her psychic contact blared into Salla's mind like a trumpet blast.

"Finally, I sense your mind open! Salla?" her thoughts blared.

"I am here," he softly replied.

"Where are you?" Filla demanded.

"Still in the lab," he answered. He did not want her to know he had been testing blood samples. Yet, he had opened his mind to her.

"Would you mind washing up quickly and getting over here! You were supposed to meet me an hour ago… Ugh! Salla! You're testing blood samples?" she noticed. "Why are you working so late tonight? This dinner is important to me, to us, to the hospital. Important people from the central government are here, hopefully to increase our funding," she linked.

"When I arrived back at the lab this afternoon, Kim gave me a note along with a sample of blood," he explained.

"All that can wait," she implored. "This dinner is more important! Drop what you're doing and get over here fast. I need you and that wonderful charm you possess. Please!"

Salla hesitated to leave. Preparing the specimen took precious time for a man who measured his day in minutes. He touched a place on the screen, which ran a series of digital images and recorded them into a memory file. He used his laptop to download the images directly from the microscope.

"I guess, my little friend, you'll just have to wait until tomorrow," he thought during the transfer.

After several minutes of carefully decontaminating his precious instrument, he went to the rack, took off his lab coat, and thoroughly scrubbed before he went to his office. He put on a clean white shirt, tie, and jacket for the occasion. As he dressed for dinner, he heard a distant rumble.

"Rain?" he wondered.

Before he left the lab, Salla returned to the examination room and placed the blood sample tubes the nurse sent him inside a special container meant for controlled-freezing. He labeled the tubes, "Extremely hazardous." He placed that container inside one of his specimen freezers that sat in his viral storage room. Salla made certain he turned on the lab's computer security systems. He did not want someone breaking into this room and spreading this specimen or any of his viruses around Africa. His research included several deadly strains.

"God help the poor sod that breaks in here," he thought as he started the lock down procedure.

He knew the night security officer, who mostly stayed at their station near the front door, would guard over his very expensive gifts until morning. Salla called out to the officers at the front desk that he was leaving before he headed toward the back door. He reached inside his coat pocket for his keys and found the black Rollo communication card in his hand. He nearly activated the device as he considered notifying Zhiwei or Chou of this new development. Su Lin was well versed in biology, too. Han could conjecture on its origins. Cecilia was nearly as much an expert in microbiology as he was. He and Rollo's physician had a connection that he never revealed to anyone, including Filla.

"Filla needs me at the party. I'll have time later to notify the WPO," he thought and pushed the card back into his pocket. He exited the building's back door and put in the lockdown security code. He could hear the steel bolts slide into the wall.

"Thanks to Zinian, no one can break down that door," he thought.

The walk to his car normally took less than a minute. He always parked at the far end of the lot. Salla still had the same old fuel-hybrid energy powered vehicle he had ever since he and Filla married in 2017. Just as Dr. Motambou pulled out his key to open the door, he heard a great commotion. At first, he thought it was more thunder and looked up at a clear sky overhead. He reached out with his psychic senses. Then he heard what sounded like firecrackers, only louder. He turned his head in that direction to listen. He thought he heard screams, shouting in the distance; or was it the honking of horns. He heard those, too. He took a few steps away from his car and tried to focus on the sounds. More firecrackers erupted.

"What the devil?" he wondered.

All at once, the ground around him shook and the air roared with a thunderous sound. Salla glanced up as a giant fireball filled the entire night sky. Salla stared with disbelief at the distant horizon. The military's fuel depot erupted into one great explosion after another as their five-year reserve fuel tanks went up in flames. Each explosion shook the ground like an earthquake. He heard the firecrackers again, only this time closer, followed by more screams... screams he recognized as people in terror.

"Those aren't firecrackers or cars honking. They sound like gunshots and screams of people in fear. What's going on?" he wondered. Before he had time to reach out with his mind and scan the countryside, Filla broke into his thoughts.

"Salla!" he heard his wife's voice burst into his mind. "Salla! Come quick! The entire city has erupted into chaos and confusion! People are rioting in the streets. I'm not sure what is happening. Several mobs are working their way across town. They've begun to burn houses. None of the city's agencies answers my calls. I can't raise the ambulance service. I'm afraid for the hospital and its staff. I need you here, now! This is an emergency!"

"On my way," Salla thought back as the ground shook with more explosions and the air cracked with occasional gunfire.

Now as he looked east toward Gao, the sky began to glow orange. To his surprise and horror, Salla realized parts of Gao were on fire!

"Salla!" Filla's linked voice returned. "They've called out the militia. The military commander reported roving gangs with weapons. They've heard multiple gunfire shots in your part of town. Please be careful."

"I'll be careful," Salla replied as he stepped into his vehicle.

He spun the wheels on the gravel parking lot and turned onto the road that headed north to the main road that led from the river into the city. The streetlights flickered and went out. Only the headlights of his vehicle illuminated the road. Occasionally he saw bright flashes of light coming from the other side of buildings on the main road. He realized he must use his power to scan the area ahead.

"I must know what is happening," he thought.

He slammed on the brakes and came to a skidding halt. Using his psychic ability, he scanned over the area. The Level III psychic's vision rose above the area. Not far from his position, he could see cars on fire in the street and a large angry mob drag people from their homes and shoot them. Then they took their possessions and threw them into large pyres that burned in the middle of the street. The fires grew taller as he watched the mob empty house after house. Horrified by what he saw, Salla considered his options.

"I'll never be able to cross the city if I take the main avenue," he surmised. "I'll check one of the side streets."

Salla shut off his headlights and pulled his vehicle off the main road. He eased down a parallel side street and quietly crept along to avoid making any noise. When he arrived at the ravine where the riverbed cut through the center of Gao, he hesitated. A deep riverbed, spanned by bridges in two locations, separated the east and western sides of the town. The bridge to the south would mean a long delay and he would need to backtrack. Although the water level dropped to a matter of inches deep, his vehicle could not go down the steep angles of the ravine.Therefore, he could either turn back or go one block north to the central street bridge and hope no one noticed him. He turned up the road along the ravine.

As Salla approached this side of the bridge, he slowed the vehicle down and lowered the windows, listening for the mob. The sound of breaking glass and women's screams shattered the night air. Every few minutes another explosion went off somewhere, which startled the peace-loving man. His heart pounded inside his chest. Sweat trickled down the sides of his face. Darkness swallowed up very building and object around him. Without any streetlights, he could not make out how far he was from the bridge. Slowly, he inched forward.

As his vehicle emerged onto the central artery and he turned his vehicle toward the bridge, he could make out the mob's handiwork everywhere. The orange glow from the fires illuminated a ghastly scene. Men, women, and even children of all ages lay butchered in the streets, some shot, others had their heads bashed in. The mob set furniture, buildings, and cars ablaze.

"Those poor people," he thought.

In the chaos and confusion, no one noticed his vehicle as it neared the bridge. Instead, the mob made its way in the opposite direction as they worked their way toward the river.

"This is my chance," he thought. Slowly he crept the vehicle forward and started to cross the bridge.

"Hey!" a man yelled. "He's trying to escape. Get him!"

All at once, men sprang from the shadows. They called out to the mob, while at the same time, they rushed toward the vehicle and tried to stop him. Salla turned on his headlights, hit the gas pedal, and sped forward, trying to make a run for it. The vehicle roared across the bridge in the darkness. He frowned as he peered ahead through the smoke that partially obscured his vision toward the eastern side of the bridge.

"What is that?" he frowned as he tried to make out the other side.

A hastily erected barricade blocked the road on the other end of the bridge. The military erected a barrier so tall and with so many large objects, they made it impossible for Salla to get through.

"I don't care what's over there. I'm coming through!" he thought.

He slammed his right foot down. His heavy vehicle picked up speed. As his car flew across the bridge, he pushed the engine hard, hoping to avoid the chasing mob.

A shot rang out. It struck his right headlight. Salla felt the impact as the bullet smashed into the light and snuffed it out. He tried to see where the shot originated when another bullet struck his car and then another. From behind the barrier, someone was shooting bullets at him.

Suddenly, a hail of bullets erupted from behind the barricade and struck the moving vehicle, with four shots striking the front windshield. The fractured glass burst around Salla and made him swerve. More shots fired into his car and some struck his tires.

He heard a loud bang as first one, and then the other front tire went flat from bullet fire. The back end of his car began to swing around. His vehicle started to go sideways and finally turned completely around, sliding backward toward the barrier in reverse. The forward momentum kept him on a collision course with the other side of the bridge. The front wheels snapped off. Sparks flew out from underneath, as metal scraped hard against the concrete.

Careening out of control, the back end of his car struck the barricade with full force and punched a hole in the barrier. The car brought a great deal of debris as it broke through. Soldiers jumped for their lives as Salla's hefty vehicle smashed into their stronghold and scraped along the road until the battered bullet-riddled car screeched to a halt some thirty meters beyond the barrier.

A bright light swung around and fell upon the vehicle. It lit up the interior. Salla put up his hand to see. He shook with fear and his body was wet with sweat. He heard men shout. A few more bullets struck the vehicle's frame, some ricocheting off the wreck. He feared he would never see his beloved Filla again.

An officer began to bark orders at the men.

"Stop firing your weapons!" he ordered as he motioned for two men.

Salla cautiously stuck his head up over the dash. Two uniformed men ran up to the car.

"Dr. Motambou!" a man shouted. "Are you hurt?" he asked. "I'm sorry, sir. We did not recognize your vehicle on the bridge."

A young officer pried the car door open and gazed down at the trembling black man who cowered on the front seat.

"Were you hit by any bullets, sir?" the man asked.

Salla ran his hands over his body.

"I don't think so," he said visibly shaken.

He tried to see the young face that stared down at him. He blinked his eyes against the bright spotlight focused on the car.

"Turn that spotlight away!" the officer yelled up to a soldier on a special truck. "Do you want to make us a target?"

The bright light swerved back toward the bridge and turned off. Salla's vision took a moment to readjust to the relative darkness that enveloped them. As his eyesight returned, he noticed some temporary electric lights put up by the military strung around a staging area. Salla wondered why the military stopped here. Why didn't they go into the western sector to stop the violence and bloodshed? Soldiers scrambled to rebuild the barrier.

"What has happened?" he asked as his hands still trembled.

"I'm sorry, sir, we don't know. A riot broke out and spread everywhere. We took care of the pockets of resistance on this side of the bridge," the officer informed him.

"Why haven't you stopped the protestors over there?" Salla pointed across the bridge.

"I had orders to stay on this side of the bridge, sir," the officer quickly responded. "I just received word that if you showed up, I should have you escorted to the secure part of town. This way, sir."

The young officer helped Salla from the bullet-riddled vehicle. Salla glanced back at his poor old car and thanked his lucky stars for having purchased such a large sturdy vehicle in the first place.

"Well, Filla," he thought. "I guess this as good an excuse as any for me to finally buy a new car."

The officer placed him in a smaller open military vehicle and told the driver to take Salla directly to an address. The driver sped through the city streets in the darkness with reckless abandon. As they left, Salla looked back over his shoulder and noticed a number of the militia push his vehicle into the barrier to fill the hole he had made.

"I'm glad someone's going to get some use out of it," he mused.

"Why? What happened to your car?" Filla's thoughts intruded.

"To put it mildly, dear, it's in tatters. I barely made it across the bridge in one piece," he explained.

"Are you alright?" she asked.

"You mean in spite of the bullets? I'm still in one piece," he told her.

"Bullets?"

"I'm ok!"

"Oh, thank goodness," she linked. "Hurry!"

Salla detected her elevated level of tension.

"I'm in a military vehicle headed your way," he linked to reassure her. "The army's bringing me."

"Whatever you see along the way, make no comment and say nothing," she warned.

His driver tore through the darkened streets so fast that Salla could not watch the road out of nervousness. He looked around for a seatbelt, but the two-man vehicle had none. To keep from being sick, he chose avoidance and clamped his eyelids shut. Obviously, the soldier knew the streets of Gao well or he would not drive so recklessly, Salla hoped.

After a mile or two of wildly rushing down one street after another, they finally reached an area where temporary lights ran off portable generators. Salla recognized the neighborhood at once as being near his house. He noticed military vehicles lined the streets as the driver stopped at a checkpoint. They created an area large enough for only one vehicle to pass. Armed guards flanked both sides of the street.

A tall uniformed man approached the car with his rifle pointed at the driver. "State your business!" the man's gruff voice demanded.

"Dr. Motambou!" the driver barked back.

The uniformed man flashed a light on the passenger and then waved the driver on.

"Hurry along then!" the sentry responded.

After a block or two, they came upon a large well-lit house with thick black cables that ran from the back of the house to two generators outside. Salla knew the house well. He had been here many times. It was the regional governor's house where he should have been nearly an hour ago. A large number of armed men and military vehicles surrounded the place. Inside, Salla could sense a crowd of nervous people milling about. Another sentry stepped into the road and ordered the car to stop. The driver pulled up to an abrupt halt in the middle of the street.

"Halt!" the sentry shouted and pointed his rifle at the driver.

"I have Dr. Motambou!" the driver quickly shot back.

"Oh," the man said after he noticed Salla in the front seat. "Follow me," he requested.

Salla stepped from the car and looked around at the other houses in the neighborhood. He could see his home about four houses away. He wanted to check on the condition of their things. He had many mementos of their trips over the years, personal items that he treasured. His heart sank when he noticed that two homes in the same area had burnt to the ground, friends of theirs, the contents of which still smoldered. Bullet holes riddled several other houses. He glanced down at the street. He noticed several bloodstains on the pavement. Salla assumed a battle took place here recently.

As he approached the regional governor's house, everything seemed intact, except for a bullet hole through the front window. He realized why the regional governor had drawn the binds and the curtains – everyone inside must be afraid. Salla stopped at a pool of blood on the front walk that someone had tried to clean off with some water. An obvious dark red stain remained on what he knew was a clean walkway only yesterday. He reached out for Filla with his mind.

"Filla?" he called.

"Come inside and act pleasantly surprised," she replied. "Say nothing about what you've seen on the western side of the town or mention the mob," she told him.

"They nearly killed me coming here!" he thought angrily to her. "What in blue blazes is going on? Is it a coup d'etat?"

"Darling, please say nothing and don't ask questions until we are alone. Just act glad to see me… please," she pleaded with him.

"Fine," he muttered back to her.

At the front door, Salla waited for permission to enter. His escort waved for him to enter the house. Ordinarily when Salla entered a party, a great cheer would go up, as he was the hero of Mali. Not tonight. The room had an errie silence that hung over the room in an oppressive way – it stifled conversation or even expressing one's opinion. Once inside, Salla saw the military had commandeered the regional governor's house. They pushed most of the furniture out of the dining room leaving only the large table. A number of officers hovered around a major in command of what was left of the military garrison. He kept pointing to a map on the table. The commanding officer spouted out theories of how the riot started. Salla heard the word "madness" mentioned several times as the reason for the crowd's aberrant behavior.

"What is it?" one frightened woman asked.

"We don't know why they've gone berserk," the major told the group of people. "But let me reassure you. We will stop this madness and make everything right again."

"The man's an idiot," Salla thought. "How can they place their trust in him?"

A sea of nervous faces lurked about the walls of the nearby "living room." People gathered in groups of four or six. No one seemed to notice Salla when he entered the room or paid him any attention. Several people made repeated trips to the regional governor's bar and a few appeared inebriated. Salla searched for one familiar face. Filla bolted out from the kitchen and rushed past the officers in the dining room, bearing a platter of sandwiches. She wore a broad fake smile on her face.

"At last!" he thought to her.

Filla glanced his way where he stood between the two rooms. He glanced over and noticed the bullet hole on the opposite wall. He also saw pieces of glassware and dishes on the floor that someone hastily swept to the edge. Gunman must have rudely interrupted the formal dinner.

"I'll be with you after I pass these," she said. Although just a second later, she placed the tray in someone else's hands. She made her way over to Salla and tightly embraced him. "I'm so relieved that you're ok," she sighed as she clung to him. "I tried to follow your progress. It drove me mad with fright," she linked to his mind.

"Where can we go?" he thought to her privately, while aloud he said, "Darling! It's so good to see you!"

Filla smiled up at him, "Yes, good to see you, too. We were so worried."

Several people turned around and finally noticed two of the town's most renowned citizens embracing. At that moment, some of those invited guests started to press Dr. Motambou with questions. Filla wisely turned him around toward the kitchen.

"Hungry? You must be famished!" she said to him. She made a quick gesture toward the kitchen with an ulterior motive.

"Starved!" he said with a grin.

The couple fled the curious crowd and headed into the kitchen. No one followed them.

"Go through the kitchen and head outside," she thought to him.

"Outside?" he thought back.

"We can go out the backdoor to talk," she linked to him, "but not in here, too many ears."

Filla took her husband's elbow and guided him through the servants crowding around in the kitchen. They occasionally acknowledged some of those present while they moved constantly toward the back of the house. Filla grabbed Salla a sandwich and a cold drink as they passed another tray, which she prepared, as hardly anyone had eaten and the governor had not given the staff any directives. Once outside, Salla stuffed his hungry face with food and drink while she linked to him.

"This way," she thought. The couple walked further from the house as Salla continued to feed his hunger.

"Hungry?" he offered her the other half.

"No appetite… I've seen too much," she thought to him.

She pulled him further away until the couple stood in the regional governor's flower garden. Even the soldiers were out of hearing range.

"I've tried to piece together the answers to a rather interesting puzzle, my fine learned husband," Filla began to explain. "The origins to this chaos and misery actually begin with you, my sweet," she said.

Then, peering closely at her husband, Filla quickly probed his mind.

"Are you working on something new in your lab? Did you receive a fresh sample of a viral specimen?" She stood only a few centimeters from his chewing jaw and probed his thoughts. "This evening's riot started when rumors of illness swept inland from the river and had spread through Gao like a fire in the dry season, inciting the crowd. Do you know anything of this?"

Salla paused a moment, uncertain how to proceed with an explanation. Filla felt frustrated with his lack of candor. She wanted answers now. She searched his mind and quickly found them.

"A strain of virus? Of course! Salla, why didn't you tell me? What are its origins? How is it spread? How long have you known?" she peppered him with questions.

Salla had little time to study it, let alone know its properties. He had suspicions as to its origins and how someone's government probably manufactured the stuff. But he needed proof to substantiate any allegation. He took a long drink to clear his throat.

"I received a blood sample and a note from a nurse visiting another village upstream," he told her. "In her note, she stated some people floated into their village on a ferryboat, dead. They had... well, it sounded like... it might be... hemorrhagic fever."

Salla had hesitated to say the last two words. Simply saying the words, "hemorrhagic fever" struck as much fear in the hearts of those in Central Africa just as the word "cancer" strikes fear into the heart of a newly diagnosed patient. He stopped speaking for a moment to gauge her reaction.

"Ebola?" she asked, wary of the answer.

"I know what you're assuming, but this is not Ebola," he told her. "To tell the truth, I don't know what it is. The structure is similar Ebola, but this virus appears to be some kind of fast-acting variant, perhaps... it could be tailored. I found the victim's blood riddled with the stuff. You linked with me, so I put the virus on hold. As I walked from the lab, I heard the explosions and the power went out across town. That's about it."

"How bad are things... on the west side?" Filla asked.

"Bad," he simply stated. Salla linked to her everything he witnessed, the killings, the torture, and the bodies.

Filla closed her eyes and waved her hand. She could not tolerate any more of his recall. She took in a deep breath.

"I'm so sorry you had that experience," she commented. "After seeing that, I'm amazed you survived. I'm glad you're here, though."

"Me, too. What happened here, Filla? How did this start?" he wondered.

Salla sensed she might be holding back.

"From what I could gather, the whole thing started at the river," she began. "Apparently, a messenger asked at a local bar about the location of the lab and said he had a specimen to deliver. Shortly after he left, several people began to bleed to death right in front of everyone inside the bar. Panic set in. Rumors spread that the military brought the virus. A mob formed and headed toward the garrison. Other people in different locations broke out with the disease. Before the infection could spread, the mob fanned out and started to kill or destroy anyone they suspected as having the sickness. Fortunately, the major headed straight for the regional governor's house and ordered his troops to open fire on the mob, otherwise… you saw in front of the house. When they gunned down some of the mob's leaders, the rest fled on foot," she told him.

"The regional governor demanded that the major restore order," Filla continued. "Since the gunfire destroyed our dinner, I went to the kitchen and made sandwiches for the guests. I just brought out the first platter when you showed up," she explained. "What could have started the resurgence of this disease, Salla?" she asked her knowing husband.

Salla put down the sandwich. After he realized all that happened, he lost his appetite as well. He looked off toward the river. The night sky had turned a sickly yellow with the light of burning fires.

"I don't know," he confessed. "I don't believe the sample spread the disease. The nurse put it in a sealed container. The messenger may have been immune and carried it to Gao, but I doubt it. I have a strange feeling the disease originated from the river water. It may be moving downstream and spreading the disease with the current. If that is the case, the government and the military might be helpless to stop the spread unless we can obtain international help," he commented.

"The commander called for the garrison from Segou. I fear they will never arrive," Filla added. "If it is as you suspect, all traffic along the river route will be contaminated."

Filla paced away from Salla as she thought through the problem.

"It's up to you, Salla," she said as she turned to face him. "You have the best laboratory on the continent outside Cairo. We can set up runners to bring you samples of river water. You can compare those elements to the virus you found in the blood sample. Perhaps you can come up with some sort of correlation," she suggested. "I know it's too early to develop a treatment…"

"The lab, Filla," Salla interrupted, "It's on the west side of the bridge and unprotected. What will happen if the mob destroys it? They were headed in that direction."

"What do you suggest we do?" she asked.

Salla reached into his pocket and pulled out his black card.

"I thought we should contact the WPO or Camille for help. Perhaps, I can send them a sample. I left everything back at the lab. I won't be able to do anything without my equipment! I've worked so hard to obtain that equipment. If it's destroyed, Filla, all the years of research and results I've worked so hard to achieve will be lost forever," he linked.

Salla seemed to lose sight of answers. He could only picture the mob destroying his precious building and burning it down.

"Salla, look at me," Filla took his face in her hands. "I love you. I know your research means everything to you, sometimes more than I do."

"You know that's not true," he weakly protested.

She shook her head and smiled.

"I wish that were true but you and I both know it isn't. At any rate, we must be practical, Salla. If this new 'moballa' virus is airborne, it may be too late," she observed.

"You saw Nurse Beluna's note from my mind?" he asked.

She nodded. "What will happen if the virus starts to spread through the countryside? Do you think we are immortal? Our own lives may be at risk," she observed. "Those people inside that house will turn into preservationists when it comes to their lives versus ours. This is a time for survival, and you must survive. Do you understand?"

Tears flowed down his face. He slowly nodded and pulled her close.

"Oh, Filla. I'm behaving like such a fool," he confessed. "You are the most important thing in the world to me."

"I know you love me," she quickly reassured him. "You and I must go to the lab at once and salvage whatever we can," she thought. "Then we should have a contingency plan if the crowd attacks and the military cannot restore order."

Filla began to pace. "If the virus is in the water, we can't travel by boat on the river. We'll need a reliable car that can quickly traverse some of these roads, whose condition you and I both know is tenuous at best."

Filla glanced across open yard to the side area of the regional governor's house where the guests parked several vehicles. The sentries were not guarding them.

"The major's car is a heavy duty military vehicle from America. They say it has a very long range due to its capacitors and the ability to use different sources of fuel. I say we use our powers, take the major's vehicle, and head west to the ravine. After we avoid the crowd and go to the lab, we take the south road to Tacharane. Then we use our cards..."

A huge explosion rocked the ground. A giant fireball, in the direction of the military base, rose above the eastern edge of the city in the form of a mushroom cloud. This time it did not sound like ignited fuel. The percussion sounded like a bomb. The explosion lit up the entire countryside and broke some windows out of the houses. Several explosions quickly followed the large explosion. Each one shook the ground like the pounding from a thunderstorm. The couple watched as the major and his staff ran out the back door to witness the source first hand. Several officers stood in the doorway behind him. A foot soldier ran up to them.

"Major! They hit the ammunitions depot," he shouted. "I've just received a report that a gang of thugs has broken into the base!"

"Shut up, fool!" the major yelled back, "You want those idiots inside to hear you?"

Salla turned to Filla with a determined expression on his face.

"I say, let's take his vehicle right now and head over to the lab," Salla suggested. "I may not be able to save my equipment, but I must save my computer. If we get there after the lab is destroyed, I'll have nothing." He shook with emotion. "Years of research, Filla, down the drain and lost forever!"

In his imagination, he pictured a senseless angry mob broke into his lab and smashed the place up. Seeing the events unfold within his mind, Filla grabbed Salla's arm. She pulled him through the side yard toward the driveway and away from the back of the house.

"I agree with our plan," she said as they walked faster side by side. "We need to make our escape. If the military can't take control of this situation, they may only save a handful of dignitaries, if that. A hospital administrator is probably very low on the priority list. You've convinced me. Let's go... now!"

They burst out of the backyard through the bushes onto the governor's driveway, just as another explosion rocked the area with its percussive blast. All the soldiers stared eastward at the sky while Salla and Filla quietly moved inside the major's vehicle. Filla knew that once they started the car, its loud rumbling engine would give them away. They would only have seconds to flee before the guards heard them and rushed them. She went to reach for the keys. They were missing.

"How will I start it?" she turned to Salla.

"Filla! Use your mind," he motioned to the ignition. Like Salla, Filla was a Level III psychic, unable to create a psychic bubble but capable of incredible power, most of which she and Salla seldom used.

"Here goes," she said and closed her eyes.

The car's systems and motor sprang to life. Sure enough, one of the soldiers turned toward them when he heard the engine.

"Stop!" he yelled. He pulled out his side arm and took aim at the driver. "That belongs to the major!"

Filla stamped her right foot down and decided to use the heavy-duty vehicle as a battering ram. The soldier leapt aside to save his life. Before other soldiers knew what had happened, the vehicle fled into the darkness. Several shots rang out but the bullets only "pinged" off the back windshield.

"Bulletproof! Huh!" Filla said as she smiled.

Despite the soldier's gunshots, Filla made good their escape. At the first street, she turned left to avoid the roadblock at the end of the next block. She knew the military did not have enough men to guard every street, so she took as many side streets as necessary to avoid the main streets. As she headed west, she wondered if the tough vehicle could pass the next obstacle, the steep gully around the dried riverbed. If the rainy season hadn't finished months ago, escape this way would be impossible through the river. With less than a meter in depth, she could traverse the water without a problem in this behemouth of a vehicle.

"I can hardly see," Salla complained.

However, Filla did not dare turn the headlights on for fear a stray gunman or a soldier might spot them. She peered through the darkness. She knew this street came to a dead end at the gully. A caution sign indicated as much.

"You'd better slow down," Salla cautioned.

"I will… soon," she answered.

"What about the…" Salla started.

"…ravine up ahead?" she finished his sentence. "We're about to find out."

Chapter Fifteen

A Man of Mystery

Salla decided he should feel grateful that his wife could drive this monstrosity. Its size alone challenged the lab bound scientist. Yet, Filla seemed at home behind the wheel. Before Salla could probe as to why, she sensed his question and revealed the answer to him.

"I didn't have time for a download, so I took the knowledge about this 'truck' from the major's mind," she said as she smiled. "I only hope I don't become lost in the dark."

"I hope nothing can penetrate this armor," Salla said as he recalled how the bullets bounced off the bulletproof glass.

He also noted what appeared to be reinforced armor around the vehicle. Essentially, this vehicle represented a tank in comparison to the heavy-duty vehicle that Salla used to drive around Gao on a daily basis. That brand of car was known for its toughness, another present from Camille. This big thing served one principle purpose – survival. At least, they felt safe inside it.

Filla slowed their speed down until she finally came to a halt.

"What is it?" Salla asked as he leaned forward. A light flashed off to their right. Another house burst into flames and partially lit their way. Salla could barely see the bottom of the riverbed. The water moved so slowly it had an almost mirror like quality to its surface. The sides appeared rather steep. "What are you doing?" Salla gasped. "We're not going to make it!"

"Are you kidding?" she said, matter-of-factly. "This kind of heavy-duty vehicle is made to go anywhere! You need to get out of the lab more, Salla," she exuded with confidence. "Buckled in tight? This is going to be steep."

She slowly moved the large vehicle over the lip of the gorge and gradually eased the great lumbering wide vehicle down the steep decline until they leveled out on the relatively flat streambed below. The large-wheeled, heavy-duty vehicle crept over the rocky wet river bottom with ease. The water never came close to the bottom of the doorframe. Filla proceeded to drive up the opposite steep incline on the other side. The rocks and debris in the riverbed would have hung up any other vehicle with a low clearance. This tributary, expanded by their country's engineers many years ago, prevented flooding in the city during the rainy season.

Up the other side they crept, the low-ratio gears and powerful engine pulled the versatile vehicle into the western section of the town that lay adjacent to the Niger River. This street ran due west, parallel to the central street through town. Filla used to her mind to turn off the engine. They lowered the windows and listened.

"Seems quiet," Salla cautiously and optimistically spoke.

"Too quiet," Filla added. "Let's get to the lab."

She started the car and floored the accelerator pedal. She sped as quickly as she dared in the direction of the lab. Filla turned the vehicle onto the southbound road and headed toward Salla's laboratory.

"No sign of the mob yet," she linked to him.

"Yet," he agreed as he nervously gripped his seat.

The southwestern section of the city appeared untouched, though the couple noticed the street lights out. This made the surrounding countryside exceptionally dark with details difficult to make out.The houses appeared deserted. Filla wondered if people had heard the disturbance and already fled the district.

"Where is everyone?" she wondered aloud.

She did not take the time to scan the area with her mind. Instead, she concentrated on the area around the lab ahead. She aimed the speeding vehicle for the gravel parking lot in the back of the building. Although the outside power appeared out, Salla had emergency generators inside that kept the lab's freezers working for days or even longer if he used the solar cells on the roof. The thick metal and concrete walls with hardly a window in its structure made the lab more like a fortress. Its only weak point, the front entrance, usually was staffed with security. Unfortunately, Salla was certain that no guards could keep back a determined mob.

"With the power off, is your…" she wondered.

"The system automatically switches over to power generators," Salla reminded her.

"You were worried about the lab? This place looks more secure than the rest of the city," she commented as they pulled into the back lot.

Something troubled Filla. She sensed danger.

"Do you feel that?" she asked. A feeling, like a chill, ran through her body and spooked her. She decided they had better hurry.

"I don't sense anything," he told her.

"Just go inside as fast as you can, grab whatever you need so we can leave," she pleaded. "Please, Salla. Don't take too long. I can't tell where these people might be. You know how difficult it is to penetrate an angry person's mind. I'm safe as long as I stay in this vehicle. Hurry up!"

She fired off her comments as she put the major's vehicle through its paces. She geared down, spun the wheels, and turned them around 180-degrees on the loose gravel.

"That major must have some mind," Salla commented as the vehicle skidded to a halt. "You learned that maneuver from his mind?"

"You don't want to know what was in his mind," Filla quipped back as she shut down the engine.

"Use the power station… if that thing has an adapter," he pointed toward the station that kept his car charged.

"It does," she answered, and jumped out her side to hook it up.

Salla leapt from the vehicle and ran straight for the locked private door at the back end of the building. Nervously, he fumbled with the keys as he tried to insert the right one into the door. In the far distance, he heard a scream followed by a gunshot.

"Why am I so afraid?" he thought as he tried to calm down. "Filla's right. I see no sign of the riot here. I need to stay focused on my task."

He took in a deep breath. The key slid easily into the slot at that moment and Salla pushed open the door. On the wall to his left, he put in the code that shut off the alarm system. He noticed at once that the alarm was switched off and the security station at the front door was deserted.

"Where is security?" he wondered. "Why isn't the alarm on?"

He was certain he turned on the lab's automated systems when he left. Security had the codes but they would not have shut it off. The blinking yellow lights on the control panel indicated loss of outside power to different areas of the lab. Only the incubators, specimen freezers, and the refrigerators remained green. They held his samples and, in some cases, their antidotes in the form of vaccines. Salla switched the remainder of the lab over to the emergency power generator located in the substructure. The whole panel turned green. This restored the emergency yellow hall lights and some of the lab's other functions.

"That's odd," Salla noted as his eyes noted one other light already green. "I wonder how the microscope room switched over. It shouldn't do that automatically," he thought. He reasoned that someone from security must be in the building. Only they could perform such an action. However, he saw on the panel's video screen that the front desk security station was deserted.

Salla walked through the building toward the electron microscope. Of all the things he had to leave behind, he cherished his microscope the most. As he slowly pushed open the door to the room, he could see the distinct bluish-white glow of the microscope's screen fill the room with ambient light.

"I know I shut that off..." he thought as he pushed on the door.

"I'm glad you decided to return for your computer, doctor," a deep voice spoke. "It saves me the trouble of having to find you."

Salla stopped dead in his tracks, gripped by fear.

"Please, come in, Doctor Motambou," the deep voice spoke again. The tone had the most compelling sound.

He cautiously pushed the door all the way open. A huge figure, outlined by the light coming from his beloved electron microscope, sat in a chair, hunched over the display screen. A very large black man wearing a long dark trench coat over his wide body frame stared at the image of the tailored virus.

"Fascinating structure… you managed to find it right away," the man stated.

Salla made several rapid observations. He could see part of the figure from this angle. This man seemed a little too clean, a little too perfect compared to other people from Mali. Underneath the trench coat, he wore a hand tailored suit made from some remarkable cloth, unlike any he'd seen in Mali. The cut of his clothes resembled the men he worked with years ago in Oxford. He noticed the man spoke with a cultured English accent. Obviously, this man worked for someone outside the country, perhaps sent here to contact him. Salla tried to probe his thoughts, yet found to his surprise, he could not penetrate a very solid mental block.

"Do you know what this is?" the man asked, never turning around.

Salla saw the picture of the specimen he prepared earlier in the evening on the screen. He forgot to erase the digital pictures from the memory. The answer to this mysterious virus seemed tantalizingly close. He wondered what this stranger knew. He pondered over its mode of transmission.

"Is the virus in the river water? How could it survive in the water? Perhaps insects transport the virus. Parasites?" Salla wondered as he peered over the man's shoulder. He suddenly felt a chill regarding the man's volatility. "This man is very dangerous," he sensed. He became concerned for Filla's safety. Before he could think anything else, the man spoke with the same commanding voice.

"Are you going to answer me?" the man asked. "Or should I begin by throwing out a guess or two? I'm waiting, Dr. Motambou."

His voice sounded menacing, as if he could easily carry out a threat.

"Who are you?" Salla asked.

The man pushed away the swivel screen and stood up. He threw back his shoulders and flexed his muscles. He was a very large and imposing man. Salla stood close to 200 cm in height. This man's head appeared nearly 20 cm above that. When the stranger turned around, his position placed his face in shadow, far above the glowing screen. Salla took a deep gulp as he stared upward. His throat instantly grew dry with fear. The huge figure seemed threatening.

The man relaxed his posture and spoke in softer tones.

"I work for some very knowledgeable and concerned parties, Dr. Motambou. These people admire your work and need your help. A virus is on the move. You are an expert in the field. They want to know what you know, the minute you know it," the man said with a slight touch of sarcasm. "Your current work has great potential."

"Are you some sort of spy?" Salla privately and instinctively surmised. "But for whom?" he thought as his head cocked over to one side.

He stared at the man for an instant. His mind kept changing its focus. He thought he would try a different tact.

"Mali can't afford a secret police," he said aloud to the man. "They can barely afford to pay the military every week. Who do you work for?"

"Let us say, I work for a rather unusual organization," the man said quietly. He had not moved from where he stood.

"I've never seen a Russian or an American in this area. Therefore, you must work for some other western government, or the opposite side, like China," Salla said as he shuffled slightly closer to try to see the man's face.

"You're a very clever man, Dr. Motambou. We like to think we're the good guys," the man said with an ominous tone. "You know, stopping terrorism or people who are on the bad list this year."

The huge figure of a man bent his large frame down so that Salla could at last see his face. He had a large black face, very much like Salla's, and yet, his features seemed foreign. The man was definitely not from Mali, he decided. Behind his very large brown eyes, Salla could sense a man of mystery.

"He's performed many clandestine operations," he thought. "Traveled to many countries, broken into buildings, and taken files," he detected. "He's also killed others when ordered to," Salla felt, "without remorse."

Bits and pieces of this man's personal history leaked out of an imperfect block.

"His mind must be disciplined in the eastern art of focused attention in order to partially block my probe," Salla thought. "Although he displays signs of being psychic, he hasn't received a conversion from Galactic Central or he would know how to block better," he quickly reasoned.

Except for the few details, this man's mind remained virtually blank, except one aspect of the man Salla could detect.

"So… you are a NATO spy," Salla spoke when he saw it in the man's mind, "and they sent you here to find me, is that it? That seems a bit fantastic. How did you discover this disease so quickly? Were you part of the promised convoy on its way along the river road?"

"You are indeed as intelligent and perceptive as your file indicates, Dr. Motambou," the man spoke reassuringly. "I haven't encountered anyone quite like you."

Then he reached over with his big arm and turned on a lamp. It's deep golden light filled the room and brought out more details about this stranger. Salla could see at once, he definitely wore finely tailored European style clothes.

"You might say, I'm a scout, sent to scope out the situation and report back," the large man said. He stepped forward and reached around Salla to push the door closed.

Salla slid to one side and allowed the man to do so. He felt that if the man was going to kill him, he would have done so already, or would do so soon once he had his information. However, Salla had a hidden asset. While he spoke, he opened a telepathic link to Filla and filled her in on the stranger.

"How did you sneak past my security?" Salla requested.

"Breaking in is a specialty of mine, doctor," the man of mystery stated.

Salla did not press the issue. He was certain that if he probed deeper, he would discover his security officers were probably disabled or dead.

"What brought you here? Uh, to my lab, that is," Salla asked. He was still curious to find out what the man knew and reluctant to start discussing his theories about the new virus.

"Hemorrhagic fever is on the rampage, doctor. Yet, this virus behaves unlike any form of Ebola on record. Don't you agree?" the stranger put to him. "It struck upstream three days ago. The world is not aware of this. Those with the power to do so, cut the lines of communication to the outside world. The Malian army is in chaos and cannot regroup."

The large man turned around and stared down at the screen again.

"Judging from the date and time of this entry, I'd say you received this specimen today and examined it for the first time this evening. I'd like to know if you've made any conjecture as to its properties," the man asked.

He very calmly and deliberately put on a pair of disposable gloves. He reached inside his jacket and produced an unusual flat gray device about the size of a cigarette case. He squeezed its sides, reached in with two fingers and pulled out the blood sample that Salla thought he put in the freezer. The man held one test tube up to the light. Salla noted other tubes, with clear substances, inside the carrier. He wondered what they contained.

"I don't know how stable that sample is. I'd be extremely careful if I were you," Salla warned the man.

"You didn't use many precautions when you examined it earlier, yet you stand before me, unaffected. Why, Dr. Motambou? Haven't you asked yourself that question?" the large black face seemed to press forward on Salla's more timid presence.

"I'm not certain how the virus is transmitted or how it enters the blood stream," he confessed. "I'm not even certain how long it lives."

The large black man stood up erect, as if he were stretching. He replaced the tube, closed the gray apparatus, and placed it back into his inside jacket pocket. He glanced around the room as if searching for something.

"You are not alone tonight," the man suddenly stated. He turned toward the direction of the parking lot. "Is Filla outside, waiting for you?" the man asked and glanced over at Salla's face. "You should never play poker, doctor. I've been trained to read faces. Is Filla outside?"

"Yes, she is," Salla confessed. "Please don't hurt her, I beg you..."

"Rest assured, hurting either you or Filla is the last thing on my mind tonight, Dr. Motambou. I'm actually here to help get you out of the country."

Salla sensed he told the truth. Relief spread over him.

"We need you," the man said, "and you need this. Your laptop computer," he pointed out. "Its memory must contain your research. What a mistake to leave it behind."

"I can transfer all the stored data from the microscope's memory into the computer, if I may," Salla asked the stranger.

"Go ahead, doctor. I'm not here to hinder you, but to make certain you survive," the big man pointed out. "You might be the only person on earth with the necessary knowledge to stop the spread of this disease."

That last statement, Salla sensed, was a lie. Yet, he decided not to challenge the big man.

The stranger moved to one side and took out a small, hand-held shiny silver object. He flipped open the lid and a screen came on. He turned his back on Salla and began to touch the surface. Salla sensed he put some coded numbers in as signals to another party. He was not a mathematician, although well versed on the subject. He could not decipher the coded message he heard made up of numbers. While the man said he would not harm him, Salla did not trust him. He sensed a dark purpose to this man, as if wickedness and evil were aspects of his personality.

Salla reluctantly moved to the microscope and transferred the last of his data files before he wiped the microscope's memory clean. He also grabbed a portable testing kit that he often used when out in the countryside. He might be able to perform rudimentary tests in another location while he waited for supplies.

The man's screen rapidly flashed a series of numbers. He closed the device and returned the thin object to his inside jacket pocket. He turned around and spoke in a hurried voice.

"We have to leave, now, Doctor Motambou," the man stated. "According to the satellite observation, a large crowd is heading this way. Unfortunately, I cannot stop them. They will probably destroy your lab."

"How do you know that?" Salla asked.

The large black man ignored him. "Take you computer and whatever else you need. We should go. I will inform your wife," the man said as he started to open the door.

"That won't be necessary," Filla spoke up. She stepped into the doorway and pointed a gun at the man. "Stop right there or I will be forced to shoot," she said with a slight quiver to her voice.

"I can assure you, Mrs. Motambou, I am here to help you, not to harm anyone," the man said, slightly unnerved by the sight of the gun. He glanced around. "The crowd is approaching. You know that fact, too. We all need to leave. Please, allow me to do my job and help you."

"You just show up inside a locked laboratory, barge in here, take whatever you want without any explanation, and expect us to trust you?" she blurted. "We don't even know who you are? You've not shown us any plausible credentials," Filla stated as her grip on the gun grew stronger and her voice confident. "You're a spy for NATO? I've never heard of a NATO spy!"

Salla moved around the man and quickly crossed to his wife still holding the gun. The man's face twisted into a puzzled expression.

"How do you know about Salla's comment regarding NATO? Is this room bugged?" he gazed from one face to the other. He carefully reached inside his jacket.

"I know how to use this. I'm a crack shot," she told him.

"Yes, you are Filla. If you will just give me a chance, I'll answer your questions," he requested.

Filla pulled back on the firing pin and made the pistol ready to fire at a second's notice. She aimed directly at the right side of the large man's chest.

Slowly he reached in with one hand and produced an official document about the size of a checkbook. The inside had his picture and a three-dimensional holographic symbol of the NATO seal.

"I can assure you, my identification is quite genuine. I do indeed work for NATO as Salla guessed," he told them. "I've just informed my superiors where I am and that I've contacted you. If you shoot me, they will have a pretty good idea who did it."

Filla reaffirmed her grip on the gun.

"If I had wanted to take this information by force, you would not have been able to stop me, Mrs. Motambou," he told her. "Believe me… I could have ambushed you. I am not here to harm you. I am here to help you."

He gazed right into Filla's eyes. She read his thoughts for that moment and felt the sincerity of his words.

Finally, after several tense moments, she lowered the gun and everyone in the room including Salla, breathed a sigh of relief.

"Where did you get the gun?" Salla thought to her.

"The major's glove box," she thought back.

"He had a gun?" Salla queried.

"I sensed it the moment we got in the vehicle," Filla linked to him. "For being a psychic, Salla, you don't seem to know what's going on around you." She addressed the stranger directly. "We don't know your name. You could tell us who you are and what you intend to do next," she said pointedly. She still held the gun in her hand by her side.

"My name is Reginald Atwater," he said and inclined his head. "Most of my friends call me either Reg or Reggie. My superiors sent me to ask you about Bamako. Evidently, the news has not reached this region or you would have known," Reg spoke matter-of-factly. "I have the only line out over a scrambled network. I speak code to my superiors. Authorities cut all other forms of communication three days ago."

"Three days!" Filla gasped. "Did you say that this disease struck Bamako? I wondered why my calls were not answered."

"They couldn't reply," Reg explained. "All lines of communication out of Bamako are cut off… radio, satellite, telephone, cable, cellular… everything is out, kaput, finished. The city was in chaos. The airport tower had no power. They dropped me by parachute. I volunteered after they pumped me full of drugs. I was to investigate why someone cut off the sudden calls for help. The central government's last signal cancelled all flights in or out of the country. After two US military helicopters crashed, they restricted helicopters and all flyovers. Within hours, all activity in Bamako ceased. I found no one in the city alive."

Filla glanced down and read his name on the document that he held in his hand. She nodded and acknowledged the ID as genuine. Reg put his credentials back inside his jacket pocket.

"I took a car and drove along the river road. I ran into the same thing in nearly every village that I passed… dead bodies everywhere. Fortunately, I remained unaffected as I made my way here. I'm not certain if I simply avoided the plague or if I am immune. Tonight, when I arrived in Gao, I saw the flames and heard the explosions. I assumed the mob ravaged the village as the plague spread. I realized it was impossible for me to reach the hospital. I avoided the mob and headed straight here," the agent continued. "The front door was open. Your security staff must have fled for their lives. I found the security panel and activated this room. Not knowing if you were still alive, I came here to salvage your work. Now, you know everything I know."

Filla did not know what to do next. The news about Bamako bothered her more than the truth of his story. She could only focus on her family, relatives, and the many friends who lived in Bamako. The thought they might be dead tore at her heart.

Salla sensed a flood of emotion pouring from her mind.

"We don't know who survived," he linked quietly. "Reginald only saw parts of the city. Perhaps the north end was spared. Let's try to remain hopeful." He turned to Reginald Atwater and spoke aloud. "We have family and many friends in the capital city."

Instead of sadness, anger rose in Salla as he clenched his fist. He glanced over at Reggie and his scientific brain won over his emotional thought processes.

"You suggested you were immune, Mr. Atwater," he said.

"Reggie… please call me Reg or Reggie," the man requested.

"Reggie…" Salla spoke. "Let's take a look at that immunity. Roll up your sleeve. I want to test your blood," Salla insisted.

He went to the cabinet to obtain blood-drawing supplies.

"Salla..." Filla protested weakly, "you're forgetting the mob."

"Dr. Motambou, we don't have time, sir. My superiors said a large group of people were heading this way!" Reginald protested.

"Do want the whole world to succumb to this disease?" Salla suddenly burst out. "Damn the satellite and damn the unruly crowd! I must know more about your blood chemistry!" he said nearly seething.

Salla never lost his temper. Filla realized the news about Bamako upset him. She had not seen him this passionate in many years.

"I'm asking again," Salla continued, "roll up your sleeve! This will only take a few minutes. Did you lock the front door?"

"I did…" Reg told him.

"That front door can repel most gunfire and I doubt they have any explosives," he declared.

Salla picked up a sterile package, tore off the paper cover and produced a large needle. He screwed one end into a device and picked up some test tubes. Before Reggie could protest further, Salla pushed up his sleeve, quickly swabbed his skin with alcohol, and plunged the 18-gauged needle into Reg's fat protruding antecubital vein. First one tube quickly filled, then another, and another, and still another.

"I need you to be my guinea pig tonight," Salla muttered.

"Whoa! Doc! Are you trying to bleed me to death!" Reg said as his eyes widened with apprehension.

"Buck it up, soldier," Salla tossed back. "Consider this one of the hazards of the job. It's going to take a bit of blood to isolate the compound you possess, which makes you immune."

Reggie grimaced and started to sweat.

"Don't let a little needle scare you," Salla said as he took a cotton ball and pushed it over the puncture site. "Hold your arm up and press this over that puncture for a minute. I'm sure your clotting factor is just fine. I'll be right back!"

Salla ran up the hall to the blood testing equipment room at the other end of the lab. He had analyzers that could produce results in a matter of minutes.

Reginald Atwater gulped as he glanced from his raised arm over to Filla. He started to ask her for an elastic bandage in the container next to her. However, the beautiful African woman started to fall apart. She dropped the gun to the floor and collapsed as she broke into deep heaving sobs. She knew the virus killed her mother. She could feel it. She wondered why her mother did not answer her calls or reply by message. She had not seen her in nearly a year. She and Salla had planned to fly to Bamako next month.

"I know this is small consolation," Reggie spoke quietly. "I'm really very sorry about your family," he said.

She glared at the large well-dressed black man through streaming tears. Her mental probe detected some form of sincerity in his voice, yet he carefully guarded his inner mind.

"It's just a shock when something like this happens, that's all," she said as she tried to regain her composure. "I'll be alright in a minute or two."

She looked around for a tissue to wipe the moisture from her face. Reggie reached into his front dress coat pocket and offered Filla his linen handkerchief. She felt the exquisite soft cloth in her hand.

"Be a shame to mess it up," she said almost playfully.

"I have dozens of them," he confessed.

She looked up at his big frame and muttered, "Thanks."

She took the handkerchief and carefully dabbed at her eyes. She tried not to smear her make-up on the beautiful woven cloth with the white monogrammed RA.

Inside, Reginald stared down unfeeling at the small frail woman before him. His hands were so large, they could complete encircle her neck. He resented the fact she had the "drop" on him with that gun. He did not sense her in the hall – a mistake he would not make with them again. He gazed at her for a moment before he carefully chose words to sound sympathetic.

"I've lost a few friends over the years. It's never easy when it happens," he quietly spoke. "Sometimes when I look back, those memories feel like an old wound that hurts on certain days," he told her.

Reg kept a far away expression on his face. For a second, Filla caught the image of a beautiful Russian woman. Then Reggie's mind went blank. This startled her as only Camille or an advanced member of the WPO had that capacity.

"How did he do that?" she wondered.

"Hey!" they heard Salla's voice shout from down the hall. "I found it!"

For a moment, they exchanged glances. Filla and Reggie leapt from their positions in the microscope room and flew up the hallway in the direction of Salla's voice.

"Come here! Look at this!" Salla cried as he motioned the two closer when they burst through the doorway. "I found a component in your blood." He stood up, not nearly as tall or large as Reg, but he squared off in front of the big man. "You were right. They administered an anti-viral drug that imparts immunity to this virus," Salla stated. This confirmed in his mind some suspicions he had about the virus, its origins, and Reggie's role in all of this.

"Just the usual shots," Reg lied.

"Shots?" Salla asked. "What kind of shots?"

"The kind they always give before I set out for these assignments. They're supposed to help provide general immunity against…"

Reginald never completed his sentence. An explosion on the side of the building cut the reserve power to the lab by destroying the natural gas pipeline. The whole building shook. The sound drowned out anything that anyone could say. The generator died and all the lights failed. The three stood in total darkness as debris shot up the hallway. Although the mob had not breached a hole in the wall, they managed to mangle a major portion of the structure.

"I guess they do have explosives!" a frustrated Salla shouted. "They just destroyed a three centimeter thick pipe!" he declared.

"Salla," Filla whispered. "They may go away if they can't gain entry."

"Go away?" Salla shot back. "Sounds like they're determined to me!"

The three waited in the dark and listened in the silence that followed. The room remained quiet with only the sound of their breathing.

"I know how the virus is being spread," Salla whispered.

"How?" Reg asked with a poker face.

"Something moving down river is spreading the disease," Salla stated.

"Why do you suspect that?" Reggie questioned.

"It's just speculation," Salla said dismissively.

At that moment, another explosion went off at the front doors, which sent shards of glass into the building like missiles. Tiny deadly fragments flew up the hall past the room where the three stood in darkness.

"The mob has arrived with vengeance on their minds," Reggie stated. "Let's go!"

All three realized in that instant that their time had run out. The mob would not hesitate any longer. They intended to rush inside. Reggie directed Filla and Salla to take whatever lab supplies they might deem important. Salla grabbed the bag that held his computer and his testing equipment. The three escapees quickly made their way down the hall to the back door that led directly to the major's vehicle.

"My Nobel medal…" Salla thought at the door.

Filla took his hand and gave it a tug.

"The next explosion could kill us," she reminded. "I can replace a medal… I can't replace you."

A group of rioters gathered around the partially broken front door – some had flashlights, some had guns, many threw rocks through the narrow opening. Yet, despite their best effort, no one could squeeze through. As the Filla, Salla, and Reggie fled out the backdoor of the lab, they could hear the growing frustration in the crowd.

"This is where the disease started!" one in the mob shouted.

"Let's burn the place to the ground!" another one added.

While Reggie and Filla ran across the lot toward the vehicle, Salla paused outside the backdoor. "I should disable the fail-safe system," he thought. The special code would take a few minutes to enter.

"No time!" Reggie told him. "The mob is moving around the building."

Salla actually feared for the crowd if the fail-safe system went off.

"If they breach the storage unit circuits…" he considered.

"Salla!" Filla yelled into his mind.

Thinking of Filla's safety, Salla gave up and ran across the parking lot to where the vehicle sat alone in the dark, plugged into Salla's charging station. Only the faint green glow around the unit, that obtained power via underground cables, remained lit. The dark flat paint tones easily hid the large vehicle with no exterior light around. Once Filla disconnected the line, the station went dark – the last bit of energy that flowed along the line now discharged.

"Nice choice of vehicle," Reg noted.

"I only steal the best," Filla replied as she headed for the driver's seat.

"Filla, give me the keys," Reggie requested. He put out a large hand in front of her. "Believe me. You'll want me to drive in situations like this."

Filla shot Salla a glance.

"No keys… she'll start the car for you," Salla told Reg.

Reggie glanced over at the ignition and shrugged. He did not want his thoughts or suspicions to betray his true purpose. The big vehicle sprang to life when he sat in the driver's seat. He calmly eased them out of the parking lot, quieter than Filla did when she drove more aggressively. She had to agree that he used more finesse than she did. The large bulky vehicle quietly moved out onto the road where Reg could get better traction. He turned south and gradually built up speed to put as much distance between them and the rioters. Finally, he hit the accelerator and the engine switched over from electric to fuel. They quickly left the lab far behind and out of side. The rioters heard the sound of the retreating vehicle too late. They fired a few shots in its direction but missed the vehicle entirely. Reggie drove as fast as conditions allowed. He did not turn the lights on until he assumed they were beyond the range of a sniper's rifle. Still, he pressed hard on the accelerator pedal to give them more speed.

In the back seat, Salla nervously glanced back over his shoulder out the rear window.

"Gee, I hope they don't break into the cold storage and trigger the fail-safe," he muttered. "I didn't have time to dismantle it."

"Did you just say, 'gee'?" Reggie asked. "No one says gee anymore."

"I hate it when you do that," Filla interrupted. "You hope they don't trigger what?" she asked.

"The fail-safe device," Salla whispered back.

"What fail-safe device?" Filla and Reggie asked at the same time.

"Well…" Salla said as he cleared his throat. "I tried to tell you before we left the lab."

"Please," Reggie requested as he tried to drive even faster. "Tell us about the fail-safe device."

"My friend," he began as he refrained from mentioning Zhiwei or Chou, "made me a special device… I did not want the microbs to leak out and cause a pandemic… therefore, it had to reach a certain temperature without being thermonuclear, you see," Salla mumbled. "I experiment with some of the deadliest viruses in the world – we equipped the lab with a self-destruct mechanism. The government knew about it. That's why I kept a full-time security staff, so they could maintain the lab's safety. I'm surprised you broke into the storage and did not activate the countdown, Reggie," he pointed out.

"I told you," Reg replied. "I break into top secret labs… you might say it's a specialty of mine."

"Anyway," Salla continued, "should someone *normal* break in and try to force open the nitrogen freezer that contains several strains of lethal samples without the proper code, it will automatically trigger a warning system with a countdown… the chain reaction will destroy any…"

However, Salla never finished his sentence. A brilliant flash of white light filled the sky all around them and lit up everything as if it were daylight for a second. Almost immediately after that, the impact of an enormous explosion rocked the car back and forth. The sound nearly shattered the windows in the vehicle. The three could see the shock wave as it ripped through the countryside. A second later, flaming debris began to rain down all around them. Reggie had to swerve to miss large chunks of burning material that fell into the road.

"What the hell was that?" he asked. "That sounded like a nuclear explosion!"

"It was… nearly," Salla muttered. "So much for the lab…"

Reggie looked into the mirror at Filla. They both glanced over at Salla who shrugged his shoulders but said nothing.

"I guess the mob received more justice than they bargained for tonight," Filla reflected. Although she had little sympathy for their fate, when she thought about the innocent men, women, and children the mob senselessly slaughtered.

"I'm glad I knew what I was doing when I broke in," Reggie uttered as he pushed the vehicle to its limit. He did not detect the fail-safe device when he disposed of the security guards or carefully bypassed the security on the locked freezers.

As the big vehicle quickly made its way south, no one spoke any further about the lab or the disease. Instead, the two occupants of the car's rear seat wondered about their next move. While Reggie concentrated on the road, Filla nudged Salla.

"Take out your card," she linked to him.

Both psychics slipped their communication cards out and placed their fingers on the front. Filla tried to keep watch on Reggie as she quietly sent a message. Salla sent a quick message in another direction before he put his card away.

In Paris, Camille reclined into the soft faux-leather surface of her limousine. The hour grew late. She had not heard from Filla at all today, no message, no well wishes, no results of the fund raising party in Gao. She was worried. She been to the theater with an old friend, but skipped out on a late dinner and party with her friends. She made an excuse and decided to retire alone this evening. She asked Charles if he would take her to one of the townhouses she owned.

"Please leave a call to Louisa," she requested. "She'll want to know where I am."

"Yes, Camille," he informally replied.

While relatively still young and handsome, she had never crossed that line and slept with her chauffeur. They often spoke and talked about love or lovers. Yet, she considered him more like an older brother than her chauffeur. She was sorry she had to watch him age while she never grew any older. Of course, she had to make her face age normally for appearances sake. Yet, no matter how many years passed, the great French Industrialist would never age thanks to Cecilia's serum coursing through her veins that imparted perpetual youth.

At that moment, she sensed a call coming through her black card.

"Excuse me, Charles," she said and put up her limousine's privacy screen. She slipped the thin device from her purse. She placed three fingers on the front. She smiled at first when Filla's face appeared.

"I was wondering when you were going to…" she began.

"Camille!" Filla's thoughts urgently called to her. "Something terrible has happened. We're in danger and need your help! The citizens of Gao have taken to the streets. There are riots and death everywhere. A terrible disease causes rapid hemoptysis and people are bleeding to death. Salla and I are travelling south along the Niger River away from the scene …"

Reggie glanced up in his rearview mirror. He could not believe what he saw. Some weird kind of screen expanded in Filla Motambou's hand and she bent her head over it, as if she were communicating. He realized this was a rare opportunity to possess advanced technology. He expertly let go of the wheel while he steered with his knees. He quickly spun around and grabbed the screen from her hand. It instantly crumbled into dust in his fingers.

"What the hell?" he muttered.

As he struggled to make sense of that, Salla reacted with amazing speed. He pulled out another small thin black card and pressed it against Reggie's hand. It instantly turned into dust. Salla glared at Reggie. He had a fierce yet helpless expression on his face. In that moment of uncertainty, Reggie let his guard fall. Filla stared at their driver with fear in her eyes as she could now clearly read his mind and his intentions.

"Go ahead, blackguard," she told Reggie. "Salla and I know who you are. We also know your mission. Carry out your orders."

With both of his large hands, Reggie, the consummate professional, swiftly slammed the heads of the Motambou's together before they knew what hit them and rendered them unconscious. Unfortunately, for the paid assassin, he did not see the car that pulled into the road at that precise moment. A second later, the air filled with the sound of screams and twisting sheet metal.

Chapter Sixteen

The Enlightened Ones

THE SUN DISC HAD RISEN only an hour ago on this quiet day in late April of 2024. Life in the non-exisitant village of Rollo, Kansas continued as had since its founding in 2016. An eager group of children sat around a teacher in the park adjacent to the school on Main Street, focused on her every word. No teacher could hold its class with such spellbinding rhetoric as could Su Lin, no matter the age of her pupils. In the medical clinic on the other side of the park – the site of the old general store – two patients waited in the open lobby to see the local physician, Cecilia Beaton-Tyler. While many knew the "gifted ones" could instantly cure many maladies, this young woman had repeatedly proven her ability to handle real medical emergencies and tackle diseases that needed a doctor's special wisdom, counsel, and intervention.

Throughout the village, workers streamed off to their daily assignments. Some helped to maintain the three park ecosystems that held unique living environments – the forest environ on the southside, the pond/river environ on the north side, and the park off Main Street, which held a variety of flowering plants, bushes, trees, and gardens. Villagers also worked on a variety of construction projects that continued the transformation of Rollo village. With each generation born to the Native Americans, new homes went up, couples formed new relationships, and the complexity of life expressed itself in the form of controlled growth within the confines of this special yet isolated slice of humanity in southwestern Kansas, oblivious to the world around it.

"Look out!" an outsider might cry out if they saw one of the floating vehicles silently cruise up the street. No matter the speed, should something sudden appear in its path, the restraining devices on the platforms would hold its occupants while it immediately came to a halt. Available all over town, every resident had several parked near their home. The identical platforms whisked the local residents from one location to the next in complete safety as they hovered 21cm above the ground.

The houses of Rollo never needed to be cleaned. A city circulation system cleaned the dust from the air and recycled the contaminants into its fusor, which offered a balance of oxygen, carbon dioxide, and nitrogen into Rollo's air. The trees never lost the majority of their needles or leaves, only those needed to recycle their plant material. Special formulas kept plant life in the same perpetual state with no genetic change or alteration, since the stable climate and the chemical inducement introduced through their water supply kept them in that condition. The air temperature never changed from a balmy 21.2 C (about 72 degrees Fahrenheit) with fifty-five percent humidity in the air every single day.

The sun disc moved into the nine o'clock position. Rollo buzzed with activity. Zhiwei kissed his Comanche wife goodbye, opened the day shift of security, and had his morning breakfast with his crew, Selena and Jennifer. They reviewed the computer's reports regarding the World Psychic Organization while they slept. Had any emergency occurred, the computer would have roused Zhiwei from his sleep. He kept his black card on him at all times. His wife and assistants knew never to touch the unique gift given to him by his friend, Chou Lo just two days after Rollo's technical wizard turned on the fusion-like device for the very first time in the fall of 2016. They held similar but different devices that did not rely on psychic energy to activate.

Michael Tyler had already finished his rounds of Rollo. After he shared an early breakfast with his lifemate, Cecilia, he headed out to walk from location to location and inspected every part of the village. He took personal requests, asked about people's lives, and examined every sewage, water treatment, or recycling systems on a daily basis.

In the large underground complex that held Rollo's flyers and built the ground transportation system used by all of its residents, Villi started to work with his crew, Edward and Victor. The two young men lived inside the complex on a floor just above the control tower. Their love interests – Zhiwei's assistants Jennifer and Selena – often visited the two males inside their cozy place. Likewise, the men would sometimes trade off by one of them spending the night at Jennifer and Selena home in the village. Unfortunately, someone had to "man" the huge underground complex 24-hours-a-day in case of an emergency mission.

Zinian, head of Rollo's construction division, currently directed his crew on two projects. He and his men had to update systems on three homes and they continued their work on the parks' recycling systems, which needed special care to maintain such uniquely conrolled ecosystems.

In the enormous structure at the east end of Main Street, two wise and powerful men sat in the morning room, as had been their routine since they occupied this great building in the fall of 2018. Master Li and Han had only just finished their wonderful breakfast created by their chef and companion, Running Elk, whose culinary mastery no one could question. They silently walked through the vast hall to the structure's most interesting room.

In the library of the building known locally as the manor house, one man sat in high-backed, green, leather chair of which nine were arranged in a semi-circle around the front of the large fireplace. He stared at the glowing fire of burning wood, an illusion he created with his incredible power. The image of the fire provided a diversion for him. Its shimmering bed of orange coals and yellow flames licked the sides of large round perpetual logs that rested upon a large, beautifully shaped, wrought-iron grate. This image brought to Master Li's mind a timeless historical method of primitive man's way to fight back against his entrapped world of cold and darkness.

"Michael Tyler…" he whispered, "The lesson of Michael Tyler…"

He brought the edge of a porcelain cup to his lips and sipped his hot green tea with lemon and a touch of honey. Master Li, who normally contemplated his world, his life, and everything as far as his all-encompassing thoughts could entail, focused on one detail today, his pupil and friend Michael Tyler. He marveled at how their lives had changed since a ten-year-old boy kept going in the face of great adversity. For when that boy grew up, he made the wise decision not to commit suicide on his twentieth birthday. Instead, on that fateful day, Michael listened to the voice that had plagued his mind for ten years. He allowed the voice to change the ruffian into a new man. Nearly a year later, he journeyed thousands of miles around the world just to find an old Chinese man whom the young man woke from a seventy-year slumber.

"Has eight years passed since we arrived in Rollo, Kansas?" Li's mind reflected. "Eight years…"

"Is that what occupies your mind today?" another voice spoke aloud into the vastness of the library. He overheard Li's mutterings. "Of all the things you consider, you've chosen to dwell on the life of Michael Tyler? I thought you were contemplating the meaning of the universe or some such rot."

Li smiled at his friend Han's comment.

"That was yesterday," Li quipped back. "For some reason, I'm thinking about Michael today."

"He has been on your mind lately," Han stated as he perused the shelves for a particular title.

"Yes," Li replied.

"Do you wonder why? Perhaps it is this new construction proposal of Michael's?" Han offered. "The size of this house, which was no small feat, pales in comparison to that monstrosity he contemplates," he commented.

"Perhaps that is it," Li again replied absently.

On the second level of the mansion's most impressive room, Han Su Yeng, master strategist and trusted friend of Master Li, reached out with his mind. He finally found the book he needed, one that might shed some light on his current feelings. The unique book, made of pressed linen paper and hand written – whose pages and form predated "printed books" by centuries – was snatched from destruction by one of Master Li's time travels. Han floated the object over to his hands. He strolled down the narrow walkway along the wall of books that ascended nearly 17 meters (55 feet) on this side of the room. He slowly descended the lavish, black, wrought iron, spiral staircase to the floor of the library with the book in his hand.

"Which of the one hundred axioms in Aesop's "Philosophical Discourses" is relevant to our situation?" Master Li asked of Han. "That, to perpetuate the species, humanity must share common purposes? Or is it, in order to achieve a mutual goal to benefit society, we must form cooperative ventures?"

"This Aesop from Lebanon was certainly ahead of his time in many ways," Han thought as he moved toward the fireplace. "By your question, do you infer some of Aesop's conclusions relate to your particular inquiry?"

"No, I meant to imply the case of our living situation here in Rollo," Li answered, "the one Michael envisioned."

"So, I'm to be included in your thoughts?" Han asked.

"I seem to recall we have an open society," Li tossed off. He clicked his tongue and expressed his frustration. "I don't know what is wrong with me. I simply cannot stop these reoccurring images of Michael."

"This coming from our all-knowing spiritual guide," Han muttered.

"Mmm," Master Li nodded his reply.

"All you can think about is Michael's past and how it relates to our present?" Han wondered.

The orange glow from the fire reflected in Master Li's eyes as his lips turned upward at his friend's comment.

"The human world knows nothing of what we've accomplished these past eight years," Li reminded Han. "We've amassed a great deal of knowledge and an immesurable treasure trove of historical artifacts. Imagine how differently the world would appear if Michael took the rogue path. He was certainly tempted in New York. Would we be here if he had? The Shi-Tien would most certainly have destroyed you and I would have perished from a broken heart. Now consider the paths of other rogues. What would have happened if they carried on without our interference? Michael chose the moral path and that has made all the difference for us, for humanity."

"True," Han replied as he walked toward Li.

"Since those first days when we arrived here in Rollo, no one has faltered in their progress because we chose to take this same moral stance," Li continued. "Even with our advances, the world continues… stumbling around, blind, making mistakes…"

"You've managed to mention our local psychic group," Han said as he reached for a sugar biscuit to go with his tea. "You cannot leave out the influence of our overseas members… or…"

"…or mention the children?" Li said to finish Han's thought.

"Yes, the children of Rollo's psychics," Han pointed out. "Five years ago when we returned from Australia, some of us started to turn out little psychics… powerful beings…"

"Yes…" Li's voice faded as he contemplated the children's impact on their community. "We cannot begin to predict their impact on humanity."

"One thing is certain, we all feel their power," Han related. "I've never felt such unique psychic signatures in any of our membership."

"All five are very powerful psychics," Li concurred.

"From this beginning, we've been able to create a very fine existence, one I would never have believed possible," Han stated with pride.

"Fine existence, true. However we may face new challenges ahead," Master Li spoke quietly as he stared at the flames.

Han glanced over at his friend. He sensed that Master has seen something. Perhaps he had been to the timeline recently and looked at the forbidden future made up probabilities. Perhaps he saw some forboding event and could not share it with him, Han speculated.

"Messing with the future again? What *challenges* are you referring to now? What have you seen?" he asked.

"You know I can't tell you that," Li reminded him. "Knowledge of the future can change…"

"…alter present history," Han broke in. "How many times have you spoken those words? Why must you taunt me so with these tantalizing tidbits?"

"I can tell you this," Li's eyes lifted. "For the past eight years, our community has enjoyed relative peace, prosperity, and obscurity. We took every precaution to create this perfect place. As far as we could tell, the outside world is not aware of our existence, giving us a feeling of safety and security." Suddenly he slammed his open hand on the arm of the chair. "We have been living in a fool's paradise! Any day now, we could be attacked and my master strategist hasn't a clue of its origins!" Li exclaimed.

Han slowly put down his tea and stared at Li.

"I'll take that as a warning that I've been too complacent," Han said as he stared over at his friend. "Does Zhiwei suspect a breach in our defenses?"

"He has been complacent, too," Li pointed out. "The world is a changing place, Han. These humans are clever people. They've been secretive and inventive. Their level of technology has changed."

Han floated his cup, saucer, and plate over to the tray. He rose from his chair.

"How much time do we… do I have?" he put to his friend.

"Time slips away quickly," Li muttered.

"Allow me a day or two of contemplation," Han requested. "Do I have that much time?"

"Barely," Li said and dismissively waved his hand.

Han preferred quiet contemplation to any further conversation that might cloud his thoughts. The master strategist walked from the library while he brooded over a problem, which he could not fathom. However, he considered that a challenge.

"I must assume that what we have to fear is… everything," he thought as he headed toward the north greenhouse.

Chapter Seventeen

The unofficial Mayor of Rollo

"Exlkd lskdi lskh xx?" the Xiltilian said. Galactic Central instantly translated the meaning of its utterances to, "Why does your culture expend valuable resources on weapons and security forces?"

Michael sent his reply via his voice in Galactic Central.

"As you know, we do not pursue that course," he linked back to his alien friend. "You speak of the planet's population in general. I will try to explain some these strange aspects of human nature. Ours is a violent world, full of natural forces that make extreme and rapid changes," he told the scholar. "Violence in our environment has influenced our evolution as a species, reflected in our propensity toward violent acts. You should recognize this by now, Yuii."

Yuii, the principle curator of the Artane Intergalactic Library, admired and respected Michael's quick mental grasp and homespun philosophy.

"For some in your history that is true... yet this 'survival of the fittest' axiom has its downside, does it not?" the great scholar challenged Michael's logic. "Your Indigenous Native American population lived in relative peace, until the European settlers..."

"They warred amongst themselves..." Michael interjected.

"... without the use of gunpowder and with fewer casualties," Yuii concluded.

"I see you've amassed more knowledge on the human species," Michael chuckled.

"The study of Earth occupies many of my underlings who pass their information to me," Yuii replied. He referred to the thousands of fellow creatures who performed the vast majority of the research.

Artane, the largest city on Xiltil, is renown throughout the Intergalactic

Psychic Collective (IPC) for its magnificent central library, perhaps the largest in the universe – a city that houses trillions of works in hundreds of buildings. Psychics from all over the universe frequently tapped into Artane's vast resources.

Just then, Michael felt a contact from Master Li.

"Sorry to interrupt, Michael," Master Li's soft voice entered Michael's mind. "I need you here, as soon as possible."

"Oh, I beg to end the audience, Yuii," Michael interjected. "I must depart. I would link in two cycles of your large moon, Een. Do you agree?"

"Agreed, two cycles," the Xiltilian quickly replied. "Good-bye, Michael Tyler of planet Earth," it formally concluded.

"May Een's moonlight always shine on Xiltil. End transmission from Earth," Michael linked from his side of the mental conversation.

Galactic Central terminated the conversation between the two worlds, which freed the two voices to assist psychics on other worlds.

Michael Tyler rose from one of Chou's floating lounge chairs. All the psychics used them when going on extended missions through Galactic Central. This morning, he spent two hours visiting four different planets after he sent his son and daughter to school and made his rounds.

Yuii and Michael previously interacted via their voices several times over the past eight years. For his part, Yuii gained further understanding of a new species whenever the two met. He catalogued each encounter as part of a larger "chronicle" he intended for the library, entitled "The Humans of Earth" by Yuii, Head Librarian. He made a subcategory in regards to the individual psychic humans, especially Master Li.

When Michael rose from the couch, he checked in with Cecilia, before he made his way out to Main Street.

"Master Li called," he linked to her. "I'm on my way to the manor house."

"Busy... I'll link with you later," she linked back.

He walked out his front door, made the short stroll east along Main Street for about thirty meters, before he crossed the mostly deserted street that once marked the eastern edge of town to the large structure clearly visible outside his master bedroom's bathroom window. Michael loved the WPO headquarters building. After all, he drew up the first designs. As Chou often expressed, "any excuse to visit Han or Master Li in that maginificent place was a good one." While the Rollo psychics stayed busy with their own projects, they always enjoyed any request for a meeting with Master Li.

"I do love this place," Michael said as he approached.

He crossed the wide piazza with its massive fountain in the center and walked toward the huge front entrance bordered by rows of tall white columns. A thudding knock from one of the knockers on the heavy ornate door announced Michael's arrival. Before any of the house staff answered, he stepped through. White marble with jewel accents adorned the floor of the entryway. Michael proceeded into the cool interior. He shut the heavy door behind him with his mind.

He turned left, away from the grand staircase under the rotunda, and walked along the green-carpeted hallway toward the towering doors on the left side of the hall that marked the entrance to the library. He raised his hand to rap politely on the thick, carved and polished wood, when a voice interrupted his action.

"Come in, Michael," Master Li linked. The huge doors to the library silently and slowly eased open.

Only the orange light from the fireplace illuminated the long dark room. Michael silently crossed the thick woven rug toward the one man in the world he respected more than he did any other. He bowed next to the high-backed chair.

"I open my mind to you," he spoke formally.

"And I accept it," Master Li replied.

"I came as soon as I could get away," Michael linked. "Yuii and I had just exchanged thoughts, when your request came through. How may I be of assistance, Master Li?" he asked. He remained standing.

The light from the fireplace cast deep shadows on the room's high ceiling, barely penetrating the great dark space. Master Li's eyes appeared sunken into his aging head as he stared at the fire.

"Please, sit next to me, Michael," Li motioned.

A highly polished, solid silver tea service from 12th century India sat on a beautiful marble-topped table between them. With his mind, Li poured the green tea into a delicate 9th century Chinese porcelain cup for Michael. He added a swirl of honey and placed a slice of freshly cut lemon next to the cup on the saucer.

Michael started to sit when he noticed two exquisite vases on the mantle. He moved closer to them.

"Something new?" he asked as he reached up to examine one.

Master Li leaned forward with a pained expression on his face. He wanted to grab Michael's arm to stop him. Michael sensed Li's anxiety and withdrew his hand. He glanced back at Li, puzzled. His eyes traveled back to the vases and he carefully examined their ornate exteriors.

"These didn't come from the Library at Alexandria, did they?" Michael asked.

Master Li took a deep sigh before he quietly linked the next part.

"The vases are Ming Dynasty porcelain, a recent acquisistion, very unique, very old, and very fragile," he linked and gestured toward the objects, still a bit anxious about them being touched. "The vase on the left is empty. The vase on the right contains the ashes of the Chinese philosopher, Wang Yangming. He once stated, 'Under heaven, nothing exists but the mind.' Powerful words that strike close to home, wouldn't you agree, Michael?"

"Perhaps these need a force field around them," Michael suggested as he sat and picked up his cup of tea. "Why the special meeting? You scheduled dinner this evening with Cecilia, Villi, and Su Lin in the dining room. I was looking forward to Running Elk's latest masterpiece. Is it something important, Master Li?" he asked as he sipped the warm brew.

Li seemed on edge. Rather than express his concerns with words, he started to link his findings over to Michael. As more information filtered into Michael's mind, he grew fearful for his family and all of Rollo. Finally, Michael could not take any more. The subject overwhelmed him.

"Stop!" he cried out.

Master Li halted the images.

"Have you shared these concerns with Han or Zhiwei," Michael wondered. "We must act on this at once."

"I thought you'd say that," Li sadly shook his head. "We must exercise on the side of caution before we act. I fear other forces are at work," he cautioned, "... outside forces."

"Master Li?" Michael questioned.

Li turned in his seat to face Michael. He had a worried expression on his face and took hold of Michael's arm in his hand. "You must see all sides of this," Li instructed, "or I fear great harm will befall us all. I am about to share something with you that you must share with no one. Understood?"

"Yes, Master Li," Michael softly answered. He understood that Li was about to impart something he knew about the future and could not trust this information with anyone except his pupil, not even Han.

"First, I must tell you that Zhiwei received a disturbing message from Camille Ossures. She passed on a message from Filla..."

"Filla and Salla Motambou?" Michael questioned. "Is Salla mixed up with this?"

"She gave Camille a warning. I went to the timeline and... what I am about to show you will not be easy to take... I have seen things... terrible things... things of a horrific nature," Li warned before he linked them.

Michael nodded he was ready. He gritted his teeth and struggled against the rising nausea in his stomach as Master Li's repulsive imagery flooded his mind.

"Africa... virus... river... mobs... violence... blood... blood... blood!

Chapter Eighteen

Horrorific Vision

A worried Master Li paced in front of the fireplace and occasionally glanced over at his pupil. Li wondered if he overexposed Michael's peace-loving mind to excessively graphic and violent images; such images he felt could damage a person's psyche. He wanted to apologize to Michael and make amends. He only meant to convey what had transpired in Africa and the warning contained in Filla's message.

Michael could only stare at the floor. He shook all over as if shivering from being too cold. Occasionally he urped, as if he wanted to vomit.

"How does Zhiwei do it?" he finally said. "How can he look at such horror so dispassionately?"

When Master Li mentally offered to reach into his mind and comfort his pupil, Michael waved him off. He sat up straight and took in a deep breath. He meditated for a minute in an attempt to restore a calm state.

"Michael... I wish to apologize..." Li began.

"You're concerned I experienced emotional scaring? If I feel the need, I'll consult our local psychiatrist and physician," Michael said as he recovered. "I believe I can easily arrange a private appointment," he sarcastically added. "Meanwhile, this calls for action. You must convene an emergency meeting of the WPO board, Master Li," he advised, "including Camille."

"I agree, Michael," Li responded. "I will contact everyone... including Camille, if you believe her presence is required. As soon as I obtained this information, I thought along similar lines. I... I simply wanted your opinion first," he told Michael.

"You mean this has to do with Ha..." Michael began.

Li held his finger to his lips He reached out with his mind across the room.

"Don't you agree, Han?" he asked.

"Han?" Michael wondered and twisted in his chair. "I did not detect his presence when I walked in."

"You weren't meant to," Li informed him. "Han wanted to judge your reaction."

"But what about the link…" Michael privately linked to Li.

"We'll discuss that later," Li quickly linked back.

Han sat on the settee in the dark across the room. He purposely kept the lamps off. Master Li called him back to the library just before he contacted Michael. Li told him, "Watch, observe, say nothing, keep yourself blocked." Han had not seen Zhiwei's report. When Li exposed Michael's mind to the message Filla sent, he also included Han on that part of the link. The master strategist had seen plenty in China. This information did not strike him the way it did Michael. He had his eyes closed and thought intensely over how this related to Li's revelation earlier in the day that someone in the outside may have breached Rollo's security. Yet, after Li simultaneous shared Filla's mental images, he could barely control the same reaction Michael had: disgust, revulsion, and nausea.

"I need a moment to recover," Han told them.

Li reached out across Rollo and contacted Zhiwei.

"Meeting tonight," he informed the head of security. "Pass it on."

The sun disc began to drift into the lower portion of faux western sky when Cecilia left the clinic and walked up Main Street toward home. She tried to alert the children telepathically. Curiously, they did not respond. By the time she opened the front door, she understood why. Michael did not meet the children after school. Two pairs of scuffed shoes blocked the front door along with their backpacks, dropped the moment they ran inside the house. Dirty dishes still sat on the kitchen table from this morning. Both Mark and Sandra scattered their dirty laundry around the floor in every room. Their toys were lying everywhere. She sensed the children had not eaten or bathed.

Mark, five, and Sandra, four, returned from Su Lin's school two hours earlier. They had been alone in the house the entire time. Cecilia could hear them screaming and laughing, jumping up and down on the beds upstairs, glad that no parents were around to enforce discipline. Cecilia, to put it mildly, was upset. She reached out for Michael but could not find him. Her concern and worry caught Master Li's attention. The moment he linked with her, Cecilia knew exactly where Michael spent the past few hours. She realized why she did not have access to him. Master Li blocked her from contact. She assumed his interaction with Li merited this isolation.

"Meeting at eight," she heard Li briefly say.

She contemplated bringing the children to the meeting at the mansion, when Michael's voice came through.

"Master Li is about to make an important international link. He wants you in on this contact. Can you stop what you are doing and join us?" Michael thought to her.

Cecilia stood at the top of the staircase. She stared at the mess in the middle of the bathroom, wet hand towels on the floor. The sink was a mess. The children draped their dirty clothes everywhere but inside the hamper where they belonged. She took in a deep breath. Instead of being angry or upset, she simply gave up on the feeling.

"I suppose I can," she thought back to Michael.

She noticed the children up the hall still playing in their bedroom, a game called dodge-the-flying-object, which Cecilia did not appreciate. Sandra and Mark made random objects fly about the room. The goal: avoid being struck by an object. However dangerous the game might be, Cecilia had other troubles this moment.

She sensed a tone in Michael's link that resembled fear, profound and unshakable fear. She linked with the children. Mark and Sandra stopped playing at once and stood still. They sensed their mother's strong presence in their minds and listened.

"Mark… Sandra…" she linked to them. "Mother is taking a special mind link with Master Li. Please do not disturb us. This is very important. Dinner will be a few minutes late this evening. I need you to help mommy by being calm," she told them.

"Yes, mother," the two children quickly responded.

When their mother mentioned "Master Li" in the link, the children immediately stopped giggling and paid close attention. Every psychic, including the youngest child, knew that communication with Master Li was usually very serious. Every psychic, no matter what age, recognized the power of Master Li. He never contacted anyone unless he felt it important. The children understood this without an explanation from their mother. Cecilia sensed a block go up around their room, one of the very first things the parents instructed them to perform since being a psychic in the womb.

Sensing her isolation from them, she turned her focus toward the great house and closed her eyes. Master Li and Michael stood amidst a cloud. They patiently waited for her. The shroud around her lifted. The vision of both men turned sharp and clear. Only Master Li could make something like this possible with the assistance of Michael and Cecilia's psychic energy. Li also isolated their psychic signatures from the rest of Rollo.

As if on cue, the three linked minds turned their attention to the east. The strong presence of a woman rushed into their minds. A form took shape.

"Master Li," the woman's voice sounded distant. "Michael, Cecilia."

"Camille," Li answered politely.

A tall woman with a slender build stood in their midst. As she walked closer, they could clearly see her lovely familiar face. No woman ever impressed the eye more than Camille Ossures. She deeply bowed.

"Thank you for responding so quickly," Camille started.

All three psychics could detect anxiety in her thoughts.

"I am so worried," she continued. "I take it you've seen Filla's message."

"Yes…" Li replied. "She sent you some graphic images."

"They still haunt my mind. Yet, I fear something worse happened."

"So it would seem."

"I contacted the Mali consulate. Travel to Mali is now restricted," she continued. "Mali cut communication with the outside world. I tried to contact Gao through French diplomatic channels but they gave me the same story. NATO forbids any flight over Mali air space. What should we do?"

Li turned to Michael and Cecilia.

"Unite and share your energy with me," he requested. "Join with us, Camille, in passive mode. I will guide our way."

Master Li's ethereal body flew across the globe to the continent of Africa and entered the landlocked country of Mali. His floating astral body scoured the countryside. As Li's body flew down into the capital city, they saw hundreds of Bamako's residents lying in pools of dried blood, their bodies bloated and rotting in the sun. Li blocked any other senses such as smell and the sounds of buzzing insects that preyed on the corpses.

"What is this?" Cecilia moaned as she started to waver, "This is extremely gruesome…" she said as she struggled to suppress her nausea.

"Steady now," Master Li broke in. "Remember you are the world's best physician. Treat these images clinically," he instructed.

Li's astral body moved swiftly down the river and arrived in Gao seconds later.

"Their residence is on the east side of the city," Camille pointed out. "The hospital is over that way, too. Salla's lab is near the river on this side of the bridge."

Master Li searched the city and found the African couple's home, but he could not sense either Filla or Salla. Many buildings had burned to the ground. The mob heavily damaged the hospital. They found a barricade on the west side of the bridge draped with dead soldiers, all appeared to have bled to death.

This time Cecilia did not feel nausea, the soldiers presented fresh evidence of a terrible yet natural event.

"This is a disease process... it could be hemmorhagic fever," she speculated.

"I have a feeling the Motambou's are alive," Li thought.

His astral body floated toward the river when they saw a large crater partially filled with water.

"Uuuhhh!" Camille gasped and sucked in air. "I believe that was Salla's lab!"

"Look," Michael pointed out, "car tracks leading away and headed south. Unless I'm mistaken, just before the explosion, judging by the debris on top of them," he observed.

Li's ghostly form quickly moved along the road for a few miles before they came across the scene of an accident. A large dark heavy-duty military vehicle had crashed into a car that had pulled into the road. The large vehicle smashed the car and killed the occupants, their dead bodies still inside. The big vehicle sat empty... abandon. The accident had disabled it. All at once, Li's black card in Rollo started to beep. He accessed a security sequence and the card spoke...

"...remnants of previous WPO communication card presence at site," the computer voice blurted.

Master Li must have inadvertently accessed its scanners and it analyzed his visual scan of the vehicle.

"The Motambou's black cards!" Michael spoke up.

"So they were here... and in that vehicle, too," Camille surmised.

"We have to assume so," Cecilia echoed.

"Do you think the accident... I mean, they could have..." Camille could not acknowledge that the accident may have killed them.

"Easy, Camille," Li linked as he attempted to soothe her. "I'm familiar with Salla and Filla's psychic impressions. I believe they were in this military vehicle during the accident. Yet, I perceive no evidence of their death here. They've moved on."

All four psychics took in the scene. From what they could make out, the dead passengers in the car had tried to leave Gao by the south road when the military vehicle struck them. The evidence for that was clear. However, the disease caught up to them at the same time. They saw one ghastly dead face after another with dried blood dripping from mouths and nostrils and faces frozen in grotesque masks of terror.

"The trail has grown cold... I can barely sense them." Li calmly stated. "Far to the south..."

"Where could they be?" Camille cried out.

A torrent of emotion poured out of Camille's side of the connection.

"Camille... calm down... I can't sustain..."

Suddenly, she broke away, and the French side of the connection stopped. Master Li turned his attention to Michael and Cecilia.

"Don't forget, Cecilia," he told her, "eight o'clock. I'm keeping Michael here."

Master Li and Michael withdrew. Cecilia stood alone in the untidy hall as she blinked away the horrific images.

"I won!" Mark yelled.

"You did not!" Sandra yelled back.

"I'm hungry!" Mark called to his mother.

"Me, too!" Sandra echoed.

"What's for dinner?"

"Yeah, what's for dinner?"

"Shut up!"

"No, you shut up!"

Two toys simultaneously barely missed the heads of each child as they attacked one another.

"Mom!" Mark loudly linked.

"Mom!" Sandra chimed in.

"Michael?" Cecilia quietly called out with her mind, yet she received no answer. Master Li prevented their communication.

Cecilia did not wish to confront her unruly children this evening. She feared that their powerful little undisciplined minds would see the images from Africa. She was tired and could barely form a block. Instead, she reached out to Zinian. She thought he might offer some help.

"Zinian?" she called. "I need your help... please?"

"Cecilia?" he responded at once.

"Can you please come over to our house?" she requested.

"I'm in the shower," he replied.

"I need you," she requested. "I can't raise Michael. He's with Master Li. I could use some support."

He knew from her tone that Cecilia needed emotional support. He jumped from the shower, made the water fly from his body, and quickly gathered up some clothes. Zinian's wife waited in their bedroom with some folded clothes to put away. When she saw him rush through the bedroom and urgently struggled to dress, she knew that Zinian acted on some special mental message he received.

"What's going on?" his Native American wife asked. "Who is calling for you?"

"It's Cecilia," he told her. "She linked with me and sounded desperate," he explained. "Something's going on over at the mansion."

"Do you want me to come, too?" she asked.

"I'll call if I need you," he replied as he quickly tucked his shirt.

"What about our supper?" she asked him. Rollo residents each had daily tasks. She made specialty breads and pastas. She traded those for other parts of meals her neighbors prepared.

"I'll throw something on a plate before I go," he told her and then hesitated. "I don't mean to run out," he said as he stood before her. "Look, I'm sorry…"

"Believe me, I understand…" she said and started to turn away.

He took hold of her arms, turned her back, and kissed her tenderly. When he pulled his lips away, he tried to explain.

"Cecilia sounded terrible… almost in pain. This must be very urgent or she would not want me to come over so quick," he told her. "Thank you for understanding. I'm very lucky to have you," he said and held her close.

"I'm the lucky one," she said as she slipped her arms around him. This time they kissed with greater passion. She had never known a lover like Zinian and doubted she ever would. She pushed him away. "If Rollo's doctor says something is urgent, she knows what she means," she said to him. "You'd better hurry."

Zinian paused as he gazed into his wife's eyes.

"I'm certain Master Li is involved," he confessed to her.

"Oh," she replied. Everyone knew that dealings with the old Chinese man up the street could be very stressful. "Give my love to Mark and Sandra."

Inside the manor house's library, three men contemplated the new information from Africa. The moment Camille withdrew on the French side of the connection and Cecilia withdrew on the Rollo side, Michael took in a deep breath. He tried to review the facts based on their observations. He rubbed his eyes and glanced over at Master Li. Li needed a few minutes to recover his energy. The eighty-three-year-old psychic replenished psychic energy from their Native American source.

"Han?" Li finally called out. "Did you see what happened?"

Both men sensed Han in the background during their link with Camille. They knew the master strategist would have monitored the connection. Michael turned around in the chair and noticed Han held his expanded card in his hands. His fingers touched the screen several times. When he did not respond to Li, the elderly psychic turned to the man next to him.

"Michael," Li finally linked, "I have a favor to ask. You may refuse if you wish. I fear the people of Mali and our two agents are in grave danger. I believe they are alive, yet..."

"I'll go… I'll go to Gao at once!" Michael blurted out. "We have no agents in Africa except Tahir. I understand he is in northern Iraq with Seel and Tabor working to infiltrate a renegade tribe of terrorists. Of course, I'll go to Africa!"

"No one said anything about going to Africa," Li murmured.

"I thought you wanted me to rescue Salla and Filla. I'm certain I can find them," Michael stated.

"Confound it, Michael; for once give me time to formulate a plan!" Li said with a frown. "What about Cecilia and the children? Surly you don't want to leave them alone."

"You're going to need someone with the ability to adapt in foreign environments," Michael retorted. "You know my history. I have more experience than any psychic on the planet. I'll study the maps and find the quickest route. Villi can drop me along the Niger River. I should be back in a few hours!" Michael said triumphantly.

Li studied his face for a moment and shook his head.

"I love your enthusiasm," he linked while he suppressed a smile. "The mission to Africa is unlike any previous attempt of resolution. This case presents many complex levels and some mysterious unexplainable forces at work," Li pointed out. "First, we must consider the environment. Viruses are tiny and undetectable. They can easily invade a body. If airborne, they would kill you before you got two miles inside Mali. A psychic shield will keep out most harm but it will not keep out a virus."

Michael relaxed his posture. He had not considered that.

"I'm open to suggestion," Michael offered.

"Let us consider two possibilities," Li continued. "Someone or something has blocked the psychic signatures of Filla and Salla. I cannot detect them or trace a route to their body. Since they did not fall through a rift in space, I must assume someone is blocking their power. If that is the case, we may be dealing with an extremely dangerous individual or group."

"You believe they are alive," Michael questioned.

"Galactic Central informs me they detect their heart rate and breathing, but that is all," Li stated. "There is another explanation. Perhaps as Filla suggested, the Niger River carries a deadly virus, bacterium, or even a parasite that rapidly enters the bloodstream. If it is new, they may be in a coma enroute to a hospital," he contemplated.

Li stared into the fireplace, the yellow flames licked up the side of a golden log with a shimmering bed of orange coals underneath. Michael could sense Li's mind working.

"However, if the disease is airborne and we fly the team into Mali," Li reasoned, "we could breathe in the virus without being aware of its presence... even with all of our technology. Filla and Salla have fled south toward Niger. If they follow the river road, their position will constantly change. Others may be fleeing as well. The roads will be jammed with refugees. Satellite surveillance will not help. We'd have to sift through thousands of images… and that will take too much time, even for our computers."

"If the river is carrying the disease, why follow it?" Michael questioned. "Why not go away from it?"

"It may be the fastest way out of Mali," Li countered. "If we are going to find them, we should approach from the opposite direction, by moving up the Niger River. Hopefully, we shall find them as they head downstream."

"We'd have to navigate the river system upstream," Michael added.

"…and for that, we'll need a powerful boat," Li suggested. "That is why I want every psychic here tonight for a roundtable discussion," Li insisted. "We need their expertise."

"I'll ask Star Wind to watch the children," Michael suggested. "By the way, what did you mean, *we* are going to find them? You're eighty-three. You haven't been on a mission since we went to Australia. You're not thinking of going…"

"Of course I'm going," Li quickly responded. "You don't think I'm staying here, do you – with our friend's lives at stake? Besides, I've never been to this part of Africa."

"Just a minute," Han's voice interrupted. "I have something to say about this cockeyed scheme that you two have begun to concoct. I happen to be a voting member of the WPO," he spoke with aplomb. "The vote must be unanimous… remember?" At that moment, Han rose from the dark end of the library and walked toward them. "I just left an emergency meeting with Yuii…"

"How on earth did you arrange a meeting with Yuii so fast," Michael wondered. "It takes me weeks…"

"I have connections in high places," Han said and glanced over at Master Li. "I find it unconscionable that men with your intelligence would attempt any strategic plan without the master strategist's input," he said as he sat next to Michael. "I can see that I'm back just in time and the news – as you feared Li – is not good. We not only have a leak in our organization, metaphorically speaking, the crack has spread and the whole foundation is about to give way," he told the two surprised men. "Gentlemen, the WPO is on the verge of collapse… and from its supposed strongest part, it's center."

"Han?" Michael questioned.

"They dangle the bait," Han continued in riddle fashion, "therefore, we must bite. It is predictable. We must not only go to Africa. We must prepare to do battle with a diabolical mind… and one who has planned this operation for a very long time. This is methodical from every aspect. We have one dilemma," he said as if he weighed an object in each hand and he was the scale, "that will outweigh another. The way ahead is fraught with peril and difficult decisions. Either way, we affect the future… or it affects us."

Han looked at Master Li when he made the last statement. Michael glanced over at Master Li, too. The powerful man looked back at Han and Michael before he nodded.

"You are correct. This is a two prong problem that requires a fight on two fronts," Li linked.

"… and we may only fight one while we lose the other," Han added.

"Perhaps," Li commented.

CHAPTER NINETEEN

RETURN OF THE STRIKE TEAM

THE KITCHEN STAFF QUICKLY CLEARED the dining room table and withdrew. The doors sealed shut. The room quieted. The group seated around the table turned toward the man at the head and waited for Master Li to open the official meeting after the group finished a wonderful meal prepared by Running Elk. Anticipation ran high. Villi, Su Lin, Zinian, and Chou did not have access to the information shared by the rest of the group. Yet they could sense more of the unspoken during dinner than what was linked in friendship.

"The time has come for us to come together and link minds," Master Li said.

The lights dimmed. Master Li bypassed Zhiwei, Han, Michael and Cecilia while he enlightened the rest of the group with what took place in Africa. Audible gasps of revulsion echoed around the room as the ghastly imagery filled each mind. After a few minutes of review, Master Li broke the link and brought the lights in the room back up.

"I see why Michael had such a poor appetite," Villi linked to Su Lin.

"I'm feeling a bit nauseous myself," she linked back.

"As you may surmise," Li told them, "a rescue effort to find Salla and Filla will take a team of experts. Zhiwei has informed me that our satellite indicated the presence of a highly contagious micro-organism in the air over Mali's capital, Bamako. Due to the extreme danger involved, I will not order anyone on this assignment. This is strictly volunteers only. Han..."

Han took the three-dimensional projector used for the Australian mission and set it up in the middle of the dining room table. The planet Earth floated in the air around them as realistic as could be... and this one in real time, since Chou launched a series of satellites with Kiran's catapult. Han reached in, pulled out the continent of Africa, and enlarged the west coast before he resumed his seat. Master Li used his finger to trace a yellow line on the projection.

"Can't we track them from space?" Villi asked before Han spoke.

"The roads leading south away from Gao are choked with refugees. It could take us weeks to pinpoint their location. By that time, they could be…" Han replied.

"I believe the simple answer, Villi, is no," Li interjected. "Han has devised a systematic search to find the Motambou's."

"I propose we enter at the mouth of the Niger," Han said and made a yellow "X" on the coast of Nigeria. "Gradually, we can make our way upstream. We can examine the environment along the way and hopefully meet the Motambou's as they make their way downstream. We feel that is their most logical route and the original direction they started when their signal stopped. Since Mali and Niger have few major highways, the river is the quickest route away from the plague."

Master Li looked around at the concerned faces.

"As I stated, since we are dealing with many unknowns," he linked, "this journey is not without considerable risk. That is why I am only asking for volunteers."

Li signaled Han to turn off the globe. He brought the lights back up and waited for a response. Very quickly, several members exchanged brief thoughts that turned into a jumble of thought. Li cleared his throat.

"One at a time… please," he requested.

"If some of us are going to Africa," Zinian spoke up, "then we will need equipment, lots of equipment." He looked over at his friend, Chou. "Do you have something that will go up a river and transport a few of us… in style, of course?"

The young man, once typified by his frumpy dark hair and glasses (no longer needed), now had perfect eyesight. Chou began to contemplate some of the major equipment pieces he would need to fabricate. He took out his black card, a variation of the one he gave everyone else. He tapped it and looked over his inventory of devices.

"We'll need a watercraft large enough to transport a group of nine people up the river in comfort," he mentioned. "It'll have to be relatively portable, lightweight, shallow keel…"

"Just a minute," Master Li said as he broke in. "First we must discuss who wants to volunteer. I'm not certain we need the entire Rollo rooster. I'll need a minimum of four members…" he paused and glanced over at Cecilia and Su Lin. "I don't expect anyone with children to go. Therefore, I volunteer to go first…"

The entire group immediately objected to Master Li going on such an arduous trip.

"Master Li… your age…" Zinian linked.

"Your health…" Zhiwei put in.

Li held up his hands to silence their objections.

"What you say is true," Li responded. "I am old… if you call eighty-three old."

"Eighty-three *is* old," Michael spoke up. "Only one person really needs to go. I'll go," Michael interjected.

Cecilia cleared her throat so loudly that silence fell over the room.

"That's very noble, Michael," she linked sarcastically. "So you just walk out the door and leave behind a family that you say you love you very much – without any regard for your safety?" she pointed out. Before he could respond, she cut him off. "I will not be some lonely wife who waits for her man to return while he runs off to save the world. You will not go to Africa without me," she told him, "and we are not going to Africa without a detailed plan from our master strategist and some extensive back up. Master Li is correct to point out – this trip sounds dangerous on many levels."

She turned to the head of the table, her eyes pleading.

"Master Li, don't you feel we should contact the voices," she linked with additional concern. "This doesn't make sense. What happened to the Motambou's? I sense something wrong, something terribly wrong with every aspect of this entire travesty," she warned. "I feel the presence of evil behind all of this, worse than we felt in Shenyang or Adelaide," she linked.

"We cannot go to Galactic Central for help," Master Li responded, "not this time. Their hands are figuratively tied."

"No one in this room needs to go except me… I have no family… If anything happens to me, the WPO can easily replace me," Han quietly linked.

Nearly everyone in the room scoffed at that suggestion. The two ex-college roommates poked one another.

"The WPO can ill afford to lose any member," Li reminded them.

"Here, here," many in the room echoed.

"We'll go," Zinian Lang and Zhwei Huang spoke up together.

"You'll need me to fly you in," Villi chimed in. "Who else in this room can fly my latest design? None of you can," he linked to them. "Su Lin will look after the children."

Su Lin kicked Villi under the table.

"Ow!" he cried out.

"I'm with Cecilia on this one," Su Lin spoke up. "I won't stay home and baby-sit while my husband faces some horror in Africa," she protested. "If you go to face danger, I want to be by your side."

Her fingers entwined his. Villi leaned over and glanced up the table toward Li.

"S'cuse me," Villi wondered. "Why don't we just fly directly to their position in Mali or wherever they are and pick them up?" he asked, glancing over at Zhiwei.

"We can't pinpoint their position because..." Michael started to speak until Master Li held up his hand.

"Something or someone destroyed their cards," Li told him.

"Only a non-psychic could cause that to happen," Villi conjectured.

"Could be a non-psychic," Han added, "or someone not converted."

"What?" Su Lin spoke up. "You suspect a rogue?"

"I don't know, Su Lin," Han replied. "It's a possibility."

"A rogue? Another rogue?" Chou questioned.

"Didn't you hear him?" Zinian emphasized. "He doesn't know."

This new information left many wondering what Han and Li suspected to be true. Han sensed their questions and shrugged, as if to say he was as baffled as they were.

"I'm guessing," he muttered. "Sorry."

"That is why this journey needs a special approach," Master Li stated. "We have too many unknowns. Something silenced our only agents in the area. Was it a disease? Was it a person? Was it both or neither? We don't know," he said as he glanced over at Han. "Someone could be transporting our two agents while they exist in a coma. We don't know their mental state because Galactic Central cannot sense them. As to flying in, as Villi suggests, Zhiwei pointed out that some disease is airborne. The entry method is unknown. For all we know, it could enter the body via the drinking water, be introduced by a biting insect, or perhaps it is a parasite that directly enters the skin through contact. We can only assume the Motambou's are alive and moving south along the river or on it."

"Sounds like we'll need lots of specialty equipment," Chou muttered.

"Aren't we forgetting the village?" Su Lin spoke up. "Every person in this room is in the middle of project. We have responsibilities here. We can't just hop into one of Villi's flyers and leave as a team any longer. We haven't done that for years. Why should this mission require all of us to go?"

"I only asked for four psychics, Su Lin," Li insisted. "We created this team eight years ago to support our WPO members and answer the call to crisis..."

"That was before the children!" Su Lin insisted.

"Children or not, the lives of our agents are just as important," Li pointed out. "Would you let Salla and Filla die in Africa before they had the chance to sire a child?"

Su Lin's thoughts betrayed her torn feelings. She struggled to speak when Villi put his arm around her shoulders.

"You stay, Su Lin," he told her, "I will go."

"Excuse me," Cecilia spoke up. "I've wanted to say this since I first saw these images," she said as she stood up. She looked over at her best friend, Su Lin. "This is not easy for me to express," she began. "I have two incredible children. But, I wasn't ready for motherhood. I had it thrust upon me, just as any young mother does when she becomes pregnant. I've had to adjust and mature quickly to be a mother, a supportive wife, and also the town's only physician. I love Michael, Mark, and Sandra. I am proud of the work we do for the village and for our organization," she stated.

Su Lin stared up at her friend. She held Cecilia in the highest regard.

"I will not stand idly by, when the fate of the world is in question," Cecilia spoke and gestured toward the door. "What would happen if this disease spreads from Mali and travels around the world as a pandemic? It could, you know. One person is all it takes... board a plane and fly to New York. In hours, it's on our doorstep. This contagious disease could be completely out of control by the time it affects Rollo. As much as we feel special from the rest of the world, we are not an island in a sea of humanity. We are part of the human race. Master Li correctly pointed out – a psychic shield is no protection against a virus. I cannot coddle my children and pray that a terrible threat will simply pass me by when I may have the means to stop it at its source... *before* it spreads," she said, her emotions seething. "We are the core of the WPO. We are its founding members for a reason, based on our ability to adapt. No other group of psychics has formed a complex organization as we have. If anyone goes to Africa, I feel we must all go as a team, working together, combining our specialties as we did in the past and will continue to do so in the future, even if it costs our lives."

Tears ran down Su Lin's face. She closed her eyes and quietly wept out of fear for her children.

When Cecilia resumed her seat, she grabbed Su Lin's hand.

"Well spoken," Master Li added quietly. He glanced over at Su Lin.

"Cecilia is right, of course," Su Lin whispered aloud. "The vote, just like our participation, must be unanimous. We must all go to Africa if we are to be successful."

Master Li cleared his throat. He wanted to address Su Lin's fears.

"As to the children," he linked to the room, "I will not leave Rollo behind for one minute unless we have in place a system to monitor the children night and day during our trip. The parents must be able to link with their children anytime the mood strikes. Do you agree?" he asked Su Lin.

She nodded as she brushed the tears from her face.

"That would make me feel better," she weakly spoke.

"Chou," Li requested as he turned to Rollo's top technologist, "I want you to generate five special cards for the children and instruct them in their use. Star Wind will watch over them and guarantee their safety. Will this be enough?" He addressed the last question directly to Su Lin and Cecilia.

Su Lin took Villi by her other hand before she linked with the group.

"Villi and I will help our community as needed Master Li. We will go where and when you need us and do our part," she linked to them, trying to show more courage. "Cecilia is right. We all took a vow. I intend to uphold my obligation. As to my children… I trust Star Wind. They will be safe in her hands."

Villi slipped his arm around her waist.

"She's worried about Mey Li and Xiong Po," he linked.

"She should be," Cecilia added as she continued to hold Su Lin's hand. "Do you think I'd just run off if we couldn't keep in touch with Mey Li and Xiong Po? We'll find a way to watch over all of our children before we leave." She shifted toward Chou. "Won't we?"

"Absolutely," he sat upright. "Please Su Lin," he added sympathetically. "I don't wish to leave Robert behind either. He's more vulnerable than the rest. I'll try to cover every contingency. This is my top priority."

When Su Lin looked around the room, the entire table nodded her way. She could feel their empathy coming through the common mental connection. Cecilia put her arms around her and the two women embraced. They exchanged a private thought, which they blocked from the rest of the room. Su Lin forced a smile through moist eyes as Cecilia linked with her.

"Master Li," Han quietly broke in. "We spoke of this privately, however, I wish to go on record that I am concerned about your age and being able to travel half way around the world to an environment we know little about. Wouldn't you be better off staying here and protecting the children?"

"Old you say," Li responded. "Yes, it is true. I am old. However, I am not feeble." He leaned back and yawned. "I am not so ancient that I cannot move independently, wash and dress on my own, or have any physical limitation. I will go on this journey as a fully active participant. If I need any help to climb a sheer wall of rock or swim across a river, I will let you know."

Master Li drew psychic energy into his body until he began to glow. He leapt up from his chair, jumped into a handstand on the table, spun around and flipped backward landing perfectly in his seat. He held up his hands for either applause or approval. The psychics all shook their heads, groaned, and glanced over at Han as if to say, "You had to test him. Didn't you?"

"Then it's settled," Master Li continued. "Due to this emergency, I will allow team members three days to prepare. If you are not ready within the allotted time, you must remain behind. Agreed?" he asked. His gaze scanned each person in the room.

Each person replied to Li with an affirmative nod.

"Good! I have decided to appoint Michael as the expedition's official leader. He will handle the preparation details," Li indicated. His face took on a fierce expression. "I do not need to remind you of the dangers we face, as well as the possibility of unseen foes at work. We've faced terrible odds in Australia, yet we did not have the children to consider," his eyes traveled from one to the next. "We have not dealt with a major world crisis as a team in five years. Oh, there have been crises. Fortunately, our membership has stepped up and dealt with them… but never on this scale or complexity. In this case, we cannot allow the situation to continue without our involvement. The consequences of inaction are too great." Master Li suddenly withdrew his mind from the others. It felt as if he'd slammed a door shut in their faces. "You'll have to excuse me. I have other matters I must attend," he said aloud and exited the room.

Everyone at the table exchanged glances. They knew Li often made excuses to leave meetings early when his energy level began to deplete. Yet when he said he had "other matters," the group knew that Master Li would soon leave their presence. It surprised no one when shortly thereafter; his psychic signature disappeared from the mansion.

Michael rose and slid his black card onto the table. This time a horizontal yet three-dimensional image of western Africa projected into the air. It showed details of the coastline along with the local topography.

"First I wish to apologize to everyone," Michael said and directed most of his feelings to Cecilia. "After my briefing earlier, Master Li requested that I work out the details of our approach up the Niger River," he told them. "He assumed from the start that we would all be going with him… he only wanted to hear it from us."

The map zoomed in on the Niger delta system and the numerous small towns and villages scattered throughout the region. Michael indicated the path of their purported journey in red that superimposed on the map.

"We'll start by landing on this remote island off the coast and parking the aircraft there…"

"Leave it?" Villi wondered.

Michael only nodded and continued. "We'll take this main tributary at Okunbiri," he pointed out. "Of course, we may look at alternative routes depending on the vessel Chou can provide for us."

Chou brought out one of his special black cards. It expanded to a meter in width. He tabbed through several images of water-going vessels before he slowed down the images and started to pick out three or four different models. He pushed those images up to the top of the screen.

"One of these perhaps," he pointed out. "Of course, it should have a shallow draft and decent facilities," he went on as he indicated sleeping quarters and a galley. "I'll try to give you a variety of steering and stealth mechanisms, Villi," Chou said as he indicated the pilot's station. "Just tell me what kind of navigation system you'd prefer."

"Why don't you just invent some flying packs?" Zinian questioned Chou.

"Remember? The disease might be airborne? Where do we go if we suddenly encounter the stuff in the air?" Su Lin put to him.

Zinian grinned and shrugged.

"Flying packs are out! Besides, we can't maintain indefinite camouflage flying through the air," Zhiwei spoke up. "Someone would eventually spot us."

"You're also forgetting why we are going by boat," Han added. "We need to bring a large amount of equipment. The boat or raft will act as a mobile base."

"I could build a tank that would cross the country…" Chou speculated. "It would only take a few days to design…"

"Forget it!" everyone else chimed in.

"We go by boat… or raft," Michael confirmed.

"I suppose I'd better start to search the database for microbe detection techniques," Cecilia stated.

"We'll need a portable fusor, Chou. Can you rig one up inside this boat?" Su Lin put in.

"Ha!" he scoffed at her.

"Just thought I'd ask," she said and smiled for the first time since dinner.

"We need a shower, too!" Cecilia insisted. "We're likely to sweat profusely. After all, we will be at the equator."

"Ok, ok," Chou replied, growing flustered. He had to field questions left and right. Michael sympathized with the innovator.

"Can you pack all of that in there?" he put to the technologist. "Let me know if you are overwhelmed with requests."

"I can easily modify these designs… once everyone stops pestering me!"

Chou replied and glared at everyone. The room fell into silence. "It's the boat's physical requirements that raise most concerns… the displacement."

"Why is that a concern?" Han asked.

"Traveling on a river is not like boating across a lake or even the ocean," Chou explained. "A river's current can change rapidly, especially if the river bottom should shallow or if we experience excessive rain. We'll be in a boat pushing against the current, trying to go upstream, and probably carrying a great deal of weight. That will require a very strong motor to fight eddies, rocks, rapids, and other anomalies. The combined weight of our group and equipment will displace a hefty amount of water. One sharp rock can slice a hole in a boat like a razor through paper," Chou tried to point out. "Han's plan did not call for us to take the main channel, where the water runs deepest. The worst part will be to make it past the delta where sand bars shift and could ground our boat," he continued. "Once we leave the delta system, the river will deepen further upstream where flow is consistent. Unless they have a dredging operation that keeps the main river open to large boats, we'll need continual scanning information on water depth."

Next, Michael called on Zhiwei, Zinian, and Villi to give their needs assessments, followed by Cecilia's medical needs analysis and tactical advice provided from both Han and Su Lin. By the time the grandfather clock in the hall struck midnight, the group agreed to end the meeting. They broke up and returned to their homes except Michael and Han. The pair of psychics blocked themselves off from the rest of the group and headed off to discuss other considerations besides the physical journey.

Both men agreed they needed to address the elusive aspect of this problem, such as the dark figure that hovered near the Motambou's during Filla's last transmission.

"I feel as if someone has been watching our organizaton," Michael linked as he and Han settled into the library's chairs.

"What do you mean?" Han wondered.

"I mean…" he said as he looked over toward the library windows, "I have the strangest feeling the government had a spy in our own backyard. A few weeks ago when we started globe hopping again, I could have sworn I felt a foreign psychic's presence when I walked out to the hanger," Michael said. "I asked Zhiwei about it and he told me that the security computer reported no such activity."

"Neither Zhiwei nor his computer is infallible, Michael," Han replied.

"He's very thorough," Michael retorted. "I looked over the daily WPO reports. No one has encountered anything suspicious. Still… this business of Li's time travel and Africa are hardly a coincidence. Did you notice how Li allowed everyone to confirm their feelings of going to Africa to rescue WPO members from an advancing disease?" Michael pointed out. "Well… you're the strategist, Han."

"You believe this is a trap?" Han linked.

Michael rubbed his eyes and stared at the empty cold grate that earlier held a roaring fire. Since Master Li created the fire as an illusion, this usually indicated he had left the headquarters building and was out wandering the cosmos. He needed every ounce of psychic energy when he performed such feats. Michael yawned. Fatigue set in.

"I haven't slept well lately," he confessed. "I'm no virologist. Yet, something about this disease seems too convenient. If Salla recognized it, he would have warned Chou or Cecilia. He certainly would have filed a report. Why didn't they take the time to use their cards? It's as if they were caught up in events meant to go quickly. Everything happened so fast. But then, what if a new disease did evolve… just as we did? If that is the case, then everything I've said is wrong, and we should exercise on the side of caution. I don't like charging into the unknown as we did in Australia; nor do I relish leaving non-psychics in charge of Rollo. Things are different since the psychic children came along. They're vulnerable. We have so much at stake for our future. I don't care what kind of technology Chou leaves behind, I'd prefer if one of us stayed."

"Master Li believes otherwise… your wife agreed with him," Han indicated.

"I know they did!" Michael declared. "I can't believe it!"

Han could detect Michael's nerves seemed frayed around the edges. Still, Michael made some valid points. He had raised many questions.

"This trip to Africa seems more challenging than I first thought," Han said. "The hour is late. We can't decide anything else tonight. Go home, Michael. Try to sleep… talk to Cecilia about it in the morning."

He rose and put his hand on Michael's shoulder after the other man stood up.

"You're probably right. I am tired. Good night Han."

"Goodnight, Michael," Han said as he watched his friend leave the library.

Han turned to the wall where the tall windows faced the front of the manor house. With his mind, he parted the long heavy velvet curtains and watched as Michael crossed the piazza before he arrived at the corner of East and Main Streets, where his large Victorian mansion sat inside its picturesque yard. The curtain closed and Han turned toward the empty grate, wishing Master Li could somehow keep the illusion of the fire going even when he traveled offworld.

"We live in a community of psychics, Master Li is so fond to say," Han muttered. "You are not the only one who felt a foreign psychic presence nearby, Michael. I sense someone has watched us for a while only I never said or linked my feelings… and as Li hinted, we have more concerns than Africa. What other surprises are in store for us?"

Chapter Twenty

Special Preparations

"I'm supposed to be the master builder," Zinian complained. "I build Victorian mansions, parks and headquarter buildings. The, uh, medical field isn't exactly my, uh, specialty," he added as he followed Cecilia through her clinic. "I should be working on temporary shelters or some such rot."

"Michael wants us to work together," she told him. "He said we won't have time to leave the boat and bivouac. Therefore, a temporary shelter will not be necessary on this mission."

She brought Zinian inside her large nine-sided examination room, an entirely different place than the original one he built for Cecilia seven years ago. Special cabinets created by Chou's fusor sealed the room's supplies behind angular protrusions that stuck out from the walls and permanently kept their items inside fresh without an expiration date. All of the cabinets were smooth without seams. The unadorned table in the center of the room also hid devices and stayed lit from overhead, as if this were a stage. On this table, Cecilia could perform any diagnostic service including surgery. She only had to link with a device and it would interact with the patient on her command.

The moment she entered the room, one of the cabinet's doors opened and a small clear box with a sparkling interior floated out to the center table. The moment it dropped down, Zinian picked it up.

"What's this?" he asked as he held the complex device.

"Do I enter your worksite and start piecing together fusor parts?" she put to him.

"No," he chuckled and placed the device back on the table. "Sorry, I feel like a fish out of water," he linked.

"You'll be fine," she smiled.

"Why am I here? What have you got to show me?" he asked her.

Cecilia thought back to him reassuringly.

"Evidently, you and Chou have visited Ziddis far too often," she said as she held her hand over the box and it opened on its own. "They told Chou he owes them a hundred lines of code on their balance sheet. 'No more credit to help Master Li,' they insisted."

Zinian laughed, "We have made several trips recently for equipment designs," he agreed.

"He said he had a feeling I would call on him early this morning," she started.

"He had a feeling… he's always making jokes," Zinian quipped.

"Chou reminded me of a place to visit for my needs. A few weeks ago I visited the Ventax in the Selurian System to help them with a… problem they were having," Cecilia told Zinian.

"Problem?" Zinian questioned.

"Sex!" Cecilia blurted.

"Sex is a problem?"

"Their mating ritual."

"Oh… I've heard Chou mention them. He heard about them through Artane. But he told me they were indifferent to our species," Zinian responded.

"To one side of our species – the male humans," Cecilia jumped in. "They had only met Master Li and did not pose their mating problem to him because of his age. Once I heard about their… difficulties, I offered a solution. They were very interested in what I had to say," she smiled.

"They were attracted to you?" Zinian wondered.

"Goodness no," she answered. "Most of their planet is female. They desperately want to reproduce. But their males chronically have little to no desire. It has to do with their natural chemistry. Unlike human males that beat down your door, the Ventax females have to lead their male counterparts into the bedroom and show them what to do! They wanted me to demonstrate how we seduce our men into sex. Naturally, I tried to instruct them…"

"Naturally," Zinian chimed in. "You and Michael?"

"No…" Cecilia smiled. "I suggested shells to demonstrate…"

"Shells! Clever," Zinian responded. "The result?"

"It was… fun," Cecilia linked with a grin.

"Leave it to a woman to work her wiles," Zinian sighed.

"Anyway, after they achieved positive results, they were very receptive to my contact. I called Chou into my link. By the time we returned, he and I found them very cooperative. Seems sex broke out all over Ventax. The happy females took us to several technical sites and shared some of their confidential information kept from other member worlds. We toured their most secretive production facility," she told Zinian. "Once they constructed human shells and adjusted their knowledge based our species, they worked out biologically compatible micro-machines."

Zinian turned his attention to the sparkling box on the table. He realized why parts of it sparkled. As his eyes drew closer, he could see them, billions of them swimming around on the sides of discs. Cities of these devices filled the box, miniaturization taken to the ultimate extreme – semi-intelligent, tiny mechanisms devoted to perform multiple functions and yet disposable. Their bodies biodegrade in the atmosphere or in ordinary water once they leave the body. At least, that is how Cecilia explained it to him.

"It didn't take them long to manufacture," he observed as he examined the box. "That's faster than they develop technology on Ziddis."

"Actually they developed these over a very long period of time. They simply adapt them to be compatible with different species," she explained.

"One size fits all," Zinian muttered.

"Something like that," Cecilia replied. "An entire colony lives inside those flesh colored discs. Once applied to the skin, the disc leaks whole groups of them, which invade the body. Once in the blood stream, they scan the organism for its optimal efficiency. Since we are psychic, they assume the special area in our brain is normal and leave it alone. They will root out any cellular malfunctions and halt the progression of any foreign invader. That includes things like staph and strep that ordinarily live on our skin."

"What about a mass infusion of a mircobe that duplicates at extremely high rates of speed," a skeptical Zinian wondered.

"We ran tests," Cecilia stated. "They'll stop anything on that scale," she told him. "They especially love microscopic organisms as they consider them the easiest target to eliminate. Bacteria are larger than viruses, but also slower and cannot duplicate as quickly. The micro-machines eat them up in seconds. Viruses they mow down like cutting grass."

"They're very tiny," he said as he bravely held up the clear container and jiggled the box.

"They're extremely durable, too. Evidently, our cells and processes do not attack them. "They are completely compatible… we only have one small problem."

"Problem?" Zinian asked.

"The Ventaxians have never actually tested these devices on a real human being," she told him, "only the human shells they created from the DNA code I gave them."

"What?" Zinian said and nearly dropped the box. "So they've only tested a shell," he uttered.

"I trust the Ventaxians," she said. "They are extremely thorough in their investigations."

She picked up the box and held it up so that the light shone through.

"I'm inclined to agree," Zinian echoed. "How do we activate them?"

Cecilia linked a special code to the box and it opened. A single disc, about 1.5 centimeters in diameter, floated up into the air. One side was clear and sparkled. The other side had a neutral tone to it. The box closed and floated back down on the table. The pad remained in the air. She hesitated to act. The disc remained aloft and hovered.

"Oohhh," Zinian cried. "I see why you wanted me... I'm to be your guinea pig. Is that it?"

"Not if you don't want to," she said as the pad floated closer to her.

The pad suddenly halted between them.

"Wait a minute," Zinian stated as he exerted his force on the pad. "I don't want to enter an arm wrestling contest with you, because you know..."

"... I'd win," she smiled.

"You would," Zinian had to admit. "I only meant I would be honored if you allowed me to be the first. That way you could monitor my vital signs. We'd be in a fix if our only physician should succumb to alien technology."

"I see your point," Cecilia replied.

She removed the protective backing on the disc and then floated the object over to Zinian's arm.

"Turn your wrist up," she instructed.

The pad floated down until it rested on Zinian's forearm with the colored side up and the clear side in contact with his skin. Almost instantly, the pad's color changed and matched Zinian's flesh. It seemed to vanish and blend with his skin. Within seconds, he could feel warmth at the spot. He lightly ran his finger over the spot.

"Where did it go?" he asked her.

One of the cabinets opened and a circular device floated over. She turned its functions on. A red light started to flash.

"Warning: invasive devices," it cried out. A three-dimensional image projected into the air next to the couple. It displayed the path of the objects as they entered Zinian's bloodstream. "Patch introducing unknown microscopic mechanical particles..."

Cecilia touched a few pads on the device and changed the scanner's calibrations.

"Topical device operating within predicted parameters, micro-mechanisms activated... working... non-belligerent to functional systems," it told her. "Processes activated on insertion, removing foreign substances."

"What's going on?" Zinian asked, worried.

"Those little machines have searched out and destroyed every unhealthy cell in your body. In their place, they have stimulated the creation of new and healthy cells using parts of the old cell they've replaced. An hour from now, you will be the healthiest person on the planet… amazing," she said as she watched them work. She zoomed in on their action. "The large ones are actually sending out smaller devices and rebuilding your DNA… and they are not undoing the DNA alterations that Galactic Central made… in fact…"

She paused as she watched them.

"I don't think Master Li will like this," she said as she looked up at Zinian.

"What are they doing? Am I going to be different?" Zinian wondered.

"They can make you into anything you desire. I could instruct them to make your hair blonde or your eyes blue," she said with a sense of alarm in her voice. "They are the perfect solution to the creation of a superhuman that would conquer the world… sound familiar?" she put. "We'll need to keep these things secret once we complete the mission… and I mean a secret from even the rest of the WPO membership. This could blow up into something terrible if it fell into the wrong hands."

Zinian nodded. He understood what she implied – gene manipulation to the point of making each person identical in traits. As with the fusor being able to create any life form, these patches could manipulate a child in the womb to be identical to some idealistic prototype – someone's idea of a perfect face, perfect skin, perfect hair, teeth, sex organs, muscles – to the most frightening Nth degree; the kind of power maniacal regimes strove to achieve.

"We can't let that happen," Cecilia said. She went to the clinic's fusor and made a few quick passes over the screen. The fusor came to life and produced another box that slid out into her hands. She went to the cabinet where she stored the discs. The sparkling box floated out. She placed it inside the new box she just created. "If anyone but me opens this, they'll find goo inside and not patches."

"Did the Ventaxians tell you how long they last?" Zinian asked.

"The patch can send out as many as ten thousand tiny machines a minute, six hundred thousand an hour. They blast away at anything that tries to invade our bodies," she explained. "At that rate, the patch will wear out in… oh, I'd say about 100 years," she smiled.

"What happens to the little… things, when their done with their job?"

She pointed to her backside indicating where they went.

"I guess we no longer have a reason to fear any viruses!" he stated.

"I like the new system," Master Li suddenly broke into their minds. "Make one available for each team member."

Cecilia jumped. Zinian looked right at her.

"Yes, Master Li," Cecilia replied, "ready and waiting for application."

"Bring them to tonight's meeting," he told them.

"Another meeting?" both Zinian and Cecilia questioned.

"Very important," Li insisted. "You are not the only two in Rollo working on new research. Everyone has something to offer. I… I've come across a major breakthrough. All nine must attend. Find a sitter. Oh and Cecilia… I knew about Ventax… very funny. Li out." They felt his presence leave.

"So much for secrecy," Zinian muttered.

"I knew he would find out," Cecilia spoke up. "He is Master Li. I guess I'll be bringing the box to the meeting."

"You'll need a patch, then. Open the box. Here," Zinian offered and another disc floated up out of the box.

Cecilia turned her wrist over.

"Can it make you handsome?" he wondered as the disc melded with Cecilia's skin.

"No… but I could program it to remove your brain cells or shrink your penis if you don't behave," she quipped.

"Point taken, doc," Zinian said. He watched the screen after she moved the scanner over to her wrist. Once he saw it working, he turned his focus in the direction of the mansion. "What did he mean by a major breakthrough?" he wondered as he looked at Cecilia.

"Yeah," she said as she looked into Zinian's eyes. "I wondered about that, too."

Chapter Twenty-One

Ultimate upgrade

"This way, this way," Han urged as he met everyone in the foyer and requested that each member take a seat in the dining room while they waited for Maser Li.

"He can't expect us to be ready," Cecilia objected when she and Michael walked in. "We've only had one day to prepare."

"I understand," Han shrugged and quickly replied. "I did not request the meeting. I'm only carrying out directives. Master Li said to make certain everyone went directly into the dining room and waited."

When the last of the group assembled, Han joined them and sat down in his usual place. Although no one saw or smelled any dinner preparations, Running Elk set the table with tea and an assortment of baked goods. Su Lin poured out tea as the room buzzed with everyone's progress.

"Master Li will arrive soon…" Han announced, "I hope."

As she intended, Cecilia brought the box of special discs and her scanner. She showed everyone the devices and explained how Zinian volunteered to be the first.

"Did she promise you a new car or a cash bonus first before you signed the contract?" his friend Zhiwei quipped. Chou laughed harder than anyone did. He helped Cecilia make contact with Ventax.

"I do have a metallic taste in my mouth," Zinian said and made a chewing motion.

"Ha, ha, very funny. Everyone here must have the patch before we leave for Africa," Cecilia reminded.

Michael enjoyed the banter and yet the reason Master Li gave him for the meeting seemed a bit vague. He mulled over the link ever since he received it.

"A major breakthrough requires everyone's attention."

"Did Master Li give any specific reason why he made the meeting urgent and mandatory?" he asked Han.

The others turned toward Han and echoed the same bewilderment.

"He'd been off world all day. He returned briefly, told me I had to receive everyone at the door, and direct all of you to the dining room. Then he said he had to speak to the director and would be arriving soon," Han replied.

A sudden surge of psychic energy moved toward the dining room, a familiar sensation impossible to mistake for anything else. They halted their conversations and turned their attention at the same time toward the entry. The large dining room doors opened and Master Li walked in, his silken robe flowed behind him like a bride's train.

The group started to rise and bow out of respect when he held out his hands and bade them resume their seats. He wore a scowl on his face and gazed solemnly around the room at the eight faces that stared back. The group suddenly sensed danger. Before they had time to react, Master Li shouted one word: "NOW!"

The eight psychics fell backward into their chairs as Galactic Central invaded their brains via those special conduits. Two thousand voices for each of the eight members manipulated psychic energy from Galactic Central. A download of magnanimous proportions flooded into each mind. As member's bodies fell back, their legs flew up and struck the table underneath. The tea service started to bounce up off the table. Master Li reached out with his power and prevented any accidents. He walked around the table and watched as the people he knew and called friends twitched with the frenzy of agitation. Currents of psychic energy rippled through their bodies. Li watched with empathy.

"This will be known in the annals of the WPO's history as that download of all downloads… I will never be able to express my most sincere apology for the way I've treated you just now, my friends," Li spoke, although no one in the room could hear him at the time. "From this moment on, you will change the course of Earth history forever."

When Master Li left the meeting the night before, he wanted to flee into the time chamber. He felt fearful and anxious for the group. He also felt personally responsible for his failure to foresee what happened to Filla and Salla. He wanted to walk the timeline, mix in some comfortable place in the past, and rest his mind. However, the moment he arrived inside the tower, the director confronted Li.

"A message from the creatures of Adis," it said to him. "Are you aware of Adis?"

"Yes…" Li absently responded as he hovered outside the giant crystal, "…but only that they are alphabetically the first planet in the IPC system. Other than that…"

"Many shells constructed on Adis…"

"Oh?" Li again halted his entry into the time chamber.

"The liptil are fascinated with advanced biology," the director continued, "seems Earth's ability to manufacture, accumulate, and store psychic energy fascinates them. They have new information for you. I'd delay that time travel you have planned and travel to Adis instead."

"I will do as you suggest," Li replied.

His body shot from the top of the spire, much to the disappointment of the voices below, and zoomed out toward the Lectim Sector of space, as far from the Milky Way Galaxy as one could be in the Intergalactic Psychic Collective.

"How could they know about Earth out here?" Li wondered.

On a huge planet with a dense atmosphere, these squashed psychic members experienced gravity four times Earth's and nearly twice as much as the gravity on the planet that houses Galactic Central. Li arrived to investigate the director's request.

"Master Li! Come!" a creature called out.

Li did not need Galactic Central for translation. He found the creature located on one of the central landmasses. It sensed his presence above the planet. Li traced the signal to the surface. He found one of the nearly horizontal creatures waving an appendage to him.

"This way!" it cried out.

It rocked back and forth as it made its way through a wide slit in the bottom of a wide structure whose sides seemed massive to Li. This building seemed out of place on a planet where most life did not grow above four meters and its intelligent life hardly reached one meter in height, although they had surpassed Earth's level of human intelligence and sophistication.

"Pass through the opening we made for you over there," it pointed.

Master Li noticed that an entrance, the size which could accommodate a human body, opened in the side of the building. He walked through and a heavy door slid back into place behind him. At once, he noticed he could easily move about in this place.

"We constructed a chamber to negate the effects of our gravity," the creature informed them.

"The director said you wanted to see me," Li started.

Several of the creatures ran back and forth over a series of panels close to the ground. They sounded like giggling children as they chirped and looked up at Li on the other side of a clear wall that separated them from the inner chamber. Out of the darkness, Li noticed other human shapes.

"Give him more light to see... dim the control wall the first," one of the creatures ordered.

The clear wall that allowed Li to see his hosts darkened while the room around him brightened. All at once, he realized he stood inside a huge chamber crowded with naked men and women of different sizes, shapes, and races. They lined up before experiment stations. One by one, they entered a station for some kind of test before they moved on to the next one. It appeared as a giant factory. Li thought there might be several hundred thousand shells in the huge space – human bodies that had brains yet without memories or advanced thought processes.

"What's all this?" Li asked.

"You are interesting creatures," he heard in his mind. "You create so much psychic energy..."

"How were you given this code?" Li practically demanded. "This is slavery!" he said, upset over the number of shells they had created.

"You have judged us wrongly, Master Li," the head creature told him. "We do not grow these shells to harvest their psychic energy, although they have plenty in abundance," it stated. "We have found an anomaly... a very special quirk that no shell we construct can possess. It will only be available to those with a conduit, as you possess. Although the great Master Li does not require such a boost..."

"Boost?" Li questioned. "What is this boost?"

"A very special manipulation... one that will change your group," it explained. "You thought it was special when you learned to form a so-called psychic bubble with your energy after Galactic Central used a DNA manipulation," it continued. "You learned to do this from Galactic Central. Yet, your species is capable of so much more... more than any of us in the collective," it pointed out. "We learned this as we studied the shells. We did not mean to offend. That we will rectify shortly... but first," it communicated, "you must see this."

The lights in the factory faded as the wall turned clear once more. All the creatures on the other side had gathered into a group. They all bowed before Li.

"We offer this information to you, oh great Master Li," the leader of the group stated. "It is an honor for us to help you. Behold!"

On the wall in front of him, a visual presentation began to take shape. Master Li witnessed something he had never considered in all the years since his conversion. He backed away and nearly fell over as he stumbled.

"I can't believe it," he said breathless. "Is this true?"

"As with the conversion that alters your cellular structure, it is best if the subject is unaware," the creature said. "Your central nervous system should be relaxed, unaware, caught off guard, and your blood stream free of these alteration chemicals. We can instruct Galactic Central in the process..." it paused. "To use it will be your decision."

Li watched the demonstration as it started again, as if it played on a loop.

"This would give us the ultimate advantage for our survival," he said as he narrowed his vision on the great discovery that played before him.

"This research took us many hours in our life cycle... we had to construct many shells... we are sorry if we offended," the creature said. "We will offend no more. We consider you a great friend to our planet. So that we may clear your... conscience....You must leave, Master Li," it said. "You must leave now."

"I want to properly thank you," Li started when he noticed the clear wall start to darken.

The creatures on the other side began to slither away onto a ramp that took them underground. The door located on the side of the large building opened and Li started to turn toward the opening when he heard a loud groan of metal under great strain. At the far end of the building, the roof came down and smashed into the floor. The heavy structure crushed every human shell underneath.

"They're going to destroy all of them," Li thought, powerless to stop them. "...as a favor to me... I should not have expressed my sentiment."

He ran for the opening as the next part of the building collapsed. The shells, no longer needed by the liptil for their experiments, stood like obedient soldiers while the liptil removed supports for the massive structure overhead. One by one, the planet's force of gravity pulled down sections of the huge roof structure, which flattened anything underneath when it struck the floor with tremendous force. Li barely escaped as the remainder of the building that once had been the tallest structure on Adis was now its shortest.

"Should we tell him of the rest?" one liptil assistant said to his commander.

"It is too late... he will discover on his own... about them," the other liptil responded. "Contact Galactic Central. Inform them of the process. Let the Earthlings figure out the rest... they are a somewhat intelligent species."

On his way back through the sector that held Galactic Central, Li sensed that the Liptil had been in contact with the voices and instructed them on what to do. The voices only awaited Li's signal to enter the minds of their linked counterparts on Earth.

"It will take many voices..." the director told him.

"I will give the signal," Li replied. "Have everyone ready."

Back on Earth, Li watched over the group.

"Once I saw the Liptil process, I knew we had to take this next step," Li quietly spoke as he paced around the dining room table and monitored each psychic's vital signs.

He did not relish this "sneak attack." He only meant to follow the advice of the liptil commander and head of its science division. He knew that once the Rollo psychics possessed this change, they could continue to grow in strength as psychic beings – with a very special purpose in mind.

Master Li sympathetically watched as eight trembling bodies wiggled around with eyes closed while their faces showed expressions of pain. Unlike the level four conversion to alter DNA, this alteration had more to do with how the body processed psychic energy. The amplification technique his group could employ would nearly match his own in strength some day.

Of all the humans on planet Earth, and the universe for that matter, Master Li was unique. He learned on Adis that he could create this new phenomenon without any additional structural changes. He had only to alter his way of thinking. However, the others had to undergo a radical change in the way they absorbed, stored, and utilized psychic energy. Galactic Central utilized the Adis blueprint to alter the human central nervous system. New neurons grew. New endings connected. Their skulls slightly expanded, although cosmetically, it would not be noticeable. However, the effect would be painful on awakening and Li stood by with a remedy.

"If only I'd know five years ago... before the children... I could have performed this feat all along," he thought. "*It is unique to humans* the liptil scientist said," he recalled. "We shall see."

He worked his way around the room and carefully watched over the group while he kept this process isolated from the psychic children of Rollo. He knew their inquisitive minds could reach into the mansion. He detected their probes. After each of them failed to penetrate Li's barrier, they withdrew, knowing Master Li's deflection was far too powerful.

Two hours slowly passed and Galactic Central finally completed its work on the human central nervous system. Li breathed a sigh of relief that the process had harmed no one. Eight bodies in the room began to glow with soft golden light that surrounded each member as energy filled them like charging a battery. The dining room guests began to stir. Gradually, as consciousness returned to the group, the golden glow faded and all eight began to shift around. Master Li brought out a spray and misted the air over the table so that as they took in a deep breath, they consumed the remedy for their headache and pain. When he felt comfortable they could understand him, he entered their minds.

"Relax. Breath deep. Feel your surroundings. Do not be afraid," he spoke collectively.

"Master Li," Michael inquired, his eyes blinking, "What has happened?"

"I cannot excuse the abruptness of my action," he apologized. "Only know that a creature recently revealed this new aspect to me during my travels. They instructed me that in order for me to institute this change, I must apply it without prior knowledge. I know that my actions violated protocol." He looked at the upset faces around the room. "Galactic Central did not manipulate your DNA. Yet, only advanced psychics could tolerate these structural changes. You are the most advanced psychics on the planet. This is an entirely new level of function, call it Level V. Welcome to your future!" Master Li said and spread his arms wide.

"I can feel psychic energy from sources I never thought possible," Cecilia spoke up. "Sources beyond the village," she added.

"That is correct," Li informed her. "You have greater range with your enhanced abilities," he stated. "This new adjustment will take getting used to," Li thought to them.

"I can sense new things," Chou added.

"I can stretch out further," Zhiwei noticed.

"Break a cup," Michael asked of Zinian.

"What? This is Running Elk's favorite…" he started to protest.

"Just do it!" Michael demanded.

Zinian took a cup and smashed it down on the table. Instead of the pieces scattering about the room, the fractured cup froze in the air. The pieces slowly came together and reformed.

"I've always wanted to do that!" Michael exclaimed.

"Amazing control," Zhiwei thought.

"A word of caution," Li expressed. "This new power is untested. When you employ this function, you will use nearly twice the psychic energy as you did before."

"Twice!" the others echoed.

"That means if you perform certain deeds, you may rapidly exhaust your reserves. You must exercise caution. My friends, the hour is late. We will discuss applications of your new abilities tomorrow. Now, the group should retire," Li urged.

The group reluctantly disbanded. The room emptied except for Master Li and Han. Han did not link or speak. He stared at the table and stayed quiet while the others flexed their new powers on the way to their houses. Li noted that Han did not follow the others in charging up his increased capacity.

"What have you done to us?" Han finally asked.

"What is wrong?" Li reacted with innocence. "Did I not give you a new ability?"

"Do you want to make us super beings, capable of lording over humanity?" Han spoke with near anger in his tone. "What is to stop anyone in this group from flexing their psychic muscle and taking over the planet?"

"Actually," Li said, rising, "you have more to fear from the children than anyone in the original group."

"The children?" Han questioned. "Is that what you saw in the future?"

"Their ability to use psychic energy is greater than anyone has yet to imagine," Li told him. "Mark is five and yet he could send a tank flying across Kansas if threatened. Their only restraint is their trust in the guidance of strong loving parents and the fact I can stop them. That is why… when I made my decision to pass this new ability along… well, you see Han, I knew about them… the children, that is. I purposely had these parents start contact in the womb, so that the children understood morality, very important if nothing on the planet could stop you."

Han stared at his friend with disbelief on his face. Li cocked his head to one side.

"Do you understand me, master strategist? Once on their own, *they* are the beings capable of ruling the Earth, if they choose," Li said as he rose from his chair and started to leave when he stopped in the doorway. "Hopefully, they will assume a role of respect and restraint."

"What's to stop them?" Han asked him.

"You, Michael, Cecilia, Villi, any of you," Li explained, "because for the first time since this started, you have the ability to create tremendous power with psychic energy, and use it in far more creative ways than you ever have. At least one of you will reach the ultimate plateau."

"What do you mean, one of us?" Han retorted.

"Michael, of course. Who does he aspire to be?" Li replied and turned to face Han.

"Are you saying that Michael could one day…"

"I'm not saying anything, am I?" Li interrupted.

He left Han sitting at the table, contemplated his words.

Chapter Twenty-Two

Mark's Song

Before the sun disc rose the following morning, Master Li called upon all the psychics in Rollo, except for the children. Li invited them to an early breakfast in the morning room. Running Elk and her staff took orders and prepared a delightful fresh breakfast for everyone. Before the feast began, Master Li requested that no one try to use their new ability until he had a chance to explain a few things. He added a few provisos as well.

"Do not reveal your new power to the children," he requested.

"Kind of late," Chou muttered.

"Yeah," Michael echoed.

"That's a pretty tall order," Villi objected. "Mey Li is very sensitive. I'm certain she sensed a difference in me last night," he stated.

"Perhaps," Li continued. "Still, I do not want you to perform extraordinary feats in front of them," he instructed. "We'll speak more of this after breakfast."

An hour later, they moved from the morning room to the library where they sat around the roaring fire in their usual chairs. Li still had not revealed the purpose of the meeting, although he did promise no more "download" surprises would take place. Once Running Elk left tea for everyone, Li stood in their midst and linked with the group. He paced back and forth in front of the glorious flames he created.

"I want to share a story with you," he began, "one I was reluctant to tell, but I feel the time is right. It begins in this very room and took place a short time ago with your son… Michael… Cecilia."

"You allowed Mark in here?" Cecilia questioned. "I thought the children were banned from the library."

"I made an exception in this case," Li said with his figure silhouetted by the flames. "You spoke about reasons why we should rescue the Motambou's in Africa at such a personal risk to ourselves. Oh, the children are a good reason, of course, yes, but there are principles involved, too. We have something precious and rare in this village. Isn't that alone worth fighting for?" he put to them.

The room fell into darkness including the fireplace. Master Li projected the image of the dining room and a meeting they held two weeks ago came into view. Everyone in the room recalled the meeting well. It ran later than usual. Their Native American friends stopped by to put most of the children to bed. Cecilia let Mark remain as he insisted he was not sleepy. However, when the meeting dragged on after midnight with Zinian and Zhiwei arguing over one specific point, the five-year-old child grew bored. Young Mark played in the corner of the room alone and only half-listened as the adults discussed projects that involved the WPO. The argument between Zhiwei and Zinian escalated until Michael stepped between the two friends.

Yet, now the gathered group saw the perspective of this meeting from Master Li's point of view. He sat quietly and watched as Mark worked on a puzzle. The little boy made the 1000 piece puzzle move through the air and reform into a picture several times in different and creative ways. No one realized Mark had such control, not even his parents. Li rose from his chair, which brought the meeting at the time to a halt. Before anyone could ask his motive, he waved away their curiosity.

"Mark and I are going for a walk. Do you approve, Cecilia?" Master Li asked the young physician.

"Of… of course," she stammered, uncertain of his intent.

Master Li crossed the room as the others exchanged glances.

"Please continue," he urged them. "Zhiwei, you were saying…"

Zhiwei shrugged and charged right back into the point he was trying to make.

Master Li moved up to Mark and crouched down.

"I want to show you something in the library," he privately linked with excitement in his tone.

"You want to take me to… the library?" Mark questioned. The puzzle pieces clattered to the floor.

"A new acquisition, something I came by recently," Li added and blocked out the others as he and the little boy exited the dining room.

As they crossed under the rotunda and headed directly for the tall doors outside the library, the five-year-old's eyes widened with anticipation. Li never allowed any children in the library, including the psychic children. Only once, years ago, did he allow Su Lin to bring a class in with older children. One of them almost broke something. After that, Li forbid any more forays.

Approaching the tall doors, the idea that he would enter the forbidden room with someone as knowledgeable as Master Li excited the young man. The two briskly strolled up the wide hall, hand in hand.

"Am I really going inside the library, Master Li?" Mark wondered.

"I believe it's high time you looked inside," Master Li said.

Mark's mouth dropped opened as the doors magically parted. He glanced up at the beautiful Renaissance-style painting on the library's ceiling and the huge perfectly preserved pterodactyl specimen suspended in the southwestern corner of the ceiling. He noticed how the center table's top shined with its brilliant thick layer of solid gold and how its polished carved wooden legs glistened under the light from fancy brightly covered Tiffany lampshade that rested in the middle of the table – all of these priceless objects treasures Li rescued from destruction.

At the opposite end of the room, the infamous large sparkling jewel that rested on the mantel caught his eye. This was the famed diamond that Master Li brought back from the formation of the planet and later had cut in Amsterdam. Also on the mantle, a solid golden statue of a pagen god and other treasures spread out next to the great oval jewel, paled in comparison. Mark's face lit up as he looked from one great wonder to the next. However, Master Li did not lead Mark in the direction of those wonderful objects, whose story of origin would have fascinated any child.

Instead, he led him over to a bottom shelf about halfway along the room's right side wall. A series of crusty old books with tattered covers sat in a row on the lower shelf, their musty odor filled the boy's nostrils with a repulsive smell.

"Old books?" Mark thought. "He's going to show me old books?"

The disappointment in the boy's thoughts could not be clearer to Li. He stopped before the shelf where a series of very old and dilapidated leather bound books stood together. Li quietly reached over and placed his hand on the middle book with its thick brown leather binding that appeared to be the oldest and most cracked. The book had no title along the backing, just a few white squiggly lines for decoration. Li pulled the large heavy object down off the shelf, and gently placed it on a small granite topped table nearby.

An unsteady hand scribbled an inscription at the bottom of the cover in a language Mark did not recognize: ברה לש לפסה. Someone attached a crude small wooden cross to the middle of the cover.

Mark wrinkled his nose. He could smell the odor of rot. He thought Master Li would show him some exotic object glittering with gold and jewels, or perhaps a preserved specimen of a beast that once roamed the planet's jungles. Such were the interests of young boys. Mark showed little interest in some old musty book, and began to fidget by darting his eyes about the room.

"Sometimes, appearances are deceiving," Master Li uttered when he recognized Mark's disdain. "Take this book for example," he said as he tried to bring Mark's attention back. "This is not a book."

"It's not?" Mark questioned as he stared up at Master Li's face.

"No," Li replied.

Mark's eyes returned to the block-shaped object lying on the table. Li opened the cover. Instead of pages, the hollowed book held a plain rough-hewn stone cup inside. Li took the cup from the book and placed it into Mark's hands.

"Do you know how to be a detective?" Li asked him.

"Like fictional characters?" the brilliant child asked.

Master Li half smiled. He realized these children knew more at this age than most college graduates did.

"Yes. I'd like you to play detective," he told the boy. "What can you tell me about this cup," Li requested and watched for Mark's reaction. He peered into the lad's mind and observed as Mark deciphered clues from its surface.

The bright young lad examined the object rather closely. At first glance, the vessel in question bore no special marks or insignias. Mark judged the stone as being probably very old, based upon the amount of dirt ground into its exterior. He could see that a craftman used a crude chisel to form the vessel, based on marks made around the outside.

"Obviously hand-made, perhaps by the owner," he thought as he turned it in his hand. "A hand or mouth rubbed the lip smooth, as if repeated use through the years made it that way. The base is dirty along the bottom, and the inside heavily stained dark purple. The stains must be natural, from some kind of plant, perhaps grapes used in wine." He sniffed the inside and confirmed his hypothesis. "Yes… wine. I can smell it."

Mark looked up from the roughly hewn vessel and held it out. He informed Master Li of his findings.

"The object is very old, based upon the amount of grit worn into its surface over many years. This is a hand-carved stone cup, used quite often by its owner to drink various liquids, wine mostly, I would guess. The stone is common white limestone found in quarries all over the planet. Judging from its crude nature, I would say you recovered this object from some past civilization where such drinking vessels were common. Am I correct? Is this an antique? Whose cup is it, Master Li?"

The old man reached down, and took the stone vessel back from Mark. He held it up in the air.

"Good observations, Mark," Li began. "I applaud your analysis. You are correct. However, you can learn more about its owner from the history of this cup than one can surmise from any superficial examination or cursusory glance. This particular goblet has a very complex story that involves some of the greatest men and women in the history of the world. Many people throughout history fought wars and died in their search for this cup and its reputed qualities."

Mark frowned. He doubted Master Li's last statement.

"It is a good thing to be a skeptic, Mark. But you must believe me that I will only tell you what is true and never false," Li implored.

"I believe you, Master Li," Mark hesitated. "I can't see fighting a war over something as silly as an old stone cup."

"Wars have been fought for less," Li commented.

He placed the drinking vessel on the table and brought Mark closer as he placed his arm around the young boy's shoulder.

"I'd like to tell you a story," Li began. "On an evening similar to this one, the owner of this cup invited his family and friends to sup with him. In those days, they ate simple meals – bread, cheese, dried fruits – and they drank wine, as most water was unfit to drink. Wealthy people drank from metal or ceramic cups. Poor people drank from clay cups. This young man had his own cup made from stone, a trade he learned from his father. After he ate with his friends, the young man in question filled this very cup with wine. He wanted to impress his friends with his philosophy of life. He drew a parallel between the wine and his beliefs. He shared that cup of wine with his friends in a very special way. Many people in the world celebrate this same act of sharing every single day. Generations have passed this story down through the years. They revere the cup, but they especially revere the owner, a very unique and wise man."

"That man used this cup?" Mark asked incredulous.

Master Li nodded in affirmation.

"Master Li," Mark protested. "If the man was so special, why didn't he have a better cup, one made from gold? This cup is so… so common."

Master Li stared at the boy's face as if examining him. He picked up the stone cup from the table; his old wise eyes affectionately beheld the object in his wrinkled hand.

"Common… yes, it is quite common, Mark. This is the homemade drinking vessel of a stonemason, a profession referred to as a carpenter in those days. Modern carpenters normally used their tools to work with wood for a living. However in that region of the world, wood is scarce. Carpenters often worked with stone as they had the tools. The young man in question made this cup as a boy when his father first showed him how to shape stone. Not every man owned a chisel. Craftsmen handed the rare instruments down to their sons. In this case, the father lent the boy his tools after he instructed him on how to carve stone. The first thing the young boy made was this cup. Having a bit of satisfaction with his first creation, he grew quite fond of the cup. He carried it around in the pocket of his robe. When he grew older, he kept it with him as a reminder of his father and his mother, whom he loved very much. He kept it with him until the day he died, which occurred quite suddenly one day."

"How did you come by it, Master Li?" the boy asked, his interest peaked.

"First, let me explain the cup's journey," Li continued. "On the day of the owner's death, one of his followers went looking for the cup. He often saw his friend with the carved-stone goblet and desired that it should not pass into the wrong hands. He eventually found the object in the young man's prison cell. The jailers were not interested in an old stone cup. The man called Simon recovered his friend's beloved drinking vessel. He took it with him on his travels, and used it for many years. The day Roman soldiers arrested him, I happened to be in Rome. They gathered those arrested for preaching blasphemy in the streets and prepared them for sacrifice in the arena. When I looked in on the prisoners, I could only offer words of comfort. I could not save them. However, one man, the man called Simon, seemed to recognize some goodness in me. He gave the book to me and told me to keep it safe. He said it was the greatest treasure in the world," Li smiled. "I thought he was delusional, until he told me the story of its origin. After I realized its worth, I reassured him I would keep it safe. Had I not intervened at that moment in time, the cup's fate would have been destruction. The Roman soldiers came through the prison cells and confiscated all of the captive's goods. They destroyed any bewitched items as ordered by the Emperor. The soldiers would have tossed the cup on a large fire along with the rest of the group's blasphemous artifacts – a case of 'they know not what they do.' The heat from the blaze would have shattered the stone and destroyed the relic for all time, had I not rescued it."

"Master Li," Mark spoke up, "I still don't understand… why make such a fuss over a plain object?"

Mark examined the stone carving more closely, thinking he missed an important aspect he had not seen.

"I see nothing but a drinking vessel, Master Li," Mark commented.

"Yes, you are correct… it is just a plain piece of stone," Li said quietly. He held it up again and this time looked at it with reverence. "Yet, I tell you, Mark, this is the most precious possession I have the privilege to preserve."

"You mean of all your beautiful things, you like this old cup the best? I like your big diamond," Mark said as he looked up at the mantel. "I would think that is the most precious possession you have." Master Li chuckled as he regarded Mark's expression of wonder at the sparkling object.

"That diamond is just a bigger piece of stone, Mark. However, let me put it to you in a different way," Master Li offered. "If you were thirsty in a desert, which would you rather have, a cup or a diamond?"

"A diamond," Mark said with confidence. "I could buy a million cups with that."

"Perhaps," Li replied as he carefully set the ancient stone-carved vessel back inside the large hollowed out book. He turned to Mark. "With a diamond, you would die of thirst before you could spend it. Then what good would it be? You can carry water from a well with a cup. Sometimes, it is better to be practical about life, and realize that the most important thing is to nourish the spirit and the mind. For that, you need a cup."

Master Li closed the book and placed it back on the self, where it blended in with the other old books around it.

"Master Li…" Mark asked as he stared at the book's binding. "What do those squiggly lines mean?" he asked, referring to the markings.

"That is Hebrew," Li told him, "it translates as 'the rabbi's cup,'" he told Mark. He took the young boy by the hand and led him back to his mother and father.

At this moment, the story that Li told his friends, ended. The lights in the library came up. The fire roared back to life. Master Li had his back to his friends. Eight heads turned around and stared across the library to the tattered volumes that rested on the bottom shelf. There they were, just as LI described them, unobtrusive… no one would ever have noticed them. If the cup was in the middle one, what was in the other two? Master Li cleared his throat to bring their attention back to him.

When they turned around, he stood before them and held a glowing golden ball of shimmering light that hovered above his hand.

"You remember the psychic bubble," he said to them.

Everyone obediently nodded like schoolchildren.

"This is a golden sphere," Master Li told them. "As of this moment, only nine beings in the entire universe can create such an object or even see it. With the present power of your mind, you can go beyond the psychic bubble and form this object of power and intensity," Li said. He stepped back from them closer to the fireplacee. The ball remained suspended in the air. The moment he released it, it slowly moved in a straight line as if it defied gravity.

"Unlike the psychic bubble that we previously generated," Li explained, "this sphere defies all natural laws of the universe. One touch and it cascades off in the opposite direction as if the normal forces of gravity, friction, momentum, and motion did not exist or were an influence as part of our planetary existence. This sphere is an isolate of compacted energy, so self contained that it creates its own influence that supersedes the world around it. Human beings, and only the psychic humans in this room, can create such an object. Its interior holds the air trapped within when it forms. That means its air supply is limited. Also, it requires a tremendous amount of psychic energy to form the golden sphere, for unlike the psychic bubble, you can only form a sphereical object and no other shape."

The group stared at the glowing golden object with wonder expressed on their faces.

"The advantages are tremendous," Li went on. "No force on the planet, or even in the universe, can penetrate its exterior, none. If you are inside a golden sphere, you could travel through the interior of a star and be unaffected by the external forces exerted on the sphere."

The glowing sphere dissipated. Li took in a deep breath. The group's focus shifted to him. They saw how much energy it cost him.

"A warning…" he cautioned. "The golden sphere is also the most draining act a psychic can perform. Do it too many times and you will find your body completely drained of psychic energy and you will fall into unconsciousness," he warned. "Villi!"

"Yes, Master Li," the young Russian responded.

"We will travel to Africa tomorrow using the golden sphere around the aircraft," Li told him. "Since the golden sphere travels in a straight line…"

"…we will need to make the trip in a series of jumps, am I correct?" Villi interjected.

Master Li smiled at Villi's quick thinking.

"Quite right," Li answered. "The golden sphere travels in a straight line. The only way to change course is to dissipate and reform with a new push. Consider this method our new mode of traveling the globe. Mind you, Villi. Due to the extreme speed the golden sphere can cut through the atmosphere, we can now circumnavigate the globe in a matter of minutes, not hours, minutes!"

The members buzzed over this revelation.

Suddenly, Master Li wavered. He began to fall over. Eight people sprang from their chairs to his aid.

"I'm calling the meeting over," Michael spoke up.

Han waved the rest of the group off. He helped Master Li upstairs to rest in bed while the others returned to their homes and prepared for their eminent departure.

"The library was full of surprises today," Zinian said as he walked out with his friends.

"Seems Mark will lay claim to the best library story," Zhiwei commented as the three friends paused to glance over at the tattered books on the shelf.

"Makes you wonder what's in the other books," Chou added as he looked between the two taller men.

"No doubt we'll spend more time in the library after today," Zinian advised as the three men returned to their preparation duties.

Su Lin head over to the school to leave plans for her students. Cecilia went to the clinic to advise her assistant on what to do for any medical emergencies during her absence. Michael headed over to leave instructions with the Charge of Parks Department. Villi sprinted over the hanger complex. He had a few adjustments to make before they took off. Zinian rounded up his crew and informed them he would be gone "for an unlimited amount of time… but it will probably be just a couple of weeks." Zhiwei made preparations with Jennifer and Selena to take over security in his absence. An hour later, the psychics communicated their progress to one another.

"I've made arrangements for the children," Su Lin linked with her friends. "They'll be staying in the mansion. Star Wind intends to look after all five there," she told them. "The rest of the children will attend school as always. Star Wind promised she will teach them during the day."

"I wish her luck," Villi linked back.

"Have you tried to form a golden sphere yet?" Su Lin asked her husband. "Zhiwei's already tried three times."

"So we're leaving in the morning?" Villi wondered.

"When Master Li is involved, always plan on the unexpected," she replied.

Chapter Twenty-three

Commonalities

When Chou said he could not construct a boat within the given time constraint, Master Li relented and allowed the rescue team another day to prepare. This gave the eight psychics time to help the children adjust to the absence. It also gave Michael and Han another day to plan their strategy. When night fell, Master Li retired early and urged the others to follow suit. They knew he would probably call for them early in the morning and packed ahead accordingly.

A lone figure stood on the foredeck of a large ship at sea in the middle of a tempest. A huge wave rose up and swept him overboard. As he thrashed about in the stormy sea, the churning water threatened to drag him under. A large dark hand reached out and pushed his head under. Li Po Chin struggled to fight back and felt helpless against the onslaught. He yelled for help and no one answered his call.

"Michael! Han!" he cried in the darkness.

Master Li suddenly sat up in bed. He looked down at his body. He lay in a pool of water – his sheets soaked wet with his perspiration. He reached up to touch his face. Sweat poured off his forehead, dripped off his nose, and saturated his nightshirt. His heart pounded in his chest as he gasped for air. His eyes gradually adjusted to the darkened room. Nothing stirred around him. Everything in the house lay still and quiet. He sensed no movement. He breathed a sigh of relief that no one heard him yell. The nightmare ended.

"I never did learn to swim," he muttered, still breathing hard.

As Master Li recognized his room and the safety of his bed, the familiar surroundings allayed his fears. Using psychic energy, he pulled the moisture out of the sheets, the mattress, his pajamas, and pillowcase. He floated the pungent ball of liquid to the bathroom's sink. He relaxed into the dry bed as a sense of comfort returned. Yet, the images in the dream lingered in his thoughts and caused turmoil.

"We must act soon," he thought, "or we may be too late."

He rose from the giant bed and briefly showered. Afterward, he went to his large clothes closet where he took out a traveling outfit. He brought down a suitcase and used his mind to fill it with shirts, trousers, socks, underwear, robes, slippers, toiletries, and other necessities.

"The time has come to utilize this new power," he thought.

As he passed the wall, he jumped into his open boxer shorts, loose fitting trousers and a shirt. Next, his walking sandals rose up into the air and dropped to floor. He stepped into them last as he walked back into the bedroom. He held out his hand and a beautiful wooden cane, carved by a native artist of old Calcutta, flew over to him. The flashy diamond on its head and distinctive special black gripping tip were part of Master Li's trademarks.

"Han!" Master Li urgently called to his mind. "Han! Wake up!" he called more forcefully.

"What? What is it?" Han mumbled, still half asleep.

"Han, it's Li," he thought to his friend. "We've slept too long. We should leave right away, if we are to help our fellow agents. Alert the team for departure. The time to leave for Africa is now, my friend."

"What woke you?" Han wondered. "It's four in the morning!"

"… and noon in Africa. Did you hear my request?" Li shot back.

Han mumbled something incoherent. He stumbled out of bed toward the bathroom. He decided to take a hot shower, figuring the next chance may not happen for a while.

"Let's hope Chou included a shower on that skiff he created," he muttered.

Forty minutes later, a still sleepy team scrambled to load the last of the group's supplies into the new aircraft. Five years had passed since the group flew to Australia. During that time, Villi introduced a completely new flyer. This strange, wide, bluish-green, slick, oval design had no wings!

"How does it fly?" Zhiwei wondered. He and Villi did not interact very often. "Where are the wings?"

"Wings on demand," Villi explained. "They form out of the fuselage."

Still at least two hours before sunrise, an April chill gripped the morning air of the subterranean structure, as the psychic children, wearing slippers and robes over their pajamas, huddled into a protective group just outside the launch zone within the hanger complex. Star Wind protectively stood behind them.

"I'm adjusting the atmospherics," Edward said and warm air flooded into the cavernous space.

As team leader for the trip, Michael directed the operation and checked off a list as they finished preparing for takeoff. He stood at the rear of the flying apparatus with Chou. The two men made certain every piece of equipment they needed for the trip was loaded. Villi walked around the exterior with some sort of hand probe and made last minute checks on the propulsion system. He waved at Edward and Victor in the control room that his manual check of flight systems confirmed the automated read out.

"All yellow!" Victor chimed back through the intercom. He yawned and rubbed the sleep from his eyes. Yellow meant standby.

Little Robert stood in his maroon robe and matching pajamas in the midst of the protective group of siblings: Mark, Mey Li, Sandra, and Xiong Po.

"When will mommy and daddy come home?" the three-year-old clearly spoke. He could not penetrate the blocked psychics as they moved around the platform.

"Soon," Mark whispered in his ears, wise beyond his five years. "We must be brave for them," he went on and protectively wrapped his arms around the boy. "Do not cry, Robert."

"I wasn't going to," Robert stubbornly insisted. Yet, he already missed his father.

Star Wind stood behind the children, like some mother hen, she spread her arms like wings. She wore a long coat that hung open and emitted a warm area that encompassed the children.

"Chou's wife has all the cool gadgets," Su Lin noted as she poked Cecilia.

"She probably invented it," Cecilia linked back.

The two women had yet to say goodbye to the children. They walked over to the huddled group while Chou and Michael finished their recap of the cargo hold's list of items. The moment Star Wind noticed Chou had finished his preparations with Michael; she went to him. She wrapped her arms around her husband and planted a long deep kiss on his lips. Seldom seen in public, the normally lab-bound couple surprised everyone with this open display of passion. Robert smiled when he saw his parents.

"For luck," Star Wind said as she pulled away. Chou practically blushed when he noticed everyone staring at them.

Zhiwei discussed a list of back up instructions for emergencies with John, as he would join with Star Wind being in charge of Rollo during the psychic's absence. Master Li and Han went over several contingency plans with the brother and sister the day before, should any emergency arise. When they questioned why Master Li was so concerned this time as opposed to missions in the past, Li only had to say, "it's because of the children."

Michael and Villi added their goodbyes to their children.

"Please be supportive," Michael asked of Mark.

"We will," the entire group of children linked back. Michael smiled.

"Please keep in touch," Su Lin linked to Mey Li and Xiong Po.

"We will, mother," the two responded.

Michael thought it strange at first that he could not penetrate the four older children's blocks. Villi thought it odd, too, that they should shelter their feelings. However, Cecilia and Su Lin did not find feel that way.

"They don't want us to feel sad," Su Lin linked to the two men.

"They probably think we'll be more upset than they are with this first time separation," Cecilia added.

Running Elk walked between Master Li and Han as the trio approached the aircraft. Almost the entire Comanche tribe followed behind them. Once Running Elk spread the rumor of the dangerous mission, every tribe member available decided to give them a send off. Men and women with stern faces stood beneath the control tower and wished their friends a safe voyage. The psychics moved among them and bid their friends adieu.

While Han stayed near the entry steps to the aircraft, Master Li, sporting his beautiful ornate cane, hobbled over to the Native American crowd with Running Elk on his elbow. He sensed their concern that the 83-year-old man was too frail to make the trip. Without their realizing it, he quickly absorbed psychic energy from the powerfully emanating crowd. He jumped into the air, clicked his heels, and did a pirouette. The whole group laughed when he did. He followed up with personal farewells to everyone in that group before he joined Han going inside the aircraft. Zinian, Zhiwei, and Chou followed behind them along with Michael and Villi. Cecilia and Su Lin were last to board.

Cecilia and Su Lin fought back tears as they suffered the pangs of separation whether or not the children did.

"Please, don't worry," Star Wind tried to sound reassuring. "I will take very good care of them. I gave each child a special black card. They promised to contact you every day and leave messages, too," she told them.

Su Lin and Cecilia could not resist. They hugged and kissed the children before Michael stood in the doorway and loudly cleared his throat. Su Lin took Cecilia by the hand and the two friends walked onto the aircraft, their hands tightly grasped as they shared a few private thoughts between them. Michael called out from the open door.

"We shall return in two or three weeks," he said aloud and waved.

"Goodbye!" the crowd cheered.

Sensing all nine team members onboard the jet, Michael closed the compartment door and notifed Villi. Before they started, Li indicated he wished to address the team and stood at the front of the passenger cabin. Villi rose from his pilot's seat and stood behind him. Master Li isolated the cabin from the psychic children outside. He pointed his boney finger at his friends.

"You believe we have tricked the humans," he linked to them. "You believe we deceived humanity. You believe that to the human world, Rollo does not exist, that when they pass this place, they see nothing but an empty field with big rocks, unfit for development."

The group exchanged glances. This was the first time they heard this kind of skepticism from Master Li, especially Zhiwei, head of security. He started to question Li when the older man shook his head and held up his hands.

"If you believe that, then your faith is a delusion. Listen to me," he forcefully spoke. "It is we who are deceived, lulled into a sense of complacency, unable or unwilling to test the boundaries of humanity's technology," he continued almost as if he were scolding them. "Our initial plan to rescue the Motambou's was inadequate. Michael and Han insisted that our group needed an advantage. In my search of the cosmos, the IPC provided one. Consider yourselves fortunate. You new ability is so powerful, that nothing the humans will ever invent, now or in the future, can counter it. I have foreseen this. Perhaps this new power will give us the edge we need to survive... for your lives are in peril and everything you thought you knew about the world around is wrong, twisted in our own isolated logic. Wake up! The world is a dangerous place. Stay alert and we might live through this ordeal. We shall see."

"Master Li..." Cecilia began.

"No questions, no comments, and no retreat," Li said with a quiet voice. "We remain committed. Our resolve, firm. Our goal – to rescue the Motambou's from what surly will be their deaths if we don't arrive in time."

Li held out his hand and the golden sphere appeared, as if he held a miniature yellow star in his hand. The golden sphere on his palm winked out. Li's eyes searched their faces.

"When we surround this craft with the golden sphere, we will not need a blast of energy to transport this aircraft across the planet. Only a small burst will do. However, we will travel in a straight line. At times, we will need to drop the current sphere, change our angle, and reform the sphere to follow the curvature of the planet. Do you understand?"

Everyone onboard the aircraft chimed in their agreement.

"Absorb energy, your most powerful source lies nearby. Soak it up like a sponge. Drain these Comanches and they will not suffer one bit from what you take. They'll only manufacture more of the stuff in a never ending well that flows like a blessing to us," he told them as he gestured toward the group outside. "Our friends are our greatest treasure, worth more than all the gold and diamonds on the planet. You think they are grateful for the material goods we have given them? It is we who should be grateful for their presence. We owe the Comanche our lives. Remember that… always. Villi, prepare the ship for takeoff."

The group engorged on the psychic energy source nearby until every man and woman glowed with power. Villi moved back to his pilot's seat. He joined with the group in absorbing energy while he prepared the ship for takeoff. Victor and Edward made certain last night that all the power cells onboard were fully charged. Villi had never flown inside a golden sphere. He wondered how the aircraft would perform. Instead of inertia dampeners, he had to use gravity plates in the aircraft's floor as if they were traveling into outer space.

"Charge the floor gravity units," he ordered the computer. "Engage power to the engines. Disengage moorings. Hover mode."

The moment he engaged power to the engines, the hanger's clear blast wall rose up between the well-wishers and the ship. The exterior color of the ship turned from bluish-green to bright white.

"Make your goodbyes," Star Wind instructed the children.

They complied and linked one last goodbye to their parents.

"All systems full power," Villi instructed.

The control panel before him changed from yellow to green.

"All systems green," he spoke to Victor.

"Clear for takeoff," Edward responded via the com.

"Hover six meters zenith," Villi ordered. "Fifteen degrees up on the forward bow plane."

The aircraft gently lifted up off the launch platform and hovered above the elevator. The elevator/launch platform, originally used for a wheeled vessel, dropped down.

"We're ready Master Li," Villi informed them.

"Form the golden sphere!" Li called to their minds.

The group of nine joined minds in unison, their psychic power melded together to form a new incredible power for the first time in the universe, its energy crackled as their powerful minds intermingled.

Outside the ship, the tribe and the children instinctively moved back when the aircraft turned bright white and the clear blast wall rose. Suddenly, the aircraft vanished. The absence of its light plunged the hanger complex into comparative darkness and silence. Victor turned up the interior lights. The sudden change startled the tribe. Several gasped when it happened. Mark and Mey Li glanced at one another the moment it formed. Mark stepped forward and held up his hands to gain the gathered group's attention.

"Attention please!" the little boy shouted. "Master Li and the team members used a new way to hide to aircraft," he said and pointed up into the space where the aircraft disappeared. "They are still here and will launch shortly," he told them.

"My board shows nothing!" Edward said aloud into the hanger from the control booth.

"You cannot see them but they can see you," Mark informed them. He turned his attention back to the children and linked something to their minds. The members of the tribe, including Running Elk, looked down at little Mark and realized that he and the rest of the children stared up at the empty space and saw something there.

"This is going to be tricky," Villi thought. He knew that inside the sphere, the force of gravity no longer applied. The computer carefully adjusted the attitude of the craft. Using slight thrusters, Villi lifted the aircraft higher from the ground. The aircraft nudged the top of the sphere, which was slightly larger than the ship.

"Firing a small burst," he warned the passengers. His hand hovered over the emergency inertia dampeners.

From the children's point of view, they could still see the large brilliant aircraft as it hovered in the air. All at once, the engines ejected a single short burst of energy. In an instant, the entire sphere shot from the hanger complex and disappeared over the horizon. It traveled faster than any object that ever flew through any atmosphere in the history of flight.

For a few tense seconds, Villi wondered what would happen. Then the world around them turned into a blur. The sphere cleanly cut through the atmosphere and did not disturb the air or leave a wake. As Master Li predicted, hundreds of kilometers rapidly passed beneath them while they gradually increased their altitude.

"The atmosphere outside this ship is… weightless," Villi linked to the group as he watched trapped dust particles floating aimlessly around inside the sphere from his vantage point.

"I don't feel a thing. Are we flying?" Li asked and glanced out the window. The countryside outside the cabin turned to a blur.

"Yes, Master Li," Villi replied. "We are traveling at," he looked down at the control panel, "26 kilometers per second… that's 93,600 kilometers per hour."

"Are you sure?" Chou exclaimed as he nearly came up out of his seat. "That's escape velocity. We'll fly right off the planet!"

"Not inside this thing," Villi replied. "All we need to do is make an attitude adjustment. However, we'll have to make the change as a sphere inside a sphere," he advised. "If we suddenly hit the atmosphere at this speed, we'd instantly disintegrate."

"Understood," Li replied and linked that information to the group.

"We'll be in Florida in less than a minute," Villi informed them.

"Absorb psychic energy as we cross the continent," Master Li instructed. "We can bring it through the sphere. Good," he said as they pulled in extra energy. "We'll have to form a second sphere in our minds before we release this first one. Villi will make his course correction at the same time. We won't feel the change inside the sphere because the new sphere will instantly go in the new direction. Are you ready, Villi?"

"I hope," the pilot muttered. "Here goes… change in three, two, one… now!"

Villi did not bother to follow the events with his eyes. He sensed it the microsecond the first sphere dropped and fired a burst from engines whether the group erected the new sphere or not. Fortunately, they did and the aircraft shot off at a new angle out over the Carribean Sea. In less than two minutes, they would approach the African coast.

"Do you know how to stop us?" Li wondered.

"I only know that we should not feel any gravity when the sphere slows to a stop, just as we felt nothing when we started – no laws of physics apply. Remember?" he linked.

Villi pivoted the aircraft around to face in the opposite direct. He spun them upside down and then rotated the frame until they looked in reverse at the ocean whizzing away from them.

"Time to form one last sphere," he requested. "Three, two, one... now! Manual thrusters," he ordered to the computer.

A fresh golden sphere formed just as he fired a short burst of the maneuvering thrusters. The sphere slowed considerably. He waited until they came to within a kilometer of the island. Then he gave one last burst of thrusters and the sphere came to a sudden halt.

"We just flew half way around the world in less than five minutes," he called out.

Villi rotated the aircraft back into a forward perspective. While the whole flight practically frightened Villi out of his wits, Master Li had confidence in his pilot's knowledge of flight.

"Well done, Villi," Li openly linked.

The team, which held its collective breath the entire trip, broke into cheers.

"Release the golden sphere," Villi requested. "I can use maneuvering thrusters from here to our landing point with normal stealth on. Is that satisfactory, Master Li?" he asked.

"Fine, Villi," Li answered.

The sphere instantly winked out. The group sensed that the combined process of forming the large golden sphere did not tax them the way they anticipated. Everyone had plenty of psychic energy. This pleased Master Li.

"You've used your power judiciously," Li congratulated them.

The aircraft hovered above a small yet very tall island located off the coast of Nigeria. From his perspective, bright yellow "X" flashed in the air.

"We have reached our destination," he linked to the cabin.

"Please land, Villi," Michael linked back.

Villi extended a soft landing platform that this new aircraft gently rested upon and kept them level, despite the irregular rocky surface.

"We have landed," he informed the team. "Power down systems."

Michael chose a tiny island just off the coast of Nigeria as the safest place to leave the aircraft. The small piece of land, home to nesting birds during mating season, sat high above the water like a pedestal. This was the largest island in a group of six small islands a few kilometers from shore, located not far from the delta system of the Niger River.

Zhiwei immediately pulled out his card and sent a message to Mark. He informed the young man they safely landed. Mark immediately sent back his reply and stated to nearly the kph speed that they must have traveled to reach their destination in such a short time period. Zhiwei closed his card and put it away.

"Thanks, Zhiwei," Cecilia and Su Lin linked to him.

"The main branch of the Niger is about 18 kilometers south of a point due east," Michael informed them. "We will enter a tributary and join up with the main branch of the river. This way, we will avoid most of the traffic in the central port towns. Oh, and by the way, I must spray every team member before you leave the aircraft," he reminded.

He stood up and pulled open a carrying case. He removed a large can with a special applicator sprayer attachment. He activated the device and stood ready for the first victim.

"I'll go first," Cecilia offered.

"Perfect! All you need to do is disrobe," he added with a slight grin, "Everything off!"

"Just what did you have in mind?" she shot back.

"You have to be naked," he winked at his wife. "No one's looking."

Cecilia turned around. They were all staring at her.

"Do I really need to...?" she started to ask, when Michael closed his eyes and nodded.

"Sorry. The penetrating mist must touch all the exposed areas of your body, including," he pointed, "down there. This is no time for modesty."

"If I must, I must," she sighed.

Reluctantly, Cecilia stripped down completely naked. She stood by the door and allowed Michael to spray her head to foot including the palms of her hands and the bottoms of her feet. The red mist dried on contact and immediately matched her skin color.

Su Lin stood in line behind her, already naked, ready for Michael to spray her. Cecilia stepped to one side and dressed.

"We may not mind share," Su Lin quipped, "but we couldn't know each other better," she said as she stepped up to receive her spray.

"I can think of ways better than this," Michael shot back.

"You've seen everything inside my mind; you might as well as see everything on the outside of it!" Su Lin linked with a light-hearted tone.

Michael smiled as he started to spray her.

"I'll tell Villi I didn't notice a thing," he quipped.

"Then you'd be blind my friend," Villi added as he watched from the cockpit doorway, "and very unfortunate."

The whole group chuckled, even Su Lin smiled, amused, except of course, Cecilia.

"Michael had better keep his mind on what he is doing or he will find spray where it was never intended!" Cecilia thought to him.

Michael decided to spray faster. As each person finished the prep, they dressed and disembarked from the plane. Cecilia and Su Lin headed for the cargo hold to take out the supplies. In short order, Michael quickly sprayed Zinian, Zhiwei, Chou, Han, and Master Li. He sprayed Villi last.

"You couldn't talk Su Lin into spraying me," Michael linked to Villi.

"She'd do it in a heartbeat," Villi replied. "Only once Cecilia finds out, we'll need to find another team leader. Ok, strip!"

Michael chuckled as he prepared for the application. After his spray, he and Villi joined the others.

By the time Michael emerged from the aircraft, Chou had created the next vessel in their journey – a large metallic raft-type boat whose weight was a fraction of its hefty appearance. When Han questioned the material he used, Chou started to talk about metallic foams that automatically expanded. The group groaned and silenced Chou before he could bore them to death.

Eager to start moving inland, the team quickly transferred their supplies onto the large inflatable "metal foam" boat. They planned to take the specialized raft upstream as far as they could. Chou figured the power cubes for the engine might last a week or two before they gave out. He designed special thrusters on the outside that allowed the raft to float in the air temporarily, so it could hover down to the ocean below. Since Villi usually piloted or drove any craft they used, Chou briefly explained the controls so that Villi could better understand the newly constructed boat.

"Like this," he began. "See the hand grips? Mentally activate the control panel…here you have rudder, pitch controls fore and aft, breaking with exterior flaps that extend…similar to your aircraft… without the takeoffs and landings," Chou mused.

"Got it," Villi said as he moved into the pilot's seat and activated the control panel.

Han escorted Master Li onto the boat, adjusting the safety belt on his seat once he sat down. Master Li glanced around at the amazing raft.

"You never do anything small, do you Chou?" Li observed.

"I didn't build it for compactness," he commented with a bit of pride in his voice. "I built it for function. We could take the thing to sea for a month if we had the right power source."

"Any amenities?" Han wondered.

"Any amenities…" Chou muttered and looked around at the others. "Is he kidding?" Chou explained what he installed on the new boat. "One doesn't travel with the Beaton-Tylers and not go in style," he said as he glanced toward Michael and Cecilia. "This rather large and complex structure has a deck that wraps around a cabin, which protrudes up in the middle of the craft. This is to allow our tall psychics standing room. The area below includes a galley, a central eating area, and two complete bathrooms between semi-private sleeping areas – no doors, just sound proof curtains. Insect repellent, of course…"

"Of course!" the group echoed.

"Two beds are wider for couples," Chou continued without a beat. "The rest are single rooms. The galley has fresh running water and a fusor, which we will have to ignite eventually."

Several team members sighed relief.

"You do know how to spoil us, Chou," Han relented.

"Hmm?" Master Li nodded impressed. "Where's the swimming pool?" he asked sarcastically.

"Is this belt too tight?" Chou asked and gave Li's safety belt a tug. "I can make it tighter."

"I got the point," Master Li said as he brushed Chou's hand away.

Villi jumped off the raft and walked over to the aircraft. He touched an area on the side and a panel appeared. He rapidly put in some kind of code and spoke softly. The aircraft's sidedoor closed as he stepped back. The aircraft vanished.

"All aboard?" Michael asked as he looked around. "Take us down, Villi."

Villi returned to the pilot's seat, activated the control panel, and engaged the airborne maneuvering thrusters. The boat quietly lifted from the ground and hovered in place.

"Come together," Master Li linked to their minds. "This will make it easier," he informed the pilot.

The ensemble mentally unified and a golden sphere formed around the large inflatable boat.

"Proceed, pilot," Li instructed.

Villi backed off on the power. He carefully gave the thrusters short bursts, which started their craft toward the edge of the sheer drop off. Seeing they cleared the cliff, Villi bumped the sphere's interior to start them down toward the sea. The sphere gracefully moved out over the sea and gradually descended away from the tall cliff wall to the dark water below. Large foaming waves crashed on the jagged rocks – cold black undulating seas, far from calm waters. Instead of trying to set down in the rough water and risk the surf, Villi applied rear thrusters and nudged the sphere beyond the jagged reefs that surrounded the island.

"Release the sphere," he requested, just as he applied increased thrust. With the sphere gone, the vessel shot out away from the tiny tall island and skimmed over the surface toward the shore like a skipping stone. The clouds parted and rays of sunlight shone down upon the dark green sea.

"That's a good omen," Master Li noted as he gazed up at the fleeting patch of blue.

Michael turned to his mentor, "Did you do that?"

"No," Li replied, "convenient sunshine is compliments of nature."

The rear open deck had a semi-circular cushioned bench that wrapped around the aft section. Li sat in the center with Michael, Cecilia, and Su Lin on one side, while Chou, Zinian, and Zhiwei sat on the other.

Villi sat in the pilot's seat and watched the sensors next to the control panel. Han sat alone in the bow section, which had four seats. A sturdy canopy covered the deck in front where Han acted as lookout. He used the scanners in his expanded black card to scope the shoreline ahead.

Michael reached over and took Cecilia's hand in his. The couple leaned back and stared up at the clouds while the salty air blew through their hair.

"Better than the trawler," he linked to her mind in reference to their crossing the Sea of Okhotsk.

"But not as fun," she whispered back and leaned against his shoulder.

"Controls are easy… smooth sailing," Villi reported.

"I'm not picking up anything on the scanner," Han added.

Chou decided to go below and check for leaks. Zinian joined him.

"All clear below," Chou put in. "Equipment's aboard and secure. No leaks. Engines operating nominally."

"This ship's built to last. That's certain," Zinian added.

"No military within a hundred kilometers," Zhiwei reported as he looked up from his black card.

Michael glanced over at his mentor. Master Li sat with his eyes closed as he absorbed the sound of the churning sea around them. He looked over at Su Lin. She had her black card open, checking the weather. She glanced up at him and shrugged, as if to say, "Nothing to report." Michael and Villi exchanged looks.

"Orders?" his friend linked.

"All ahead, full speed," Michael ordered

"Aye, captain," Villi replied.

He brought up the power level to the navigation controls and turned on a display that showed their point of entry into the river system. He turned the inflatable boat toward that location on the coastline. The raft gradually moved faster. The sleek craft Chou created effortlessly glided across the top of the Atlantic Ocean waters to the mouth of the Niger River. The propulsion system gave off no sound as if they were traveling in a sailboat.

Had the team landed further north and taken a straight-line course overland to Mali from the sea, the straighter, more direct path would have led them through mountainous terrain. Even after they reached Bamako, they would still have to travel across another 800 kilometers to reach Gao, a city already in ruin. With the Motambou's presumably on the move south along the Niger River, the group reasoned they would being playing a game of catch up if they chose to cross the land. By going up river, they hoped to meet the Motambou's as they made their way down stream… they hoped.

"Do you sense them yet, being this close?" Michael asked Master Li.

Li blinked his eyes a few time until he stared into Michael's face. His blank expression did not betray his thoughts.

"I do not sense them, Michael. However, I believe they are alive."

"I hope we can find them in time," Han muttered aloud.

"I hope they survive their current predicament," Li privately thought.

Chapter Twenty-Four

Up the Niger River

The rescue party approached the Niger Delta from the Bight of Benin, the sea located on the northern side of the gulf outside the delta. The Atlantic coastline had large sand dunes built up from the strong ocean current that flowed southward from Ghana. The group decided to avoid the remains of the large oil drilling platforms along the main tributary.

The sleek silvery craft neared the coastline at speeds not even Chou thought possible. The craft seemed to defy the displacement he thought would make the vessel too heavy for river travel. The foam-like material actually repelled the water around it and made the craft more buoyant, which allowed it to ride on the water rather than wade through it.

The group kept their minds open to monitor each other's thoughts.

"Villi, initiate stealth mode on the control panel," Chou advised.

"Good idea," he replied. "Never know who's watching."

A field of graviton waves swept around the boat and bent light rays, which made the boat invisible to the naked eye on the horizontal plane.

"We're invisible," Villi proudly announced.

"Not entirely," Chou countered. "From the horizon, we appear as a slight distortion, easily dismissed. Graviton waves are perspective dependent. From most people's point of view, the waves bend the light around the object. The object inside the field appears as a heat anomaly. However, viewed from directly above, light swirls around the object and creates an oval-shaped dead zone about a half meter long at its center. Therefore, we are mostly invisible," Chou commented.

"Mostly?" Su Lin questioned.

"It's not perfect," Chou shrugged, "but we can avoid detection while we save our core energy for emergencies."

"Don't be too sure," Han spoke cautiously as he stared at his screen. "Spy drones cover wide zones and can hover over one area for hours."

"I'm not worried. My security scans can spot a drone," Zhiwei confidently said as he pointed to a small metal shaft that stuck up from the roof of the boat. He activated the scanner via his black card. "No drones... no spy planes... no satellites focused on us."

"Good," Michael spoke up. "Let me know when you need a break," he offered Villi.

"Thanks," he replied, "but I should be good until dark."

Cecilia closed her eyes and drifted off to sleep against Michael's side. He turned to Master Li, but the venerable wise man suspiciously cast his eye toward the approaching coastline. Michael did not wish to break his concentration as he probably contemplated some distant problem.

"How can you see through that?" Zinian linked to Han in the bow.

"From my perspective, I see very little distortion," he offered.

Inside the field, the further one is from the bow or stern, the more pronounced the distortion becomes. For those seated in the aft, the bow seemed like a swirl of color. Otherwise, right or left, the field of view is practically clear. However, for the navigator, visual acuity quickly became a problem, like trying to see through thick warped glass.

"Oh, I almost forgot," Chou said. He reached over and touched something on Villi's panel. A large wide clear curved shield rose up. When it locked into place, all of the distortion disappeared from Villi's perspective.

"Thanks," Villi linked to him.

"Zhiwei," Michael spoke up. He noticed Zhiwei had his black card out of the coast. "Instead of entering here, what about further north... here."

"Too many patrol boats," Zhiwei warned. "Even with invisibility, they may spot us."

Villi kept on the original planned course. The route on the screen automatically adjusted to his current position. He poured on the power at the last moment to push the craft against the flow of the rapid moving fresh water and the waves that clashed just off shore near a reef. For a few moments, he struggled with the controls while the sea tossed the front of the craft into the air.

"Hold onto something," he warned.

Han barely had time to reach out and grab the railing. More than any person on the craft, he had the most difficult time trying to stay in the bow, which shot nearly straight up before it crashed back into the surf. However, within minutes, they passed the breakers and the ship soon glided onto smooth river water. Once Villi started up the tributary, the watercraft settled into calm, steady, forward progress with only large mangrove trees and their entangling roots as obstacles to avoid.

From Han's point of view, the way ahead started coming at them too rapidly. He wanted to shout out warnings when he caught Villi's keen sense of perception. A natural driver whether it be a car, plane, or boat, Villi had the fastest reaction time of anyone in their group. He could steer anything with precision that would make a racecar driver insanely jealous. Soon the watercraft picked up speed and practically flew up the river. Han nervously glanced away, as the vessel dodged and sprinted around obstacles at breathtaking speed. The others learned to ignore the wild ride, as they trusted Villi's judgment.

"I think I'm going to be sick," Han moaned as he moved out of his snug position in the bow. He walked along the side deck and held onto the rail as the scenery flew past.

"Join us for some tea," Master Li beckoned. He made a hand signal to Michael.

"I'll whip something up," the team leader offered as he gently moved Cecilia off to the side. "I'll have to ignite the fusor..."

"I will muffle the start up," Li volunteered.

Michael went to the galley and activated the automated systems Chou installed. The fusor slid out from a hidden compartment.

"Initiate fusion reaction," a computer's voice chimed.

Michael touched a control.

"Please stand behind screen," the voice instructed.

A screen came out of the wall. Michael leaned back and looked up the stairs.

"Master Li!" he called out instead of linking.

He felt Li's power reach down and place a powerful psychic shield around the fusor. Li did not use a golden sphere during the initial energy release. He feared that in the weightless environ, the energy would rebound inward on the fusor and set off an uncontrolled fusion reaction – in other words, a hydrogen bomb!

Chou loudly cleared his throat when he caught Li's thoughts.

"I have installed a few safety features," he chirped up. "Give me a little credit. Uncontrolled reactions are not possible, even with a golden sphere. However, you would have one very damaged fusor and psychic when you released your golden sphere."

While Michael worked on cranking out treats, everyone gathered at the aft section of the boat and made small talk about what they could or could not do with a golden sphere. Villi kept his eyes forward and rapidly pressed their forward progress up stream at break neck speed. At first, the surrounding country consisted of open flat plains covered with sand, sparse islands of mangroves, and some shrubs. These offered little cover for the large silvery boat. Even in stealth mode, the distortion probably seemed conspicuous as they pushed upstream through the treacherous shallows that pushed swiftly against their progress at times.

Although the boat seemed to glide easily through the water, the engine strained to push the nine passengers and their heavy gear against the rapidly moving current. Villi hoped they would soon make their way toward deeper inland waters where the surface currents ran slower. Gradually, as the boat moved further upstream, the landscape eventually gave way to thicker cover until the stream wound through great bunches of mangroves.

Michael returned with a large tray: butter and cognac-brazed sea scallops, Beluga caviar, thin slices of raw Pacific salmon marinated in teriyaki sauce, caraway wafers made with organic Georgian wheat, a crock of whipped orange blossom honey, hot salsa, tahini, garlic paste, onion butter, dried cured dates, fresh figs, fresh slices of carrots, cucumbers, red peppers, and tomatoes. A freshly brewed pot of an herbal tea mix added to the delicious aroma. He floated down a stack of plates, silverware, and napkins.

"Dig in!" he declared.

"The fusor is an amazing device," Li considered when he saw the rare delicacies that Michael chose, "Is it not?"

No one could disagree. The group sighed with delight when they beheld the feast. The nice thing about the fusor is that you could produce clean, pure, animal by-products such as caviar – fusor created, fusor recycled, without the guilt of capturing, killing, or penning a naturally wild creature. The fusor perfectly duplicated the epitome of an item without harming any living thing. The luncheon diversion helped to take everyone's mind off the terrible task that lie ahead.

"Can't this boat steer itself?" Villi asked as he jealously glanced over his shoulder.

"If we were at sea, the answer would be yes," Chou told him, "but not on this river."

"Open, love," Su Lin said to him as she floated a wafer spread with caviar. Villi opened his mouth and thought back his gratitude to his wife.

Even Cecilia woke to the smell of food and joined the others as they partook. Villi minimized his side-to-side movements of the boat while they ate. The Niger Delta, like most river delta systems, is a vast web of tributaries and fabricated waterways. Literally hundreds of tributaries break from the main Niger River nears its end, winding their way through a maze that covers an area over two hundred square kilometers. Thick underbrush covers parts of this area, clogging water channels, while clouds of swarming insects, mostly the biting kind, strike if you move too slowly.

Unfortunately, Villi could no longer speed as the stream narrowed and the curves did not offer a clear view ahead. At last Villi had to slow down to the point where they inched their way through the delta. Off to the side, the team noticed people crowded the shorelines. Nearly naked women washed clothes in the dirty river water, a life of abject poverty and squalor.

"I want to come back here," Cecilia said as she stared at the passing villages. "I see much work that needs to be done."

"Mind if I join you in that venture?" Michael broke into her thoughts.

"I'd like that," she said as she turned to him.

Su Lin noticed that Li, Han, Zinian, and Zhiwei all had teacups in their laps. It seemed strange to her that they were on this African expedition and the men looked so… effeminate.

"This is a sight!" she laughed. "We've become the teetotaling society."

"I'd like to see any man knock it from my lap!" Zhiwei shot back.

Despite his small size, he had the highest degree of martial arts in several disciplines of any member in the WPO. Michael and Zinian studied and practiced as well. Villi specialized in a variety of martial arts. The four men often sparred.

"I should think she'd be glad we aren't the liquor guzzling, cigar smoking psychics?" Han muttered.

"That might make us a bit more appealing to some and perhaps even more human to others," Zinian spoke up. "My crew believes I am rather strange for not partaking in a beer after work. I told them that if I did, they would regret it far more than I would."

"Yes," Li spoke up. "Let's get stuporous on drugs like alcohol. Then we could use our power in some stupid way that would surly gain the attention of the Americans! Give into those urges, Zinian, and you'll wind up on a dissecting table yet!"

"It was just a comment, Master Li, nothing more," he said as he took a sip of tea. "Besides, I loathe the smell of beer, let alone the taste of it."

"Really! As I recall, when you met Master Li during your first year of college, you were drafting a fraternity pledge," Han commented. "I would suggest you come clean on your taste for beer."

"Well… I suppose I used to like it… a little," Zinian confessed.

"You do see the dangers, don't you Zinian?" Li pressed.

"I see that I freely chose this life. If I wanted to drink beer, I'll give up being a psychic as a choice. However, if I did give up being psychic just to drink beer, that would be incredibly stupid!" he grinned. "No, I have to agree wholeheartedly with you on this one, Master Li. Anything we consume that alters our state of consciousness might have disastrous consequences… especially now that we are Level V's."

"Amen," Cecilia added. "The use of opiates to dull pain is barbaric compared to inducing nerve blocks or altering the flow of neurochemicals. You won't find sophomoric depressants in my doctor's bag."

"I don't mean to interrupt, but an impassible obstacle is quickly approaching, Michael," Villi linked.

Michael glanced over Villi's shoulder and quickly appraised the situation.

"Golden sphere!" he called out. "Villi, use your thrusters and take us over it!"

The sphere-shaped field snapped into place around the boat and sliced down into the water, trapping some of the liquid inside, adding its volume to the effort. When Villi tried to use the thrusters, the boat pushed the sphere up out of the river while still going forward. Yet it also trapped the river water inside, which was now as weightless as the boat. Huge brownish-colored globes floated up around them. They hovered or bounced into one another. The weightlessness also sent people bouncing off their chairs. The tea floated up out of the cups. No one anticipated that the river water would slosh about inside the golden sphere and bounce off the interior surface.

Having passed over the logjam, Villi maneuvered the thrusters down and set the boat back into the river. The trapped water ominously rose up around them.

"Release the sphere!" he requested.

The second the sphere vanished, smelly dirty river water cascaded down all around them, dousing each person with buckets of the dirty brown stuff, except Master Li, who comfortably nestled into his dry portion of the bench. He had the presence of mind to make a psychic bubble around him that protected him from the water. Villi had the added protection of the navigator's cubby. He turned around and saw the chaos of the team floundering in filthy river water. Villi burst out laughing when he noticed Master Li completely dry.

"Now that's thinking ahead!" he chuckled.

Remembering how to remove particulate, the seven wet psychics pulled the dirty river water from their clothes. However, the beautiful brunch that Michael prepared lay in ruins. Whatever food they managed to consume before the onslaught would be it for a while.

"That was fun," Li linked to the pilot, "Let's do that again some time."

About twenty minutes later, after everyone cleaned up and Michael returned the disastrous feast to the fusor for recycling, the boat began to move slower and slower. The engine could not match the power of the river that pushed against it. Despite the fact the foam metal rose high in the water, the overweighted craft with its small engine could not fight the current of the river.

"I hate to break the news," Villi linked to Michael. "But we're going to need a more powerful motor with our extra weight."

"Your extra weight," Su Lin linked kiddingly.

"Very funny," Villi shot back. "Seriously, we need a much bigger boat. The river is deep enough to take on larger craft," he pointed out, "if we can find one."

Michael began to notice how the embankment moved past at a jogging pace. At this rate, it would several days to travel upstream.

"I'm forced to agree," he acknowledged. "I thought you said you could make a boat that would take us up the river?" he asked Chou.

"The power needed to propel our weight plus the cargo would mean a boat of much larger proportions. I could not squeeze such a craft into the cargo hold of Villi's aircraft, even with alien technology!" he stated.

"We'll have to find another solution," Michael countered. "Zhiwei, can you locate a boat we could adapt, perhaps something we could borrow?" he asked and cast a wary eye at Cecilia.

She disliked the idea of stealing people's property or taking money from banks when they were on one of these missions. Although in all fairness, the group always compensated the person with more than they originally had. Villi, being a former police officer, agreed with her stand. He and Cecilia often sided together in this regard. Michael and Su Lin tended to be pragmatic. Michael did not wait for Cecilia to object.

"I know you're going to object. But what would you have us do?" he asked. "Every hour we delay may be the Motambou's last."

She gave the matter a great deal of thought before she glanced over at Villi and shrugged.

"I give up on this one," she finally said.

"Allow me," Zhiwei replied. "I'll start scanning for a larger boat."

"We're entering the main branch of the Niger," Villi linked to Michael.

"How do ferryboats do it?" Michael wondered.

"You mean those small six person things that could tip over if you leaned to one side?" Chou put to him. "Or perhaps you refer to those ancient tubs they call river boats. They're entirely unsafe."

"I don't know how much longer the boat's small engine will hold out," Villi told them. "We may have to ditch and go ashore."

"Must we travel upstream in this… dingy?" Master Li suddenly spoke up. "Why not travel in style?"

"I wasn't aware of any other method," Michael replied.

"I don't mind tagging along on this mission, Michael," Master Li linked to him openly. "Let's go with a little class this time, shall we? Zhiwei!" he shouted into his mind, which startled the group.

"Master Li?" Zhiwei responded.

"Zhiwei, I thought you were locating a boat!" Li asked.

"I'm working on it, Master Li!" Zhiwei quickly thought back. "With so much traffic and varying types of vessels, it's difficult to sort out. Would you like the commercial fishing boat I found? It's a little smelly but it bunks nine."

"I would not!" Michael stood up. The tall slender young man quickly sat down when a low branch flew past overhead. That brought chuckles from all quarters of the craft.

"I'll help you look, Zhiwei," Han offered. "I know the busy river traffic is distracting."

"Actually, I'm fine, Han," Zhiwei told him. "Thanks for offering. I simply haven't found anything good enough for either Michael or Master Li!"

Zhiwei continued to search for a ferry of proper dimensions. Knowing Michael and Master Li's tastes, he tried to find one with more amenities, but his choices were rather limited, considering the local level of poverty.

"Perhaps a ship with a passenger's quarters," Su Lin offered.

"Yes, what about a cruise ship?" Zinian kidded his friend.

"Perhaps you'd like the QEII?" Zhiwei shot back.

"Her draft is too deep," Han commented.

"I'm using my brain too much, it hurts," Zinian cried.

He leaned over and put his head in Su Lin's lap. She giggled and started to massage his scalp.

"I'd like a boat with a masseuse," he requested. "This is the life," he sighed and closed his eyes.

"I expect the same treatment at the end of my shift," Villi broke in.

"I was hoping for more," Su Lin added.

Zinian opened his eyes and quickly sat up.

"Don't look at me!" he declared embarrassed.

Villi burst out laughing.

Han noticed clouds of insects swarming over the water.

"I hope this spray repels these biting insects," he said.

"Supposedly it not only repels insects, it also delays the need to shower for several days if we can't find any facilities," Michael put in.

"That simply will not do," Master Li spoke up. "Not shower for days? That's fine for you young people. You can tolerate the stink, but not for old people. We start to decay."

"I'm with him!" Cecilia chimed in.

"An alien formulated the stuff," Michael told them. "I wonder if they considered human odor into the ingredients.

"If everyone applies deodorant daily, we'll all be fine," Han added.

"Yes, but the heat and humidity are murder," Zinian muttered.

"Perhaps taking a shower won't be necessary," Su Lin announced as she gazed skyward. "We're traveling in the tropics," she reminded as she looked down at the screen. "Unfortunately, it's too early for the rainy season. The river level seems fine for some reason. Still, I wouldn't expect any heavy downpours."

As they rounded the next bend in the river, everyone could see the sky darkening ahead. Su Lin pulled out her black card and tapped into a weather satellite.

"I spoke too soon… a storm system *is* coming in," she informed them. "You have your shower, Cecilia. Rain will be here in less than two hours."

Villi had the engine throttle wide open. Still, the silvery craft crept along. The sun dropped lower in the afternoon sky and the shadows grew longer. With the engines strained to their limit, Villi could not outrun the storm and arrive at the next port in time. They began to see flashes of light and hear rumbles of thunder in the distance. As they rounded another bend, boats choked the passage ahead.

"Villi, the traffic is too congested," Zhiwei observed. "We must switch over to a disguise. Otherwise, I'm afraid we'll collide with someone."

Villi glanced over at Chou. The technologist pointed to Villi's control panel. The pilot found the application and activated it.

"Found it," he replied.

He switched the boat's exterior projection system to show them as a different vessel. Instead of being invisible, a special light filter projected an image around the boat. To anyone outside the boat, they appeared as a crowded riverboat, instead of a large metallic craft.

"The disguise is working," Han announced.

Several people waved as their boats passed.

"What the hell is that?" Zhiwei suddenly declared.

"Zhiwei? What is it?" Michael asked.

The security chief held up his expanded card so the others could see it. They stared at the screen in his hands with disbelief.

Chapter Twenty-five

Poseidon

"I can't believe it," Zhiwei suddenly linked. "Master Li?"

He passed his black card over to Li, whose trembling hand accepted it.

"It is here..." Li whispered when he saw the ship.

"What's here?" Su Lin asked and sat up.

Li handed the expanded card back to Zhiwei.

"Looks like a yacht," Li responded.

"Wait a second," Cecilia spoke up. "You mean to say that thing is on the river... near us?"

"You sounded as though you recognized it," Michael put to Li.

"Let me see that," Han requested. "I know this boat. It's been in the news. That's not just any yacht," he stated. "That's a billionaire's yacht."

"Billionaire?" Chou questioned. "How do you know that?"

"Look at the name on the aft section," Han pointed out on Zhiwei's screen. "The *Poseidon* launched just two weeks ago from Italy. It's one of the most expensive yachts ever built!"

Han took Zhiwei's card and brought up a newswire item. The whole group took in a collective breath when they watched the broadcast. He stopped the image.

"No technical information about the boat," he commented.

"Strange he picked the name Poseidon – ruler of the oceans," Su Lin stated.

Michael never stopped looking at Master Li. He wondered if he was the only one who heard his whisper. He finally glanced over at Zhiwei.

"Security?" he asked. "What do you say? Is it safe?"

Zhiwei put his card into scan mode.

"Some bodyguards and staff here and there," Zhiwei informed them.

"Very convenient," Su Lin commented.

"Too convenient if you ask me," Han linked and shot Master Li a quick glance. "Why take a cruise up the Niger River? Why not go to Capri?"

"You're always suspicious," Zinian linked back.

"Maybe he likes to travel in style," Chou put in, "like someone else we know," he said as he looked over at Michael.

"One thing is certain," Master Li stated the obvious, "it solves many of our problems."

"I've tapped into its security files," Zhiwei spoke up. "The yacht belongs to an oil magnate. He's come up the Niger is to settle a long time debt with an oil minister who lives in the village of Bolougbene. He also brought along a small army of security personnel and some special guests to help launch the vessel on her maiden voyage. If you were concerned about the draft, Chou, don't be. Two large tributaries of the Niger River merge near Bolougbene. The engines on this enormous boat can easily handle any current."

"Look at the size of that thing. How many levels does it have? Four?" Zinian speculated.

"Five," Michael said as he peered closer at Zhiwei's card.

"It's definitely big," Su Lin mentioned as she crowded in.

"I'm still concerned about its displacement," Chou wondered. "She'll flounder."

Villi took an advanced reading on the river ahead. He found the river had the depth required to carry a vessel of that size without grounding.

"I'm surprised," he said and shared his findings with them. "Judging from her keel, her displacement, and draft… I've also checked the water table up ahead, depth of river, shallows, number of sand bars, rocks… I estimate the yacht should be able to navigate the river for another three or four hundred kilometers," he guessed. "That should take us well into Nigeria, probably past Lokoja."

"What will we do after Lokoja? Walk?" Su Lin asked.

"Cross that bridge when we come to it," Michael threw out.

"Don't you think we'll be a little conspicuous," Cecilia offered, "sailing up the Niger River in a giant stolen yacht?"

"Is it possible to adapt a camouflage device?" Zhiwei put to Chou.

Chou looked at the picture of the yacht and began to make a series of mental calculations.

"I suppose we'll have to… if we want to use it," he responded. "Thank goodness we have a fusor. I had only intended its use for food. I always bring a reader with me…"

"Always?" Michael questioned.

Chou only stared back at him, which gave his answer.

"I could probably cannibalize parts off this tin can and manufacture several small power cubes," he stated, "enough to keep the projectors running for the next two weeks... if the mission takes that much time."

"Start on it right away, Chou," Michael instructed. "We'll need to transfer everything over to that boat the minute we land."

"Then we're taking the yacht?" Cecilia questioned.

"So it would seem," Master Li answered. "Any objections?"

"The owners might have a few," Cecilia tossed back.

"I back Cecilia on that objection!" Villi chimed in.

"I'm force to agree," Han added. "Taking a riverboat is one thing. This is the world's most expensive yacht. We're stealing. That violates our charter."

"I can tell you this billionaire stocked his galley with practically everything you'd need for a gourmet meal," Su Lin said with her black card scanning the ship. "You won't need the fusor for food."

"The yacht has plenty of extra fuel, too," Zinian added with his expanded black card out, too.

"Did anyone bother to check the sleeping quarters? No? Well, I did," Master Li slyly linked. "I'd like the master suite on the fifth level."

"All yours Master Li," Michael linked and patted the elderly man's knee. "I'll make the other assignments once we move onboard."

"The yacht has extremely sumptuous sleeping accommodations for ten guests," Zhiwei informed them. "That doesn't including the staff quarters below the main deck..."

"This is very mean spirited," Cecilia interrupted. "We're the wealthiest people on the globe and we haven't brought along the proper gear? We can't just leave these people stranded in the Niger Delta with no means of travel... *and* a rain storm on the way! It's not ethical," she objected and stood up. "I won't allow it to happen."

"I still agree with Cecilia," Villi put in.

"I believe on this point, I agree with Cecilia, too," Su Lin voiced.

"I'm with them," Han echoed.

"You're right," Master Li stated. He held up his hands to stop any further objection. "I have an idea. Would you care to hear it?"

"Don't try to trick me," Cecilia warned.

"I propose a purchase. How would it be if we buy this vessel?"

"They won't sell it out here. They'll be stranded Master Li," she countered.

"No one will be stranded without their creature comforts, for very long," he reassured her. "I'll have a helicopter come to their rescue. As to the compensation for the yacht, I will go far beyond the current value, will that be satisfactory?"

"I suppose," she said hesitantly.

Master Li took out his black card, placed three fingers on the front and it sprang to life.

"Steven Harper," he spoke aloud.

Within seconds the screen sputtered to life with a life-like image of Steven Harper, the current CEO of the Tyler Foundation located in New York City. The word, "pending," flashed over his picture. Master Li knew that meant Steven had to find a private place to use his card. He patiently waited until the picture turned from static to a live view of Steven in a private restroom.

"Master Li," Steven said as he bowed his head, "to what do I owe the honor," he asked.

"We'd like to buy a yacht," Li began.

"Certainly," Steven said. "I know of several in the marketplace or would you like one built to order," he wondered.

"No, we've decided to take this one instead," Li told him and flashed the picture through to him along with the information on the owner.

"I know this man," Steven responded at once, "a Nigerian oil magnate who sold his corporate interest in GYR Oil for a reputed 30 billion, although most governments had trouble tracking the funds. He's a sleaze, Master Li," he told him. "This must be about his new yacht, the Poseidon. Am I right?"

Master Li nodded.

"You intended to compensate him?" Steven wondered. "I'd just take it. He's not a nice fellow, Master Li. He has many ties with drug lords and weapons dealers, slave trade, prostitution… the list goes on."

"We're not interested in a character assassination. You know that isn't our style," Li half-smiled and glanced over at Cecilia. She sheepishly shrugged. "Compensate him for his loss via insurance and stock, Steven," Master Li instructed.

"Cecilia or Villi insisted on this course of action, didn't they?" the CEO of the Tyler Foundation correctly guessed.

"… and I'm proud of that, too!" she added from the background.

Everyone laughed. Even Steven Harper smiled.

"Ok, Cecilia," Steven spoke from the screen, "you win. Full compensation. Though the next time you have a free minute, you might look into the owner's background. This is less like stealing and more like payback for all of his victims. However, I will grant your wishes. Anything else?"

"Thank you, Steven," Master Li said. "We'll speak later, after the mission."

"Just a word," Steven added, "please give the warmest regards to… that is, when you rescue Salla and Filla."

Master Li and the rest of team caught Steven's sincere sentiment.

"I will," Li replied. "Li out."

The screen shrank to credit card size and Master Li slipped it back into his pocket. "Satisfied?" he said to the group. When no one complained, he turned toward Michael. "You have a green light, Michael. Make the arrangements for our transfer."

"What about their personal items, pictures, computers, things like that?" Cecilia spoke up.

"Michael will see they are left on the docks. Won't you Michael?" Li threw to him.

"Yes, sir," Michael concurred, "as if I didn't have enough on my plate," he privately thought.

The group sat poised, waiting for Cecilia's reaction.

"If I didn't know any better, I'd say you tricked me," she privately linked to Li.

"We must travel on this boat," Li privately linked back. "It is essential for our survival."

"What an odd thing to say," she considered.

Cecilia stared back at Li confused.

"Master Li, a word… in private," Han spoke up.

Before Cecilia could address her suspicions, Han caught Master Li's attention and the two men raised a block around their interaction. Li and Han privately communicated for a few seconds. Li seemed to do all of the linking. Han barely nodded back at him. In an instant, Cecilia knew she stumbled onto an aspect of events that only Master Li knew and Han probably suspected.

"What did Michael know? He spent a great of time at the mansion," she wondered. "Master Li can see into the future of probabilities," she remembered. "Does he know something about the yacht that no one else knows?"

She glanced over at Han. She was the only one in position to catch the exchange between them but heard nothing. She halted any further objections and decided to go along. Li would no longer give her eye contact and seemed to avoid her. That bothered her.

As the boat that carried the nine psychics rounded a river bend, the yacht in all of its glory, came into view.

"Whoa!" Zinian stood up, astonishment written across his face. "It's gargantuan! I don't care what you say. That'll never make it up stream!"

"Easy, Zinian," Chou said. He reached up and pulled him back down. "I checked over Villi's scan. He's right," he linked and showed Zinian his screen to prove it.

Su Lin turned to Zhiwei.

"Next time, give us some scale," she linked. "That's a floating city."

"It's bigger than even I thought," Villi muttered and for a moment, he forgot to steer the raft.

The most expensive yacht in the entire world sat moored at the dock, its white and silver surface glistened in the afternoon sunlight. The vessel seemed more like a cruise-ship than a yacht. At 180 meters in length, and twenty-three meters wide, this behemoth appeared totally out of place in such a remote section of Africa.

"Look at how much water she displaces," Chou observed. He took his black card and scanned the vessel. He whistled and looked around at the others. "Unbelievable."

"Are you sure we can sail a boat that size upriver?" Michael asked. "She'll scrape the bottom. The river isn't that deep!"

Chou turned his card around and expanded its size. He showed the others a complete read out of the vessel.

"Her hull is wide at the bottom which makes her ride shallower than she appears," he gestured as he spoke. The builder knew how to make a versatile boat."

"Why do you say that?" Master Li asked.

"Look at this. You can alter the hull shape to compensate for the environment," Chou informed them. "Over-lapping plates will allow you take the ship from sea and up river by altering its keel. She'll actually sail into fairly shallow bays while also be sea worthy. It takes a lot of money to make a boat of that quality. If Villi's figures about the river depth are correct, we could continue up the river for… who knows… four hundred, possibly a six hundred kilometers," Chou figured. "If it rains, the runoff will bolster the water level. The engines are powerful enough to handle any current."

"What will we do after we travel four hundred kilometers?" Michael wondered, yet no one answered him.

"How did it get here?" Su Lin asked.

"The main channel to the sea is dredged," Zhiwei informed them. "They probably navigated up that tributary from the coast. When you are a billionaire, anything is possible."

Han frowned as he puzzled over the craft's design. He said nothing but glanced sidelong at Master Li. Curiously, Li turned his head away from Han and gazed at the shore, as if he could sense something far away in the jungle. Han could not penetrate his thoughts. No one could, unless Li allowed it.

Michael stood up and stared in the direction of the large ship. Like Han, he also wore an expression of concern.

"This is all wrong… I sense something awry… that boat did not travel up the river," he blurted. "I believe someone airlifted the thing in and set it right in front of that dock. This river is filthy with pollution. Look at its sides… no oil along the starboard side!"

This time when Han and Li exchanged glances, Michael and Cecilia caught it.

"Excellent observation," Han quickly spoke up. "If you discover how they managed to lift such an enormous vessel in the air, Michael, we might just fit another piece to our growing puzzle."

Michael carefully regarded Han after he made that remark.

"Don't you believe someone put it here deliberately?" Michael wondered.

Han did not acknowledge Michael's question.

"Han and Michael are correct to observe the coincidence of just the right size and type of boat that just happened to be exactly where we needed it," Master Li linked. "However, Michael, to address your skepticism, I don't believe someone airlifted the boat. It is clean because of its crew and its owner's insistence on cleanliness."

Zinian, Zhiwei, Su Lin and Chou went forward and stood in the bow while they used their ability to scan the yacht.

"Some of you need to sit down so I can navigate!" Villi mentally shouted.

As the disguised craft drew nearer, the immense proportions of the yacht loomed ever larger. From water level to the very top of the communications tower must have spanned a height of over thirty-five meters. The command bridge alone took one entire forward section of the second level.

"The closer we come… I'm beginning to wonder… Can we navigate a boat that size safely up the river?" Zhiwei asked. "It's too big."

"I have my doubts with all that gear on top," Zinian said. He pointed at the various radar and communications towers. "What will happen when we encounter low lying bridges, narrow passages, or trees overhead?"

"I suppose we'll find out," Villi commented as he maneuvered their boat along side. "Anyone for giving up or finding a better mode of transportation, other than the world's most expensive yacht?" No one commented. "Then, I suggest we follow Master Li's advice and Michael's guidance."

Just as the large metallic raft began to pull alongside the yacht, rain started to fall from the sky in the form of a sprinkle. The few drops of moisture that pelted them did not restrain the team with determined expressions. Despite their piracy, they knew the real objective involved the safety and security of their friends. While they looked out for humanity in general, their small numbers mattered in personal ways when one of them was threatened. They kept this in perspective as they advanced on the huge ship parked next to them.

Security conscious Zhiwei reached out with his mind. Using his new Level V ability, the remaining crew and passengers aboard the yacht suddenly decided to go ashore. They managed to grab most of their personal things in the process, which he knew would help save Michael a step. Soon, a procession of people poured down the gangplank onto the docks. The security personnel stationed at the base of entry ramp stood still with strange blank expressions on their faces. They stared straight ahead as if transfixed on some point in space, not minding that the yacht behind was now empty of a crew.

"Did you do that?" Michael wondered and turned to Master Li.

Before Li could answer, Zhiwei chimed in.

"That's my job Michael," he linked, "I did."

"Great work," Michael commented, "and fast, too."

Zinian jumped out and secured the bowline to the dock. Michael secured the aft. One by one, the crew disembarked the much smaller metallic boat, every person tasked with some burden. They quickly stripped off every gadget and mentally carried every piece of luggage over to the yacht. Even Master Li contributed his part by helping to float supplies and his luggage.

Once emptied, Chou took out his black card and formed a complex keyboard out of it. He touched a few areas that lit up. The bottom of the raft began to dissolve, which scuttled the craft. Its molecular bonds broke apart and the boat literally melted into oblivion without a trace. Once he knew the mechanism left no residual to poison the water, he brushed his hands together and joined the rest of the team already aboard the yacht.

"The team is underway with preparations to leave, Master Li," Michael informed him. "They've fanned out to explore the ship and find out its workings."

"Carry on, Michael," Li directed.

Michael mentally reminded each team member where they should concentrate.

"Villi, bridge; Chou, engine room; Su Lin, galley; Han and Cecilia, crews quarters; Zhiwei, address security; Zinian, mooring system; I will inspect the upper decks for personal items. Let's move… we only have a matter of a few minutes. Hurry!"

The psychic group quickly moved to take over the big boat by becoming acquainted with its facilities. Villi headed straight for the bridge and set about learning the controls. Chou went to the engine room to inspect the mechanics of the ship's propulsion. Su Lin headed to the galley to look over the food preparation system. She also held the fusor and its power system in the air behind her as she moved in that direction. Zinian looked over the anchor system control panel located near the bow. He loosened the exterior moorings after they carried the last of the supplies aboard. Zhiwei found and then disabled any tracking or security devices placed on the yacht by the billionaire. He also set up the camouflage electronic devices Chou brought onto the yacht. He hurriedly ran along the deck and placed power cubes with projectors at strategic locations. Cecilia looked over the crew's quarters, pulled out any personal items and left them on deck. Then she took over an office to set up a lab with the equipment they brought. After he assisted Cecilia, Han moved to the bedroom suites on the higher floors to help Michael clear out personal items.

Michael headed directly to the master suite where he collected the owner's personal items, which he promised to leave behind. He opened the boat's safe and emptied its contents into a secure metal container he found. He knew that the owner, still ashore, had the key. He locked the box before he left it on the deck along with all the other personal items their team assembled. Cecilia signaled to Michael that she had finished her sweep. Michael moved all the items on deck to the dock below and covered everything with a plastic drop cloth.

"I can't find Li. Are you certain he's aboard?" he linked to Han.

"Yes, I just sensed him a moment ago," Han told him. "He walked toward the bow."

"I can't sense him, Han," Michael linked back.

"You know Master Li," Han linked, "if he wants to be private, he can disappear. He might even be in time travel. Who knows? I'm with Zinian. He and I have figured out the mooring panel. We can operate the system from the bridge."

"Right. Villi? Have you learned the engine controls?" Michael asked.

"I'm working on it," he quickly linked back. "This may take a few minutes. For being rather simple in construction, the ship's controls are hard-wired into the navigation system. I have to decipher the codes."

"Use your black card. Please hurry. We may only have seconds instead of minutes. Chou?" Michael switched his focus.

"We've got plenty of fuel," he chimed up from below. "The ship is enormous and displaces a great deal of water. Despite the altered shape for river travel, the hull sits deeper than I thought. We may run aground if Villi ventures out of the main channel."

"Zhiwei?" Michael checked next.

"I've turned off the installed security systems and the tracking devices. We don't need GPS, so I switched that off as well, anything they might use to locate the vessel. I'm heading to the conning tower to set up the last of our holo-projectors. I already placed them, port, starboard, fore and aft. If you have finished with the engines, Chou, I could use your help," he hinted.

"Heading up now, Zhiwei," Chou replied.

"Take the elevator from below," Zhiwei offered.

"Elevator? Nice!" Chou replied as he ran toward the shaft's access doors in the engine room.

"Cecilia?" Michael checked next.

"I found a few additional things. I added them to the personal items on the dock, Michael," she told him, "and withdrew the automated gangplank."

"Su Lin?" Michael called out. "What's the situation like in the galley? Do we have enough fresh water?"

"The galley has more supplies than Running Elk's kitchen. It's incredible," she pointed out. "I know they didn't stop here for food! Plus, we have the fusor from the raft. I checked the water system. They have a very sophisticated recycling system that should keep us in fresh water for a long period before it needs recharging. By long period, we're talking weeks. Cecilia… the showers have timers!"

"What?" Cecilia shot back.

"I thought that would get your attention," Su Lin chuckled.

"Very good team," Michael acknowledged. "Be ready to disembark when Zhiwei has the final camouflage projector in place and Villi gives the signal," Michael piped to the team.

"Steering a vehicle this size will be difficult at first," Villi muttered as his mind probed the controls. "When you finish on the conning tower, you might give me a hand, Chou," he requested.

Chou acknowledged and hummed as he rode the lavish elevator to the very top.

Cecilia thoroughly inspected every bedroom, in case someone fell asleep in a bed or was in the shower when Zhiwei encouraged the crew and passengers to leave. She agreed with the Michael. The ship appeared to be so new that the owners had yet to use many of the rooms. She turned a corner and practically ran into Master Li on the fifth floor just as she entered the master suite.

"Oh! There you are!" she declared. "I found Master Li!"

"You were concerned of my whereabouts," Li linked. "I'm checking out my bedroom."

"Han said you went to the bow," she commented.

"I've been to several places on the ship," he quietly stated as he ran his hands over the thick satin comforter. "Very nice."

"I'd like to take the bedroom down the hall on the same level," Michael requested. "No objections?"

Since no one linked anything in return, Michael took that as an affirmation he could take the second suite on that floor. He walked out on the main deck and looked around. Zhiwei managed to maintain control over the bodyguards while he carried out his duty on the tower with Chou. Michael swept over the minds of those assembled on the dock. He altered their thoughts and memories accordingly. He knew the owners would return once the rain fell harder than it had. He felt sorry for the crew they left standing in the rain, but he had little choice. Cecilia decided to join Michael on the main deck and took the elevator down.

"We'll be ready on our end in a few minutes, Michael," Zhiwei told him.

"We're running out of time, people," Michael piped to his crew. "The owner will return with his guests to the boat. I sense he doesn't like the rain. We must leave in two minutes! Zhiwei! Chou! Villi! Hurry!"

Villi's mind searched through the electronic controls until he found the ones that started the engines and manipulated the thrust controls. The yacht rumbled to life – its engine complex sent an alert hum through the giant vessel.

"Moorings clear?" he called out via a general link.

"Moorings clear," Zinian and Han answered as they checked the status of the four anchors. "Thruster controls at your discretion."

Zhiwei and Chou just finished connecting the last power cube. Chou pulled out his black card that reverted into a special all-in-one remote. He touched the face. The second he activated the holo-projectors, the great yacht vanished from view. Michael took that moment from the minds of those around them. He could feel Master Li at his figurative side in assisting with a memory erasure. Li's power passed out over the surrounding area like great pulsing waves of energy. Michael appreciated his help.

"Takes us out of here, Villi," Michael ordered.

"Huh! This thing has side thrusters and stabilizer motors," Villi realized as his mind touched the control board. The yacht pushed sideways away from the dock into the center of the river. "Master Li!" Villi cried out when he realized they took up a great deal of room. "I'm going to need some interference..."

"I'm way ahead of you," Master Li said as he stepped through the doors onto the third floor deck. From this vantage point, he could see the entire river. Surprised ferryboat owners began to veer right and left as the large invisible object pushed into the river's center.

"Prepare for forward thrust," Villi told them.

A shudder passed through the boat as if the propeller were moving for the very first time, followed by a loud, "whoosh, whoosh, whoosh, whoosh," as the cavitation pushed the big boat upstream. Almost at once, the sound died out and the yacht lurched forward, moving much faster than their previous vessel did. Villi sat in the command chair and propped his feet up.

"Piece of cake," he said with a grin.

"We're leaving a wake!" Han pointed out.

"No… we're not," Master Li interjected. The river water miraculously flattened behind the great boat with no telltale trail as they moved out of port.

"Sweet!" Villi said with a grin as he glanced up at the aft screen.

Outside on the docks, the security team remained at their post. The ship's crew stood still and stared at the river. As far as they were concerned, the yacht remained at station while a small ferry parked nearby pulled away. Michael and Li completely altered the perception in their minds and in the minds of those standing around on the docks. Soon, the yacht left its previous passengers stranded in a steady downpour of tropical rain. When the poor depraved billionaire returned to the docks a few minutes later with his umbrella-covered entourage in tow, he found his security bodyguards and his crew standing amidst their belongings, getting soaked. He exploded with fury.

"Where the hell is my boat?" he roared.

"Right here," the head of security said as he turned around. The illusion planted in his mind vanished and revealed an empty mooring. "What?" the man shrieked when he only saw an empty dock. He swore that he and his team had not moved from the spot the entire time.

"That's right," the others around them honestly chimed in.

"I'll have you all arrested," the upset wealthy man declared as he left in search of local authorities. He could not believe anyone could misplace such an immense object without aiding in its theft.

However, the local police suddenly had multiple problems. A riot broke out at the local market. In fact, an unexplained number of incidents broke out all over town. Overwhelmed with trouble, the police captain declined repeated requests to assist the billionaire with his missing yacht.

"Do you own a cell phone?" the police captain put to him.

"Yes!" the billionaire angrily answered.

"Then I suggest you call for help!" the captain shot back in broken English. "I've got problems of my own to solve. This town's gone crazy!"

Frustrated, the billionaire returned to the docks and grilled the security team who remained at their post. He started to rant when his security chief spoke up.

"Honestly sir, I don't know what happened," the man said with all sincerity. "You can have me arrested. I just wanted you to know, I haven't been idle. While you went looking for the police, I notified the river authorities in Nembe. They'll be searching the river up and down for the yacht. They promised to involve the central government when I mentioned your name. Also, a large rescue helicopter is on the way to pick you up. They should be arriving shortly. They will fly you and your guests out of here no later than twenty minutes from now. I also found this… over here, with other things," the man told his boss.

He held out a metal case. The wealthy man took out his key and opened the case. It held all of his personal effects, a computer, money, his wife's jewelry and many important papers he had in the safe. Another case contained things such as his favorite pictures, books, and mementos.

"This is very odd," he said as he examined the box's contents. He looked at his head of security. "It's as if they only wanted the boat." He looked at the box and then at his bodyguard, a man he thought he knew well after all the years the man served him. "What should I do with you?" the billionaire wondered. "I am extremely upset… to say the least."

"If I were you, sir, I'd fire me immediately," the man spoke with all sincerity. "I let you down. I failed in my job. You can't afford to have a failure like me around."

The seventy-eight-year-old retired billionaire shook his head. He could not recall the number of times he placed his wife and children in the hands of this man and knew they would be safe. He never trusted anyone else in his life as much as he trusted this man. Still, he could not explain the yacht or the way the crew seemed so genuinely confused. Nothing added up, and yachts of this size don't disappear. He decided to leave the yacht business to the government. Let them find the thieves. He would deal with them later. He had to think of his wife and their guests. He moved in closer to his bodyguard so that only the man could hear him.

"I'm afraid can't fire you," the rich man spoke with honest feelings. "You've saved my life too many times. Beside, who could replace you? I can buy another boat. It's just a thing. However, I could never find another man I can trust like you," he said.

It did not sound like the heartless money barron who "screwed" so many people through the years. Something inside the man changed in that moment. He no longer felt tied to his possessions or material things. He felt differently about his guests and this man. He wanted to reform his ways. He wanted to cut his ties get to the illegal businesses that had brought him wealth. If this was a sign from one of his enemies, that they could sneak up and take something this large away, then perhaps he had better heed this as a warning. He turned to face his wife and their guests.

"Obviously, I haven't figured out what happened… yet," he said aloud, "bandits somehow drugged my security team. When I returned to the dock, I saw them, just as you did, staring straight ahead when we walked up. Judging by the sophistication of this operation, and the fact there were no witnesses anywhere on the dock, it could have been the work of highly trained and organized terrorists. I'm certain the authorities will eventually find the boat. When they do, then perhaps we'll have some answers."

The expression on his wife's face at that moment changed from one of hardness to one of love. She gazed deeply into her husband's eyes and found something that had been missing for a very long time. He nodded that acknowledgment and continued. He looked at the case in his hands.

"What I can't figure out is why someone would purposely take my personal things off the boat and then leave them in water proof containers, as if they were being considerate," the man said as he looked over at the stack of containers on the dock.

"Perhaps it is a sign," his wife whispered.

Once more, he nodded to her. He turned around and placed his hand on his security chief's arm.

"Helicopter's on the way, you say?" he asked.

"Yes, sir," the man replied.

"Guide the helicopter in. I will call for another helicopter for you and the crew," the billionaire told him. "We'll meet you back at Nembe. Bring my things. Understood?"

"Yes, sir!" the man said.

Later after the dust settled, and the billionaire quickly recovered the money he lost, he gave up the idea of owning a yacht, and retired to an island off the coast of Argentina to the end of his days with his wife and the same security man who loyally watched over the man. So much for his obsession with being Poseidon, ruler of the seas.

Chapter Twenty-six

Motivation

"I've been spoiled in the mansion so long, I never thought about going to sea in similar fashion," Han noted as he ran his hand along the polished hardwood-panel. "I never knew a regular human builder could put this much luxury into a ship."

"The world is full of many wonders. The Tyler Foundation is flush with petty cash. Perhaps you should take the time to travel," Li said as he walked down the staircase with Han from the fourth level to the third.

"I might take you up on that offer… some day," Han replied.

A wide polished wooden staircase in the ship's middle connected the third, fourth, and fifth levels with the elevator nearby. As they turned the corner, Han noted the opulent hallway: in addition to the carved wooden panels, the polished brass railings, the marble floors and gold trim, the sides had lights behind beveled cut-crystal faces. The ceiling bowed with recessed lights behind a curved relief. Painted cumulous clouds adorned the artificial blue sky.

The fifth level had two large "four-room" suites and two "three-room" suites. The fourth level had six "two room" suites, not quite as large but just as luxurious. The third level had other amenities that Li and Han noticed when they descended the staircase and inspected the long hallway.

The two men moved up the third level corridor toward the bow. They found an open room with a long table and twelve chairs around it, obviously a dining room. The ceiling had a sparkling chandelier fixed into a large half-globe. Glass cases in the walls held sets of beautiful expensive matching china; crystal cut stemware, sterling silver warming plates, exquisite bone china, and a complete set of sterling silver tableware: a variety of forks, knives, and spoons, all polished to perfection in rich, dark velvet holders. The place glistened and shined with first-class elegance.

"Quite nice," Han declared as they entered the overly indulgent space with its emphasis on highly polished carved woods, gold trim, and natural granite surfaces.

"Now this reminds me of home," Master Li quipped.

Han shot Li a glance. Master Li shrugged his shoulders.

"Are you referring to that monstrosity your devoted pupil designed and built?" Han threw at him.

"I believe they refer to it as the WPO headquarters and not my house," Li said as he smiled back innocently at Han.

"Get a load of this!" Zinian linked from the aft third floor deck. "An outdoor hot tub!" he declared. "I also saw his and hers saunas, a steam room, and a movie theater with overstuffed chairs. It has a popcorn machine!" he declared. "The game room has a billiards table and a long bar next to a walk-in humidor for cigars."

"I see you found the liquor and cigars," Su Lin quipped from the galley. "I'd like to add, FYI," she linked, "the ship's galley has every food indulgence you can imagine, from caviar to pâté de foie gras, stuff that's been outlawed in several nations. The prep cooks have airtight bins of chopped onions, celery, carrots, turnips, potatoes, tomatoes, sliced lemons, oranges, limes… I'm overwhelmed. I've enough prime rib and filet mignon in the walk-in cooler to choke a lion. Chateaubriand, anyone?"

Han and Master Li walked from the dining room back into the hall and headed toward the large third floor deck in the bow. They stopped at the interior lounge surrounded with large windows and sliding glass doors that led to the outside deck, which had four seating areas that included tables, upright chairs, and chaise lounges. On the beautiful inside table, someone placed a bottle of Bollinger's, wrapped with thick white linen inside a silver ice bucket next to a spray of fresh flowers. A large three-tiered box of hand-made Belgian chocolates rested on the other side of the wine.

"Oh, welcoming gifts! They were expecting us," Han dryly commented.

"Someone expected anyone but us," Li said as he glanced around. "Notice… everything is untouched. If they journeyed up river…"

"The steward set it out for returning guests…" Han quickly shot back.

"I'll grant that," Li replied. "However, the question remains, strategist, is the billionaire intended for this boat, or are we?"

Han started out the deck's doors when he stopped in his tracks and stared at Li's poker face.

"You and I both know the answer to that question," Han shot back.

"You've been playing cat and mouse with me long enough. What did you mean by that comment you made to Cecilia?" he questioned.

"Nothing," Li casually tossed off as he moved the glass doors open with his mind. "But don't you think it's an odd coincidence…" he said, his voice trailed off.

"Now what?" Han practically demanded.

"A luxury yacht that surly cost several hundred million euros should be in this unique spot at this moment, as if someone knew we would need a vessel of this size…" Li pointed out.

"No… Li, I…" Han stammered.

He started to link further when Master Li turned away and put his block up. Han nearly exploded with anger when he sensed Michael stepping off the elevator down the hall. While he revealed a great deal at the manor house, he realized that Master Li wanted to withhold certain information from his star pupil. He put up his block, too.

"Have you seen everything on the boat?" Michael cheerfully asked when he entered, oblivious to the conversation that just took place. However, almost at once, he detected the level of discomfort between the two men as well as their high-level mental blocks. "Ok…" he said as he backed off and looked around. "I love the hand-made chocolates," he observed. He reached over and popped one into his mouth. He closed his eyes and sighed as the pricey confection melted its sweet gooey insides over his tongue. "The delights of the wealthy," he finally linked. "I once saw a box like that in Germany when we visited Jonathan and Maria," he noted.

He looked back and forth between the two men and noticed the way they avoided each other. He had intruded on a private meeting and felt he should leave.

"Oh, by the way," he mentioned before he left, "running a ship this size will take cooperation. Thankfully, we have a specialized team: Villi as navigator, Su Lin in the galley, Cecilia with her lab equipment, Chou in the engine compartment, and Zinian inspecting the hull and the mechanics. Zhiwei is installing additional security devices…" he stopped and noticed the two men continued to avoid him. "I don't know what you two are up to… but I'll bet it spells trouble."

Michael turned around and headed back down the hall.

"Is it trouble?" Han verbally put to Li after Michael disappeared.

Master Li would not respond. He only shrugged as he walked through the sliding glass doors to the bow and gazed upstream while the large ship silently sliced its way up the Niger River.

Chapter Twenty-Seven

The Natural Flow of Things

The bed assignment turned out to be relatively easy. Master Li kept the huge owner's suite that included its own deck, a baby grand piano, a living room, and its own "mini-galley" (meant for a private chef, no longer aboard). Michael and Cecilia took one of the fifth floor suites. Villi and Su Lin took another suite on that level, each with its own outside deck. Han, Chou, Zinian, and Zhiwei did not want to fight over who would take the last suite on that floor. Rather, they jockeyed for the fore and aft positions on the fourth level that had their own smaller end decks.

Michael rose during the late evening hours after a short nap and relieved Villi on the bridge after his friend explained the controls. The following morning, Villi resumed his bridge duty. Michael put off going to sleep for a little while. He went to the first level deck that encircled the ship. He jogged around the deck, despite the rain that continued to plague their journey. The ship's first level held some of the crew's quarters along with the machinery for air filtration, water purification, and additional batteries. After a few minutes jogging, he walked to the bow, removed his shirt, and sat in a lounge chair. Momentarily at least, the rain stopped and the equatorial sun beat down upon his pale skin.

"Villi informed me you did not go to bed. Care for some tea?" Su Lin linked to his mind.

"You read my mind," Michael kidded.

"May I join you?" Han spoke up. He walked along the deck from the elevator and sensed Michael on the forward deck. He first removed the moisture before he sat in one of the lounge chairs and put up his feet. He also took off his shirt. Surprisingly, Han was in better physical shape than Michael realized when he happened to glance over at the strategist. Cecilia really took care of the members in that regard. Michael supposed that every Rollo psychic was in perfect physical shape. When Master Li walked out on deck, neither Michael nor Han greeted the elderly man. Li said nothing, but headed over to another chair. Su Lin arrived with a loaded trolley. She offered Master Li tea first, which he gladly accepted.

"May I offer to negotiate peace in this somber group?" she linked with all three. "I come cheap."

"There's nothing cheap about you, Su Lin," Michael said quietly. "I believe we can work things out. Thanks for the offer."

She served the men tea with a light breakfast before heading to the bridge. Cecilia appeared as the men quietly enjoyed their breakfast. She noticed the lack of communication between the three men who normally could not be quiet between them. She tactfully remained silent as she sat next to Michael. He reached over and took her hand. She linked to him that she spoke with Mark and replayed the conversation. Michael listened yet seemed tired. She glanced over at Master Li who stared straight ahead at the river.

Han sensed Li's isolation and resolved to end their differences. Yet, before he could interfere, Michael, Cecilia, and Han noted that Master Li emitted tremendous power. He seemed to gather energy from sources offshore in anticipation of some event. To the amazement of everyone present, Li's chair rose in the air and turned around to face the other three psychics.

"Mastering the moment is less important than seeing the overall picture," he linked to them. "You've placed a burden of responsibility on me from the start of our relationship. As a group, you created my position, that of spiritual advisor. I accepted your decision then and will continue in that role. You must know that, despite my foreknowledge, I will only act on our behalf when the time is right and not before. It therefore becomes necessary for me to determine when that moment has arrived. No matter what apprehension my strategist displays, I cannot act on my knowledge until I see no other course. He finds this difficult to accept. You, on the other hand," he said and indicated Michael, "show blind faith and devotion. Han cannot accept that premise. Normally, his skepticism serves him well." Li commented. "Cecilia shares Han's skepticism. Her whole life is based on scientific fact. She conjectures on reality and not on probable futures. If you are to master this new level of psychic ability, you must learn that the time for action can be as important as the knowledge of the future."

"I have never doubted you, Master Li," Michael stated to him. "I will always say to you, based upon my faith alone, that I open my mind to you, and it will forever be open to you."

"And I will always accept it," Li replied. "But in this instance, Michael, faith is not enough... facts are not enough... strategy is not enough... timing is everything."

Master Li's chair rose into the air, turned around, and he resumed his posture of staring straight ahead. Han sat in silence. He did not move or link. Cecilia looked at all three men and wondered what just transpired. The whole business confused her. She knew that Li shared part of what he knew about the future with the other two. She felt something between anger and frustration. Before she could speak her mind, Michael stood up.

"I'm going to bed," he said and headed for the elevator.

A moment later, Zinian arrived. He was in a good mood when he walked into the solemn scene. He stopped and glanced over at Cecilia.

"Did I miss something? Are the kids, ok?" he asked.

"They're fine, Zinian. Thanks for asking," she told him.

She felt the need to address what she, Han, and Michael just witnessed from Li, when Han interrupted her.

"Master Li was just telling us that he wants us to stay focused on our environment, Zinian," Han informed him. "Anything could happen at any time," he told his friend. Cecilia glanced over at Han.

Zhiwei walked out on deck at that moment. Zinian rose and cut him off. He took his friend by the elbow and spun him around.

"Let's go see what Su Lin can make for breakfast," he suggested. "Then I think we should play a few games of billiards," he offered.

"What's going on?" Zhiwei asked as he fought to look over his friend's shoulder.

"They wouldn't tell us if we used torture," he commented.

Villi made good progress up the river that first day. With occasional relief help from Chou, or whoever happened to be handy, they kept the river traffic away from the yacht while Villi pushed the big boat upstream. Michael rose from his nap around two. The moment he sensed his special pupil awake, Master Li urged Michael to call a team meeting. Villi pulled the ship off to one side and put the moorings in place so he could attend. They held the impromptu gathering in the open third floor lounge room with its wide windows that overlooked the river.

"Michael, you are the team leader," Li began. "Tell us how next to proceed."

Anxious faces looked at Michael. The mantle of authority and leadership seemed as comfortable to Michael as lounge slippers.

"First, we should tackle this problem of disease and pinpoint how the sickness is spread," he pointed out. "Cecilia... Chou... you should test the air, water, and even insects as we move up the river," he advised. "So far we haven't seen any sign of local people being sick or ill with the same general malaise we saw in Gao or Bamako. If those cities were the only areas hit, a slim chance may exist that this disease will be confined."

"I'll help Cecilia construct sensors," Chou spoke up. "I know she brought some testing equipment. I did, too."

"To that end, I brought analysis and testing equipment that will define the kind of virus or bacteria, if we should find a live sample," Cecilia offered.

Michael took out his black card and adopted it into a note pad. He'd prepared a list of things he wanted the team to accomplish before they found the Motambou's.

"We should know what we're up against," he stated. "We don't want this disease to slip past our defenses and catch us by surprise. If you and Chou can start right away, I'd like samples taken at intervals so that you can determine when we leave a disease free zone and enter a zone with disease present; specify whether you find it in the air, water, or both. Are you certain our little... machines will protect us?"

"They should," Cecilia reassured them.

"Good," Michael responded. "Zhiwei, check with some of our WPO agents. See what they've heard about Mali. Tahir is operating outside of Africa. He has Seel with him and Sarah. Tabor knows Africa well. Sir Charles is always a good source. Ask Catherine Olsen what she's heard through diplomatic channels. She usually operates out of her office in Washington."

"What about Camille?" Zhiwei asked.

"Leave her out of this," Li spoke up.

"Ok," Zhiwei replied.

"Zinian, I'd like you to watch over the boat's mechanics. Check the maintanence logs in the engine room periodically. Look over the power plant. I know Chou did this already, but we should keep a close watch on the equipment. I need Chou to test and monitor scanning devices..."

"My pleasure, Michael," Zinian responded.

"I know this will sound sexist," Michael began.

"Then don't go there," Su Lin spoke up as she knew Michael was about to comment about her role in the kitchen. The gourmand enjoyed that position.

"He's *so* understanding," Cecilia said to her friend.

"...and handsome, too!" Su Lin added. The two women smiled.

"I need you to concentrate on finding the Motambou's, Han," Michael put to their strategist. "Before you pitch in on one of these projects, go over our strategy approaches and take your time. I promise you, no one will bother you if you say you aren't free. Please keep me alerted to anything you might... conjecture."

"I will, Michael," Han politely replied.

"I don't need to review your job, do I Villi?" he asked his friend.

"Only that you need rest, too," Villi replied. "I can do longer shifts," he stared.

"That won't be necessary," Michael reassured him. "12 on, 12 off. Hospitals and cops have done it for years. We can, too. Listen group! I would also like to add this caveat. Salla Motambou is the greatest virologist in the world. If he set out on the road south away from Gao, he did so for a reason. The border with Niger is only a day's journey by car, if he and Filla were persistent. We know he did not head west for the capital or east. He went south, along the river. That is significant. Wouldn't you agree?" he put to Han.

"Yes, Michael," Han agreed.

"Therefore it is logical to conclude he would continue to follow the river away from an advancing disease. However, Master Li, Han, and I believe he is under restraint. I believe that does it, Master Li," Michael said. "If no one has anything else to add…"

"Good luck everyone," Master Li spoke quietly. "We shall know more in a few days… until then, continue what you are doing. Believe it or not, it helps."

The meeting broke up. The group went to their tasks.

"I'll volunteer for some of these relief posts…" Han started to link when Master Li cut him off.

"I need you here with me," Li linked to him. "I wish to discuss several things with you in private.

Han noticed that the link with Michael went cold as the young man headed off to tackle some problem or project.

"I know you mean well," Li began as Han turned to him. "This future stuff is very tricky, even for clever men. As I see so many things, certain variables often cloud the truth. I know you seek the truth. I'll need your blind trust, too, on this trip, Han," Li spoke sincerely to him.

"Master Li, I didn't mean to question…" Han humbly began.

"No, you were right to be suspicious," Li told him. "However, the time has come for me to allay some of those fears you have about my frequent journeys through time, my very good and trusted friend."

Master Li shifted in his chair and turned to face his friend.

"You and I have an important task that needs to be done," Li explained. "This ship will carry us up the river, of that I have no doubt. I can tell you this: nothing on this river will stop us or slow us down; no enemy, no disease, no attacking force. None of those things worries me," Li said as he rose and motioned for Han to follow him. "We have other considerations…"

The two men walked up the hall toward the aft deck. Behind them, two bottles of iced tea floated in the air. The doors opened as the men approached.

Li sat in one chair and Han next to him. One bottle floated down next to each man.

"I'm worried about this vision of water," Li suddenly whispered as if he were afraid to link it.

"Water?" Han quietly asked.

"I may know some important facts about our future," Li said as he took a breath. "Yet there are aspect to this journey that remain a mystery to me," he explained. "I have a bad feeling that something terrible is going to happen… and this vision of water is involved."

"Of course," Han leaned back. "It is understandable you would fear drowning in water since you cannot swim," he quickly replied. "If the ship should sink by some unknown means, we may not be able to use our power and save ourselves. Is that what you saw?"

"Our lives are in peril… and I'm worried about him," Li corrected.

What Han believed were paths to answers just turned into a tangle of questions.

"Him?" he said as he cocked his head.

Li struggled against revealing the future.

"Didn't you feel him… in Kansas," Li put to him. "He's been there all along… I thought for certain, you detected him… Of all people, I thought for certain… that you…" Li said as his voice faded and he stared at Han.

Han began to think back about his feelings… things he suspected but dismissed for one reason or another. Had something or someone manipulated his senses? His eyes widened as he began to apply what Li just reveal to his formulas. A new idea began take shape in his mind.

"Detect him… there all along… open… vulnerable on all sides…" Han closed his eyes and groaned. "Oh, no! Han! You've been so stupid! Of course, I sensed him… I thought it was an anomaly," he whispered. "You hinted as much yesterday! This ship… this journey is a trap!"

Master Li looked his friend in the eyes and slowly nodded his head.

"We might be facing an enemy so powerful, that he has predicted and guided our moves from the start," Master Li continued to whisper. "He may have blocked our thoughts, manipulated our emotions, our motives, and even read our minds, when I thought the probe I felt might be Mark's or Xiong Po's," Li said barely above a hush. "He didn't do this last week or even last month," Li privately linked. "He's been doing this for years!"

Han looked all around him. All at once, the gift of the boat did not seem such a welcome thing. He saw it in a completely different light.

"Some spiders will collect dew from flowers and weave it into their webs to entice certain insects," Han stated. He finally understood that the chessboard showed only a few moves before capitulation and checkmate. "We cannot stop him," Han said with conviction. "It's too late. We're doomed…"

"It's not too late," Li whispered, unwilling to risk a link.

"What do you propose? Sacrifice the queen?" Han stated the blatant chess move.

"You wonder if some of us are going to die?" Master Li still whispered as he turned to stare out at the rain-swollen river. "I wish I could say, my dear friend. That part of our future has yet to form."

"… and it is vital to our understanding of the outcome," Han completed the thought.

Chapter Twenty-eight

The Queen's Gambit

NATO agent Reginald Atwater sat behind the wheel of an older model car that ran on liquid fuel. He methodically drove along the river road that snaked back and forth, parallel to the Niger River's edge, contemplating his next move. The rain started several kilometers back and continued to pour down around the countryside. It rained so strong at times, he could barely make out of the road. The wipers seemed to smear the water around the windshield rather than clear it, which slowed his pace. He had to pay careful attention to the road's surface, or he'd run afoul of large potholes that kept cropping up.

"Rainy season is early this year. I hate rain," he grumbled as the car jostled its occupants and dipped in and out of large puddles. "It used to rain in England for days," he recalled. "I hated that."

The first part of Reggie's plan proceeded as he predicted it would. He shut down the government of Mali, spread fear and panic, and intercepted the Motambou's in Gao. His scheme to win their trust ran smoothly with the exception of the strange alien technology they possessed. In the years he covered Rollo, he never saw one of the psychics use such devices. He wished now he had not grabbed them. He should have observed their use and waited until he persuaded Filla to show him how they worked. He had a gut feeling that Filla used hers to communicate a message to the outside. Since they crumbled to dust, he no longer cared about them. He knew they did nothing to deter his plans or stop him from attaining his goal. The more he thought about it, he realized they might have helped spur his plan on.

He entered the next phase of his operation. Shortly after he subdued the two psychics, he inoculated them with the antibody serum that he took when he stole the vials of virus. That immunity kept him alive, and it would keep them alive, too, as he continued to spread the virus along the river. For a while at least, he contributed to the myth that the river carried the disease.

The Niger government already expressed disdain for this NATO imposed embargo. The ambassadors from both Mali and Niger appeared in the United Nations general assembly and expressed their outrage over the news blackout imposed by NATO. When questioned, the Mali ambassador withdrew from the press without further comment. He did not show up at the UN the following day and no one in the embassy would give out any information as to his whereabouts.

The Niger government announced plans to seal off the country's border with Mali and stop the exodus of people fleeing the advancing plague. They were sending troops to the border to protect the dam at Kandadji and to prevent the spread of disease into Niger. The rain continued to pour from the sky without end, threatening to burst the dam at Kandadji. Officials had no choice but to open its gates and allow the Niger River to flow, even though privately they feared the consequences of that action.

"I'd be making faster progress now if I hadn't acted so stupidly," Reggie thought as he pressed on. "Must get the Motambou's out of Mali…"

The night Reg stole the Motambou's from Gao, he glanced away from road for only a moment to render the couple unconscious. How could he have predicted a car would stray into their path? Unfortunately, the Motambou's received some injuries in the accident, which presently left them in a coma. At first, Reg felt certain they would recover within a day or two. When they did not and began to deteriorate, he pressed on south even faster to the border.

He could not take a boat as the dam prevented river traffic from moving past that point. Therefore, he drove the road that ran parallel to the Niger River. Occasionally, he made stops to maintain the Motambou's health. He attempted to give them water and clean them. Yet, nothing he did worked to reverse their condition. He practically drove nonstop for 24 hours until he could no longer stay awake.

He finally found a suitable isolated house outside a small village close to the river. He easily subdued the tenants and physically brought the Motambou's inside. He laid them on a bed, cleaned them up and tried to force some fluids into them. They actually managed to swallow some of the liquid Reggie poured down their throats.

After about five or six hours of rest, he headed south along the main river route. He figured if he kept the Motambou's alive, they could tell him more about their international organization, its membership, and the mysterious village in Kansas. From that information, he could find out their weaknesses and how to exploit them. Most of what he learned he did from eavesdropping on Rollo. He kept most of that information from his commander, General

Andrews. He figured he could torture Filla so that Salla would surrender the information he needed. That was *his* plan. He convinced the general, as he convinced the colonel and the sergeant, to eliminate the rest of the psychics as a threat.

As Reg drove recklessly through the rain along this rough stretch of road, his special cell phone/communicator rang. This was a unique device, created just for Reg. General Andrews could connect to Reg anywhere in the world with this device and pass along coded numbers.

Reginald opened the device inside his coat pocket. He could not contact them, except in a dire emergency. When the phone vibrated, it meant only one thing – his superiors wanted an update. He opened the thin device and propped it up on the dash in front of him. Code began to crawl across the screen that Reggie translated…

"Pretty Baby. This is uncle."

Reg touched the screen and a numerical keypad appeared. He typed code back.

"Pretty Baby," Reginald quickly replied.

"Acquired package?" more code scrolled.

"Package acquired, but damaged. Await location for pickup," he shot back.

A series of numbers followed. He glanced down at the numbers. Each one spelled out a cryptic message. Lower numbers indicated common usage, while higher numbers had catagories that dealt with specific circumstances.

"127 – Continue on course. 189 – We have your position. 633 – Will advise later as to pick-up time and method. 298 – Weather permitting. 244 – Heavy rain in your area. 654 – Helicopter landing impossible. 112 – Send report on package condition. 79 – Soon. 121 – Keep package intact. 19 – at all costs. 4 – Uncle out."

Reginald's incredible memory held over four thousand such code combinations, which was why they chose him for such clandestine operations. He closed the phone's connection and the phone's memory automatically erased each time he did.

"If you were my real uncle, you'd take better care of me, rather than leaving me here to rot in this jungle!" Reg complained.

He glanced in the rearview mirror of the car and looked at Dr. Motambou. His body jostled around without any indication he was awake or alert – just a flaccid body. In the reclined front seat next to Reg sat Filla, also comatose. Neither had spoken or uttered a sound since the accident happened, just after they left Gao. It bothered Reg that these two annoying people should slow down his important pace.

He should have been far inside Niger by now and moving toward his supposed rendezvous location where he could fly the doctor and his wife out. He had not counted on that accident and thought he had establish their trust in the lab. The rain was another factor that seemed to fly in the face of wisdom. He purposely planned this operation before the start of the rainy season. Normally, a meticulous person, Reggie seldom made mistakes. These blunders cost his mission valuable time. Reggie knew he could ill afford to act so foolishly.

He considered the coded phone message.

"Keep the package intact," he recalled, "at all costs."

He knew that General Andrews sent this particular order. He wanted him to keep the Motambou's alive. Like Reg, the general felt he could manipulate Salla into giving him secrets. He let Reg plan the other things, but insisted his agent return with "at least one of those freaks alive!" The disease brought the psychics to Africa and Reg had to protect his package. When the United States sent investigators to Mali, as he knew they eventually would, Reg had to cover his tracks and leave no trace of his influence. That's why he chose this strain of infection.

"Thank god, the Russians put in a self-destruct code," Reg said as he patted the remaining vials in his pocket. He had plans for those viles, plans that included the secret NATO building in Canada.

His phone vibrated. Reg flipped it open. A number flashed across the screen.

"They took the bait!" he declared. For the first time since he landed in Mali, that stone-like face broke into a broad smile. "Let's hope they stay nice and snug and feel right at home… queen's gambit!"

Chapter Twenty-nine

A FRIEND IN NEED

Camille Ossures felt isolated and alone in Paris. She knew of the Rollo psychic's mission to Africa. However, with Master Li and the others preoccupied, she needed a sympathetic ear. Yet, none of the usual psychics were available for conversation. The Showalter's were on a mission to meet secretly with Leni. Sir Charles and William were at a business meeting in Mumbai. The Middle East group was away on a mission in Turkey as Zhiwei discovered when he tried to raise Tabor. The newest Canadian psychic and the two new Japanese psychics were studying volcanic activity along the Pacific plate. Even Kiran and the two Indian psychics that recently joined the WPO, along with the Liong's, were in Australia with Major Pollack for a symposium on the fifth anniversary of the Brisbane bombing. Master Li placed Catherine Olsen temporarily in charge of the WPO until the Rollo psychics returned from Africa. When Camille requested an update on the African mission from Catherine, she had nothing to report other than they were working their way up the Niger River.

The whole membership of the WPO seemed busy saving the world while she attended parties with politicians and bankers. As she pushed away from another dinner table, bored with the conversation, her world seemed pointless and shallow. She called Charles for the car and intended to return home. A cold wind blew through her before she entered the back seat.

"The country estate, Charles," she requested. "Brrrr.... Chilly night."

"Would you like the seat warmers on?" he asked her.

"No, makes me feel alive," she said and briskly rubbed her arms.

She drew her faux-fur collar up around her neck and stared at the city of Paris as it moved past her limousine window on their way out of town. More than anything in the world, she needed her friends, Salla and Filla. She missed them. She was worried for them.

Her repeated attempts to communicate with her long-time friend, Filla, frustrated the young French industrialist. Not a day had passed since their psychic transformation years earlier when she and Filla did not speak through the special cards Chou provided them. They were only in Paris a short time ago for that brief yet joyous celebration of Salla's prize. The future seemed so bright, so vibrant, so alive for the African couple. She flew them to Sweden on her jet where Salla gave a wonderful speech before the Stockholm crowd and then accepted the Nobel Prize in Medicine. He gave the five million dollar prize money to the Paris Institute and set up a grant for new researchers. Camille was so proud of him.

Now she felt as if someone dropped them off a ledge and they fell into a bottomless pit, a black abyss that swallowed them without a trace. As hard as she tried, Camille could not sense her two friends. Three days passed since she called upon Master Li in Rollo.

"Have you gone very far? Do you still sense them? Oh, why am I here and not on this mission?" Camille wondered as her frustration mounted.

She reached over and touched an electronic control panel in front of her. A list of names came up arranged alphabetically. She touched "F;" the name and face of an old familiar friend appeared. She touched his picture. Camille leaned back in her seat as the private number rang.

"Hello?" a masculine voice answered.

"Oh, François… Are you alone?"

"Camille?" he questioned. "Yes, but…"

"I need you," she sighed.

"Darling, I…"

"I must see you tonight…"

"Of course… it sounds urgent."

"It cannot wait… it must be now."

"Then we should meet…"

"I just need to… to talk."

"By all means…"

She knew it was late. She did not care. She needed his big shoulders to cry upon tonight. She hear the rumors about François. His girlfriend left him. She knew he was alone. She did not wish to take advantage of his vulnerability. Yet, she needed her old friend. The fact they were once lovers did not matter to her, although it might to François. She bade Charles drive faster.

"It seems strange… to find you alone so late in the evening," she commented. She knew his girlfriend, Charlene, and did not care for her.

"Ah, well…" he sighed, "surly you know about my state of affairs lately.

I will not burden you with the stories. She left three months ago. Believe me, you are the breath of fresh air I needed tonight. What will you have me do?"

"May I come by?" she asked.

"I'm at the estate," he told her.

"I… I must confess…" she hesitantly spoke. "I'm nearly in Rouen."

She heard him laugh, not a cynical laugh but one of genuine amusement. She knew he was not upset with her.

"I will be ready when you arrive," he offered.

"Ten minutes?" she wondered.

"Ten! Oh, Camille…" he groaned.

"I am sorry…"

"Ten it must be," François said, resigned to his fate.

When she walked through his front door, he stood in the hall wearing his robe. Camille did not care. She went straight to him and wrapped her arms around him.

"This is sudden," he whispered.

"Not soon enough… I never liked the way Charlene treated you," she told him. "You deserve better than that. I want to make it up to you."

"If you wish," he replied and smiled.

She spent the night wrapped up in François' arms as a young woman who sought refuge in an older man's embrace. Still, the CEO of the most profitable business in Europe tossed and turned in bed. She had a dark terrible dream that a large menacing man tortured Filla. She could not wake from the nightmare, as if some power held her imprisoned. François tried to wake her.

"Camille," he shook her repeatedly, "Camille! Wake up!"

"Filla!" she shouted, her eyes wide with fear. "Filla!"

She sat up in the bed, her face wet with perspiration. Her eyes darted around with fear until she reached out and felt someone next to her. The moment she saw François, she relaxed and fell back.

"Camille, easy," he took her into his arms. "You are safe with me. Let me help you."

"Oh, François," she sighed and began to sob. "Hold me close," she begged. "I… I don't know where to turn. We have been friends a long time. You were the first person I thought of."

"I'm glad you called, Camille. I've been concerned about you lately," he told her. "Do you know the time? Perhaps you should get ready. I believe you are running late. Charles will need to drive you back to Paris."

She lost all concept of time.

"Oh!" she declared when she saw his clock. "I can't work like this…" she whined.

"Yes you can," he calmly stated. François gave her a brief hug before he pulled her from the bed and led her into the bathroom.

"We both have obligations today," he said and pushed her into the shower. "Your corporation will call out the military if you do not show up!" he kidded. "I'm too old to go to prison."

After her shower, he lingered nearby and reminded her to put on make-up. She finally sauntered out to the kitchen wearing an appropriate outfit Charlene left. Her friend noticed that Camille moved about the room absentmindedly, as if she floated in a dream world.

"Camille, darling. Would you like cream in your coffee?" François asked as she gazed out the window.

"Yes... two spoons," she replied absently.

He smiled and prepared the coffee the way she always enjoyed it. He set the cup next to her, but she did not touch it. He purposely made his own cup of coffee as noisily as he could just to annoy her. Camille did not flick an eyelash.

"What is wrong?" he finally asked. "I've seen you distracted when you were trying to settle a contract or about to land a large donor. But lately, it's as if your mind is far away." He leaned closer to her face. She did not move or glance his way. "Camille? Camille!"

Finally, she blinked as if she just awoke from a trance.

"I'm sorry, darling," she whispered. "I've been a bore, haven't I?" she suggested and took a sip of coffee. "It's just that... well, I have these two friends, very dear old friends... and I haven't heard from them…"

"How long?" he asked.

"I know this sounds silly. Three days," she told him.

François coughed and choked on his coffee.

"Three days! Really, Camille..." François protested. "We've hardly spoken in four months!"

"Well, normally, I hear from Filla every day," she told him. "It's not like her. She hasn't contacted me!"

"Filla? Filla Zambi? The one who married the married the Nobel Prize winner? The same beautiful Filla who ran the speaker program?" he inquired. "I didn't know she called you every day. Isn't that expensive for someone from Mali?"

"It's not like that. We trade off," Camille brushed aside his remark.

"I know her husband's a doctor… What's he paid with, chickens?" the man laughed.

Camille did not smile. In fact, her eyes began to fill with tears.

"How callus of me," François said as he moved to her. He took out his handkerchief, dabbed her eyes. "Forgive me, Camille. She's your friend." He begged. "What can I do? You name it."

"Anything?" she asked shyly.

"Anything in my power, yes," he said with all the sincerity he could muster.

"Let me borrow your jet," she blurted.

"Darling, you have three..." he started when more tears fell down her face.

"You have one of the newest and fastest jets on the continent..." she began and burst into tears.

"Ok! Ok!" he quickly added. "I'll make the arrangements!"

Three hours later, Camille Ossures sat inside a new private jet on the tarmac that awaited clearance from the tower for a flight plan to Algiers. From there, the jet would refuel and take her to Dakar, Senegal. The final leg involved a charter plane that would take her to the capital of Mali, Bamako.

She picked up the telephone that rang next to her large leather reclining seat.

"Camille, darling," François wondered, "I still want to know how you talked me into using my corporate jet. This is absurd! I'm certain Filla is fine. You'll see!" Then he added, "Are you sure you don't want me to come along?"

"No, I must go alone," she told him.

"Very well, I will wait for a telephone call from you to let me know how you are. Agreed?" François requested.

"Agreed," she told him. "Thank you, so much, François. This means so much to me. I will repay you ten-fold for this favor."

"Repayment I don't need. Just return to me, alive," François told her. "I could never forgive myself if something terrible happened. Good luck, Camille."

"Good bye, François," she said softly and placed the phone back on the cradle.

Camille leaned back into her seat as she watched the runway speed past the window and the roar of the engines blasted her skyward to her African destination. She wondered about Filla and Salla's condition. Camille closed her eyes and decided on a nap as the aircraft left French airspace, crossed over the Mediterranean Sea, and approached the coastline of Africa.

"Mademoiselle?" a female attendant softly spoke as she touched her shoulder.

"Yes?" Camille blinked her eyes open. She gazed up at a tall woman in a uniform who stared down at her with a look of concern on her face.

"We have a problem..." the woman told her.

Chapter Thirty

Into the Heart

Master Li sat on the covered aft deck of their newly acquired prize, having an iced tea with his friend, Han Su Yeng. Special cooling fans blew dehumidified air down upon them as they enjoyed the shade. The two men focused on the board game in front of them, used this moment to divert their minds from the slow chase of their lost friends.

While the game of weiqi originated in China over 4000 years ago, many consider "Go" as a national pastime. Han took pride that he only lost twice in his lifetime, each time to the same national champion, a competitor friend of his living in Beijing. Most of the Rollo group played him for experience, even Master Li. Yet no one ever beat Han at Go.

The board between them barely held Li's passing interest, or so he told Han. While the younger man concentrated on his *eyes*, special areas between the stones.

"What do you think happened to the Motambou's?" Master Li asked Han. He absently tossed out the comment as he reached inside his burlwood bowl and placed a white stone on the board.

"And you call yourself a master! Ha! A foolish move! I will finish you off in no time!" Han bragged and quickly added a black stone while he attempted to surround Li's position.

Master Li glanced at the board and then his friend.

"Not even speculation?" Master Li asked. "About our friends from Mali, I mean."

"I hate to say it, and I don't mean to sound disrespectful, but I think they are dead," Han finally said as he stared down intently at the board.

Without appearing callous, Han spoke as a realist. He did not think the doctor and his wife stood a chance after what they witnessed. Besides, Han's competitive spirit held him riveted to the game.

"If anyone on this planet could find them, it would be you, my friend," Han reminded Li as he counted the few remaining squares versus moves. "But your foresight is not going to help you today!" he exclaimed as he placed a key stone on the board.

Han leaned back, content he had beaten Master Li. He took a long draft of iced tea.

"Ha, yourself," Master Li smiled. He placed the final stone and won the game. "My game."

"What? How did you do that?" Han sat up as he figuratively scratched his head and stared at the stones. The arrangement favored Master Li.

"I could have sworn... Did you do some hocus-pocus stuff?" Han accused.

Master Li made some comical gestures in the air.

"Cheat?" Li said with feigned astonishment. "How dare you suggest such a thing of me, the great Master Li."

He made a hand gesture as if he were crowning his own head.

"The great master cheat!" Han said as he rose and made a hand gesture of his own.

"Tsk, tsk. Such a poor loser," Li quipped.

"An honest one!" Han shot back.

"Excuse me for interrupting the weiqi battle of the century, gentlemen," Michael said as he strolled onto the deck.

"Michael," Han spoke up, "Just in time. I was about to rip your master to shreds for cheating!"

"Master Li? Cheat? Han, how could you even suggest such a thing? Why I've played Go with Master Li many times and I have never recalled him cheating. Master Li is the most honorable of men," Michael rattled off.

Michael stood there with a blank expression, blinking. Han glanced up at Michael and frowned. He suspiciously looked over at Master Li, who stared up at the overcast sky.

"Hmm, could rain," Li commented.

"Did you make him say that?" Han accused.

"Beg your pardon?" Li said with an innocent expression.

Michael shook his head as if waking up.

"Come to think of it," he said as he scratched his head, "I can't recall I ever played Go with Master Li." He turned to Li. "Say! Master Li!"

"Michael," Li spoke up to change the subject. "You stopped by to tell us something important?"

"Yes... yes, I did," Michael responded. "We'll be stopping in Onitsha.

It's a large port town on the river. Villi wants Chou to install some navigation tools into the bridge. We need everyone's help to watch the shore while we dock. Zhiwei thinks we might be visible due to some small breaks of the camouflage field. Chou promises to run a diagnostic soon. Su Lin wants to recycle the water treatment system. We shouldn't be longer than an hour or so."

"Han and I will join you on deck," Master Li responded.

"Onitsha is a fairly large port," Michael pointed out. "If some of our team don disguises… move among the populous…"

"You can pick up local gossip. News spreads faster from relatives. Is that it?" Han inferred.

"Something like that," Michael said.

"A stop at this port is definitely in order," Han concurred.

"What else?" Master Li requested.

"Cecilia's experiments with river water and the insects produced negative results," Michael linked. "If some plague is moving down the river, word of it might precede its arrival. Mali is under a news blackout. We'll have to be cautious. We don't want to arouse suspicion."

Han pulled out his card and expanded its size. He pulled up an older satellite image of the local Niger River and the approaching port town.

"If Zhiwei is correct, with a port town of this size," he pointed out, "people on shore or in boats might see parts of the yacht from many different angles. Every member of the team will need to scan minds and alter the perception of those who see anything strange," he offered.

"I've anticipated that," Michael linked. "The others are waiting on deck."

"Zhiwei, checking in," he openly linked.

"Go ahead," Michael linked.

"The docks hold twenty moored boats, some in the process of both loading or unloading cargo and passengers. Three small boats approach from upstream and another is in line behind us. For the most part, the boat's disguise is holding up," he linked. "It's the congestion around the main dock I'm worried about…"

"Perhaps we should wait until dark," Han suggested.

"I believe our group can handle this," Michael interjected, "Master Li?"

"You are in charge, Michael," Li stated. "Direct us."

"Villi, take us in," Michael directed, "easy."

Villi slowly guided the great vessel into the largest clear area at one end of the sprawling network of wooden docks. The psychic group, with Villi as the exception, moved to the port side facing the dock to act as interference. Master Li took the elevator up to the crow's nest just below the antenna tower. Han intervened first when he entered the minds of dockworkers. Chou scanned the mind of the harbormaster and his support crew. Michael and Cecilia scanned people walking around nearby that happen to look in their direction. Zhiwei jogged over to the starboard side and scanned the minds of people approaching in other boats. To almost everyone outside the yacht, a large yet dilapidated covered ferryboat had moved into a mooring position next to the docks. Only a few people noted anything unusual.

"I think we managed to cover every angle," Zhiwei said from the other side of the ship.

Li oversaw their activity from above and patiently waited to see what developed. He made wide sweeps of the crowd. Any mind with the thought, "… that's weird/strange/bizarre/etc.," he quickly changed their perception to "ferry."

Villi moved the ship as close as he could without wrecking the wooden dock. A dockworker routinely moved in to assist with mooring what he perceived to be a very large water taxi. Imaginary people aboard grabbed imaginary ropes at one end and then the other. When he started to jump on board, Cecilia changed his mind. The man moved away instead. Zinian activated the anchor system and the automated gangplank. The whole team worked to secure the large boat to its slip.

Michael linked up to Master Li.

"What do you advise as our next course of action?" he asked.

"Go ashore disguised with psychic bubbles and ask questions, just as you suggested," Li pointed out as he scanned the perimeter of the inlet bay.

"Zinian and Zhiwei promised to watch the dock area. Su Lin has decided to shop. Chou is very busy… being Chou," Michael pointed out, "and Villi is integrating new navigation components."

"What will you do?" Master Li asked of Michael.

"Cecilia and Han want to stroll through the public market," he told Li. "I thought I would snoop around the dock on my own. And you?"

"I'll keep my mind open for any trouble," Master Li said as he pulled energy from the people ashore.

Yet even as he settled into his conning tower vantage point, he sensed a dark presence not far away, a brooding mind, possibly psychic, and very powerful. Master Li moved toward the railing and looked out at Onitsha, past the marketplace.

"Could the Motambou's have made this far that fast?" he wondered.

The rest of the team started away from the boat or headed to their projects below. Michael tarried when he glanced up and saw the queer expression cross Li's face when he leaned out over the railing.

"Something wrong?" Michael quickly sensed. "What is it?"

"I wish I knew," Li said as he gazed beyond the docks. "I have a strange feeling about this place."

"Do you want me to stay?" Michael linked.

"Go, mix with the locals," Li waved him off. "I'll be fine."

The midday heat surrounded Master Li. The rain had only stopped a short while ago. The air felt hot and humid. When the sunlight returned, the air quickly changed into an oppressive steam bath. His eyes squinted back the bright light from the equatorial sun. He felt it beating down on his head. He held out his hand and a big wide straw hat floated up from the docks. Li sniffed it before he placed it on his sweating head. Using his mind, he pulled out any dirt, mites, old sweat, and debris. What remained largely consisted of clean woven straw. Pleased with his thorough scrubbing, he placed it on his head.

"Clean enough," he muttered, thankful for something to shade his eyes.

He sat in a chair that Zhiwei dragged up to this perch and tried to relax. It did not take much exertion to sweat. Even breathing could be a chore. He noticed how slowly the dockworkers moved and paced their laborious tasks. Just beyond the docks, Li watched market patrons buy fish and other commodities that rested under tattered awnings.

Li closed his eyes and tried to empty his mind of troublesome thoughts. Yet, the peculiar feeling of a powerful psychic nearby made him uncomfortable, an irritant like a piece of food stuck in his teeth. This feeling gnawed at his sense of calm and would not go away.

"I must see if this place holds any significance," he thought.

Within the time it takes to take a few deep breaths, his ethereal body streaked across the universe to Galactic Central. A great echo of salutations and greetings filled the great spire when Li's presence arrived. Ignoring his fan base, Li thrust his ghostly body upward to the top of the spire and entered the crystal which allowed him access to the timeline.

He quickly formed the event horizon. The lines of probability fanned out and converged at his feet. These represented the future. He gazed upon their forbidden form, hoping for a clue.

"So many to engage," he thought as he quickly scanned them.

Unfortunately, Li's engagement with the lines of probably took him far too long. He wanted to scrutinize the endless variables and countless probabilities that comprise the future – days from now, hours from now, minutes away. Yet any hesitation on his part slows the flow of time. The future glistened and sparkled and sang its enticing song.

"Linger… stay!" it called to him.

"Clumsy human!" the director's voice echoed. "Are you trying to rob the universe of its existence? You should know better than to tarry and risk imbalance," it said. "I am pulling you out!"

Before the director could act, Li withdrew. He rushed back to the Milky Way galaxy before another second of time could pass.

"Be careful Li," the director's voice trailed off. "This future you seek is fraught with peril... for all of us..." Uncharacteristically, it added, "Good luck."

"That was a very human thing to say," Li responded. "Sorry to disrupt the chamber. However, I have the information I need." he thought. "I hope." He blinked his eyes and took a few seconds adjusting to the bright sunlight.

Unfortunately, Master Li received more information than he bargained for on this trip to the timeline. In the center of the near future, a thousand lines of uncertainty converged around his energy. His very presence seemed to bend the fabric of space around him. This visit confirmed the fears that Li experienced lately. Many dangers lay ahead, serious danger that involved his friends, their families, and the Motambou's with Master Li found smack dab in the middle of it. It wasn't the rescue team's efforts he had to watch. His influence, his choices were what mattered most... and the timing was crucial.

"How will I know when to act?" he wondered.

For the first time in years, the future existence of Earth's psychic community seemed clouded with doubt. Even the fate of Galactic Central was uncertain. The voices relied on Master Li to resolve this situation... for they could see what Master Li saw and they knew what Li knew.

"I'm so thirsty," he thought as he smacked his lips together.

Li used his power to open the refrigerator in his suite and pull out a bottle of cold iced tea. It floated up the staircase, out the door, and over to his hand. He took a long drink before he pulled the empty upturned bottle from his parched lips. He cast his eyes toward the marketplace and watched the team as they worked their way through the locals. Each person had a psychic bubble around them and cast a disguise into it. He watched Michael question one of the dockworkers near the boss's shack. Although Michael thought in English and heard the man in English, the two men spoke aloud using the local native dialect.

"What news upstream? Any?" Michael asked.

"What? I tought you came that way?" the man gestured. "What you here for anyway?" he asked using a thick accent. He stared suspiciously at Michael, whom he saw as a ferryboat operator.

"Naw! We been laid up in dry dock for tree weeks," Michael told him. "We had to leave. Food runnin out! We headed for this here port to re-supply.

I was just wonderin, that's all. You sayin you didn hear nothin?" Michael asked, trying to duplicate the accent.

"We heard 'bout some rich man… got his ship stolen down river," the dockworker told him. "Nobody's seen it though. How ya gonna lose a five-story yacht on a river wif a buncha junks like dose? I ask you?" he laughed, bearing his crooked stained teeth and pointed to the boats in the river.

Michael shrugged his shoulders

"We figured they stripped it," the man said, "an scuttled what was left. Udderwise, where would they be hiden such a beeg sheep?" The man shrugged his shoulders back at Michael.

"How big is dat boat?" Michael asked.

"Never mind dat boat," the man dismissed him with a wave of his arm. "What have you heard 'bout Mali?" he asked in a strange whisper. He glanced around to see if anyone overheard his question. "People are sayin a great plague is sweepin down dee rivah. Day say many have died. You heard of dis?"

"Haven't hurd da ting. 'Specially bout Mali," Michael threw his arms up and walked away.

When the dockworker returned to his work, he did not recall the conversation. He glanced over his shoulder. The docks seemed strangely quiet today.

Chapter Thirty-One

Mirage

Zhiwei, Zinian, Cecilia, Han, along with Michael and Su Lin donned their outside appearances via the psychic bubble, which they had created in the past and used as a disguise. Although they originally called the energy shield a bubble, they held a field of psychic energy close to the outline of their body. Into this field, they could cast a different image for others to see. For the past eight years, they taught other Level IV psychics to use the psychic bubble as a means of stealth. Thus far, in the WPO's short history, no one outside the organization had ever detected one of its psychic members.

In the public market, sellers displayed many spices, fruits, and vegetables for sale. They shaded their produce from the weather with loose canopies. Yet, flies swarmed everywhere, mostly all over the food.

"If Su Lin were at this stall, she could choose among this stuff," Cecilia said as she wrinkled her nose. "What would be considered fresh for a third world country?" she asked.

"Yes, you westerners are rather spoiled with your new 'fangled' inventions, like refrigeration," Han said with as much sarcasm as he could muster. "The grocery store still has not arrived in all corners of the globe."

Han's sarcasm caught her off guard. Cecilia burst into laughter, which drew attention to them. People from villages such as this one enjoyed a good joke. The best humor came from travelers. Like celebrities, people engulfed the two and asked to hear the joke. Cecilia and Han struggled quickly to explain she suffered from a sudden outburst of coughing and not laughter.

"No, look, see… Ha!" Cecilia fumbled. "Ha!"

"Poor thing," Han said as he hustled her away.

After the crowd around them thinned, Cecilia whispered to Han.

"I forget the huge cultural differences that exist between us," she said.

"You should get out more, Cecilia," Han shot back. "It'll do you some good."

"Me?" she replied, disingenuous.

She suppressed her laughter this time and diverted her attention by throwing more rotten fruit inside a large burlap bag that she carried. Han did the same with the vegetables. They paid with paper money they had seen others use. Instead of paying, they made a motion of placing an illusionary bill into the merchant's hand and actually put nothing there.

From his perch atop the great silver and white sailing ship, Master Li carefully monitored the situation. He continuously scanned the surrounding area while he kept abreast of most activity. One thing continued to puzzle him – the uneasy feeling of a powerful psychic source, which explained why he tore into the timeline to find out if he missed some important detail. That act of inquisition on his part turned out to be a mistake.

Rushing off to the other side of the cosmos cost him a great deal of energy. The heat was bad enough, but this presence he could not locate only added to his physical state of unease. He sensed a threat nearby, a menacing presence that grew closer to their location on docks. Li peered over the side through the haze until the anomaly caught his eye.

A strange fat man wearing a white broad-brimmed panama hat and a white vested suit walked in Zhiwei's direction. He slowly moved along with an unsteady gait. He had a beautiful black ornate cane which had a crystal gold-trimmed head that he used for support. A gold watch chain swung back and forth as he dawdled along. He paused, pulled out a white linen hanky, and mopped his forehead.

"Where did *he* come from?" Li wondered. "He appeared from nowhere!"

Clearly, the man – an obvious outsider and possibly British – stood completely out of place. In contrast to all the black or brown-skinned people who wore drab clothing, the sweating white fat man stuffed into the bursting white suit appeared dazzling in the equatorial sunlight that bounced off the pristine fabric and created a blaze of reflection.

"He looks like a mirage," Li immediately thought. "Obviously the man is very wealthy and usually the center of attention," he surmised by his appearance and bearing. He scanned the area to see how the other members of the team reacted to this man's presence. "This buffoon may be watched by someone else, an accomplice, someone spying to see who might interact with him," Li thought.

He had to know what was going on and why this character should suddenly show up at this moment. He reached out with his mind across the dock. Yet, he could not read the other man's mind. This bizarre character erected a strong block that prevented Li reading him. Li reacted immediately with alarm.

"That's what bothered me!" Li exclaimed. "It's him! This could be the agent sent to take us out!" he thought in relation to what he saw on the timeline.

He picked up a pair of binoculars that Zhiwei left next to the com-line. This brought the stranger into closer focus. The man walked over to Zhiwei and started to speak. Li entered Zhiwei's thoughts so he could hear the conversation.

"... sorry, sir," Zhiwei humbly spoke.

"What? Are you certain you cannot take me?" the man demanded. He spoke with the thick Oxfordian British accent of the aristocracy.

"I knew it, English," Li thought, which confirmed his suspicion.

"I'll pay you very well," the rotund character spouted. "After all, you are operating a passenger service."

He took his heavy cane and gestured toward the boat.

"For being someone from England," Li pondered, "the man's manner seems a little too stiff, as if he were an archetype instead of a real person."

He had another English lord to compare. One of Li's best friends was Sir Charles Bickford, an English duke and psychic. He continued listening to the conversation through Zhiwei while he watched with the binoculars.

"No passengers," Zhiwei said in his best native accent. "Boat goes to dry dock for repairs," he told him. The fat man distracted Zhiwei from helping Zinian. Li could sense the unease Zhiwei felt in the man's presence.

"You're loading supplies! I overheard one of the crewmen saying you just *came* from dry-dock," the Englishman said as he questioned Zhiwei's excuse.

"Tell him to take another taxi," Li thought to Zhiwei.

"I'm afraid sir, you must take another taxi," Zhiwei said and shrugged his shoulders. He started to move away.

The man put out his rather ornate cane in an aggressive gesture. He cut off Zhiwei's path and stopped him from retreat.

"I don't think you understand my friend," the Englishman said with almost sinister tones. "There are no other passenger boats. This ship is all that has passed through here for many days, and my business upstream is urgent."

Zhiwei stared up at the big fat man, uncertain of his next move.

"I'll pay in cash," the man said and slapped his breast coat pocket.

"Tell him he must speak with the captain for approval. Make a gesture toward the boat and move away as quickly as you can," Li whispered into Zhiwei's mind. "He may be dangerous."

"Yes, Master Li," Zhiwei linked back. He addressed the pompous man with a loud voice. "If you insist, sir," he told him. "You'll have to talk to the Captain. He's on the boat." Zhiwei made a broad gesture in the general direction of the yacht.

"That is all I ask," the man in the white suit said with a false smile. "Lead on."

Zhiwei hesitated as Li specifically told him to move away.

The fat well-groomed man again mopped his forehead with his large white handkerchief and motioned once more with his rather expensive-looking cane. The moment he turned, Zhiwei quickly ran over to assist Zinian with the remainder of the water.

"Oh, these local urchins," the man muttered as he dabbed more sweat. "They can't give you a straight answer to anything!" However, instead of folding his handkerchief, he flung it around for a second or two before he folded and pocketed it.

"A signal?" Master Li wondered.

He whipped the binoculars around to see if anyone else responded. A man in dark clothing did move away at that moment. Li scratched his chin. Three things troubled him.

First, this man appeared a little too perfect. He seemed to be wearing a costume rather than the kind of business suit as would someone real. Secondly, he wondered how this man could block his thoughts, when even Michael had difficulty. Third, the man did not lean on his cane properly when he walked. If he had a bad hip or back, he would lean consistently the same way. Perhaps the man used the cane as a weapon in disguise. He could be the mastermind behind the trouble in Mali and looked for an excuse to board the boat. Once aboard, he could surprise Villi and take over the yacht.

"That man is a powerful psychic!" Li realized.

Sweat trickled down the sides of his face. His heartbeat quickened as he saw a strategic disaster about to explode in their faces. They made an error in judgment and were vulnerable to attack. This psychic caught them unaware. Nearly the entire team was off the boat and this man was seconds away from coming aboard. Li strained his eyes but could not find any members of his team nearby.

"Villi…" Li linked. Villi did not respond. "I'm weak… no energy," he thought. He tried to pull psychic energy but had trouble. "What's wrong with me?"

Li clicked the com-link and called to Villi in the pilot's room.

"Villi, we have an urgent situation. Try to contact the team. Get everyone back onboard the boat as quickly and quietly as possible without arousing too much suspicion," Li said through the mic. Villi did not respond. "Villi?" Li pressed the button and called. Again, silence.

Master Li returned his focus to the dock. He watched with increasing dread as the gleaming white fat man with his white hat approached the side of the ship. The big man strutted across the creaking boards of the dock with confidence that spelled trouble to Li's instincts. Li slammed his hand down on the com-link.

"Villi! Tell them to hurry!" he called out.

Unfortunately, Villi chose that moment to go down to the galley and make a cold roast beef sandwich with onion and horseradish on rye bread – his favorite. He was unaware of Master Li's attempts to contact him.

"I've got to get down there," Li spoke as he dragged his weakened body over the stairs. He stared down at the steps. He had expended too much energy scanning the countryside and going to Galactic Central. Without realizing it, the heat and humidity took its toll on his energy depletion. He stared at the steep staircase – the only way down. They seemed too much for an old man in his current state of health, more like an obstacle to his path.

He looked again over the side at the man coming closer by the second. Once on the fifth level, he could call for the elevator. But it would take too long. He had to move quickly or it would be too late. Yet, one misstep and it could mean a broken hip or leg. Even with psychic powers, he had to be careful. If he fell from trying to hurry too quickly, it could be fatal.

He started down the stairs as fast as he could move. He was determined not to stop until he stepped out onto the first deck. On level five, he pressed the button for the elevator and realized it was on the first sublevel. Villi took it to the galley!

He started down the main staircase. Each turn, each step cost him energy. By the time he reached the main deck, the stairs had emptied his reserve. He swayed as he emerged on the main deck. The mid-day sun relentlessly beat down like a drum that pounded in his head. He let go of the railing and started across the deck. The air started to swim.

"Oooo, I'm going to faint," he thought, feeling lightheaded.

The fat white-suited man took large strides as he approached the gangplank. Any second he would cross over onto the ship.

Gasping for breath, Li tried to cry out for help, as he could not link.

"Michael…" he called. "Cecilia!"

Yet with his lungs so taxed, he could hardly breathe, let alone cry out. As he stumbled along the main deck, the last of his energy drained away. The deck seemed kilometers long.

"Must try to stop him," he thought as he moved ever slower.

The large phosphorescent man grew closer. His pace quickened. He swung the heavy ornate cane as he briskly started up the gangplank. Master Li lost the race. He dropped to the deck several meters from the gangplank. The fat man in the white suit stepped onto the boat and turned toward Li.

He started across the deck, his figure grew large and sinister as he towered over the frail old man. He raised his cane as if he were going to strike. Li felt his power fade. He could not stop the fat man. He panted for air. His heart pounded in his chest, while sweat poured down the sides of his face.

"Is this the end?" he wondered, as the light grew dim.

The last thing he saw was the fat man standing over him, the cane raised in the air. After that, Master Li lost consciousness.

Chapter Thirty-two

Shared Vision

Michael suddenly sensed the rising danger in Master Li's thoughts. He jerked his head in the direction of the boat. He left in the middle of a conversation and ran across the docks like a sprinter.

"It's Master Li," Michael linked to the group, "he's having a stroke!"

When Zhiwei sensed Michael's fearful reaction, he moved toward the boat's gangplank.

"Master Li!" Cecilia reacted as she picked up Michael's thoughts and took off.

Han sensed the general alarm and ran after Cecilia.

Soon, all of the psychics raced for the gangplank.

"What's going on?" Su Lin linked to Villi.

"I don't know?" he responded about to take a big bite of his sandwich. "Is something wrong?"

"Michael says that Master Li's energy is fading," Su Lin linked. "He fell on the main deck! Have you checked in with him?"

"I'm heading there now," he replied. Villi dropped his sandwich on the plate and sprang toward the stairs.

Although Zhiwei was near the bow, Michael's long legs won the race. He reached the gangplank first and bound up the incline, taking long strides. Just as he reached the top, he noticed a hefty round man in a white suit reach down for his master with both hands. Michael jumped over the top of the gangplank and prepared to send the man flying into the river if necessary. The man held Master Li in his arms. Michael knew he could not fling him away without harming Li in the process. The other team members who rushed up the gangplank behind him saw what happened, too. They charged forward to save Master Li.

Michael reach over with his hands about to separate them, when the fat man leaned back and revealed a different picture underneath his wide brimmed hat. He actually held Li's head in his lap and tenderly stroked his hair. He took off his hat and started to fan the old man's face when the hat disappeared and turned into only his hand going back and forth.

The man began to transform as he spoke with a strange voice.

"Master Li," a French accent said, "You must move slower in zees heat. Eet will be the death of you!" The rest of the disguise melted away to reveal a beautiful woman wearing a white dress. She poured some of her energy into Li and instantly revived the elderly sage. His eyes fluttered and he took in a deep breath. He glanced up at one of the most beautiful faces on the planet.

"Camille?" he asked.

"Yes, you old goat," she replied. "Who else would have the audacity to dress up like the old Belgium detective?"

"That's who you were!" Li said with a long sigh. "I knew it was someone familiar. What are you doing here?" he croaked, still unable to link yet.

"I was too worried to stay in Paris, so I decided to fly to Bamako," she explained. "The country is closed to all flights, but no one knows that unless you try to fly in!" she told them. She leaned closer to his face. "Do not speak or link. You are too weak. I can hardly sense your presence. Serves you right for poking around the timeline," she winked to him.

"You know about that?" he whispered.

Camille nodded with a knowing expression.

"I sensed you wink in and out. Please allow me to share more of my energy," she offered. No psychic is to use another psychic as a source of energy. It is a violation of the WPO charter. "I insist on this course of action, monsieur," she whispered in his ear.

She pressed her lips to his forehead. Her energy flowed directly into his mind and refreshed his level, but only enough to attempt a link. Villi walked up behind Michael. Cecilia and the others arrived at the same time.

"What's going on?" Cecilia asked as she quickly changed to physician mode and applied her knowledge to Master Li. "Dehydration, hypertension, hyponatremia, and hyperthermia," she correctly diagnosed. "You're a mess! Let's move him out of this sun and start PO liquids right away," she ordered. "Good to see you, Camille," she added. "I believe you took us all by surprise," she stated and glanced over at Li.

The French woman briefly smiled in return.

"How did you arrive, Camille? I didn't sense a plane or helicopter land?" Michael asked.

"I couldn't fly into Mali," Camille explained. "So, I asked the pilot to fly me to Lagos, on the northern coast of Niger. The big news is that someone had stolen a billionaire's yacht; seems it disappeared without a trace."

Camille glanced from one face to the other. The whole party's guilty expressions avoided her penetrating gaze.

"Hmm, just as I thought! Psychic pirates!" she said and returned her attention to Li for a moment. "I searched for strong psychic energy until I finally caught up with you and your brave crew going up the river in this luxurious yacht. Your thoughts informed me of your position," Camille linked. "Master Li isn't the only one who can eavesdrop."

"You came by way of the roads?" Han questioned.

Camille nodded in reply.

"I persuaded a helicopter pilot to bring me here on a short flight from Lagos," she continued. "From the landing strip, my driver brought me through the town out to the docks. I only arrived at Onitsha just an hour before you. I could see the distortion wave around your ship. I assumed it held the yacht under heavy camouflage. Who else would have the audacity to steal from a billionaire than your notorious gang of psychic thugs, eh Li?"

Camille's light laughter replaced her stern face, nervously followed by the other's laughter.

"Didn't you recognize me?" Zhiwei wondered.

"You are too good with your psychic bubble, Zhiwei. I am too good with mine. We both have practice, no?"

"No… I mean, yes!" Zhiwei replied and grinned.

Camille looked around at the yacht.

"Not bad, not bad," she commented. "I hope I can take a shower and find a bed perhaps, no?" she asked. "Permission to come aboard?"

"Permission granted," Michael linked to her. "I'd like to help," he said as he reached down to assist both Camille and Li to their feet. "We have a beautiful suite all ready for you."

"You were expecting me?" she wondered.

"He means we have an extra one," Cecilia spoke up.

"You had me completely fooled, Camille," Li said sheepishly as Michael supported his arms. "How could I have been so blind to that corny disguise?"

"Darling, you have so much on your mind," Camille reassured him. "I left my things on the dock. If someone…"

"I'll get them," Zinian offered, though he and Zhiwei fought over the honor.

"After I clean up," Camille continued, "I think it's time we convene the board and have a serious discussion about Africa."

"Agreed," Li said in a weak voice. "Camille is right. Let's meet in the dining room in one hour. Michael?" Li spoke and inferred that Michael should resume his duties.

Taking his cue, Michael sprang into action.

"Let's get underway. Z's: store those supplies, cast off all lines, finish refueling. Villi, prepare to take the boat out of the port. Su Lin, stow your supplies. I'll let Han escort Camille to her quarters. Cecilia will look after Master Li. I will watch the shore," he ordered. "Su Lin… can you prepare something for us?"

She saluted back.

"Time is valuable. Let's move!" Michael ordered.

Zinian and Zhiwei took off at a sprinter's pace.

"Villi, set your course upstream," Michael instructed. "In about an hour, find a place to weigh anchor so you can attend the meeting," he ordered. "But grab your sandwich in the galley first!" he added.

"Aye," Villi saluted and ran back to the galley before he headed to the bridge.

Chou, who had been oblivious to all of the events, linked in with Michael. He was working in a crew's room that he changed into a technology lab.

"I've converted the power supplies and integrated the new system," he started. "There'll be no more gaps in the…"

"We need to get underway, Chou," Michael told him. "Oh, and we're convening the WPO Board in about an hour."

"Too bad Camille can't attend," Chou commented.

"She just arrived," Michael informed him.

"She's here? Camille Ossures?"

"I'm here," she linked. "Hello, Chou."

"Oh… Oh!" Chou said with surprise. "Everything is ready to implement, Michael," he said. "Welcome aboard, Camille."

"I'm heading below," Su Lin indicated to Michael.

She went directly to the galley and started to prepare the meal. In addition to teaching, Su Lin made one of her goals to become a gourmet chef. She did not need to attend cooking school. She went through several downloads and amassed a great deal of "chef" knowledge. While she never tried to complete with Running Elk, she often held private parties at home where she could show off her skill.

She whipped together a sumptuous feast for everyone onboard the yacht. She pounded chicken breasts to make scaloppini, and tossed them into some beaten egg, breadcrumbs mixed with salt, pepper with a touch of thyme and rosemary. She braised them in extra virgin olive oil along with cloves of garlic, shallots, parsley, ginger, and sliced mushrooms. She added freshly grated Parmesan cheese and garnished with some chopped fresh parsley.

She also prepared steamed wild rice with blanched almonds and a large mound of locally grown vegetables, which she sautéed in the same pan that cooked the chicken. A puree of mango, peppers, and blanched fresh fruit she placed next to the chicken, adding slices of almonds for garnish. She served a chilled white wine.

Michael gave up his usual seat next to Master Li so that Camille could sit opposite Han. He sat at the opposite head with four members seated along each side. With Camille present, they completed the official circle known as the WPO board. Villi parked the boat off to the side of the main river with perimeter and drift alarms on. Chou's new projectors wrapped the vessel in any disguise at the pilot's discretion. Villi made the boat resemble a rocky island. The anchors held the yacht fast so that Villi could join the feast. Su Lin served before she sat with them.

"This wine tastes… different," Camille commented.

"Master Li…" Su Lin gestured, as he removed the alcohol.

"I'm sorry I missed the action on deck," Chou linked apologetically.

"No one could miss me!" Camille commented with a smile. "I tried to make my character as conspicuous and pompous as possible."

She crossed her eyes, puffed out her cheeks, and used her arms to imitate being fat. Everyone laughed including Li. When the laughter died down, Camille went on to describe her reason for coming.

"I know this sounds strange," she began. "I had this terrible dream. A large man attacked Filla…" she said with a faraway look in her eyes. She had to pause as her emotions took over. "I know it sounds absurd. But I believe I had the same dream when you came to visit."

No one else spoke, but Camille could feel tension in the room, as if she struck a collective nerve. Master Li broke the silence.

"Before we talk shop, let's eat! Su Lin made a beautiful meal without the fusor. Shall we begin?" Li said and motioned to the plates.

Everyone enjoyed the meal. The chicken was tender and juicy, the vegetables bright in color, and the rice just enough starch. The mango puree added an unusual element as a condiment. When it seemed as if everyone enjoyed enough dinner, Li clinked his wineglass with his sterling silver chopsticks he usually carried.

"I am please we have so distinguished a guest with us," Li said. "The pleasure of her company," he raised his glass, inclined his head and took a sip of wine.

"The pleasure of her company," the others echoed his sentiment.

Li set his wine glass down and continued.

"Camille does not bring us good news," Master Li said as his thoughts took on a somber tone. "As some of you heard, Mali is closed to all outsiders.

Reports indicate the disease practically wiped out the cities of Bamako and Gao. No one can say the extent of the casualties with any certainty."

Master Li grew quiet as the room settled to silence.

"Despite the negative news, Camille and I both feel that Filla and Salla Motambou are still alive," Li continued on an upbeat note. A visible sigh of relief passed around the table. "However, we also feel they are in danger and under some kind of restraint."

At this point, he cleared his throat and glanced toward Camille.

"We disagree as to whether the restraint is caused from the disease or from some other unknown force. Therefore, we must move with all haste upstream... to what fate, none of us can say," he told them.

Master Li stopped and Camille stared at her glass, saying nothing. She missed her friends and feared for their lives.

"Report," Master Li said as he cast his eyes toward Michael.

"It's just as you've described, Master Li," Michael started. "We heard the same story from many different members of the community we encountered. They said the same thing... stories of massive deaths, especially along the river. None of the wire services or satellite news channels are allowed to carry the story. It's as if someone has drawn a curtain around Mali and blocked the outside world from knowing the truth. If anyone in Mali had a cell phone or other device, they couldn't use them. Someone has blocked all satellite communication."

"The dock workers are frightened," Zinian spoke up. "They refuse service to anyone coming from too far up stream. They've heard rumors and are fearful."

Master Li privately linked to Han who then linked to Michael.

"We need to get underway, Villi," Michael ordered.

Camille placed her hand on top of Li's and squeezed it.

Villi pushed away from the table and leaned over to Su Lin.

"Great dinner," he whispered in her ear, "as always." He kissed her cheek. He stood up and prepared to leave. "Good to see you, even if it was brief," he directed to Camille.

"I'll relieve you on the bridge at twenty-three hundred hours," Michael told him.

Villi squeezed Su Lin's shoulder and headed off for the bridge.

Su Lin pushed away and began to clear the table.

"Very nice meal, Su Lin. Thank you," Camille put in.

Su Lin nodded to Camille.

"We're all so glad to see you, Camille. I only wish it were under better circumstances," she replied.

"I'll help," Chou offered.

"Thanks," Su Lin replied.

The two left the room with stacks of floating dishes.

"Cecilia?" Master Li spoke up.

Cecilia shook her head. "I can find nothing wrong in the environment." She added, "Oh, by the way, Camille, you must come to my room. You'll need a patch and a spray."

"If you insist," the Frenchwoman replied.

"I do," Rollo's physician stated. "If we encounter a lethal micro-organism, you must have the same level of defense the rest of us have."

Master Li used a link that included all the psychics on the ship.

"Camille and I have spoke and feel we need to share some of our thoughts with the rest of the team," he commented. "We don't know why the Motambou's cannot think thoughts or feelings. Only a drug induced coma or a brain injury would prevent that. We also do not understand why we perceive them as alive yet cannot precisely locate their psychic presence. Unfortunately, the voices cannot help us in this regard."

"Excuse me," Zhiwei spoke up. "When Camille said she had a dream before the meal started, I remembered something that happened to me back in Rollo. It's not like me to have nightmares," he explained. "I dreamed we were all on a large boat, but not on a river. A great body of water surrounded us. I could not see the shore. I assumed it must be the ocean."

Zhiwei glanced around the table at the faces focused on him.

"This part of the dream disturbed me the most," he explained. "One by one, this unidentifiable evil force knocked us from the boat. We helplessly sank into the icy cold depths of that steely blue water."

Cecilia and Michael exchanged looks. He nodded toward her. She wanted to share their experience with the group.

"Michael and I experienced a similar dream about a week ago," she informed the group. "It shook up both of us."

Michael nodded as he gazed sympathetically at Camille.

"I remembered the dream and its affect on us," he linked. "We had no idea that someone else had the same dream."

"I never saw the end of my dream," Zinian spoke up. "I'm afraid the intensity woke me. The experience left me in a frightful sweat. I'm sorry I never mentioned it before now. I didn't see the significance. I only told my wife about it."

Every head in the room turned to Master Li.

"Well, it seems we've all had some terrible dreams," Master Li sighed as he leaned back from the table. "Han and I shared our dream experiences after the fact. We wondered about the coincidence, that we should both experience nightmarish visions at the same time."

Han closed his eyes and took in the facts each person stated. All at once, he bristled as if irritated by some detail, which caught their attention. Everyone focused on their expert strategist.

"Our dreams have some commonalities – those who included visions of water found they were not on a river, but on a large body of water," he linked to them. "Additionally, we were sailing in a large boat. At some point in the dream, a despicable act results in death or destruction..."

Han opened his eyes and looked over at Master Li. He knew the older man had knowledge of the future but could not or would not share that information.

"Is that it?" Michael questioned.

"I'm sorry that I can't draw any conclusions. I have too few facts," Han said. "I cannot extrapolate any meaning from this."

Michael started to leave.

"So the meeting is over?" Cecilia wondered.

"Not yet," Camille spoke up. "I am familiar with Salla Motambou's work in virology. To have a disease suddenly show up and start wiping out thousands of people is too convenient without cause or reason," she commented. "Most bacteria, and even viruses, do not behave in this fashion. I feel there is more behind this. Yet for what purpose, I cannot imagine."

"Has anyone considered the children's safety? They are unprotected in Rollo," Su Lin linked from the galley.

"What?" Chou linked in. "This is news to me. Has my barrier failed?"

"No, Chou, it hasn't," Zhiwei informed them. "I monitor Rollo's security constantly."

"I can assure you," Master Li said calmly, "that the disease has simply incapacitated the Motambou's. We will find them within a few days alive. We left the children well protected. Rollo is the safest place on the planet."

However, Master Li's reassurances settled uneasily with the group. Li finally pushed away from the table and stood up to leave. Michael gave the last orders for the night.

"Run engines at increased capacity, Villi," Michael ordered. "Zinian and Zhiwei will take the first watch of security. Cecilia and Chou will relieve them at midnight," he told them. "We'll change shifts in the morning. Everyone needs their rest. I suggest those relieving get some sleep."

Michael received acknowledgements from the group. He kissed Cecilia on the lips and left. He wanted to walk around the main deck before he turned in.

"I apologize for being such an alarmist," Camille linked to Li. "I'm sure you're version is the right one. I was just worried. That's all."

Master Li gave her a reassuring smile while he blocked his thoughts.

"I wish I could do more to relieve your worry," he told her.

As Camille returned to her room, she wondered about the significance and timing of those dreams.

"What could have caused all of us to have nightmares?" she wondered.

Chapter Thirty-Three

Bogged down

While April is ordinarily toward the end of the dry season in Africa, this year the sky opened up and a deluge of water poured down over the entire tropical region adjacent to the Niger River. Only minutes after their meeting, the rain returned and seemed to come with even more intensity. The level of the Niger River rose to record highs and began to flood certain areas of Niger and Nigeria. The speed of the river's current also increased while the boat's engines worked harder to push the great vessel upstream. The rain came down so hard, at times it sounded like someone pounding on the roof of the boat all through the night.

The psychic team had a difficult time sleeping. Master Li paced restlessly in his room. Occasionally the strains of Chopin's Etude or Liebestraum drifted from the suite as he mentally pushed the keys on the baby grand. Camille went to her balcony several times and tried to peer into the darkness. She searched with her mind for her friends, yet her efforts produced no inkling of their existence.

"Try a French composer… Debussy," she linked to Li. The sound of Clair de lune met her ears as she started inside.

On level four, Han played electronic chess and go with his black card to keep his mind occupied while he contemplated their situation. Su Lin sensed their restlessness. She could not sleep either. Instead, she went to the galley and brought Camille, Han, and Master Li warm pots of tea on a trolley that she pushed from room to room.

"I sensed you were awake," she said as she moved from room to room. She also brought fresh fruit and biscotti.

The ship plowed east through the muddy water during the night. Michael had to stay alert for debris that washed into the river. The Niger had overflowed its banks in places and flooded small villages, their huts half-filled with water looked eerily abandon as the yacht made its way past them in the dark. The heavy rain also kept river traffic to a minimum, which made steering easier for Michael.

Despite the weather, the yacht kept a steady pace and moved swiftly upstream. While the continuous strain on the motor may have worried most mechanics, Chou encouraged Michael to push the engines just as hard as he wanted.

"Those new engines can take it," Chou informed him.

By morning, they had reached the great junction at Lokoja. Although Li, Camille, and Han eventually fell asleep before three, they rose around eight and met in the third floor lounge.

"Master, Li," Michael linked with a sense of urgency, "We're approaching the junction with the Benue tributary."

"What the significance?" Camille asked.

"The Benue River originates in Cameroon and joins with the Niger to form the large river system that leads to the ocean," Han explained to her. "The town of Lokoja rests at the junction where the Niger River splits off to the northwest and crosses Nigeria to the border of Mali. Lokoja has about 200,000 people."

"I thought we might stop to investigate," Michael offered.

"Good idea, Michael," Master Li chimed in. "Wake your team."

Before he could wake Villi, the pilot was already headed toward the bridge to relieve Michael when he heard Master Li's request.

"Su Lin's in the galley," Villi informed Michael. "I believe she's rustling up some breakfast."

The big Russian man came around the corner with his usual exuberance.

"Rustling…" Michael echoed. "The last vestiges of Russia have given way to American colloquialisms, my friend," he grinned as he relinquished his navigation duties to his friend.

"Only because you forced me to think like you," Villi shot back. "Pervert!"

"Jackass!"

"American wart!"

"Russian sloth!"

"I've spent too much time in your head," they both said together and then laughed.

Thirty minutes later, a team of psychics moved to the outer decks of the yacht to run interference as the big ship pulled into a slip. Although thoroughly disguised this time, they did not want to take any chances. Villi tried to move them as far from the main docks as he could negotiate. Zinian and Zhiwei ran to fake the mooring ropes while Han operated the anchor system and lowered the gangplank.

The moment they docked, Michael coordinated the groups' efforts to move among the masses, not easy in a relatively impoverished community like this. He called a short meeting to discuss their actions before they disembarked. Su Lin managed to whip up a quick breakfast, which she brought with her to the meeting. As they settled over tea, and whatever else they wanted from a buffet Su Lin laid out, they awaited their instructions from Michael.

"Anyone going ashore should try to gather as much information as they can while we keep our time in the port brief," Michael reminded them. "Please be mindful of any contacts. We aren't certain how far the Motambou's have traveled. I'm going to take a nap."

After the debacle with Camille, Zhiwei decided to remain aboard this time and monitor security concerns. He also wanted to check with Rollo and look in on Star Wind. He knew it was night in Kansas. If she did not respond, he wanted to leave a message for her. Michael turned in for some much-needed rest. Cecilia continued to test the air and water.

Su Lin, Zinian, Chou, Han, and Villi all headed ashore to investigate the local port while Master Li and Camille monitored their activity from the third level aft deck aboard the yacht. Su Lin decided to shop in the local markets for nearly an hour before she returned with bags of special items difficult to replicate. She would use the fusor's reader to add their unique DNA sequences to the computer's memory banks. She stocked the galley with a variety of local delicacies and busily entered recipes in the database that she discovered after she spoke to local cooks who sold their prepared dishes in the marketplace.

As midday passed into early afternoon, Michael rose after an all too brief nap. He managed to catch the gathering in the lounge. The shore teams returned with little in the way of gossip. Michael asked Cecilia if she would like to join him in doing a little clandestine snooping around Lokoja. Rollo's most famous couple sauntered around the town not far from the docks and asked questions about Mali while they gathered intelligence.

Their incessant questioning stirred up even more rumors and turned heads. Soon, the psychic couple realized they had a shadow of not one but three men behind them.

Han and Zhiwei joined Camille and Li. The group sat together and drank some lemonade with fresh slices of lemon tossed into the pitcher.

"Uh, oh," Camille said as she shaded her eyes and stared intently toward the shore. "Cecilia just signaled trouble," she noted. She saw the young physician use hand-gestures, which Camille learned from the Rollo group.

"She and Michael are coming in, but she signaled company. I see what she means."

"Police," Han observed. "Michael and Cecilia have been asking too many questions. They're being followed."

Michael and Cecilia picked up their pace as they started to move faster through the crowd while trying not to arouse suspicion. The two practically ran toward the yacht parked at the end of the docks. Right behind them, two large men and a smaller man separated to head them off, the smaller man obviously giving orders to the other two men.

"I can't get through to them," Cecilia linked as she and Michael rushed toward the boat's gangplank that resembled a wooden board to anyone else on the docks.

Han and Zhiwei exchanged glances after they appraised the situation. This group had participated in running interference in other chases. All at once, piles of goods stacked along the docks toppled over in front of the smaller man. A container of soap spilled out on the dock. The two larger men slipped on the surface and slid right off into the river. They splashed around and sought assistance. Some workers nearby threw them lengths of mooring ropes. A few of the locals laughed when they saw how the meddlesome police seemed to receive a little of what they usually dished out.

"Whew!" Cecilia linked as she and Michael walked aboard the yacht. "Thanks. That was close! Their stress levels were so high that we weren't able to break through to stop them. I guess we're just too tired. See you in a few minutes," she told them.

They soon joined the others on the third level deck and sat underneath the overhanging shade. Once more, the rain halted its onslaught on the river basin. The clouds parted and the equatorial sun beat down on the area. The humidity became almost unbearable. Michael smacked his lips together until Su Lin gestured toward a large sweating pitcher that contained several floating slices of lemon and chunks of ice.

"Oh, that looks so good," he said as he moved toward the tray.

"The ultimate thirst quencher," Su Lin stated.

"Over here!" Cecilia called out. She grabbed Michael by the elbow and pulled him into a seat.

With her mind, Su Lin poured out tall cool glasses of ice-cold lemonade, which she made specifically from scratch, knowning Michael's penchant for the tart yet sweet drink. She pulled out two fresh slices of lemon from the pitcher and dropped one into each glass of the yellowish colored liquid. The two glasses floated over to their recipients. They gratefully took a long draft and breathed a sigh of relief when the refreshment cooled their dry throats.

"I made cane syrup and lemon extract from locally grown organic sugar cane and lemons," Su Lin pointed out. "I even made the ice cubes with fusor water to complete the purity and flavor. How is the lemonade?"

"Are you kidding?" Cecilia shot back with a big smile.

"Perfect," Michael sighed as he pulled his lips from the glass.

"You had time to make the cane syrup?" Cecilia questioned.

"Uh, huh," Su Lin put in, "from an old recipe with boiled water and chopped up sugar cane," she explained. "I had to reconstruct a special kettle from an old drawing. Ordinarily, it takes a much longer to make syrup. Thanks to some help from Chou, I sped the process up a little."

"Thanks, Su Lin," Michael sang. "This is delicious."

Han and Zhiwei stared at the couple rather expectantly, but Camille and Master Li patiently waited as they enjoyed the yacht's special fans that blew cool dry air down upon them. Michael poured out a second tall glass.

"What did you learn?" Han finally asked Michael.

"We found out that no river traffic has come south of the Kainji Dam," Michael thought back as he drank more of the precious liquid. "The dam authorities have allowed overflow due to the excessive rains but that's it. They're not permitting any river traffic, no delivery boats, taxis, or ferries, nothing. It seems everyone in Nigeria is extremely worried about this unmentionable plague. The water in the reservoir is an important resource of drinking water for the entire region. The Nigerian Government suspects that someone has poisoned the river water in Mali. They closed the border with Niger, just as Niger's officials closed the border with Mali, but the move in Niger may have been too late. We overheard the police say that the infection spread south of Mali into northern Niger. Locals stated that the capital city of Niamey is in panic. Thousands of people have either fled the capital and are headed further down the river toward Nigeria, or spread into the countryside, including the president and the cabinet. The Niger military has blocked access to Kainji Reservoir. We also heard that the highest casualties so far are only in villages near the river. The infection has not spread inland."

"You heard all of that on the docks?" Zhiwei questioned.

"Michael also tapped into the police band before it went dead," Cecilia explained.

"What do mean?" Han questioned.

"There's more," Michael continued. "The Niger government put out a call for international assistance when communication from that country mysteriously stopped, just as it did in Mali. Seems NATO cordoned off both countries."

"NATO…" Master Li whispered, which only Camille caught.

"Did you say NATO?" Camille spoke up.

"Yes… Are you certain they said NATO?" Zhiwei added.

"Yes, I'm sure," Michael replied. "NATO is in charge of the operation."

Han frowned as he stared into his drink, but said nothing.

Michael wiped the sweat from his face and finished his second glass of ice-cold lemonade before he continued.

"Oh, yes, I almost forgot. The military closed the river to all traffic. We can't go upstream as a water taxi. They won't allow anyone to approach the dam," Michael added as he drained the glass. "At least we don't have to worry about the water level. With all the rain, they've had the sluice gates nearly wide open for two days. The river is more like a lake!"

Camille sat up as if shocked from a stupor.

"Oh mon dieu! Of course! Why did I not see it? Camille, you imbecile!" she declared. "It's not the ocean we saw in our dreams, it's the reservoir! The Kainji Reservoir! It's where the Niger River opens into a huge lake made by the Kainji Hydroelectric Dam!" she exclaimed as she glanced around the space at the others. "Don't you see?"

"You're right!" Han declared.

"Wait, we have a bigger problem!" Zhiwei mentioned.

"Zhiwei?" Han asked.

"We'll have to abandon the yacht long before we reach the dam," he informed them. "The Niger River is only deep enough for a fishing boat or a ferry. Can a yacht of this size travel in a stream that shallow? We've been fortunate with the rain making the river deep..."

"Send the boat upstream anyway," Master Li interrupted.

"But Li, you heard him," Camille protested. "It is impossible."

"Master Li," Chou broke in. "We won't go ten kilometers before this boat will be grounded on a sandbar or run into shallows."

"I believe we can go as far as Shankadade just past the river town of Jebba," Li informed them. "There is a smaller hydroelectric dam at Jebba. Perhaps we can find another means of travel to the reservoir lake after that," Li spoke in an open link. "Alert me when we reach Jebba," he said. He rose from his chair and retreated.

Those seated nearby stared at each other and wondered why Master Li seemed so abrupt. Camille turned to Michael.

"How does he plan to go from Jebba to the reservoir?" she wondered.

"If anyone can accomplish such a thing, Master Li can," Michael said. "Villi," he thought to the bridge. "Is the ship ready to leave port?"

"All members are onboard," he replied. "I see no reason to delay."

"We can certainly bypass the patrol boats if the yacht is invisible," Zhiwei pointed out.

"Arrange that when no one is looking," Michael said with a touch of sarcasm.

Su Lin looked up from the expanded rectangle in her lap.

"The rains have returned, Michael," she informed him. "Another system is quickly moving our way."

"Villi, let's get out of here before the rain hits," Michael requested. "Zinian? Cast off all lines."

"I'm heading to the anchor controls," Zinian informed him.

The great ship hummed to life, backed away from the dock, and turned its bow toward the upstream branch of the Niger River.

"All ahead, full," Michael ordered. "We have some friends to rescue."

The big Russian steered the huge craft slowly away from the docks with the ship's maneuvering thrusters below the water line on the starboard and port sides. Once in midstream, he opened up the large yacht's powerful engines and moved the craft into the center of the swiftly flowing Niger River. Just as the bow pressed forward, the sky opened and the tropical rain began to fall twice as heavy a downpour as before. The group moved inside just as the deluge struck the countryside like a great tidal wave.

"Now would be a good time to go invisible," Michael linked to Zhiwei.

The yacht seemed to shimmer in the heavy downpour before it slowly faded away like some ghostly Flying Dutchman while it moved deeper into the heart of Nigeria.

Chapter Thirty-four

Departure cancelled

NORMALLY FASTIDIOUS TO THE POINT of obsession, Reg showered twice a day.

"Whew! I stink," he muttered.

His nasty sweat-saturated clothes hung on him like filthy rags. Four days of traveling down bad roads in torrential rains and Reginald Atwater finally ran out of options. The spy could hardly stand the stench that permeated the car. He stripped off his jacket, tie, and white shirt to reveal those bulging muscles underneath that covering. The humidity and the constant rain ruined his hand-tailored London suit. He only wore a tank top as he drove the car. His rank armpits filled his nostrils with an odor he never smelled from his body until now. Growing increasingly frustrated and ill-tempered, he frequently hit the horn and shouted at pedestrians to move out of the road as he passed them. A steady stream of refugees fled from the river communities, heading south.

Things were not going as he planned. He could not find a flight out of Niger, not even a clandestine one. For one thing, the unchanging weather would not cooperate. The heavy rain and sheer wind made it impossible for a helicopter to land near him on the road. No airstrips in the region seemed long enough for a military jet unless he drove all the way to Niamey. However, Reggie had other more serious problems than his escape.

He looked into the rearview mirror.

"Shit!" he declared and slammed his foot on the accelerator.

The Motambou's appeared seriously ill and were probably close to death. Salla's breathing turned erratic at times and his skin took on an unhealthy pallor. Reggie could barely keep the man alive. He needed medical help and soon. He spent most of his life being an assassin. He knew nothing about being a doctor, although he certainly knew death when he saw it. Since the accident, neither Filla nor Salla ever regained consciousness. Lack of proper nutrition and fluids emaciated the couple. If he did not provide medical attention soon, he could kiss his future plans goodbye.

Reggie continued to spread the virus as he drove south. He had to continue this onslaught to perpetuate the myth of a spreading plague. Unfortunately, the road was so congested with traffic, it slowed his progress as well. He wanted to clear the road. He pulled out a vial and popped the top. Soon, screams of terror broke out and hundreds of people started to run as panic set in.

An infected man ran toward the car. His disease-ravaged body bled from every orifice.

"Get out of the way, fool!" Reg yelled out the window.

Unable to stop in time, the accelerating car struck the oozing body full force. Red liquid gushed everywhere as the man's flesh disintegrated. The body flipped up and splattered red goo everywhere. The rain slowly rinsed the human fluid from the vehicle.

"Huh," he thought. "Even in the rain… this stuff spreads like wildfire."

He had barely pulled back onto the road when a military vehicle heading north, blew its siren to clear the road. Reg swerved to avoid truck after truck, filled with soldiers that passed by as part of a great convoy. They were sent to reinforce the troops already on the border with Mali and halt the flow of refugees. Reg took the rest of a vial and flung its contents on the lead truck.

"So much for the relief," he smugly spoke.

He could reach Niamey by dawn if he drove the rest of the night. The capital city had over a million people with a large hospital, the only one of its kind in the entire region. Reggie was unaware of the panic that preceded him. Thousands of people were on the move. Vehicles of every type jammed the road south. People used whatever they could, whether it was wheels or hooves, to flee the oncoming plague.

He knew at least one doctor who could help him, a doctor who patched up many agents. He also had a secret contact in Naimey – a man he knew from his dormitory days in England, when they bunked together as teenagers. Despite Reg's aggressive nature, this was the only young man with whom Reg formed a close relationship in his youth, the only person in the world he could call friend. When they grew up, MI-6 recruited both men. They worked together on assignments several times in Africa. They were responsible for tempting the old doctor out of retirement to patch up agents for a fee and never ask any questions.

"Perhaps the butcher is sober today," he thought as he wiped his dry mouth. He needed a stiff drink and some blessed sleep.

When Reg returned to the road, he took out his special cell phone. The moment he opened the device, it created a special connection to the NAT-IX satellite parked overhead. The rain never let up and poured out of the sky. Reg's fingers worked the numerical keyboard rapidly as he sent code…

"Baby calling uncle," he typed. "Urgent."

"Uncle," the code flashed.

Reg typed with his right hand while he steered with his left, never taking his eyes off the road this time. He wanted no more accidents. The road was too crowded as he weaved in and out of traffic. His thumb knew the exact key to push.

"Will arrive soon in Niamey… cargo in poor condition… need medical help," Reg informed them.

"Understood," the numerical code responded. "Stand-by."

Reg could hear the labored breathing of Salla Motambou from the back of the car. The interior of the car smelled like a morgue. The phone vibrated in his hand. He glanced down before the numbers faded and the phone automatically shut off.

"Rendezvous point C, 69. Code 20. End."

Reg closed his communicator. Code 20 meant to use the current greeting for spies in their network. The "69" indicated a special joke that he and his African friend made up when MI-6 first assigned their codes. Reggie took the code 5-2-5 for his name. His friend Zinder took a low number, not usually allowed. Since Reg only used the number when he went to Africa, the corps allowed it. When he changed service, Reginald carried this code over to NATO – code 69 stood for his old buddy from spy school. Reggie smiled when he saw the number. He looked forward to seeing Zinder again. Perhaps they had enough time to catch up on each other's life.

"Code 20," Reg muttered. "I hope I memorized the latest greeting before I left… and I hope my pal has the same one."

Code 20, the latest standard spy greet, also meant complications involved – no additional communication over this channel. He wondered if the local spy network compromised the secrecy of their coded transmissions. At any rate, he could no longer speak with uncle after they issued a Code 20, no matter how scrambled or secure the line may seem. His hand slammed into the steering wheel out of frustration. Reggie was used to having things go his way. He had never failed on a mission and did not intend to upset that record.

"Bad weather… Motambou's injured… and now communications compromised. This deal keeps getting worse," he muttered.

He drove straight through until he reached the neighborhood in Niamey, which he knew as well as the streets of London. During his stint with MI-6,

Reg lived here for six months with Zinder in a "safe house" where the two men posed as local graphic artists. It was one of the few times in his life he enjoyed having one place to call home – regardless of the fact he assassinated sixteen targets during that period.

"Too bad we're no longer on assignment, Zin," he thought as he turned up the familiar street.

He pulled up outside the small residence he used to call home. He noticed that several of the homes in this area were already vacant – the front doors to these homes hung wide open, debris scattered in the yard, vehicles missing from open garages. For some reason, the lights in Zinder's house were on. He could see them through the open front window. Reg pulled the car into a driveway next to the house and shut the engine off. He reached over into the glove compartment and pulled out a 9mm pistol. From an inside pocket, he produced a silencer and slowly screwed the custom-made piece onto the front barrel of the gun. He slipped the gun into his right coat pocket, small enough so that its bulge would be undetectable.

As he opened the car door, he kept his right hand clasped around the gun in his pocket. He heard a voice from the shadowed side of the garage.

"Hold it. Don't move," the voice spoke with a British accent. "I don't recognize you stranger."

"That's because I forgot my hat," Reg responded. "You'd know me… I wear a white hat." Reg slowly raised his gun in the direction of the voice.

"You'd look damn silly in a white hat, Reginald Atwater," the voice said as a large black man emerged from the shadow. "You'd look much better in a blonde wig!" A tall black man wore a huge grin on his face. His right hand held a gun pointed right at Reggie's head as he approached the car. "If your right hand moves one more centimeter, I might have to shoot!"

"Zinder?" Reg asked. "Is that you?"

"In the flesh," the man responded.

Reggie's hand relaxed at his side as he visibly sighed. He pulled his hand out and showed it was empty. Zinder holstered his pistol.

"I only got the message of your… request… a short time ago," Zinder said as he walked up to Reg.

Side by side, the two men appeared practically identical in physical stature. Both were tall, broad-shouldered black men with big bulging muscular arms and chiseled good looks. Reggie had forgotten his pal's great physique. It was nice to find another man in equally good shape. Yet, as he gazed at Zinder's face, he noticed the other man seemed to have aged. That disappointed him.

"Come here you," Zinder said.

The two men embraced and kissed each other's cheek. This was the way of the corps. This was the way of two warriors. Between them, these men assassinated over a hundred targets. They knew about life and death.

"Sorry, I don't have much of an English breakfast for you, old chum. Not much time to prepare," Zinder explained. His eyes darted left and right as he looked to see if any of remaining neighbors saw them. He looked into the back seat and wrinkled his nose. "However, I think I can provide what you need," he told his friend. "Come inside. The cargo stay will keep until we leave. I need to brief you."

Inside the house, Zinder turned around and appraised his friend.

"Good to see you, old sport," Zinder said with a grin.

"You too, cricket," Reg replied.

"I haven't heard that name since we worked together for MI-6. Now we're both working with NATO. How long has it been since we tore up the town, my old friend," Zinder said. "We had a lot of fun back then, didn't we? I hear you've been busy."

"New mission," Reg sighed, "Can't tell you anything... need to know basis... sorry," he reminded his friend.

"I hate to say this, but the Americans have intervened on this case. They feel that NATO's over stepped its bounds," Zinder informed Reg. His smile faded. "The plan has changed. MI-6 is involved. They've contacted me and activated my old number..."

"Have they?" Reg asked while his face remained unreadable.

He knew that General Andrews would not share his most secret program with anyone else. As far as he knew, Andrews hated the head of MI-6. He read it from his mind, along with many other things. More likely, the Prime Minister, under pressure from the Americans, went to the head of MI-6 and pleaded the case that they needed to take over the operation. Too many collateral casualties. However, Reg was certain General Andrews would not let that happen. He knew Andrews had ties that went deep inside the American agencies and the British military. He could delay their involvement, but not forever. The news that Zinder reported to MI-6 probably prompted the code 20.

"They consider Zinder a possible leak," Reg thought.

For now, he would play along with his turncoat buddy.

"We've much to discuss and time is short," Zinder told him. "Let's go."

"After you," Reginald gestured. "I like to keep my back covered."

"Ok, Reggie," Zinder replied. "I can see you haven't changed."

"You got that right," Reggie said with a smile. He looked at the man's back for a moment. "If you get in the way, my friend, I may have to severe our ties," he thought.

Chapter Thirty-Five

An Ill Wind Blows

John loved to lie in the big hammock on his back porch and gently swing back and forth on his days off. He often borrowed a book from Master Li's library, laid in his hammock, and read while he relaxed. Zinian glued blocks with eyelets to the wall so John could hang his hammock, big enough for two. As second under Zinian, he had a large three-story Victorian house built on the south side of Rollo, not far from Zinian's construction offices.

The head of the local Comanche tribe remained single, although he dated one particular woman now and again. She came down to visit John and was preparing to make lunch for him. She brought out a bottle of beer.

"I thought you might be thirsty," she said.

"You read my mind," he whispered to her. He reached over and grabbed her around the waste.

"Don't start," she as she pulled away. However, when she twisted around, she noticed what looked like a dust cloud on the horizon.

"What's that?" she said and shaded her eyes.

From this perspective, they could see into the southern horizon through Chou's holographic field. It was only slightly above the horizon that it projected an image of "the perfect day."

"I don't know," he replied as he came up out of his hammock and put his beer down. "If I didn't know better… Looks like a lotta trucks comin' up the road…"

"More like a convoy," she commented. "A circus or a county fair?"

All at once, John had a terrible feeling in the pit of his stomach. He could make out more details as the column of vehicles grew closer. This was not a line of four or five regular semitrailer trucks. This looked like a whole division of military vehicles, with two tanks on flat bed trucks partially covered by tarps. They started to slow down as they approached the south end of Rollo.

"I thought Master Li told us… outsiders can't see us," his girlfriend wondered. She turned to John with a worried expression. "Can they?"

The column of military vehicles had already passed the shield that protected the Native American village south of Rollo. These trucks were deliberately slowing down where the southwest corner of Chou's shield came closest to the highway. That was too much of a coincidence to John. He rose from the hammock and stood up.

"I don't like this," he said as they came to a stop. "Do me a favor. Go to my desk. In the upper right hand drawer, I have a pair of binoculars…"

His girlfriend did not wait for him to finish. She ran through the house, grabbed the item from his desk and ran back. John put them up to his eyes. The column of military trucks and equipment stopped just south of town. He saw men with maps. They were pointing in their direction.

All at once, a booming voice filled the air around them.

"Warning! Warning!" the voice shouted into the air. "Impending threat! Take cover! Warning! Impending threat! Take cover!" it repeated.

The moment the loud warning went off, people started to pour out of their houses into the street or away from their projects. Soon, a whole crowd of bewildered people stood mulling around in Main Street, wondering what was going on. John looked over at this girlfriend.

"Go to Main Street. Tell everyone to run, don't walk, to the manor house," he said as he turned toward her. "Have each adult grab a child and run… RUN!" he yelled. "Run for your life!"

His girlfriend sprinted off the porch and ran up the street as the voice continued to yell out its warning overhead.

"Warning, impending threat… take cover!"

"Go to manor house!" she shouted as ran north up the street for Main Street. "Grab a kid and go to manor house! Everyone! Leave no person behind. Everyone take cover in the manor house!" she yelled.

John kept the binoculars to his face. He watched as an officer stepped out of the lead vehicle. He took the map with him and checked it. Then he gestured toward something on the ground about two hundred meters between John and the officer. Several men gathered around the commander. He kept pointing toward the same spot. Then, it suddenly occurred to John.

"They know were here," he realized. "This is a government invasion!"

John took a moment to reason out his next course of action.

"Why now?" he wondered. "Why this moment?"

Quickly, the reason became apparent. With Master Li and the others out of town, that only left one group of psychics vulnerable.

"They're after the children!" he thought. "But how did they know..."

John expressed his thought so loudly that his overt concern leapt from his mind. Mark picked up John's thoughts inside the classroom building. Inside the structure, the schoolchildren had not heard the warning. The five-year-old stood up and waved his hand.

"Teacher," he linked to Star Wind's mind. "Your brother John says someone is coming for us."

Star Wind frowned. Mark never spoke to her mind like this. She brought the psychic children to the school building, along with the other children this morning, hoping to resume some normalcy in their lives. All at once, the psychic children stood together as a group. Mey Li and Mark turned in the direction of the road. They could feel the growing menace. Sandra, Xiong Po, and Robert joined the other two staring in the same direction.

"They're coming for us," Mark said in a loud voice.

Little Robert started to cry. "We can't stop them without Master Li," the littlest psychic stated. "They'll kill us!" he said.

Mey Li stood behind him and patted his shoulder.

"Don't worry, Robert," she told him. "I won't let them hurt you."

Star Wind's expression immediately changed to one of fear. She did not doubt the children's word. She only wondered to whom Mark referred.

"Who are *they*?" she asked the children.

Running Elk, nearly out of breath, suddenly burst through the schoolhouse door as she frantically searched for Star Wind. When she heard the noise, Star Wind walked into hall and saw her mother. Running Elk ran over to her daughter, her chest heaved up and down. She gasped for air as she tried to collect her composure enough to speak.

"They're coming," her dry voice gasped. "They're coming for the children!" She reached out and grabbed Star Wind's arm for balance as she almost slid down onto the floor.

"Who mother?" Star Wind demanded. "Who's coming for the children?"

"No time to explain," the elderly woman gasped. "We must move all of the children back to the manor house. The rest of the village is on their way... everyone is waiting for us. Now let's go!"

Star Wind turned around and noticed that all of the children had gathered into a group behind her with Mark at the head and Mey Li at the back as they herded both the psychic and non-psychic children into a group.

"We need to go to Master Li's house now," Mark said as he stared up at Star Wind with wide eyes. "Running Elk is right. It is the only place that is safe."

The other psychic children nodded their heads. At that moment, they heard a vehicle honk its horn outside. The group moved to the front door. John had the large hovercraft used to transport big items from the construction area. He waved at his sister.

"Come on!" he shouted. "Hurry!"

Without saying another word, Star Wind had Running Elk lead the children toward the floating platform. Some of them giggled and laughed.

"Jump on!" she told them.

When they had the last child aboard, Star Wind, still standing in the school's front doorway, touched the wall. A panel lit up.

"By authority of Star Wind," she stated, "Rollo emergency override 996; complete shutdown of all municipal facilities; override WPO order number 9. Theta, phi, epsilon, seven, now, now, now," she said.

The moment she stepped from the building, the door behind her sealed and the building began to drop into the ground. Across the park, the medical clinic started to drop down as did the security building across the street. Selene and Jennifer monitored Star Wind's actions and cut off all electronic monitoring devices, which also cut Rollo off from the rest of the world. They decided to remain inside the security building.

At the north end of town, Victor and Edward heard the alarms go off. They knew they were safe inside the subterranean chamber, especially when they heard the exterior doors seal tight. Villi trained them well for all contingencies. Every hover platform on the street swiftly moved across town and entered the hanger before it shut itself off from the surface. Protective shields went up around each park. Every house sealed itself.

Satisfied she accomplished her task, Star Wind ran to the platform and jumped on. She noticed that John had the main remote control device on the dashboard that her husband gave him. The screen showed a map of Rollo. A red wave went off on the south end of town around the invasion force clearly visible on the screen.

The moment the children and Star Wind were safely aboard, John drove the floating platform up Main Street toward the headquarters. The last person on foot ran through the piazza toward the front door. The platform just passed through the front gate when an explosion shook the air around them. John brought the platform to a halt inside the piazza and jumped up on his seat to give him some height advantage.

Across town, the picture did not look good. Part of the force field that also acted as camouflage collapsed. The wall of energy that normally protected them had a huge gaping hole. Immediately, military vehicles and soldiers began to pour through the opening. John dropped down into the driver's seat and drove the platform up to the front door. He spun around to face the children.

"Mark… Mey Li… Sandra… Xiong… Robert… you must listen to Star

Wind," he told them. "Do not use your power unless an adult directs you to do so. Understood?" he asked.

The psychic children all nodded their heads in unison.

"Thank you," he said with a slight smile. "Star Wind, take the children inside and see to their comfort," he requested. "Mother, would you look after the town's people. I must do something. I'll be fine. Just hurry… please."

Everyone scrambled down from the platform. John moved the device over to the side of the piazza. It was too large to park inside the garage. Adrenaline pumped through his arteries as he stood in front of the mansion with the remote in his hand and tried to remember Chou's instructions.

"*If there ever is an emergency and you cannot reach us in time, use this special code*," Chou's words echoed in his mind.

John gazed down at the controller in his shaking hand. He placed three fingers on the front part that had a black blank screen. The screen moved up off the controller and expanded in his hands.

"*You only have to speak to it, John*," Chou's voice echoed in his memory.

"Steady," he thought. "You must stay calm. Trust Chou's device," he thought. "This is John Smith," he spoke to the screen.

"Recognize John Smith," it spoke back to him.

"I'll marvel over this later," he thought. "Emergency," he said aloud. "Security breach. Rollo is under attack by the military."

"Security breach acknowledged. Proceed to enter WPO headquarters building and await further instructions," it told him. "Defensive systems activated."

John turned around and walked toward the front door. As he did, the hair on the back of his neck went up. All at once, he could feel a strong energy field surround the grounds that held the mansion. When he turned around, the town of Rollo and everything else vanished from sight.

"Wow!" he reacted.

"John Smith," the remote spoke to him. "You must go inside the WPO headquarters."

"Sure, sure," John said as he went to the mansion's front door and walked inside. "Let's hope this works."

Chapter Thirty-six

The second trap is sprung

"A JACK OR BETTER TO open," Villi said as the crowded table of gamblers pressed in under the light over the table, the only light on in the room. "Ante up!" He started to deal, when he sensed a rise in psychic activity. "Don't try to use your power, Cecilia," he admonished. "Besides, all the cards will be face up."

He dealt the first card face up, going around the table and asked each person if they wanted to bet or not.

"I'll bet a hundred," Cecilia said after Villi tossed out a king of spades and ten of diamonds on the table in front of her.

"It's tough to play poker with psychics," Su Lin openly thought.

"That's why the cards are face up," Villi countered.

"You're right, Villi. No need to scan. I feel lucky tonight!" she bragged.

"We'll see. Hmm, an ace!" Villi noted as he flipped the heart card in front of Su Lin followed by a nine of clubs.

"I'll see your hundred," Su Lin offered, "and raise you another hundred!"

"I'm in," Cecilia said as she tossed another chip confidently.

"Five of hearts, six of spades," Villi comment when he tossed the next two cards to Han. "No help and no raise, but two hundred to stay in..."

"I want a new shuffle," Han complained. "Is that possible in this game?" he asked innocently as he reluctantly tossed in two chips.

"This is a game of chance and luck, my boy," Cecilia grinned over at Han. "You don't get to build up one of your strategies tonight."

"Pair of diamonds, no face cards, possible flush," he said as he tossed the next two cards to Chou, "two hundred to stay in."

"Might as well," Chou spoke up and tossed out two chips.

"The pot is growing!" Su Li said as she rubbed her hands together. "More suckers!"

Zinian and Zhiwei sat quietly in the corner as they watched the game.

"Nothing," Villi said as he gave Cecilia a six of clubs. "Another ace!" he smiled when he tossed the card in front of Su Lin.

"Look at the genius who shuffled the cards, will ya?" Su Lin posed with two aces on the table. "I think your luck, Cecilia, is about to change."

"Hey! No cheating you two!" Cecilia cried with fake passion.

"That ace is worth another two hundred," Su Lin said.

"That's another two hundred to you, Han," Villi said as he turned to the Go master. He pulled another card from the top of the deck and let it fly across the table.

"This hand's getting awfully expensive," Han said as he noticed the three of clubs land. "Too much for me," he complained. "I fold," he said as he turned his cards over.

"Han's out," Villi said and turned to Chou. "You're up next," he said as he flipped another card out. "Queen of diamonds!"

"That's gotta be worth another hundred on top of your two," Chou said smiling. He grabbed his chips, "make that another hundred more," he added as he looked around the table.

"Four hundred to Cecilia," Villi exclaimed. "Feeling lucky?" he asked her.

Before Villi could throw out the next card, Michael chimed in from the bridge.

"Just about the end of my shift, Villi," Michael told the dealer. "Who's ahead in the poker game? My guess is, it's Han," Michael thought knowing Han's gaming abilities.

"Su Lin," Cecilia muttered.

"Really? You folks are lucky Master Li has been hibernating. If he was there, you'd all be..." his thoughts trailed off.

Everyone looked at each other. No one could sense Michael.

"Michael? We'd all be what?" Villi asked.

At that precise moment, a loud piercing sound shot into their ears and mind. None of the psychics aboard the yacht could stop it.

Deck of cards in his hand went flying as Villi tried to block the sound in his ears with his hands. Nearly the entire group of card players collapsed onto the floor in pain. The sound grew to a deafening roar and rendered all of them helpless. They could only writhe in misery from the intense pain that bombarded their brains.

Chou tried to shout above it. He struggled to speak. No sound came out. The others tried as well. They could not link to one another. The piercing sound ripped through their minds like a knife that stabbed deep into their psyche. The light bulbs shattered and plunged the room into darkness.

After a few minutes of steady attack, the deafening noise, which crippled every psychic in the room, stopped. At that moment, the yacht's camouflage devices that hid the craft quit working. Then the ship's engines died. All power to the yacht ceased. Lights all over the boat went out. Nothing moved. Silence and darkness descended on the large yacht that drifted down the Niger River toward the embankment with no apparent signs of life aboard.

An ultra-high frequency wave of energy cascaded outward from the yacht and destroyed every living thing within fifty meters of the huge vessel. The psychics aboard never stood a chance against its onslaught. The yacht had served its intended purpose.

Chapter Thirty-seven

Mountebank

"Get up, you old fool," Zinder said as he shook the elderly, white-haired, black man who was lying in bed. "Get up!" he yelled and jerked the covers off the man. "We have a special package for you."

The elderly man shook all over and shivered, but not from cold. Next to the man's bed sat an empty bottle of whiskey and an empty glass. The stale air in the room smelled of cigarettes and exhaled booze coming from the man's decayed mouth.

Zinder pushed a small window open and waved his hand.

"Whew! I thought the back end of that car was bad. This place stinks!" he declared.

"What did you say? A package?" the white-haired balding man said as he slowly rose. He scratched at his body and blinked against the brightness that streamed into the room.

"There's a couple in the next room that needs your special touch, doc," Zinder informed him.

The doctor's old, wrinkled, black face scowled. He definitely did not like the idea that he would start his day by patching up some shooting victim only to send him to prison. He rubbed his tired bloodshot eyes, pushed back his fuzzy white mane, and decided to button his lip. Once a proud surgeon for thirty years, his practice slipped when he started to drink after he lost his wife. The medical board finally forced Doctor Liander to retire years ago after he showed up too many times for work inebriated. Gambling left the doctor broke until Zinder approached him to help with a special case, for which he received a large amount of cash. After that, Zinder recruited Dr. Liander into their service, which required the doctor to remove bullets or stitch wounds with no questions asked as long as Zinder paid him with cash. He was broke and needed the money.

"What did you do to them this time?" Doctor Liander's squeaky voice asked.

"Reggie brought them. I didn't do a thing… this time," Zinder added.

"Reginald Atwater is back? Well," Liander said as he yawned and pulled up his suspenders. "Let's have a look."

He reached over on the dresser and picked up his bifocal glasses. His eyes searched the room until he found what he needed. His hand slipped behind a stack of books and pulled out a flask. He took a quick swig of his morning "medicine" to chase away his shakes and put the bottle back. Taking in a deep breath, he went into the other room to inspect his patients.

Reg dragged two sofas close together as makeshift beds for Salla and Filla Motambou. He stripped off their foul smelling clothing, when the half-asleep hung-over doctor came stumbling into the room.

"Oh, my... oh, my! What has happened to these poor people?" the doctor asked as he pushed his wire-framed spectacles further up on the bridge of his nose. He noticed at once their wretched color and malodor. "Whew! They need a bath!"

Zinder shook his head and pointed at Reg, who just pursed his lips. The old doctor bent low over each body for a moment and performed a rapid assessment. He picked up each wrist, gazed at their faces, pulled open their eyes and mouths, then "tsked" at the other two men in the room.

"Rapid, thready pulse, shallow breathing, emaciation, poor turgor, dry sclera... these people are suffering from malnutrition and dehydration," the old man observed.

"Is that all?" Reggie muttered.

"Possible concussion…" the elderly man muttered.

"Can you do anything doc?" Zinder asked.

"Let me get a closer look at the rest of him," Dr. Liander offered.

He examined Salla's trunk and mid-section. He palpated his abdomen.

"This man's had some blunt trauma," he accused and looked over at Reggie. "Were they beaten? I need to know."

Reggie shook his head and munched a piece of fruit.

"Car accident," he mumbled through his teeth.

The physician scowled. He doubted his statement.

"Honest!" Reg declared as he carelessly discarded the snack. "No seatbelt!"

"I suppose I'll have to believe you," the doctor replied, "I'll check them for spinal cord injuries." After that, he began to bark orders. "Zinder, go get me the IV supplies. I need to start a line in each of them," the old man ordered.

He pointed to the room that appeared to be a doctor's office toward the side of the house.

Zinder saluted sarcastically. The big man casually walked toward the room in question.

"They haven't bathed in days. Their bodies are covered in excrement," the doctor exclaimed as he reeled from the odor.

"Get him. He thinks *they* stink," Reg spoke sneering.

"Reggie… get me a basin of hot water and some soap!" the little black man requested. "I must clean their skin. Please wash their clothes," he requested.

Reginald returned shortly with a basin of hot water and soap as the doctor suggested.

"Good," Dr. Liander said as he picked up a washcloth with a bar of soap. "You know where the washer and dryer are in the back."

Reggie picked up the offensive clothes and took them to a stoop behind the doctor's home where he found an old washer and dryer. He started the noisy washer, dumped in some detergent and dropped in the clothes. When he returned, Reg watched as the doctor sponged off Salla's naked body.

"Can't you go a little faster?" Reg asked as he turned away.

"I suspect that you're in a hurry as usual, Reg. Aren't you?" the doctor shot back. Reggie simply shrugged his shoulders. "I'm trying to save you some time, unless you'd like to do this?" Reggie shook his head. "I filled up on supplies yesterday before the panic set in. Go to the kitchen and help yourself."

"Thanks, doc," Reg grunted. He ventured off to the kitchen where he intended to make some breakfast.

Zinder finally returned with the IV supplies. Moments later, he stood by a nearby table and spread out the "kits" on the table. He had two big plastic bags with a 1000cc's of fluid and two silver-capped bottles with yellowish fluid inside, lengths of tubing, along with some IV catheters inside sterile packaging.

"Thanks, Zinder," the older man told him. "Go join your friend. I'll finish," he said. Within minutes, the smells of brewing coffee, fried eggs, potatoes, and sausage wafted through the kitchen door.

In the living room, the old physician found his mark when he penetrated a vein he knew from years of experience. He opened the line and began re-hydrating his patients intravenously while he made a more thorough examination. He pulled out another kit, catheterized Salla's bladder, but received no urine. Relieved he had only been incontinent, he did the same to Filla with similar results. He put diapers around the two patients to keep the caustic urine from breaking out their skin.

He hung a second IV on both patients. This time he added multivitamins to the IV's and piggybacked some albumin to help their emaciated bodies. He probed their abdomens, shined his otoscope into their ears and shined the optometric scope into their eyes while he searched for other damage.

Dr. Liander backed up and scratched his head.

"These two should be dead," he said quietly. "If they were in a car accident, they should have bled internally instead of healing so rapidly on their own accord. What has caused this phenomenon?" he mumbled. "It seems as if their cerebral contusions are rapidly healing of their own accord as well. This is weird," Dr. Liander observed. "I wish I had access to the hospital... I could test their blood, take x-rays..."

"No questions, doc," Reg said from behind the doctor, which shocked the old man and caused him to spin around.

"I didn't hear you, Reg," Liander nervously spoke.

"You weren't meant to," Reggie said as he chewed on a piece of toast. "Just treat them and make them stable so they can travel, understood?"

The frightened doctor nodded his head. He had good reason to fear Reginald Atwater, having reluctantly become part of the spy business in Africa. Doctor Liander knew that the people he helped – Zinder and Reginald Atwater – were cold-blooded killers. He also knew better than to ever ask questions or let on that he knew more than he should. When he gazed into the heartless eyes of the man before him, he lowered his head.

"Whatever you want, Reggie," Liander softly replied.

"That's better," the large black man stated. "And if they start to come around, doc, knock them out with something. I want to keep them unconscious, understand?" he requested with a rather threatening tone. "I'll know if you don't do it."

"Yes, Reg," Liander humbly answered.

The doctor previously dealt with this ruthless killer. He had seen some of Reggie's victims. He knew the large black Englishman would not hesitate to shoot anyone who stood in his way.

"Zinder!" Reg called to his friend in the kitchen. "Show me where I can clean up!"

Zinder grunted something from the kitchen when Reggie turned his back on the doctor and returned to his old friend.

The doctor worked on his two patients all morning while Reg took a shower and used the bathroom to clean up. Zinder sat outside the bathroom and talked to Reg about England. The two men reminesed after Reggie scrubbed the filthy malodor from his body. The Motambou's breathing improved during this period, while their blood pressure and heart rate returned to normal readings. Liander heard a moan from the woman. Filla started to regain consciousness. The old corrupt physician pulled out a vial from his nearby cabinet and gave her a long-acting injection directly into a port of her IV tubing. Filla soon drifted out before she could form a single thought. The doctor carefully re-examined Salla and noted that he had never moved. He went and adjusted his position, checked his pulse and respiration.

A refreshed Reg along with Zinder appeared in the living room doorway. Zinder kept some suits of clothes at the doctor's house in case he had to make a change if he showed up covered with blood. He and Reg were nearly identical in size and weight.

"How is my package?" Reggie also wondered.

"Improving," the doctor replied. "However, they still cannot travel in this condition. You'll have to give me more time, if you want them to survive."

Reggie fought off sleep for several hours. Noon came and went. Finally, he had to sleep.

"We're going upstairs for some rest, doc," Reg told him as he glanced over at Zinder. "Wake us up in a few hours. Then we'll take over." Reggie winked at Zinder and touched the special cell phone on his side.

Zinder caught Reggie's implication that he wanted to talk.

"Oh… oh, sure," he agreed and followed Reg up the stairs to the attic.

Dr. Liander had two cots there for the agents to sleep when they sometimes dropped by unannounced. The two big men walked up the staircase. The creaking stairs groaned under their weight. Reg did need to lie down for some needed rest.

Dr. Liander followed them with his eyes. All at once, he had the sensation that one of his patients awoke. He spun around and stared at Salla. Dr. Liander rubbed his tired eyes. His patient's eyes were closed. He poked Salla's arm hard with a sharp needle to get a reaction. Not the slighted flinch passed over his face or even a flutter of the eyelids. The old man figured he just imagined the feeling.

Upstairs, Zinder wondered what would be Reggie's next move. He did not hear Reggie's communicator when it vibrated a few minutes ago. Instead, he took off his jacket and thought he would join Reg in stretching out on the cot for a few hours.

The second Zinder turned around to hang up his coat, Reggie pulled out the device and looked at the numbers as they flashed across the screen.

"I'm glad you showed up in Niamey," Zinder said as he hung up his coat and started to face Reg. "Seems like old times."

When he turned around, he saw Reggie held a silenced gun pointed at him. To his astonishment, he gazed into Reggie's cold eyes. A puzzled expression crossed his face. Before he could open his mouth, poor Zinder did not have time to question his fate. Reg did not hesitate. He accurately fired one shot through Zinder's right bare chest. He never missed. The bullet tore right through the right side of Zinder's heart. He had less than a heartbeat to live.

"My friend," Zinder muttered as he staggered a moment and clutched his chest. A second shot zipped through the air and struck Zinder between the eyes. The professionally constructed bullet easily crushed the bone, exited the back of his skull, and scattered his brains all over the wall. His body fell backward onto the bed, dead before he hit the mattress.

Reg walked up to Zinder's lifeless body and prodded him with the barrel of the gun. The number he had seen on the screen of his cell phone did not bother him one second – a special message for him directly from General Andrews. He had no problem carrying out that order.

"Code 37," Reggie muttered. "Kill all witnesses."

He heard a noise downstairs and glanced over at the attic door. As quietly as he could, he walked to the open doorway and listened. He could hear the doctor downstairs busily tending his patients. Reg quietly closed the door. He walked back over to Zinder and covered his body with the bed sheet. He would take care of the doctor later, once he knew the Motambou's were stable. He went back to his phone.

His fingers furiously typed out the coded message: *"Complied with code 37. Await further orders."*

More numbers appeared that Reggie immediately translated.

"Attention: Code 92, imperative."

Reg sat back on his bed as a smug sense of satisfaction spread through his thoughts. Code 92, orders to carry out a special execution, in this case, kill the Rollo psychics. He wondered if General Andrews had the guts to issue it. He tried to convince the general they were a danger to the organization. Evidently, the general came around to his way of thinking. They knew the Rollo psychics would seek revenge if the military attacked the children. He and the general were of similar mind.

He waited a long time for this moment. The plans he worked on for five years would finally pay off. He knew they took the first bait and moved onto the yacht. He only hoped they wouldn't notice the amplifiers. He glanced down at the remote in his hand. They were still active. The moment he activated them, he would eliminate his only real threat. After that, he would kill off the rest of the psychics. One by one, he would find and eliminate them. Salla would reveal their locations.

"Well… things are beginning to look up," he thought.

He recalled the meeting with the general when he convinced the man to make a crucial decision… one that Reggie knew would result in his being the most powerful psychic on the planet.

Reginald, General Andrews and Colonel Brighton were present.

"…even if you do have this yacht built and put it out there on the Niger River," the general questioned, "what makes you think they'll take the bait?"

"Are you kidding?" Reggie replied. "First of all, I'll instill in them to over pack for the trip. Their boat will be inadequate. Once they see the yacht, they'll feel they can take it. Besides, they love to travel in style. I'll modify the hull so they can take it up river. Secondly, they know the Motambou's will be going down river. I'll find a way for them to communicate that before I disable them. They'll do anything to rescue one of their own. Once they step onboard, we run the risk they'll find the devices and disable them. I'll know because it will trigger a light on my phone… if they try to disable the setup, I'll set it off…"

"Without my order?" the general put to him.

"Make it a standing order…" Reggie countered.

The general looked down at the plans for the yacht.

"This is going to cost us a bundle…" the general objected.

"You'll be reimbursed," Reg told them. "My wealthy friend has agreed to help the military with dozens of weapon smugglers, if he can have the boat at half price. I figure this will save the military hundreds of millions. The yacht is a small investment."

"He's welcome to it," the general said. "How much are we talking?"

"Probably three… five hundred million… give or take a hundred or so," Reggie calmly put to him and Brighton.

"Five hundred…" Brighton started to object when the general signaled.

"How much will your Nigerian friend donate," the general asked as he chewed on a cigar. "And don't tell me any less than two hundred million, Reg. I know how you're playing this thing," the general grinned. "I've a few contacts, too!"

All three men laughed, but all during that meeting, Reggie knew he had another ace up his sleeve.

"If you only knew what I intend to do with that money," he thought as he covered Zinder's body.

That meeting took place over two years ago when Reggie first brought the idea to them. During construction of the boat in Italy, scientists from their division installed hundreds of sonic devices and placed them all over the ship with the intended purpose to disrupt and destroy all forms of life. Reg had them spread all over the boat. A few minutes exposure to those waves would scramble anyone's brain. The psychics would never know what hit them.

With sensors also onboard, Reg knew the minute the psychics took over the vessel. Their mere presence activated the special sensors he instructed the scientists to create. His billionaire friend only had to deliver the yacht to a specified location. The rich elderly man wasn't certain if he was going to take possession of the yacht or not and had his luggage taken aboard the freshly delivered vessel. He'd been double-crossed by Atwater in the past and decided he wanted the yacht after he saw it.

However, Reggie had different plans. He suspected the psychics would procure the boat when he planted the suggestion in their minds while they slept. He only had to place it in their path at the right time – what he considered another of his chess moves. He found out that they could not resist this form of temptation when they had inadequate means, as when they took the general's jet to escape China, or stole cars in Russia. Reggie planted several suggestions into the minds of the psychics while they slept as part of his plan.

Now as he stood in Dr. Liander's attic, Reggie held the phone in his hand and put in the activation code. He smiled as with his finger poised over the screen. The sensors showed ten vital signs. He wasn't certain about the tenth person. He could probably guess as to who it might be. Reggie did not care. One less psychic to worry about later.

"Good bye… Mr. Li," Reggie said as he activated the code. "Checkmate!"

A signal bounced off a satellite and triggered the sonic devices onboard the yacht. For a moment, a red light flashed that indicated the devices had activated. He watched for a nervous few minutes when the light first flash yellow before it finally burned a steady green. The sensors indicated no life forms aboard the yacht. He killed the ten people whom he assumed could pose as a problem for him. Now that they were eliminated, he chuckled at the ease he had carried out his mission.

"23," Reg put into his phone – the code for "mission kill completed and successful."

"Only one more little detail to resolve," he thought as he remembered the doctor downstairs. He glanced over at Zinder's body. "Sorry old chum we didn't have a chance to renew our acquaintances," he muttered. Reg turned to his own cot and loosened his tie, prepared to take a nap.

He lay on the bed, closed his eyes, and envisioned the Special Forces unit sent to Kansas with orders to kill the children. He planned that, too. They were as much a threat to him as the adults were. He implanted the fear of their dangerous nature into the operation's two officers. Newly promoted Colonel Brighton along with Sergeant Peterson headed that task force. They personally planned to carry out the "kill" orders while their men rounded up the citizens of Rollo and brought them back for processing.

"I can't wait to see what kind of futuristic devices they find in Rollo," he thought. "Perhaps only a psychic can use them… in which case, I will be both rich and powerful."

Reginald Atwater rolled over and took in a deep breath before he drifted off to sleep, filled with the satisfaction that, despite the weather delay and the accident, everything had turned out the way he had planned for this operation.

"Nothing can stop me," he sighed as he confidently closed his eyes.

Chapter Thirty-Eight

Terror Plain

When Colonel Brighton's big cargo planes, loaded with NATO tanks, trucks, and officer's car, landed at a private airstrip outside Libbey, Oklahoma, no one in America – not the CIA, the FBI, the NSA, or even Rollo's residents – knew about this secret commando raid. Only one man had the authority to order such a domestic invasion without a directive from the Pentagon. General Andrews gave the green light to Colonel Brighton and ordered his men to invade a place they had never seen and only suspected existed.

"We'll be running an exercise," the general reassured America's Homeland Security, "and nothing more. We promise that no civilian will even know we've been there. We'll be finished in less than three hours," he reassured the American government when he made the arrangements.

After he received his permission for the secret mission, he gave Colonel Brighton the greenlight. Yet, the general did not know what his commando team would find. After all, he only had Reginald Atwater's word a place called Rollo actually existed. Andrews managed to keep the operation a complete secret the entire time, even from his staff. However, Colonel Brighton had serious doubts that he would find a village called Rollo.

"Don't express those views in front of the men," Andrews told him.

While reluctant at first to lead the attack, Colonel Brighton could not argue with the promotion or the increase in his department budget. He did squawk over the waves he might make when he landed an invasion force in America. Therefore, General Andrews invented the cover of exercises. He wanted this operation kept as quiet as possible. In their strategy meeting, they even made certain the landing site was close to Rollo without alerting the public or the military of their true mission.

"Make it fast, quick, and get out!" he ordered.

Brighton had every intension of following those orders… only when he arrived in Kansas, the stark evidence of nothing being there, glared back at him and made him look like a fool in front of his men.

"Halt!" Colonel Brighton ordered into his mouthpiece.

The column behind him ground to a stop. He overheard some skeptical comments from the men. He pulled his satellite photograph out, with two areas circled in red. *"Line up your sites with these GPS coordinates and destroy this area!"* A hand scrawled message in red across the photo acted as instructions.

"I hope Atwater is correct," Brighton muttered. He turned to the man next to him. "Call General Andrews. Tell him we arrived at the position just outside of Rollo. We are about to enter the village," he said and muttered, "if it's there…"

"Village? What Village?" the com-officer scoffed.

"Gunner!" the colonel yelled into his mouthpiece. "Do you have the target coordinates I gave you?"

"Yes, sir," the man replied.

The colonel turned to his assistant. "Just call the general and give him the message," he said as he pointed to the communicator in the man's hand.

Until this moment, only four people from the outside world knew of the mysterious place called Rollo. Yet, no one but Reginald Atwater ever saw the place. No one knew of its appearance or size. Colonel Brighton had orders to take his company of men and equipment into Rollo and remove its population, load them on the trucks, and take everyone back to Labrador.

"Use whatever force is necessary," the general ordered.

Unknown to the rest of his men, the colonel and the sergeant also had strict orders to kill the psychic children. Despite Peterson's protests, Brighton threatened him with desertion until his promotion to sergeant helped persuade the young man to perform the delicate task. Brighton also reminded Peterson that let loose on the world, these "children" could cause untold damage, or so Reginald Atwater convinced him. He fingered the canister in his pocket. He had to gather the children into an enclosure, like a closet and open the cannister. The chemical would kill them instantaneously.

"Gunner… fire your weapon at those coordinates when you are ready," Colonel Brighton ordered.

"At that bush?" the man questioned.

"I gave you an order soldier!" Brighton barked. "Carry it out!"

The man swiveled his big gun into position until the numbers on the readout matched those he'd been given. General Andrews sent the latest armor piercing shells made for advanced tanks and guns mounted on light armored vehicles. The firing mechanism automatically loaded the small but powerful shell and the gunner's panel lit up green.

"Fire in the hole!" he called out.

Several soldiers put their hands over their ears. The soldier pressed the button that fired the shell at the spot a hundred and fifty meters away. The ensuing explosion destroyed the black box that powered this corner of the holographic shell. The inclusive and protective mirage that covered the entrance to the south part of Rollo faded and left a wide gap in the great shield that stretched over the village. From their point of view, they could see the village through the opening with the illusive flat plain of Kansas on either side. It seemed surreal and dreamlike that a person could find an idyllic oasis in such a desolate place. The men saw streets lined with large ornate buildings, a different sky inside, birds that flocked from one huge tree to another, beautiful parks, large civic sculptures, a veritable paradise, and yet they saw no people.

Amazed, the stunned soldiers gaped with their mouths open. Even the major stood there for a few seconds amazed with the perfection he witnessed. The place looked exactly as Reggie described it to. Before this moment, he could hardly believe that everything the spy told him was true. Yet, now he could see it all as Reginald has described the place, right down to the parquet roads that seemed too pretty to tread upon. Then it sunk in, that everything else Reggie told him was also true, and that the psychic children did represent a real danger to the world. He had to act as swiftly as possible before his soldiers formed doubts.

"Where the hell did that come from?" the assistant in the car muttered.

"What is that?" one of the soldiers questioned.

"Shut your mouth! No questions!" Brighton shouted. "I want the entire company to move through that opening... Now!" he ordered. "Sergeant Peterson!" he yelled. "Have two men on the road to divert the curious should someone drive by. Tell your men to search every house. Break down doors. Pull out every citizen and be quick! Driver! Take me to the center of town!" he yelled to the man next to him.

"Yes, colonel!" his assistant responded. "I'm sorry I doubted..."

"Never mind," Brighton said dismissively. "Did you call the general?"

"Yes, sir," the assistant said as he maneuvered the vehicle across the grass and then onto the village street. "It's so clean and so perfect... Should we..." he commented.

"Can the comments," the colonel ordered. "I said no questions."

"Yes, sir," the assistant quickly replied and did not speak.

He drove the colonel's car north a few blocks before he turned to the right and pulled onto Main Street. The colonel finally told the driver to stop between the last two large houses. He stepped out and waved the two transport trucks and the flatbed truck that carried the tank to follow him as he rapidly pushed into the heart of Rollo. However, the moment the troop truck turned onto Main Street, the houses, the parks, trees, everything they saw only moments ago around them, shimmered and then vanished. Only the empty street beneath their feet remained along with the perfect sky.

"What the hell is going on?" the colonel shouted as the column of vehicles skidded to a halt.

"Sir," Sergeant Peterson spoke up when he jumped down from the flatbed truck. "How can we search the houses, when we can't find the houses?"

This frustrated Brighton to no end. Reggie assured him that everything would be clear once they enter the village. He scratched his head at a loss of what to do next. He had limited personnel, for the sake of privacy, and brought only the three drivers of the trucks, four privates, Sgt. Peterson and his assistant. He started to call the general when he noticed an odd phenomenon at the east end of Main Street.

A large black wrought-iron gate stood alone, as if it led to a cemetery that wasn't there. He could see nothing on the other side of it, no cemetery, no structure, no road, nothing – only a large open field of sun burnt grass and a huge distortion heat wave that rose up out of the ground. The other men noticed it, too. He thought that seemed peculiar.

Colonel Brighton walked up the street toward the gate and waved for Sgt. Peterson to follow him.

"What is it, sir?" Peterson asked as he came up behind the colonel.

"I'm not sure," the colonel said. "Whatever it is, it isn't normal. This way!" he directed the sergeant.

The closer he moved to the gate, the more he noticed the distortion in the space beyond the gate. Sergeant Peterson did not know what to make of the area.

"Sergeant," Brighton said to him. "Take down the tank and bring it over here. Point the main gun at that field."

The sergeant ordered two privates to set up the ramp on the flatbed. They pulled the tarpaulin covering off the tank. The sergeant climbed up on the large machine and personally drove the tank down the ramp and onto the street. The big lumbering machine made loud crunching sounds as it gradually moved into position, although it left no mark on the pavement. Peterson stopped just a few meters shy of entrance. He aimed the tank's main gun at the area just beyond the open gate.

"Don't fire until I give the order," the colonel said as he gestured toward the area on the other side of the gate, "Keep an eye on me… if I am not back in five minutes," he said as he moved inside the gate, "open fire… that's an order soldier," he told Sergeant Peterson.

Colonel Brighton stepped through the open ornate black, wrought iron gate trimmed in gold. Overhead, an oval framed beautiful cursive golden letters **WPO**.

"Why would anyone erect a huge fabulous gate like this only to have it lead to a deserted lot?" he thought aloud. He paused and stuck out his hand. At this close range, the camouflage shield seemed more like particulate fog. He walked forward in the direction of the brown grass. Colonel Brighton suddenly vanished!

"What the…" Peterson shouted.

The sight alarmed the crowd of soldiers who stood beside the tank. Peterson jumped down off the tank and shouted his name.

"Colonel Brighton! Colonel Brighton!"

Seconds later, the colonel reappeared on the same spot walking backward, which startled the group. He turned around and held a puzzled expression on his face.

"Watch this," he said.

He picked up a decorative stone and tossed it into the air toward the field. In mid flight, the stone vanished.

"What's going on?" Sgt. Peterson asked as he drew nearer. "Is this some kind of illusion?"

"This is not a trick," the colonel told him. "This is an advanced camouflaging field, different from the one at the edge of town. I could not see anything inside, but I believe it is hiding a structure." Brighton said as he stepped back outside the gate. "Funny…" he said, "it doesn't work from this perspective. Like most stealth technology, it does have its drawbacks," the colonel observed.

"What do you think is on the other side, sir?" the sergeant asked.

"Them," the colonel quickly replied, "they're inside that field, somewhere… I wonder what would happen if... go back inside the tank," he ordered.

The sergeant ran across the street and hopped into the tank.

"Fire a round into that barrier," the colonel ordered.

"That won't be necessary, Colonel Brighton," a voice rang out. "You've proved your point. What do you want?"

Every soldier stopped and stared at the air around them.

"Did you hear that sergeant?" the colonel asked Peterson.

"I heard a voice, sir. But where did it come from?" the sergeant replied.

The colonel spun around to face the gate. He noticed all the men gazing around them as they tried to find the origin of the voice.

"Never mind," the colonel said as he focused on the barrier. "I want your surrender!" he called out.

"Not possible today, Colonel Brighton. "Your weapons are useless. You will not penetrate this barrier," the obstinate voice answered back.

"We can try!" Brighton shouted.

"Colonel?" the Sergeant asked. "Is anything wrong? Why are you shouting?"

"You didn't hear that?" Brighton asked as he looked around him. He noticed the other men staring at him.

"I haven't heard anything that makes sense," the sergeant told him, "just strange sounds."

Colonel Brighton realized that the voice directed its comments only to him and not the others.

"I'll show you whose weapons are useless," he muttered. "Clear out this area!" the colonel barked and directed the men to back up. "Sergeant Peterson! When the men are safely behind your tank, open fire!" the colonel ordered and indicated the force field.

"Sir?" he replied.

"Get your men out of here and blast away. Now!" the colonel angrily shouted.

The Sergeant waved his arms.

"Fall back!" he shouted. "Move behind the trucks! Now!"

The soldiers backed up Main Street until they stood in a group.

"Standing by to fire the first round," the sergeant called out once he saw his men in a safe area.

"Fire!" Colonel Brighton ordered.

The tank fired one round into the area beyond the gate. Instantly, a bright flash of light filled the space around them. A plain small building, similar in construction to the secret building in Labrador, suddenly appeared and exploded into thousands of pieces. A strong gust of wind swept across the flat plains of Kansas and blew the particles away. Unfortunately, the force from the explosion pushed Colonel Brighton's body backward. He fell to the pavement. The men rushed forward when they saw the colonel go down. Colonel Brighton lay unconscious on the ground. He had received second and third degree burns on the front half of his body.

Sergeant Peterson jumped down from the tank and took over command.

"Medic! Help that man into the command car!" he directed. He went to the staff car and picked up Colonel Brighton's special phone. He opened a direct line to General Andrews on the other end. "We have a situation here, sir," Peterson informed the general.

"Go ahead," General Andrews replied.

"The Colonel was injured, sir, after he ordered our tank to fire at a target, which exploded when the shell impacted. We believe the whole town was inside. If the children were with them, they were killed along with everyone else," he informed him. "We don't see any technology. The whole place is deserted."

"Consider your mission accomplished," General Andrews told him. "Detonate the device after you leave," he ordered. "Quietly, Peterson, we've already attracted enough attention!"

"Yes, sir," Sergeant Peterson replied. He closed the communicator and turned to the other men. "We have orders to leave here at once," he told the other soldiers. "Move the tank back on the flatbed and cover it up. Let's move!" he ordered.

The sergeant told the medic to stay with the colonel in the back seat of the command car. Two soldiers took a heavy black box from the back of one truck and left it in the middle of Main Street. Once he had everyone onboard, Peterson led the convoy back to the road and quickly headed south to the airstrip where they started.

"Ready, sir," the sergeant signaled the general back in Labrador after the convoy put five kilometers between them and Rollo.

"Detonate," General Andrews ordered.

Peterson looked down at the live satellite image to make certain no cars were on the road. He pressed a button on the controller in his hand. That sent the signal to set off the special semi-implosive device, which obliterated everything for a kilometer around it, except that it left the highway intact. For a moment, the screen went white. When the image returned, they could see a hole in the ground with no buildings around it and no range fires. The highway next to Rollo remained unharmed.

"Detonation successful, general," Peterson stated as he closed the screen.

The general knew as much, for he watched the entire event unfold back in Labrador, live via satellite in the spec obs room. He chewed the end of an unlit cigar and grinned. Reggie's plan worked and he had a one-of-a-kind agent at his disposal, one worth every penny he spent on this over-priced project.

"So much for this... Rollo, Kansas," General Andrews spoke.

He took the physical file labeled "Nimble" from his lap.

"Shred this," he told his assistant.

He sipped his coffee, leaned back in his chair and knew he had one more mess to resolve – the situation in Africa. He had to explain NATO's involvement with Mali, for which he had the perfect cover... and he had to retrieve his top agent Reginald Atwater along with the Motambou's from Africa. Like Reggie, a smug feeling of satisfaction passed through the general.

"I'll be damned. Reggie was right. Everything *is* going our way!" he confidently spoke. "By this time tomorrow, we'll be the most powerful force on the planet. Nothing can stand in our way… not even the Chinese!" He grinned as he thought about other projects he had in mind for Reggie.

Chapter Thirty-Nine

Under Wraps

John and the others looked over at Star Wind. She turned to Mark.

"Has the danger passed?" she asked him.

"We've managed to divert the military," the five-year-old confidently spoke. "The village shield is severely damaged..."

"We can easily fix that..." Star Wind stated when Mark placed his hand on her arm.

"There is more," he told her. "They left a bomb..."

"A bomb!" John and some of the villagers echoed.

"Don't worry," Mey Li said as she stepped up next to Mark. "We've interfered with its signal. Xiong will alter the holo-projectors on the building to reflect another image overhead. I will interfere with the soldier's minds. To them, they will see and feel all the responses necessary to be convinced they ignited a bomb."

Star Wind skeptically gazed from psychic child to psychic child. However, the small group nodded in unison and convinced Star Wind of their sincerity.

"Oh, you darlings! You know exactly what to do. Bless you! That's such a relief to the rest of us," Running Elk said with a sigh. "How can we ever thank you," she told them.

She bent down, spread her arms wide, and gave the whole group a big huge. The children laughed when she did, as it seemed silly to them. However, they responded with kindness and hugged her back.

"Yes, thank you," Star Wind added.

"One moment..." Mark said.

Mark, Mey Li, Sandra, Xiong, and Robert closed their eyes. The whole village held its collective breath. Mark finally opened his eyes and turned toward Star Wind.

"It is done!" he declared. The other children opened their eyes.

Everyone breathed a collective sigh of relief.

"We'd better dispose of the bomb and quickly repair the shield," Star Wind said aloud. "John, call Jennifer and Selena and tell them to alert the other agents around the world they may in danger."

He picked up his device and spoke to them. Once he finished, she motioned for him to follow her.

"Come with me," she directed.

John activated the control in his hand. The force field around the headquarters dissipated. The large beautiful wrought iron gate that the military thought they destroyed reappeared and the large five-story mansion with its wide piazza in front along with the beautiful fountain shimmered back into view. The village and parks reappeared, too. When the townspeople shuffled out of the front door of the mansion, they broke into applause. The school, clinic, the entrance to the underground hanger, and the security buildings rose up and returned to their former states. Only the gapping hole in the southwest end of town remained. Three Comanche tribespersons jogged to the location and stood guard while the rest of the community took up their posts.

Moments later, John and three of his friends walked up Main Street, bent down, and picked up the heavy black box. They placed the weighty object onto one of Chou's floating transports. Star Wind stood outside her house and waved for the men to bring the dangerous object directly to her.

Meanwhile, Jennifer and Selena took a different device that Star Wind provided to the south end of Rollo. A new power cube and "patch" projector would fill the open spot damaged by the military. The moment the two women activated the mechanisms, the shield sent out tentacles that reattached the matrix to maintain Rollo's stealth.

Reggie correctly directed the military to exploit that position; for it was the weakest spot in the shield Chou first created in the fall of 2016. After he carefully examined the village perimeter, Reggie found the one weakness that would allow entry. Chou always assumed the attack would come at its center and fortified the shield where the highway connected to Main Street.

The young security assistants had no more active the new shield, when a truck came over the horizon and flew past the plain rock formation.

"Whew!" Jennifer exclaimed. "That was close!"

"Thank goodness Star Wind and Chou work so well together," Selena commented. "She knew exactly what was needed and returned from the lab with the right device just in time."

The townspeople and psychic children, still concerned for their safety, stayed huddled together just outside the gate at the end of Main Street. When Jennifer and Selena signaled they repaired the shield, the entire village breathed a collective sigh of relief. The children watched with satisfaction when John and his crew moved the bomb over to the side of Chou's house.

Two robots took the black box inside where she instructed them to "dispose of the item" via Chou's large fusor recycler. She quickly returned to the surface and announced the all clear for the rest of the village.

Star Wind and John walked side by side up Main Street and assured the gathering that everyone could return to their house or project.

"The defenses worked," she told them, reassuringly. "You may all resume your jobs or go home." Although shaken, they nodded or waved in return. "Mark, Sandra, Mey Li, Xiong Po, Robert…" she addressed the psychic children. "I'd like to speak with you. Are you ok?" she asked.

All of the children nodded their heads.

"Yes, Star Wind," Mark succinctly answered for the group. "We are fine."

The psychological damage to the village would take months to heal. Unfortunately, Master Li was not present to explain the situation to the children. They sensed the blind rage and hatred toward them in the soldier's minds outside the house. They could not understand why strangers would feel so much anger for someone they had never met. They did not realize that others perceived of them as a threat to society. While Mark and Su Lin partially understood the soldier's motivation, the younger children found their strong emotions overwhelming. Robert showed the most signs of confusion and concern.

"I wasn't sure Mark's ploy would work, but I guess it did," John said. He turned to the older boy. "Is your mental projection still working?" he asked.

"Yes, John," young Mark replied. "The images we planted in their minds will remain with the soldiers for some time."

"You may have to keep up the charade just a while longer," John reminded them. "They must board the planes and return with those images."

"Have no fear," Mark spoke with confidence. "They will retain the altered memories we gave them. Mey Li and I were very thorough, just as our parents and Master Li taught us."

"You saved us. I will forever be grateful," John stated. He bent down and hugged Mark.

"Thank Master Li when he returns," Mark told him as he affectionately returned the hug. "He taught us how to enter their minds and plant the images. They only thought they fired the tank, that the house exploded, and that the colonel was injured. The colonel will wake up in a few hours with no harm done."

"That might be a problem," Star Wind considered.

Star Wind worried that she could not raise Chou on her black card. She knew he never went anywhere without his card or his ring. Not one time since he gave her that card had he ever failed to respond. Even if the card were destroyed, his ring would respond. It was indestructible.

"Children… I… I have a favor to ask," she requested.

She hearded them inside the headquarters building with John in tow. Running Elk baked fresh cookies that morning. She sensed her daughter enter the house and headed their way. Despite her lack of a cranial conduit, Running Elk and her daughter had rudimentary psychic abilities.

"Ah! Just in time for milk and cookies – a proper reward for the heroes of Rollo," Running Elk said beaming. "Let go to the dining room."

She held a tray that had a large plate of cookies with a pitcher of milk. The children, using their best control, moved the plates and glasses from the nearby cabinets to the area in front of them. Running Elk began to help them set up when she noticed her daughter had pulled her son to one side.

"All of our effort will be for nothing if we can't alert Master Li and Michael's team," she quietly said to him.

"What should we do?" he asked her.

"We'll have to use the power of the children. Perhaps they can reach Master Li," she said in a low voice. "Mother," she called out and walked over to where she stood. "I need Mark for a moment," she requested.

As he sensed her need, Mark changed his focus to Star Wind and patiently waited until she addressed him.

"We must act before the military can see through the ruse and return," she said to him. "We need to contact Master Li and your parents. Chou does not respond to his card. Can any of you think of a way to…"

Mark held up his black card.

"With this," the five-year-old suggested.

"Can you find them? Can you locate Master Li?" she requested.

"I can trace the signal back to its source," the child proudly stated.

"You can?" Star Wind wondered, surprised at Mark's boast.

He placed three fingers on the front. The card expanded and he closed his eyes. To Star Wind's astonishment, she saw the list of the WPO members appear and with his mind, Mark chose Master Li's name. The other children watched as Mark quickly carried out the directive. John leaned over to Star Wind and whispered into her ear.

"What if something has happened to them?" he wondered. "If they came after us, why wouldn't they attack the adults?"

All at once, Mark began to shake all over. The other children backed away.

"No!" he cried. "It's not possible!" he said as his eyes swam with moisture.

Whatever happened in his mind had moved the rest of the psychic children to tears. The other children formed a group around Mark and sympathetically hugged him. Mark looked up at John and Star Wind as the two puzzled adults stared at them.

"They're… they're…" he sobbed as he tried to speak, "They're dead."

Chapter Forty

Mass Murder

For what seemed like an eternity, the five-story, sleek, silver and white yacht drifted down the river, silent, dark, seemingly abandone, and caught in the current that it fought for the past few days. The rain poured down on the lifeless large vessel as the river slowly pushed the great boat toward the shore.

In the dim light of the game room, the only source of light present came through the porthole when the lightening outside flashed. The young student from Changchun, China, Chou Lo, lay very still on the floor for a long time. His body, crumpled and disheveled from where it fell, had not moved; nor did he twitch or blink an eyelid. Although his heart continued to beat very weakly and his lung barely exchanged gases, his limbs were stiff and cold. From all outward appearances, he was dead.

After a prolonged period, he sensed a spark of consciousness return. Aware of his body, he eventually moved his first muscle when he blinked his eyes open. He took in a deep breath. He had no memory at first of what happened. He tried to look around, although he could only move his head with great effort. He recalled the terrible sound that pierced his ears – a horrifying noise meant to harm. The technologist realized someone used a sonic weapon to attack them. It was in that moment of revelation that he wondered if he was the only person alive. He tried to assess the situation.

Less than a meter away, Su Lin lay on the floor. She had her eyes closed as if she were either dead or unconscious. He did not have much psychic energy in his reserve. He could not scan her for vital signs. Yet to his supreme relief, Chou, with his incredible Level V senses, could hear her breathing. Judging from her twisted body posture, he assumed that she toppled over onto the floor just as he had, although her chair remained upright. Despite the severe pain in his neck, he moved his head around. He noticed that Cecilia and Villi also lay where they fell, twisted in a similar condition. He sensed their beating hearts, although he could not link with them. Zinian and Zhiwei sat slumped over, still sitting in their large chairs. They were fortunate in that they did not topple over.

Chou realized as he slowly gain energy and scanned each person in the room that no one moved and no one else had their eyes open. He did not have enough energy to scan their brains. He feared the worst. Was he the only one who survived with his brain intact? Were those around him mental cripples? What exactly happened? How long was he unconscious? Who could do such a thing to them?

He could not reason the situation. His head buzzed with pain, while his neck hurt him even more. He tried to straighten his limbs when more pain shot down his spine.

"I'm injured," he realized. "Must have hurt myself when I fell."

Chou also realized that he had clenched his teeth together so hard for the past few minutes that his jaw ached. His head pounded as his arteries throbbed from the intensity of his heartbeat. He knew his blood pressure must be extremely high. He could hear the pulses from his beating heart in his ears. He tried to relax but found it impossible as his muscles remained stiff. They had tensed tightly all over his body. Survival mode set in.

"What the hell kind of weapon was that?" he wondered.

He struggled to sit up. In the darkened shadows, he finally noticed the chips. The chips and cards in the room were floating around.

"We must be inside a golden sphere… but how? Why aren't the people floating, too?" he wondered. "Because they had not moved from when they fell," he realized.

He looked up and saw Han at the table, still in an upright position with his eyes closed and a scowled expression on his face. He appeared completely alert. He started to say something when he sensed Han's intense concentration. He could feel that Han projected some field of energy. With his weakened state, Chou could not follow its course. Yet, he instinctively knew that it was Han who had erected a golden sphere and possibly saved them.

"You are amazing my friend," he thought.

Chou reached out to the countryside through the sphere and sensed some people about 500 meters away. He pulled psychic energy to him. He had a difficult time at first. He felt as if he were trying to drink a thick liquid through a narrow straw. Finally, his reserve began to rise.

"Better," he sighed. He started to link with Han, when the strategist quickly signaled, "Wait."

Faintly, he heard Master Li's voice in conversation with Han's mind.

"Reach out and gather any psychic energy you sense nearby," Li's voice faintly spoke to him, "to maintain your golden sphere."

Chou watched breathlessly as Han reached out and quickly found the same sources he located that were scattered around the nearby countryside. A group of villagers lived adjacent to the river's edge. Han gradually rebuilt his depleted level of energy.

"I believe I can safely wake them," Li informed Han. "Chou is already alert and listening to us. I will rouse the others. Chou, help Han form his golden sphere."

"Yes, Master Li," Chou meekly replied.

"Wake up… wake up my friends," Master Li softly spoke via a general link to the rest of the psychics in the room. "You are safe. The attack is under control… for now at least."

Slowly, the people in the room began to stir and open their eyes. Villi blinked back tears that streamed down his cheeks as he experienced a great deal of pain in his head. He struck the floor hard with his skull. He had a large contusion. Su Lin pulled her body into a sitting position. Villi mustered some strength. He crawled to her side.

"Su?" he whispered, his voice barely audible. "Are you alright?"

Su Lin nodded and gazed at her husband with eyes full of questions. They tried to link, but could not. In fact, no one in the room could link except Chou. Cecilia stirred and tried to sit up. The same tears slid down her face as she placed her hands up to her head. She severely twisted her spine.

"Can you link?" Villi asked as he glanced over at Cecilia.

She barely shook her head.

"No," she whispered back.

"Master Li wants us to absorb energy from sources nearby," Chou said aloud as he continued to support Han.

Cecilia could not rid her ears of persistent ringing. The sound in the room seemed muffled and yet it filled the air around them. Everyone in the room experienced a similar level of pain. You could see it on their faces and the way they moved – the same angst and twisted expressions told the story.

"I feel as if I stood next to a cannon when it went off. I can't hear anything," Su Lin complained.

Cecilia used hand signals and said she felt the same.

The group of psychics followed Chou's suggestion and began to absorb psychic energy. As they did, their condition gradually improved. Cecilia used her new energy level help those injured, including Villi. No one could link, yet they heard Master Li link with others on the ship.

"Michael?" Master Li linked to the bridge.

"Yes, Master Li," the team leader answered.

"Bring the engines back on line and put us back on course."

"Yes, sir."

A shudder went through the ship. Everyone could feel the yacht come back to life as its engines gradually came back online. Lights turned on throughout the ship as Michael restored power to most circuits, including the attachments to Chou's power cubes. The ship resumed its invisible status as the engines roared back to health. They could feel the ship lurch forward.

"I've turned the bow back into the stream, Master Li," Michael's voice linked. "The attack shut off the main power circuits. The sonic projectors overloaded the circuit breakers and cut off all the power sources. I've bypassed the main circuits and tied the ship's power directly to Chou's power cubes. They've sent out tentacles that bypassed the main buss box. The sensors will still report the ship is dead in the water. I have full power on the bridge."

"Nice work, Michael..." Li told him.

"Please extend my apologies to those in the poker room," Michael continued. "I'm sorry..."

"Don't apologize, Michael. You acted to save that part of the ship when you sensed the attack," Li said to him. "I managed to reach our group in time. Han was only slightly distracted by losing in a game of chance. Maintain your current sphere for just a little while longer."

"Is Cecilia..." Michael asked.

"She'll be fine," Li linked back. "She cannot link to you, yet. However, I can hear her thoughts."

"Master Li," Cecilia finally linked in. "My ears are ringing. I can hardly hear anything. What happened?" she asked.

"Listen to my voice," Li said in a general link to all the psychics aboard. "I want everyone to know we were deliberately attacked just now with the sole purpose of committing mass murder," he informed them.

"By whom?" the group collectively asked.

"By a force that has plagued us since the start of this journey. He has grown in strength while he stalked us," Li explained. "His plan was to take over psychic control of the planet... if given enough time. He convinced others in powerful government positions to destroy all the psychics. He told them that we would not co-operate. We were a threat to national security. They made the decision to eliminate all of us. They believe they have just carried out that mission. Fortunately, only *he* is aware of our global network."

"You said we were attacked," Chou spoke up. "Won't he discover we are alive?"

"Han and I managed to change the return signal," Master Li told them. "The sonic devices will continue their attack until the sensors report no life aboard the yacht. They were constructed to kill any living thing within fifty meters of this vessel. Han is helping me deflect their signal until we can disable them," he informed them. "I need your help with that part."

Han still had his eyes closed while he shielded the game room.

"Camille is trying to locate the projectors," Li explained. "Have you found them?" he asked her.

"Yes," she replied. "The boat is riddled with them. They're on every deck and practically in every room. Michael was right about the bypass. Whoever put these things aboard tied them into a bypass circuit that boosts their signal."

"How did Camille survive?" Cecilia asked.

"I extended a sphere around her head first," Li replied. "That is why the rest of you had about one second of attack time, for which I am truly sorry. Although the culprit received his false all-are-dead signal, the sensors on the ship indicate lifeforms and continue their attack. We must disable these devices."

"If I can break free of Han's sphere, perhaps I can help," Chou offered.

Zinian and Zhiwei helped Han maintain his golden sphere.

"I found their power source," Chou said.

"And I followed your path," Villi said next to him.

The whole ship heard a loud pop sound.

"The devices are disabled," Chou announced.

"Drop the golden spheres," Li ordered.

Michael stopped the main engines and put the boat into hover mode.

"All I can say is…it's about time," he said.

A few moments later, he entered the game room. The floating cards and chips were scattered all over the room. He headed headed straight to Cecilia, took her into his arms, and kissed her.

Everyone watched as their team leader trembled in his wife's arms.

"Has the future caught up with the present?" Han asked Master Li.

"Not yet," Li replied.

The exchange puzzled everyone except Michael.

"What now?" Camille spoke up.

"Now we demonstrate what the WPO can really do," Li linked to them. He placed the image of what he intended.

"Can we do that?" Camille asked.

"We can do anything we put our collective minds to," Li responded. "Right, Michael?"

"Right!" Michael replied.

His Galactic Central voice once told him at the beginning in the summer of 2015, that once the psychics formed a collective group, many things were possible. The group pulled psychic energy into their bodies until the members began to take on an extra glow. At last, they reached their maximum power.

"Push!" Li ordered.

The river water pushed against the hull of the ship and forced the craft up out of the depths to the very surface. The water bubbled and boiled around the craft as psychic energy forced the heavy yacht upward defying gravity.

"Thrusters!" Li stated.

The ship shuddered all over as it began to rise even higher up out of the water.

"Golden sphere!" Master Li ordered.

A large powerful sphere of golden energy snapped into place around the giant structure. The yacht vanished and began to lift up high into the air above the Niger River Valley. This time Master Li punched small holes through the sides of the sphere and forced the trapped river water within a means of escape, something only he could accomplish. Level IV Camille never felt the presence of this much psychic energy. While she tried to support the group's effort by contributing her part, she had never participated in forming a golden psychic sphere, as it was beyond her level of comprehension.

"Steady Camille," Master Li spoke to her. "Meld your energy with ours and allow it to flow through us," Li encouraged.

The great yacht ascended into the sky.

"Remember," Li reminded them, "size and weight have no bearing inside the golden sphere. Everything is weightless. Concentrate on the bubble's construction. Now... let us apply forward maneuvering thrusters."

The great sailing construct began to fly over the countryside that stretched out below them. In the distance, off the starboard side, a star known as the sun on planet Earth, began to appear along the terminus between night and day. The poet Li Po Chin guided his flock's thoughts:

"We hold in our minds the world's most powerful light.
May it guide our future...
For light brings order out of chaos, helps life spring from rock
And beauty will emerge from the cold depths of space
When light brings warmth.
Onward my friends,
We bring the light of reason and rebirth!"

Chapter Forty-One

The Last Gambit

Reginald Atwater rolled out of bed after four hours of rest. He knew he had probably slept too long. He sent out his feelings and sensed some people in groups not far from the doctor's house. Since the plague had yet to arrive in Niamey, some began to doubt it ever would. Reg quietly dressed and silently descended the stairs, despite his weight and the wood's ability to warn via creaks from strain. His stealth ability was one of his prized assets for assassination.

The doctor helped Reggie carry his packages to the car. He left a special IV port in their arms should Reggie need to pump them full of drugs. Dr. Liander prepared some syringes for Reggie. When they were finished, Reg entered the house and killed the old man before he had a chance to say a word. Reg collected his things, and then took a kerosene lantern from the back stoop. He spilled its contents in the middle of the floor. He particularly doused the two shot bodies with the stuff. He did not care if it left a trace of accelerant or that they could tell someone shot the two bodies. It was sloppy but he did not care. He didn't have the time. He threw in a match and set the doctor's house ablaze.

Keeping the headlights out, Reg eased the car up the street as shouts of fire broke out in the background behind him. In his rearview mirror, Reggie watched as a few remaining neighbors helplessly stood by and watched the doctor's house burn. With so many people out of Niamey, the fire department no longer responded to calls. Before he pulled away, Reggie reached inside his jacket, held the last deadly vial out the window and popped off the top. Almost at the same time the neighbors noticed the house on fire, the disease began to spread into the crowd. As Reg drove through the town toward the river, he spread the deadly airborne virus. For the next few hours, the western wind would spread the lethal virus back through Niamey and start a fresh wave of panic. Just as he did when he parachuted in over Bamako, he figured his airborne release would kill most of those left in the city until the virus ran its course and expired as the scientists designed it.

As the disease spread, rioting broke out in Niamey and panic set in as people ran for their lives. Within a few hours, only piles of bloody corpses remained. The mass confusion created a perfect cover for Reggie's escape.

He felt his phone vibrate. He opened the screen. New codes scrolled across the screen. He deciphered them: *"Go to Kainji Reservoir. Pick up at these coordinates… 10.473°N 4.56°E"*

The last numbers represented latitude and longitude. Reg easily memorized them as he did all of his messages.The final code appeared: *mission accomplished.* He knew the last code well. He used it frequently.

"Acknowledged," Atwater sent back. He grinned in the darkness before he closed the phone and placed it back inside his jacket. "So Brighton had the guts to pull it off," he thought. "I didn't think he would. Anyway, they're dead and that makes me the most powerful psychic on the planet… almost. After I torture Filla, Salla will give me the locations of the rest."

He glanced over at Filla who sat in the seat next to him, limp as the car jostled her around, her facial features no longer visible in the darkness. He worried about Filla more than he did about Salla. He could handle Salla and manipulate his emotions. He knew Salla's background. The scientist never had another relationship in his life. The female, on the other hand, could be trouble. Perhaps he should just shoot her right now and push her body out on the road.

"Naw," he thought, "I'll stick with the plan, torture her and manipulate Salla."

His car approached the waterfront. He had one objective in mind – to switch over from the car and steal a fast boat. Traffic jammed the roads south – no more dams from here to the Kainji Reservoir. The fastest way for travel to the reservoir seemed by boat, if he could find a good speedboat, one that could outrun patrol boats when he reached the border with Nigeria at Lollo. He could no longer afford any more delays. Rain or not, he would arrive at the reservoir by tomorrow morning.

His eyes searched the wharf for the most expensive piece of property he could locate.

"Rich people don't know how to hide anything," he thought. "Now, that's what I mean," he responded when he saw a large grand boathouse surrounded by a tall fence and security gate. "You think a fence will keep out a determined crook? Besides, I never did like guards."

Reggie got out of the car after he stopped in front of the gate. The guard inside a small station next to the gate jumped out. He immediately pulled out his weapon and aimed it at Reg.

"Back away from the gate or I'll be forced to shoot!" the man declared.

Reggie kept walking forward. Before the man could act, the professional killer raised the gun in his hand and shot the man three times in the head and chest before the guard knew what hit him. The man stumbled backward and fell away from the gate.

"That was dumb," Reggie thought as he stood at the gate. "I should have made him open it first. Oh, well," he mumbled as he shot the bolt. The lock dropped off.

He pushed the heavy gate open and drove the car inside. He closed the gate behind him and dragged the guard's body off to the side before he drove across the wharf to the large boathouse.

"I hope they have a fast boat," he thought as he parked the car.

He practically completed his primary mission. The plan he developed through all those years of scheming and sucking up to the general worked. He patiently drove to Rollo several times, mostly at night. He entered their dreams, read their minds. He discovered they were the strike team. They ran to everyone's defense. That would be their weakness. He placed their friends in jeopardy and not with any ordinary dilemma. He used a virus, which he knew would appeal to Cecilia. She was the linchpin, the person who would convince the others to come along. By knowing their weaknesses, knowing how they would respond, he lured the original group of psychics to Africa. That would separate the parents from their children. Yet, he couldn't be in two places at once. Therefore, he convinced the general to kill the children. He had manipulated the general's staff and the Rollo psychics – all of them since the whole business started.

"It was all a chess game from the start," he remembered when he first scanned the village. The very first psychic he felt was Han. He knew Han loved chess… and he knew how to beat him. He planned every move. "Check, game, match! Now I have Salla… I can manipulate him when I torture Filla. He'll do or say anything to save her."

Reggie didn't need much persuasion to convince the general of his plan. The general drooled over the idea of information regarding alien stealth technology. He wanted to know about the holographic shield and to use its protective technology for NATO's interests.

"Salla is their top scientist," Reg lied to him. "Even if we find nothing in Kansas, Salla will share everything with us!"

Reggie snickered as he walked to the boathouse.

"… and the suckers believed every word," he sneered. "I'll bet Brighton pissed his pants when he walked into Rollo and looked around at the place.

Well, Rollo is no more. Who needs that place anyway? I have Salla, the man who won the Nobel Prize!" he thought as he pushed open the boathouse door with his foot and burst inside.

"I need to get the hell out of here!" he thought as looked at the beautiful shiny red boat in its slip.

At that moment, Reg heard explosions going off in the capital city. That did not distract him. In front of him, lay the answer to all his problems – a very new and very fast speedboat – an answer to a prayer, granted, a very twisted one. The boat's owner also made plans to leave soon via the speedboat. He was in his house collecting his things when Reg began to steal the man's means of escape. Just as he moved closer to find out how he would start it, another door opened and the wealthy man's bodyguard entered. He went to start the boat and have it ready.

"You!" the man cried, when he saw Reg. "Get out of here!" He came at Reg fast and reached out to grab him.

Reg trained for years with men like Zinder, who had a reputation as the best martial arts expert in England. He dropped down, spun to his right, and knocked the man off his feet. However, the man was not as clumsy as Reggie figured. Although he stumbled, he quickly recovered, rolled backward, and jumped back up to his feet, ready to fight. Yet, Reg sprang first. He went for the man's knees. The man had speed, too, and deflected Reggie's attack. In response, he came down hard on Reg's shoulder. The consummate professional was not used to dealing with anyone who had extensive martial arts training. He underestimated his opponent. He dropped under the man's blow to lessen its impact. Then he rolled across the floor and avoided any further blows.

The persistent man came right at Reg. The big black man deftly spun around. His swiftness caught the other man off guard. This time Reggie's leg sweep met with better success. As the man tumbled over, Reg reached inside his pocket to grab his gun. But before he could grasp his weapon, the man stretched his leg out and kicked Reg's hand away. The man rolled backward and reached for his own weapon. He pulled out a knife and threw it. The blade swung through the air and struck the boards next to Reg's face. The razor sharp edge sliced away part of Reggie's cheek. He felt a trickle of blood run down his face. No one had ever damaged his face. In fact, the secret agent had never encountered as skilled an opponent. Not even Zinder had bested him this well in a fight. The other man's skill humbled Reggie and made him feel even more determined to fight.

Anger boiled up in the trained killer's mind. He made a fade, which threw the other man off, and then shoved the man back with his foot. He flipped to the side. This time he didn't bother to take his gun from his jacket pocket. He reached in and pulled the trigger without the silencer, firing right through the fabric. The weapon noisily rang out, its loud bang echoed inside the boathouse. The precisely aimed bullets found their mark. They ripped through the bodyguard's flesh as his body twisted and turned.

Angry he had to ruin Zinder's suit, Reg continued to shoot until he emptied his clip into the man's chest. The man fell back against the wooden wall and moaned as he felt around his chest, but he was not dead. Reg realized that the man had some kind of superior body armor on that stopped his bullets. He fumbled in his pocket for another clip when the man rose up and moved on Reggie with his arms out to strangle him.

Barely a meter apart, Reg popped the clip in and fired the first shot through the man's eye less than 10 cm from his face. The man screamed with pain. The second bullet shattered the bodyguard's nose just as the determined man reached out to grab Reg. Blood spattered everywhere as the gun's blast sent the man backward onto the planked flooring. Somehow still alive, he screamed with agony as his body twitched for a few seconds. This time Reggie stood over him and shot two more times into the man's head, shattering his skull like a squashed melon. Breathing hard, Reg stared down at the man with contempt.

"Look at what you did! You made me ruin a perfectly good jacket," he complained. He searched the man and found the boat's keys before he kicked the corpse into the water.

He slipped outside the boathouse and glanced around to see if the noise from his un-silenced gun attracted attention. When nothing else moved in the darkness, he went over to the car. He carried Salla and then Filla inside the boathouse and placed them in the back seat of the speedboat. They were still unconscious yet breathing, which was good enough for Atwater. He plopped them down and no longer cared if they suffered a bruise or two.

"Good… full tanks… now for a little insurance," he thought after he checked the fuel guage and search for extra cans of fuel. He wanted to make this trip a nonstop ride.

Once he filled up the boat with extra cans of gas, Reg moved cautiously to open the front door of the boathouse. However, as quiet as he tried to be, the moment he started the engines, they reverberated with a loud rumbling noise.

"So much for stealth," he thought.

"Hey!" he heard someone yell from the house. "Someone's taking the boat!"

He revved the throttle and sent the boat flying out of its moorings onto the river. He turned the bow toward the south and accelerated the boat to full throttle as he banked left through the muddy water. He heard a shot ring out that whizzed over his head. More shots rang out. However, in the darkness, it was difficult to aim well with a handgun and the boat was soon out of range. He pushed the sleek boat at top speed down the Niger River and headed away from Niamey as fast as he could for the great Kainji Reservoir about 250 kilometers to the south. With a top speed of about 40 or 50 kph, it would take him all night to reach the reservoir. Under the cover of darkness, the boat sped along, no longer noticed by a waterfront crew that stared wide-eyed and opened-mouthed at a city under siege, rocked by explosions and set ablaze by rioters.

The yellowish-orange glow of fires raging around the city of Niamey reflected off the shiny surface of the speeding boat. Just as the boat rounded the bend in the river south of Niamey, the rain started once more. The droplets that struck his face refreshed the sweating spy as the boat picked up speed over the glassy smooth water.

"I intend to take a long hot shower and find some decent food when I get back to Labrador," he thought as he kept the boat in the center of the river. He watched as hundreds of people ran to the end of one pier and tried to force their way onto a boat. The ship toppled over, pulling many underneath when it sank. Another crowded boat tried to pull away from a dock when a crazed infected man ran up the pier and jumped on amidst the healthy passengers. People screamed with terror as the disease rapidly spread through the boat and killed everyone.

Reg reached into his jacket's left interior pocket and pulled out a small pillbox. He stuffed one of the small white pills under his tongue. His heart rate increased and his pupils dilated.

"Got to stay awake... keep alert through the night..." he thought as the pill dissolved under his tongue. "This should do the trick."

He passed through a column of smoke coming from the burning city. This did not represent some acrid foul fume. He smelled victory in the air.

"It'll be a cold day in hell before I ever come back to this place," he muttered.

Hour after hour, he kept the boat at high throttle. He buzzed past village after village. Fifty kilometers, one hundred kilometers, two hundred kilometers, the engine on the boat grew so hot that in the darkness, he could see a reddish glow coming from the engine block. After he reached the border, Reg knew he had to travel another 100 kilometers inside Nigeria to reach the Kainji Reservoir. Reggie used his persuasive power to penetrate Nigeria's border patrol. He flew past two border patrol boats as he fled Niger and rammed his craft through the flimsy barrier when he passed into the country of Nigeria. Although one guard had a machine gun, his brief spray missed the speedboat. The patrols sent one of their boats after him but they could not maintain the pace and soon gave up the chase. Reggie knew the rescue plane would pick him up before any reservoir patrol boat found him in the morning.

Just before dawn, the rain stopped. A swift wind seemed to blow the remaining clouds to the east. For the first time in nearly a week, the clouds parted and the sun began to rise over the land. The reservoir resembled a calm giant mirror when Reg's red and white speedboat cut through the surface like a sharp knife. Golden light streamed slantwise through the trees along the widening shore as the morning star we call the sun pushed higher into the sky. The lake stretched out over 30 kilometers wide and 100 kilometers long with countless huts, villages, and towns that dotted all sides. At the opposite end of the lake sat the Kainji Hydroelectric Dam, running at full capacity with the reservoir near its maximum height.

Reg reached inside his jacket pocket and pulled out his communicator. He pressed the front of the screen and a yellow light flashed. He did not need to send a message. He only had to activate the homing signal, which would allow the seaplane to pinpoint his position. He figured the plane was en route to his position. The final minutes of the mission ticked down.

"Heh, heh," he chuckled, "I just made it."

The sun's golden disk finally rose above the tree line and a bright blue sky glimmered in the reflecting water as Reggie's boat sped into the wide-open water of the great Kainji basin. He eased back on the throttle and slowed the boat while he placed his hand on his forehead to shade the morning sun's glare. He scanned the sky for signs of the seaplane.

"At last!" he sighed with relief as a black dot quickly approached from the southern sky.

A large seaplane with pontoons instead of wheels dropped down onto the surface and sent out a big splash as it drew near. The seaplane's pilot maneuvered the craft parallel to Reggie's boat. Reggie cut the boat's engines and maneuvered the craft up to the side of the large seaplane. The side door swung open. A tall handsome man stepped out and stood on the pontoons. Reg started to step forward when the tall man gestured.

"Help me load your cargo," the man requested.

Reggie reached into the back of the boat and retrieved Salla first. He helped the young man pass Salla to another man inside the plane. Then Reg took Filla in his arms and intended to simply step onto the pontoon. The young man instead blocked his path and insisted Reggie hand over Filla to him first.

"Let me pass her inside first," he told the spy.

Reggie waited as the man passed Filla over to another man inside the plane. As soon as the young man passed off Filla, he turned around to face Reggie. The spy reached out his hand. The young man stared at him for a second and then looked down. Reggie followed his line of sight. The man had his foot on the edge of the boat. He pushed the boat away. Reggie started to jump but the young man held up his hands.

"Not today… old sport," the tall man said to him. "You're staying here."

"Now wait just a minute!" Reg cried out. "This is my mission… my plan… the general will be furious…" he protested.

Even as he lectured the young man, Reg reached for his trusty gun. However, his hand did not find the familiar object in his pocket. He frantically searched for it. The gun must have somehow fallen out of his pocket through the hole he made when he shot his opponent in the boathouse. Anger swelled up inside Reggie with this betrayal as the seaplane's engines roared to life and pulled away. The aircraft sped away and lifted into the air.

"You think you're going to leave me? Me? Reginald Atwater?" he shouted. "This was my plan… MY PLAN! I'll show you! I don't need a gun. I should have done this before now, but you've forced me to use my power. Now feel what a psychic can do to your mind!" Reggie threatened.

He reached out with his mind to stop the pilot of the aircraft. He entered what he thought was the man's mind and forced him to land the seaplane. He grinned as the plane's engines sputtered and it banked around.

"Ah, ha!" he said and started to smile.

The seaplane seemed to go slower than an aircraft should and maintain flight. At that moment, Reggie realized he had made a terrible error in judgment. The object in front of him was not what it seemed. The image of the seaplane disappeared and a large five-story yacht replaced it. Reggie's eyes widened and his mouth dropped open as the yacht slowly flew past his boat at an easy pace. A small oriental man stood in the open side door of the large yacht's cargo hold. He held an object in his hand.

"Li!" Reggie exclaimed when he recognized the old man.

The old man threw the small object out and Reggie snatched it out of the air. He opened his hand. It was a chess piece… the king.

For all his scheming, Reginald Atwater had never encountered a master strategist like Han Su Yeng – for it was Han who finally pieced together the facts and discovered Atwater's plans in time. He tempted the group with a game of poker that night, knowing the evening arrived for their demise. He resurrected a golden sphere around the team in the game room, which was enough counter the sonic energy weapon and prevent the full out assault of the attack. Master Li, who could not interfere with the timeline, simply helped Han when it came time to act. Once he discovered the identity of the culprit, Han studied Reginald Atwater's file and kept his knowledge of the coming event a secret from the others lest the listening devices on the boat revealed their awareness of the devices too soon. Knowing Reggie's love of chess, Han told Li to throw him the piece and offer one final word before he passed judgment.

The psychic linked, "Checkmate!"

Chapter Forty-two

Reconciliation

Salla Motambou gently swayed back and forth as he lay in the hammock. After some assistance from Camille in terms of color and fabric choice, Zinian installed the large woven object on the veranda of Camille's magnificent villa nestled into the hillside above the deep greenish blue sea.

"I always did like a hammock," Zinian confessed.

"I do, too," Camille concurred.

The beautiful hammock actually fit in with the grand promenade deck, its carved marble pillars and majestic pathways. Some of these paving stones led to the gardens behind the villa. Their bright brilliant colorful flowers stood in sharp contrast to the pale stucco walls that wrapped around this towering palatial house overlooking the French Mediterranean.

The large black man wore khaki pants and an open white shirt that showed off his firm black chest. He no longer bore the wounds of that recent mishap. His body glistened with sweat, muscle, and taut skin – the body of a black god. He pulled the straw hat down over his eyes and slowly rocked the wide hammock back and forth with a mental push. Salla listened intently to the world around him. The recent rise in his, and Filla's psychic ability to Level IV, heightened their senses. Salla had never known a world to which his mind so acutely attuned.

The soft melody of a Mozart concerto drifted down to his ears from an upstairs window. A honeybee busily worked away as it gathered nectar from a honeysuckle bush in full bloom. In the distance, he heard the saltwater waves rhythmically slosh against the rocks along shoreline. The wind rose from the sea and carried the salty smell of ocean water on the breeze. He gazed out from under the hat over the serene sun-lit sea and took in a deep breath.

"The complexity of life unfolds before our eyes… unnoticed," he sighed.

"What a precious gift we take for granted. I will never make that mistake again."

Using his mind, he floated a tall cool glass of ice-cold lemonade over until it hovered next to him. The straw conveniently bent over to his lips. Salla took in a long sip. The cool and sweet yet tart yellowish beverage trickled down his parched throat to his great satisfaction. The control and complexity of movement he developed in the last twenty-four hours boggled his mind with possiblilities to which he could apply this new power. The glass float back to the stand. He looked up at the clouds as they slowly drifted past. He could best describe his life today as one of rest and reconciliation with his friends who came to their rescue.

"This is all I want to do for the entire day," he stated as he crossed his bare feet and placed his hands behind his head.

He relished the restitution before he resumed his former labor by using his mind to gently push the hammock and sway in the warm breeze.

"Nothing can disturb this tranquil scene," he thought.

"Have you relaxed enough, you lazy bum?" a voice chimed into his head. "I thought you might come inside and joining us for tea."

"Oh, Filla," he sighed. "I'm so comfortable here. Can't I just stay for a while?"

Although Salla dearly loved the person in his mind, he wanted to ignore the intrusion. Going to tea hardly seemed temptation enough to move from this most comfortable perch.

"Camille baked your favorite cookies," Filla added as an enticement. "She made them from scratch using real country-churned butter!"

Salla opened his eyes and took a deep breath, "so much for tranquility."

He put one foot outside the hammock and pushed his hat back.

"Filla," Salla quietly grumbled, "I don't think anything you say can tempt me from this hammock."

"Master Li has returned… he wishes to speak to us about the plot to destroy the WPO," she told him. "Some villagers finally found Reginald Atwater. He'd been adrift for two days in that speedboat. I understand the sun traumatized his exposed skin."

"Being a physician, I can tell you that a two-day sunburn will most certainly be painful," Salla observed.

The mention of Atwater brought him back from his all-too-brief reverie. Grudgingly, Salla rose from the hammock, rolled off one side, and stood up. He stretched out his big limbs. Surprisingly, he never felt better in his entire life. In fact, Cecilia's treatments rekindled vitality he could barely remember from his teens.

"Oh, my," Salla declared as he glanced down.

He heard giggling in his mind. The African physician blushed and waited until the excitement passed before he headed inside to find his wife.

"At last," Filla smiled until he zeroed in on her and gave her a big wet kiss in front of everyone. "Salla!" she admonished, but she secretly enjoyed his attention.

He plopped into the seat beside her and took her hand, something he had not done in a long time.

"Who made the lemonade?" Salla asked.

"That's a secret family recipe," Su Lin linked.

"I take it you are feeling fit as a fiddle?" Cecilia asked.

"And then some!" he added. "I feel charged, full of energy."

Cecilia and Su Lin exchanged glances and laughed.

"Oh, I feel for you," Cecilia said as she reached out and touched Filla's arm. "I remember the first night with Michael after I tested my rejuvenation formula on him. The man acted like a horny teenager!" Cecilia said as she suppressed a giggle and glanced over at Su Lin.

Filla looked from Cecilia to Su Lin for confirmation. Su Lin knowingly nodded at the same time.

"Villi did the same thing!" she confirmed. "I must admit. He's a terrific lover even without rejuv juice. But that is one evening I will never forget!"

"But I haven't had enough time to recover," Filla weakly protested. "Have I?"

She searched her mind for some sort of excuse she could use. Cecilia and Su Lin then burst out laughing. Filla smiled weakly.

"Maybe I should have let him sleep on the hammock a bit longer," she thought as she broke her hand free and poured out more tea.

"Don't worry, my dear," Camille said as she entered the room carrying a large tray of still warm cinnamon-raisin oatmeal cookies. "We'll all be pulling for you! Besides, I put some of Cecilia's elixir in the tea, too!"

All four women burst out laughing. Salla smiled as the women left him out of the private links that went between them.

"Are you conspiring against me?" he asked.

"We are conspiring for you," Camille told him, which made Salla grin and Filla shrink even more, though she too, smiled albeit meekly.

"Where is Master Li?" Su Lin asked Camille. "I don't sense him."

"Taking report… trying to sort the mess out," she informed those present. "He erected a block while he's conversing with Michael, Zhiwei, and Han. I believe they are still on location in Labrador. Zinian has completed his mission in England, and Chou has finished his work in Russia."

"He's linked to all of them at the same time?" Filla wondered.

"He's good… but he cannot split into three people," Camille said and smiled. "He used an open channel to them with his card."

In another part of the estate, Master Li had his black card expanded outward into a screen nearly two meters wide and a meter tall. With his energy, he made the screen float in front of him while he first listened to Michael. The images of Zinian and Chou waited their turn while they listened to what was said.

"Go ahead, Michael," Li requested.

"It is as bad as we feared," the tall American told his mentor. "General Andrews had agents infiltrate governments, news organizations, media outlets, military hierarchies, and businesses," Michael informed Li. "It took us two days to sort through the mess. We would have never found all of the agents except for Han's diligence and perception. He knew exactly how to work bureaucracies so we could find and replace those people without arousing suspicion," he reported.

"Zhiwei, Han, and I managed to dismantle the entire operation here," Michael continued. "We transferred or discharged every soldier or civilian involved with this place and set them up in a private life with the help from our foundation. We're making it seem as if the Labrador operation was a nightmare experience, not a pleasant memory. We shut down the NAT- IX satellites, destroyed their schematics, and sent them on a collision course with the sun. Zhiwei introduced a bug into the security systems of every NATO member country that will monitor their securities for any future clandestine developments. Han found and destroyed all references to NIMBLE and Rollo. This base will self destructed once we set off Chou's little device. The whole place will return to the nature that once existed here. That should bring you up to date on everything we've accomplished in Labrador, Master Li," he spoke respectfully.

"Thank you, Michael," Li responded. He moved Michael's image off to one side and placed Zinian's image in the center. "Zinian?"

"Master Li…" Zinian linked when he realized it was his turn.

"Report," Li requested.

"Charles Bickford and his son, William, helped me enter MI-6 and find all of the files that related to Reginald Atwater," Zinian began. "We found his school records, his birth records, even his chess records. Did you know he was born in Africa not far from Mali?"

"No," Li replied and wondered what Han thought of that.

"At any rate, we destroyed all British government traces of Reginald Atwater," Zinian concluded. "We also erased the man from anyone's memory in the building during our three visits. We taught William how to make a psychic bubble. He enjoyed the fact he could walk through the most top-secret place in Britain and no one saw him or knew he was there. As head of the Tyler Foundation in London, he frequently is seen at fund raising functions.

I understand he's quite a female following since he remains a wealthy eligible bachelor..."

"Yes, yes, thank you, Zinian," Li said and pushed that image to one side. "Chou..."

"Villi dropped me off outside the lab near St. Petersburg," Chou began. "I easily entered what is left of the lab. Atwater's little firebomb trick did not destroy everything, far from it. I scoured the place, went through the subterranean vaults that even he didn't know existed, and destroyed all of the specimens. I found a sample of the virus he used and analyzed it. If we should ever encounter any of these species again, we'll know how to instantly counter them," he told Master Li. "That's all from here."

"Thank you, Chou... Villi?" Li called upon the pilot.

The big Russian's face appeared in a new screen. Li noticed the background change as the sleek vessel crossed the terminus from night to day.

"I secured the yacht, which is now parked in New York, thanks to our buddy, Steve Harper. We can move it to Rollo later. I'm on my way to pick up Chou, Master Li," he informed him.

"Thank you, Villi... listen, everyone," Li called out to the team. "Villi will extract Chou from Russia, continue to London and pick up Zinian – by the way, Zinian, please thank Sir Charles and William Bickford for their help. Then Villi will fly to Labrador and bring the rest of our team back to Camille's villa. Meeting and afternoon tea at 1600 hours. Li out."

The screen collapsed down into a credit card size that Li pocketed. Rather than return to Camille and the others, Li took a stroll in the garden. He had much to consider before he addressed the group. He knew Villi could land his big flyer on the open lawn near the villa. He wanted to meet privately with each team member before the meeting.

Two hours and ninety-three minutes later, the Rollo men returned to the villa and entered with Master Li. He stood at one end of Camille's long dining room table and addressed those present, which included Salla and Filla Motambou.

"First of all, I must apologize to you," Master Li said and indicated the Motambou's, "and to the rest of you. Reginald Atwater played me for a fool..."

"You mean us," Camille put in.

"Actually, I must take full credit for this mistake," Li openly linked. "I've suspected his involvement for a long time but I was not certain of his identity or what he intended. Of all the rogue psychics we've ever encountered, Reginald Atwater blocked as well as a Level IV psychic. He learned that from observing us. Ability wise, he was only a Level I at best and a crude one at that. He had no telekinetic capability at all. When I first suspected his presence, I tried to clarify my suspicions by walking the timeline. Due to my hesitation – my delay, if you will – I placed us all in danger. You see, dreams are not premonitions. No psychic can see into the future, not even me. The future is nothing but probabilities and uncertainty. These have no physical manifestation. No matter how hard any psychic tries, the future is as elusive as a photon. However, in my apprehension and concern for your safety, I gave Reggie enough ammunition to project my thoughts into your minds. He looked into my mind while I slept and used things I had seen along lines of probability. No psychic has ever attacked me in my sleep, not even Cyrus. I never suspected I was so vulnerable. Naturally, you caught glimpses of these scenarios, which he purposely broadcast into your thoughts. That is why we all had a shared dream experience in Rollo. He successfully carried out the same attack with you in Paris," he said to Camille.

"What about when he was in Africa?" she questioned.

"He was good at planting suggestions. Things we did, normal things triggered those reactions. Knowing probably outcomes about the future is a double edged sword," Li explained. "I could speculate about things I had seen… even share them with Han. However, if I did, I might change the probably outcome. That would upset the natural flow of time. I had to wait until Han figured things out, which fortunately for all of us, he did. Eventually, he sought me out to confirm his hypothesis. I never had to say a word. Han could read my face, which is why he and I never play cards."

That brought some chuckles around the table. Master Li glanced over at Han who nodded back and slightly smiled.

"Master Li, when did you first suspect Reggie's influence?" Michael asked.

"It wasn't Reggie's intrusions that tipped me off to his presence," Li confessed. "It was the state patrol car that always seemed to park in the same place," he told them. "It didn't make any sense to me. We had been in Rollo for three years and then all at once, a patrol officer set up a speed trap across from our village. I was surprised when the coincidence did not rouse Zhiwei's suspicion. I had no proof. The highway patrolman pointed his radar down the road and his thoughts only dwelled on traffic. Yet, he never pulled anyone over. He would disappear for two months and show up again. During our game of Go on the yacht, I finally shared this observation with Han. He never heard about the patrol officer. Han correctly concluded that Rollo must be the officer's destination. I asked him why. Han offered no rational explanation."

"I believe I compared us to pawns," Han spoke up.

"The repeated references to chess," Li responded. "After the game of Go, Han went to his room and found one of the sonic amplifiers. Rather than bring it to your attention, Zhiwei, he made an investigation. He discovered a carrier signal. He traced its origins to Labrador. When Han broaden his investigation, he discovered one of the most classified secrets of all – that the US, France, England, and Germany created a special organization to deal with assassination and societal infiltration. They were the ultimate spy organization, run by NATO and involved with practically everyone and everything. Lastly, Han discovered Reggie's involvement. When he found out General Andrews ordered Atwater into Mali, Han fit the last piece to the puzzle."

"How on earth did you find that out?" Zhiwei wondered.

"You aren't the only person in this organization capable of breaking into encrypted computers," Han said with a wry smile.

"I shall never forget when Han came to me..." Li reminisced.

"Does the name Reginald Atwater mean anything to you?" he privately linked to me.

"No," I lied to him. But of course, I had actually seen Reggie in one of the more recent timelines.

"Did you know he's quite a chess player," Han continued to tell me. "He loves to win... plays the queen's gambit... plays people the same way he plays chess, with brutal precision. He's never lost a match."

"I'll never forget that conversation as long as I live. Han read me like a book that day," Li told them.

"Still can," Han muttered, which elicted a few chuckles.

"Why not include us?" Zhiwei asked.

"If we did, someone might have let the knowledge slip," Han answered. "The general could hear us. Those things were listening devices, too. We had to let Reggie play out his hand while we kept safe guards in place. We couldn't protect the Motambou's. They were vulnerable. However, Master Li decided to let them to find Rollo. He felt confident the children were safe behind the barrier Chou made for the mansion. Before we left, Chou instructed John to take everyone there. The fact the children expanded their role and improved the outcome... well, let us say it surprised us."

"Master Li," Cecilia broke in. "Did you know the children would interfere the way they did before we left? Did you see it on the timeline?"

Master Li gazed across the table into Cecilia's eyes and shook his head.

"I have a few things to say about Rollo's children... things I have held back. First, let's set the record straight," Li said. "From the moment of Mark's conception, Galactic Central and I have followed their progress closely. Conceived at Level IV, without conversion mind you, these five are very special. Within a month or two of their birth, they transformed themselves into Level V. They never required a conversion. Only the voices at Galactic Central have that capacity."

"Are they more powerful than you?" Filla asked.

"No," Master Li shook his head. "However, Mark made his first contact with Galactic Central before his birth! No human child ever attempted this, not even me. Mark, Mey Li, Xiong, Sandra, and Robert are destined to be very powerful psychics when they mature. Had they wished, they could have brushed the company of men easily aside. They demonstrated restraint because their teachers and their parents have instructed them to use their power wisely. During this crisis, you'll be happy to know, Cecilia, that your son chose wisdom over violence. Eventually, Mark or Mey Li would have created a golden sphere on his or her own. If they did that before we knew of its existence, no one in Rollo, not even me, could have stopped them. However, now that the parents are Level V, all of you returned to equal footing."

"That's a relief," Su Lin said with a deep sigh.

"As to the military assault," Li continued, "the children were never in danger. The military had more to fear from the Rollo security system or worse, the children's anger. With a thought, they could destroy the entire defense grid all over the planet. In the past few weeks, I have spoken to them about interfering with human history. They understand and made a solemn oath never to attempt such a thing in their lifetime, which, as we know could be hundreds of years. I told them that I would hold them to that oath for all time. This much of the future I can reveal – no psychic will dominate the globe with his or her power."

"What about you?" Camille quietly slipped in.

"I repeat, no psychic will dominate this planet," Li emphasized.

"Don't you see?" Michael spoke up. "He's not giving you a straight answer because he will not be on this planet in the future," he guessed correctly.

"My time is not quite over, Michael," Li spoke up, "but you are correct to make that conclusion. The day will come when the WPO no longer needs me. When that happens, you must be ready to take over," Li said directly to Michael's mind and to no one else in the room.

Michael stared at Master Li and did not move at first.

"Did he mean what I thought he meant?" he wondered.

"I thought I made my meaning clear… we are psychic," Li replied privately.

The others noticed this private exchange but did not hear it. Michael bowed his head and kept his eyes downcast. They knew that Li must have linked something profound to affect Michael this way. Cecilia reached over and patted his hand.

"By the way, what happened to Reginald Atwater?" Filla spoke up.

"You did punish him, Li… didn't you?" Salla wondered.

For the first time in a very long time, Master Li's face took on an expression of anger.

"This rogue business must stop!" he firmly linked. "I am sick to death of rogues using their power to threaten the stability of this planet. Reginald Atwater is no more. He no longer has psychic power or has much of a brain left. As it was with the case of Cyrus, I could not solely interfere and pass judgment. I don't feel that is my role – judge and executioner. I simply requested Galactic Central send through a tiny atom of antimatter to seal off his portal. However, we were not aware that nature constructed Reginald Atwater's brain and conduit differently. Through the years, his psychic area grew in a manner that had convoluted tissue around his portal. When Galactic Central attempted to close the portal, several blood vessels broke and bled into his skull. In effect, he experienced a severe stroke. Neither Galactic Central nor I intended for this to happen. Since we were flying the yacht to the coast of Africa so that Villi could retrieve his flyer, I was not aware of what happened. Galactic Central did not know either. They thought they closed the portal and Reggie resumed being a normal human. By the time I discovered the damage, I could not reverse it. He can walk and speak, but simply put, he is a moron. He will live out the remainder of his life dependent on others."

"How poetic," Camille commented.

"You mean he isn't dead? That doesn't seem exactly fair," Filla protested.

"He killed everyone in Bamako, Master Li," Salla added. "Our parents… our friends… the man is a mass murderer, a monster…"

Salla choked up and could not finish his sentence. He and Filla looked at one another. In addition to their parents, they found out that most of Gao burned to the ground, including their hospital. NATO would not allow any air, land, or river traffic into Mali until they launched a full investigation. Currently, they flew in relief supplies to the survivors in outlying areas.

Master Li saw the torment on Salla's face. He understood the impact that Reggie's actions made on both Motambou's. He gazed upon them with a sorrowful look in his eyes. The others around the table realized that Master Li deeply felt their pain and elicited a high level of empathy.

"What would you have me do, Salla… Filla?" Li asked of them. "Would have me obliterate Reggie with a blinding flash of psychic energy as I did to my cousin? You realize, of course, that I have such power! What would you do with my power? Would you go around handing out death sentences to those you feel deserve it?"

Filla cast her eyes down, ashamed. Yet, Salla looked Master Li straight in the eyes. He did not have an answer, only the burning desire for revenge. He hated Reginald Atwater and how the man destroyed everything they tried to do for Mali. Li could feel it. He looked around the table but no one linked.

"May I remind every psychic in this room that our organization is not in the revenge business?" Li put to them. "We stand for justice, not vengeance. We do not twist the truth to suit our feelings for the day. We seek clarity and facts, not emotional opinions that cloud judgment. We do not emulate those who violate our laws. We do not kill, torture, or maim with this power that nature gave us – we precious few. Reginald Atwater was a despicable villain who killed many people with his psychic power… and he did so without remorse. However, Reginald Atwater no longer exists. Let it end."

"Li…" Salla pleaded. "I didn't mean…"

"I… I…" Filla struggled to reply. "I'm so sorry…"

"Salla… Filla…" Li replied and looked at both of them in the eyes. "Don't you understand that if we start executing every person who is evil, where do we stop? What level of morality do we follow? Yours? Mine?"

"I only wanted to…" Salla muttered. "We've lost so much…"

"We understand what you feel," Cecilia softly spoke. "Believe me when I link to you like this, we do understand everything you feel. We are psychic, are we not?"

Filla bowed her head slightly and nodded. She recalled Reggie's victims that included her mother. Yet she finally realized that even if Reggie suffered for a thousand years, his torture would never return the life of her mother.

"This tragedy has no happy ending," Li went on. "The purpose of our life is not death. The purpose of the WPO is to leave the world a better place than how we found it. This simple premise brings me back to my earlier statement. This organization will no longer tolerate rogues. If this power is to emerge in the populous from time to time, we must be vigilant and find these pre-psychics before societal fears and prejudices' warp their evolvement. We must make it our mission to fan out across the globe and seek out anyone with psychic talent. We must determine if they are a pre-psychic candidate. If that is the case, we must nurture and help them develop into members of our organization – people whose goal is helpful and constructive. Otherwise, we may encounter Atwater's at every turn."

Master Li stood up. He absorbed psychic energy until his body glowed not with a golden color, but shone with white light, emanating more energy than any psychic in the room could. With a tremendous effort, he reached out across the planet in a display of power he seldom showed.

"The World Psychic Organization must be more than just a loose collection of psychics scattered around the planet," he linked to every psychic member everywhere. "We must have laws that govern our conduct, rules that guide our behavior, and a charter to give us cohesion. This document, to which we pledge and dedicate our purpose in life, provides a platform to steer our future course. Every psychic across the globe must renew that pledge we make here, today," Master Li announced.

Master Li stretched out his arms. Simultaneously, energy flowed from his body and out to the entire planet. Whether in the middle of sleep or in the middle of any involvement, every psychic, every member of the WPO heard his voice.

"From this day forward, no human being with a conduit will be allowed to operate outside the charter of this organization for the safety of the human race," he dramatically linked. "So shall you pledge… so shall you agree."

In a blinding flash, Li connected the mind of every psychic on the planet. They instantly agreed to the charter and the WPO pledge.

"So you are bound!" Li said with a profunctory finish.

The light faded and Master Li collaped into his chair. The blood drained from his face and his head slumped over. Camille reached over and placed Li's head in her arms.

"He's alright," she announced. "He'll be fine in a moment."

What happened just now overwhelmed Salla. Tears ran down his face. He had no idea any psychic had such power. Li's demonstration managed to impress everyone, but it made the most profound impression on Salla Motambou. He stood up.

"I pledge to do whatever it takes to reverse all the damage Reginald Atwater perpetrated on the world," he said.

Filla reached over and took Salla's hand.

"Need some help?" she offered.

Salla resumed his seat and slipped his arms around his wife. The two psychics hugged and wept.

Camille looked over at her friends, moved by Salla's sacrifice.

"You and Salla must live here," Camille spoke up. "This will be your home. I give you this villa."

"I can't let you…" Salla started to protest.

"It's done," Camille said with such finality, no one doubted her word.

Salla and Filla both reached across the table and grabbed Camille's hands. The French woman knew that from that day forward, she would never have to go far to be with her friends.

"The foundation will supply you with whatever funds you need," Michael offered. "I think that what you propose will be a noble cause, Salla."

"Here, here," everyone in the room echoed.

Silence fell over the scene until Su Lin made an open link.

"By the way," she spoke up. "While Master Li converted Camille to Level V, I came across a very interesting news item," she linked to them. "Scientists reported that the early rainy season in Africa reached record levels this year. The yacht would have never made it up the river and Atwater would have left Africa unless it had rained with such intensity. We would have perished before Han made his discovery." She turned toward Master Li, who had recovered in Camille's arms. "You didn't intentionally make it rain while we were in Africa, did you, Master Li?"

"Do you really believe I am capable of doing something like that?" he slyly replied to her question.

"After what you did a moment ago, I believe you're capable of moving heaven and earth!" she declared.

Master Li suddenly broke into laughter, which startled the rest of the group. Su Lin, uncertain how close to the mark she hit, joined in and laughed right along with him. Soon, the room filled with the kind of healing laughter that brought some solace to the grief stricken and some hope as well.

The End of "The Proximate Voices" – Book V of "The Voices Saga"

Up next, "The Outer Voices" – Book VI of "The Voices Saga"